Praise for #1 *New York Times* ~~bestselling~~

"Roberts' bestselling novels are some of the best in the romance genre. They are thoughtfully plotted, well-written stories featuring fascinating characters."
—*USA TODAY*

"A superb author... Ms. Roberts is an enormously gifted writer whose incredible range and intensity guarantee the very best of reading."
—*Rave Reviews*

"Characters that touch the heart, stories that intrigue, romance that sizzles—Nora Roberts has mastered it all."
—*Rendezvous*

"Her stories have fueled the dreams of twenty-five million readers."
—*Entertainment Weekly*

"Roberts is deservedly one of the best known and most widely read of all romance writers."
—*Literary Journal*

"Roberts has a warm feel for her characters and an eye for the evocative detail."
—*Chicago Tribune*

"When Roberts puts her expert fingers on the pulse of romance, legions of fans feel the heartbeat."
—*Publishers Weekly*

Dear Reader,

They say home is where the heart is, but as we see in these two classic romances from bestselling author Nora Roberts, sometimes you have to see the world before you can learn to cherish the place you came from—and the people you left behind.

In *Song of the West*, Samantha Evans returns to Wyoming to help her sister through her pregnancy, but it was always her intention to get back to city life as soon as possible. Of course, that was before handsome cowboy Jake Tanner moseyed on into her life, with his easy confidence and careless smile. Suddenly the range is starting feel like home again, and Samantha isn't in such a hurry to get back to the city.

In *Unfinished Business*, Vanessa Sexton thought she understood what it meant to be happy. For her, it was becoming a renowned and successful pianist. But once she achieves that goal, she realizes she has no one in her life to share it with. So she decides to retreat back home to the house she hasn't lived in since she left to start her career at sixteen. To the mother she hasn't spoken to since. And to the man she hasn't been able to stop thinking about all these years later...

We hope you enjoy these sweet stories about returning home, only to find your heart was there all along.

The Editors
Silhouette Books

NORA ROBERTS

Home at Last

Silhouette Books

Published by Silhouette Books

America's Publisher of Contemporary Romance

SILHOUETTE BOOKS

Home at Last

ISBN-13: 978-0-373-28185-5

Copyright © 2014 by Harlequin Books S.A.

The publisher acknowledges the copyright holder
of the individual works as follows:

Song of the West
Copyright © 1982 by Nora Roberts

Unfinished Business
Copyright © 1992 by Nora Roberts

Recycling programs
for this product may
not exist in your area.

CONTENTS

SONG OF THE WEST

Chapter 1

The land in southeast Wyoming is a magnificent paradox. Spreading plains and rolling hills coexist with rocky mountains and thick velvet pines. From the kitchen window, the view was astounding, and Samantha Evans halted in her duties for a moment to drink it in.

The Rockies dominated the vast curtain of sky, their peaks laced with snow, though it was late March.

Samantha wondered if she would still be in Wyoming the following winter. She dreamed of long walks with the air biting and sharp on her cheeks, or wild rides on a spirited mount with hooves kicking up a flurry of white. But none of that could happen until her sister was well enough to be left alone.

A frown creased her smooth brow. Sabrina was her reason for being in Wyoming, with its majestic moun-

tains and quiet plains, rather than in the more familiar surroundings of Philadelphia's tall buildings and
traffic-choked streets.

The two sisters had always been close, with that special, magical intimacy that twins share. They were not
identical. Though they were the same in height and
build, Samantha's eyes were a dark cornflower blue,
widely set, with thick, spiky lashes, while Sabrina's
eyes were a light gray. Both faces were oval set with
small, straight noses and well-shaped mouths, but while
Samantha's rich brown hair, with its highlights of gold,
was shoulder length with a fringe of bangs, Sabrina's
ash blond was short, framing her face with delicate
curls. The bond between them was strong and endur-
ing. Even when Sabrina had married Dan Lomax and
moved so many miles away to settle on his ranch in the
Laramie Basin, their devotion had remained constant
and unwavering.

They kept in touch by phone and letter, which helped
to mitigate Samantha's aching loneliness. And she was
happy in her sister's delight in the coming baby. The
two women had laughed and planned together over the
phone. But that was before Dan's call. Samantha had
been aroused from a deep predawn sleep by the shrill
ringing of the phone. She reached groggily for it, but
was instantly alerted by the anxious tone of her brother-
in-law's voice. "Sam," he'd said without any preamble,
"Bree's been very ill. We did manage to save the baby,
but she has to be very careful for a while now. She will
have to stay in bed and have constant round-the-clock
care. We are trying to find someone to—"

Samantha had only one thought—her sister, the person she loved best in the world. "Don't worry, Dan, I will come immediately."

She was on the plane to Wyoming less than twenty-four hours later...

The whistle of the kettle brought Samantha back to the present. She began to brew the herbal tea, placing delicate floral cups on a silver tray.

"Teatime," she called as she entered the living room. Sabrina was propped up with pillows and comforters on the long wood-edged sofa. Though her smile was warm, her cheeks still retained a delicate pallor.

"Just like the movies," Sabrina commented as her sister set a tray on the pine table. "But the role of Camille is getting to be a bore."

"I imagine so." Samantha poured the fragrant tea into cups. "But you may as well get used to it, Bree, you've got the part for a month's run." She transferred a large gray-striped cat from Sabrina's lap to her own, offered Sabrina a steaming cup and sat on the rug. "Has Shylock been keeping you company?"

"He's a terrible snob." With a wry smile, Sabrina sipped at her tea. "He did graciously allow me to scratch his ears. I have to admit, I'm glad you brought him with you, he's my biggest entertainment." She sighed and lay back against the pillows, regarding her sister seriously. "I'm ashamed to be lying here feeling sorry for myself. I'm lucky." She rested her hand on her stomach in a protective gesture. "I shall have my baby, and I sit here moaning about your waiting on me."

"You're entitled to moan a bit, Bree," said Samantha, immediately sympathetic. "You're used to being active and busy."

"I've no right to complain. You gave up your job

and left home to come out here and take care of me."
Another deep sigh escaped, and her gray eyes were
dangerously moist. "If Dan had told me what you were
planning to do, I would never have allowed it."

"You couldn't have stopped me." Samantha attempted to lighten the mood. "That's what older sisters are for."

"You never forget those seven minutes, do you?"
Sabrina's eyes cleared, and a reluctant smile curved her
generous mouth.

"Nope, it gives me seniority."

"But your job, Sam."

"Don't worry." Samantha made another dismissive
gesture. "I'll get another job in the fall. There's more
than one high school in the country, and they all have
gym teachers. Besides, I needed a vacation."

"Vacation!" Sabrina exclaimed. "Cleaning, cooking,
caring for an invalid. You call that a vacation?"

"My dear Sabrina, have you ever tried to teach an
overweight, totally uncoordinated teenager the intrica-
cies of the parallel bars? Well, the stories I could tell
you about vacations."

"Sam, what a pair we are. You with your teenagers
and me with my preadolescent Mozarts. Lord knows
how many times I cleaned peanut butter off the keys of
that old Wurlitzer before Dan came along and took me
away from scales and infant prodigies. Do you think
Mom expected us to come to this when she dragged us
to all those lessons?"

"Ah, but we're well-rounded." Samantha's grin was
faintly wicked. "Aren't you grateful? She always told
us we'd be grateful one day for the ballet and the piano
lessons."

"The voice lessons and the riding lessons," Sabrina continued, ticking them off on her fingers.

"Gymnastics and swimming lessons," Sabrina concluded with a giggle.

"Poor Mom." Samantha shifted Shylock to a more comfortable position. "I think she expected one of us to marry the president, and she wanted us to be prepared."

"We shouldn't make fun." Sabrina wiped her eyes with a tissue. "The lessons did give us our living."

"True. And I can still whip up a mean spinach soufflé."

"Ugh." Sabrina grimaced, and Samantha lifted her brows.

"Exactly."

"You have your medals," Sabrina reminded her. Her smile warmed with pride and a trace of awe.

"Yes, I have the medals and the memories. Sometimes, it feels like yesterday instead of nearly ten years ago."

Sabrina smiled. "I can still remember my terrified excitement when you first swung onto the uneven bars. Even though I'd watched the routine countless times, I couldn't quite believe it was you. When they put that first Olympic medal around your neck, it was one of the happiest moments of my life."

"I remember thinking just before that competition, after I'd botched the balance beam so badly, that I couldn't do it. My legs felt like petroleum jelly, and I was mortally afraid I was going to be sick and disgrace myself. Then I saw Mom in the stands, and it ran through my mind how much she'd sacrificed. Not the money. The bending of those rather strange values of hers to allow me those years of training and those few heady moments of competition. I had to prove it was justified, I had to pay her back with something, even though I knew she'd never be able to say she was proud of me."

"You proved it was justified." Sabrina gave her twin a soft smile. "Even if you hadn't won on the bars and the floor exercises, you'd proved it by just being there. And she was proud of you, even if she didn't say it."

"You've always understood. So get over the idea I'm doing you a favor coming here. I want to be here. I *belong* here."

"Sam." Sabrina held out a hand. "I don't know what I'd do without you. I don't know what I *ever* would have done without you."

"You'd manage," Samantha returned, giving the frail hand a squeeze. "You have Dan."

"Yeah, I do." The smile became soft. "This is the time of day that I miss him most. He should be home soon." Her gaze wandered to the glass-domed anniversary clock on the mantel above the fire.

"He said something about checking fences today. I can't quite get away from the image of him chasing rustlers or fighting off renegade Indians."

With a light laugh, Sabrina settled back among the cushions. "City slicker. You know, Sam, sometimes I can't even remember what Philadelphia looks like. Jake Tanner was riding along with Dan today to make sure the boundary fences were in good repair."

"Jake Tanner?" Samantha's question was idle.

"Oh, that's right, you haven't met him yet. The northwest corner of the ranch borders his. Of course, the Lazy L would fit into one corner of his ranch. He owns half the county."

"Ah, a land baron," Samantha concluded.

"A very apt description," Sabrina agreed. "The Double T, his ranch, is the most impressive I've seen. He runs it like clockwork, super efficient. Dan says he's not only an incredible rancher, but a very crafty businessman."

"Sounds like a bore," Samantha commented, wrinkling her nose. "Steel-gray hair around a leathered face, a handlebar mustache drooping over his mouth and a generous belly hanging over his belt..."

Sabrina's laughter rang out, high and sweet.

"You're about as far off the mark as you can get. Jake Tanner is anything but a bore, and speaking from the safety of marital bliss, he's a fascinating man to look at. And, being rich, successful and unattached, all the females under forty buzz around him like bees around honey."

"Sounds like a good catch," Samantha said dryly. "Mom would love him."

"Absolutely," Sabrina agreed. "But Jake has eluded capture so far. Though from what Dan says, he does enjoy the chase."

"Now he sounds like a conceited bore." Samantha tickled Shylock's smooth belly.

"You can hardly blame him for taking what's offered." Sabrina defended the absent Jake Tanner with a vague movement of her shoulders. "I imagine he'll settle down soon. Lesley Marshall—her father's ranch borders the other side of the Double T—has her sights set on him. She's a very determined woman, as well as being more than a little spoiled, and dreadfully rich."

"Sounds like a perfect match."

"Mmm, maybe," Sabrina murmured. Her face

creased in a small frown. "Lesley's nice enough when it suits her, and it's about time Jake had a wife and family. I'm fond of Jake. I'd like to see him set up with someone with more warmth."

"Listen to the old married woman." Samantha addressed a dozing and unconcerned Shylock. "A year of nuptial bliss, and she can't stand to see anyone unattached."

"True. I'm going to start on you next."

"Thanks for the warning."

"Wyoming's full of good-looking cowboys and handsome ranchers." Sabrina continued to smile as her sister grimaced. "You could find a worse place to settle down."

"I have no objection to settling here, Bree. I've become quite attached to the wide-open spaces. But—" she paused significantly "—cowboys and ranchers are not among my immediate plans for the future." She rose from the floor in a fluid motion. "I've got to check on that roast. Here." She handed her sister the novel that rested on the table. "Read your love stories, you incurable romantic."

"You won't be so cynical when you fall in love," Sabrina predicted with the wisdom of experience.

"Sure." Samantha's grin was indulgent.

"There'll be bells ringing and fireworks shooting and trumpets blaring." She patted her sister's hand and strolled from the room, calling over her shoulder. "Angels singing, flames leaping…"

"Just you wait," Sabrina shouted after her.

Samantha busied herself preparing vegetables for the evening meal, clucking her tongue at her sister's nonsense. *Love,* she sniffed derisively. Her only experience with that complex emotion had been fending off unwanted attentions from eager males. Not once had any man lit an answering spark in her. But whatever this love was, it worked for Bree. The younger twin had always been more delicate, softer and more dependent. And though Sabrina was trying to be brave and strong, her sister knew the fear of miscarriage still lurked in the back of her mind. She needed Dan's support and love, and right now, she needed to feel his arms around her.

Like the answer to a prayer, Samantha spotted two figures on horseback approaching from the lower pasture. Grabbing her heavy jacket from the hook by the back door, she scurried out of the kitchen and into the cold March air.

As Dan and his companion drew closer, Samantha greeted him with a smile and a wave. She had noticed, even at a distance, Dan's expression of concern. But a smile relaxed his features when he spotted Samantha.

"Sabrina's all right?" he asked as he reined in next to her.

"She's fine," Samantha assured him. "Just a trifle restless, and tremendously lonely for her husband."

"Did she eat better today?"

Samantha's smile warmed, lighting her face with a quick flash of astonishing beauty.

"Her appetite was much better. She's trying very hard." Samantha lifted a hand to stroke the smooth flank of the gelding he rode. "What she needs now is you."

"I'll be in as soon as I stable my horse."

"Oh, Dan, for heaven's sake. Let your hand do it, or I'll do it myself. Bree needs you."

"But…"

"'S all right, boss," the other horseman interrupted, and Samantha spared him a brief glance. "I'll tend to your horse. You go on and see the missus."

Dan flashed his companion a wide grin and dismounted. "Thanks," he said simply as he handed over the reins and turned to Samantha. "Coming in?"

"No." She shook her head and hunched her shoulders in the confines of her jacket. "You two could use some time alone, and I'd like some air."

"Thanks, Sam." He pinched her cheek with brotherly affection and moved off toward the house.

Waiting until the door closed behind him, Samantha walked over and dropped wearily onto the stump used for splitting wood. Resting her back against the fence, she breathed deeply, devouring the brisk, cold air. The strain of caring for her sister in addition to running the house and cooking the meals, including, over his objection, Dan's predawn breakfast, had taken its toll.

"A few more days," she whispered as she closed her eyes. "A few more days and I'll have adjusted to the routine and feel more like myself." The heavy corded jacket insulated her from the bite of the cold, and she tilted back her head, allowing the air to play on her cheeks as her mind drifted on the edge of exhaustion.

"Funny place to take a nap."

Samantha sat up with a jerk, confused and disoriented by sleep. Her eyes traveled up to the speaker's face. It was a lean face, skin bronzed by the sun and stretched tightly over cheekbones, all lines and shadows, hollows and angles. The eyes were arresting, deep-set and heavily lashed. But it was their color, a deep, pure jade that caught and held her attention. His dusky gold hair curled from under a well-battered Stetson.

"Evening, ma'am." Though he touched the brim of his hat with due respect, his extraordinary eyes were faintly mocking.

"Good evening," she returned, struggling for dignity.

"Person could catch a bad chill sitting out too long after the sun's low. Wind's picking up, too." His speech was slow and thickly drawled. His weight was distributed evenly on both legs, hands deep in pockets. "Oughtn't to be out without a hat." His comment was accompanied by a fractional movement of his head toward her unadorned one. "Hat helps keep the heat in."

"I'm not cold." She feared for a moment her teeth would chatter and betray her. "I was…I was just getting some air."

"Yes, ma'am." He nodded in agreement, glancing behind her at the last, dying brilliance of sun as it slipped behind circling peaks. "Fine evening for setting out and watching the sunset."

Her eyes flashed at the teasing. She was embarrassed to have been caught sleeping. He smiled a slow, careless smile that crept unhurried across his face. The movement of his lips caused the hollows to deepen, the shadows to shift. Unable to resist, Samantha's lips curved in response.

"All right, I confess. You caught me napping. I don't suppose you'd believe I was just resting my eyes."

"No, ma'am." His answer was grave, with just a hint of apology.

"Well." She rose from her seat and was dismayed at how far she still had to look up to meet his eyes. "If you keep quiet about it, I'll see to it that you get a piece of the apple pie I baked for dinner."

"That's a mighty tempting offer." He considered it with a long-fingered hand reaching up to stroke his chin. "I'm partial to apple pie. Only one or two things I'm more partial to." His eyes roamed over her in a thorough and intense study that caused her heart to pound with unaccustomed speed.

There was something different about this man, she thought swiftly, something unique, a vitality at odds with lazy words and careless smiles. He pushed his hat back farther on his head, revealing more disorderly curls. "You've got yourself a deal." He held out his hand to confirm the agreement, and she placed her small hand in his.

"Thanks." The single word was breathless, as she found her speech hampered by the currents running up her arm. Abruptly, she pulled her hand away, wondering what it was about him that disturbed her equilibrium. "I'm sorry if I was short before, about Dan's horse." She spoke now in a rush, to conceal a reaction she could not understand.

"No need to apologize," he assured her, and the new soft texture in his tone both warmed and unnerved her. "We're all fond of Mrs. Lomax."

"Yes, well, I…" she stammered, suddenly needing to put a safe distance between herself and this slow-talking man. "I'd better go inside. Dan must be hungry." She looked past him and spotted his horse, still saddled, waiting patiently. "You didn't stable your horse. Aren't you finished for the day?" Hearing the concern in her own voice, she marveled at it. Really, she thought, annoyed, why should I care?

"Oh, yes, ma'am, I'm finished." There was laughter in his voice now, but Samantha failed to notice. She began to study the mount with care.

It was a magnificent animal, dark, gleaming chestnut, at least sixteen hands, she estimated, classic lines, fully flowing mane and proud, dished face. Arabian. Samantha knew horses and she recognized a full-blooded Arabian stallion when she saw one. What in the world…? "That's an Arabian." Her words interrupted her thoughts.

"Yes, ma'am," he agreed easily, entirely too easily. Her eyes narrowed with suspicion as she turned to him.

"No ranch hand is going to be riding around on a horse that's worth six months' pay." She stared at him and he returned the steady survey with a bland, poker face. "Who are you?"

"Jake Tanner, ma'am." The slow grin appeared again, widening, deepening, then settling as he lifted the brim of his hat at the introduction. "Pleased to meet you."

The land baron with the women at his feet, Samantha's brain flashed. Anger darkened her eyes.

"Why didn't you say so?"

"Just did," he pointed out.

"Oh." She tossed back her thick fall of hair. "You know very well what I mean. I thought you were one of Dan's men."

"Yes, ma'am." He nodded.

"Stop *ma'aming* me," she commanded. "What a mean trick! All you had to do was open your mouth and say who you were. I would have stabled Dan's horse myself."

"I didn't mind." His expression became annoyingly agreeable. "It wasn't any trouble, and you had a nice rest."

"Well, Mr. Tanner, you had a fine laugh at my expense. I hope you enjoyed it," she said coldly.

"Yes, ma'am." The grin widened without seeming to move at all. "I did."

"I told you to stop…" She halted, biting her lip with frustration. "Oh, forget it." Tossing her head, she took a few steps toward the house, then turned back crossly. "I notice your accent has modified quite a bit, Mr. Tanner."

He did not reply, but continued to stand negligently, his hands in his pockets, his face darkened by the late-afternoon shadows. Samantha spun back around and stomped toward the house.

"Hey," he called out, and she turned toward him before she could halt the reflex. "Do I still get that pie?"

She answered his question with a glare. His laughter, deep and rich, followed her into the house.

Chapter 2

The sound of the slamming door reverberated through the ranch house as Samantha struggled out of her jacket and marched into the living room. At the sight of her sister's face Sabrina slipped down into the pillows, picked up the novel lying on her lap and buried her nose in its pages. Dan, however, did not recognize the storm warning in his sister-in-law's blue eyes and flushed cheeks. He greeted her with a friendly, ingenuous smile.

"Where's Jake?" His gaze slid past her. "Don't tell me he went home without a cup of coffee?"

"He can go straight to the devil without his coffee."

"I expect he wanted to get home before dark," Dan concluded. His nod was sober, but his eyes were brilliant with merriment.

"Don't play innocent with me, Dan Lomax." Samantha advanced on him. "That was a rotten trick, letting me think he was one of your hands, and…" A giggle escaped from behind the paperback. "I'm glad you think it's amusing that your sister's been made a fool of."

"Oh, Sam, I'm sorry." Warily, Sabrina lowered the book. "It's just hard to believe anyone could mistake Jake Tanner for a ranch hand." She burst out laughing, and Samantha was torn between the pleasure of seeing her sister laugh and irritation at being the brunt of the joke.

"Well, really, what makes him so special?" she demanded. "He dresses like every other cowboy I've seen around here, and that hat of his has certainly seen better days." But, she remembered, there *had* been something special about him that she had not quite been able to define. She firmly dismissed this disquieting thought. "The nerve of him." She rounded on Dan again. "Calling you boss, and ma'aming me in that exaggerated drawl."

"Reckon he was just being polite," Dan suggested. His smile was amiable and pure. Samantha sent him the look that terrified her students.

"Men." Raising her eyes, she searched the ceiling in hopes of finding the answer there. "You're all alike, and you all stick together." She bent and scooped up the sleeping Shylock and marched into the kitchen.

Time at the ranch passed quickly. Though her days were full and busy, Samantha fretted for some of the physical outlet that had so long been part of her life. At times, the confinement of the house was suffocating. Years of training and discipline had left her with an inherent need for activity.

Unconsciously, she separated her life into three categories: the pre-Olympic years, the Olympic years and the post-Olympic years.

The pre-Olympic years were a blur of lessons, piano teachers, dance instructors, her mother's gentle but inescapable admonishments to "be a lady." Then, the first time she had gripped the lower bar of the unevens, the new chapter had begun.

By the time she was twelve years old, she had remarkable promise. The gymnastics instructor had informed her mother, who was more distressed than pleased at the praise. Though her mother had objected to more intense training, Samantha had ultimately prevailed.

The hours of training became months, county meets became state meets, and national competitions became international competitions. When Samantha was picked for the Olympic team, it was just another step down a road she was determined to follow. Weariness and aching muscles were accepted without hesitation.

Then it was over, and at fifteen she had found it necessary to alter what had become a way of life. College had to be considered, and earning a living. The years passed into the post-Olympic period, and she remembered her days of athletic competitions as a dream. Now her life was shifting again, though she was unsure as to the direction. The mountains and plains were calling to her, inviting her to explore, but she buried her desires, remaining indoors to see to her sister's needs. Dan is a busy man, she thought as she prepared lunch, and Bree needs someone within calling distance during this critical period. When she's better, there will be plenty of time to see the country.

She arched her back and rubbed a small spot of tension at the base of her neck. The kitchen door opened and Dan burst in, accompanied by Jake Tanner. Samantha met the amused green eyes levelly, though once more she felt treacherously at a disadvantage.

Her hair had been carelessly scooped on the top of her head that morning, and now, with their usual abandonment, stray locks were beginning to escape confinement. She was dressed in a black ribbed sweater that had seen too many washings and ancient jeans, splattered, faded, patched and too tight. She resisted the urge to raise her hand to her tumbling hair, forced a smile and turned to her brother-in-law.

"Hello, Dan. What are you doing home this time of day?" Purposefully, she ignored the tall figure beside him.

"Wasn't too far out," Dan explained. Slipping off his jacket and hat, he tossed both over the hooks provided. "Jake was giving me a hand, so I figured it was only neighborly to bring him back for lunch."

"Hope I'm not imposing, ma'am." The slow smile spread, once more rearranging the angles of his face.

"No imposition, Mr. Tanner. But you'll have to settle for potluck."

"My favorite dish—" he paused, giving her a cheeky wink "—next to apple pie."

Samantha sent him a withering glance and turned away to warm the previous evening's stew.

"I'll just go tell Sabrina I'm home," Dan announced to the room in general, and strode away. Samantha did her best to ignore Jake's disturbing presence. She stirred the stew busily.

"Smells good." Jake moved over to the stove and

lounged against it. Samantha went to the cupboard to get the bowls.

When she turned back to place them on the round kitchen table, she noticed that he had shed his outdoor clothing. The slim-fitting jeans, snug and low on narrow hips, accentuated his leanness. His flannel shirt fitted over his broad shoulders and hard chest before tapering down to a narrow waist. The athlete in her immediately responded to the firm, well-proportioned body; there was not an ounce of spare flesh on him.

"Don't talk much, do you?" The drawl was there again, the exaggerated twang of the previous evening. Samantha turned her head, prepared to freeze him with her eyes.

His face was barely inches from hers as he slouched by the stove. For a moment, her mind ceased to function.

"I really have nothing to say to you, Mr. Tanner." She struggled to keep her voice cold and detached, but she could feel the blood rush to her face.

"Well, now, we'll have to see if we can change that." He spoke with easy confidence as he straightened to his full height. "We're not much on formalities around here. Just make it Jake." Though his words were spoken with his usual lazy delivery, there was an undertone of command. Samantha's chin rose in defense.

"Maybe I prefer to keep things formal between us, Mr. Tanner."

His lips were curved in his careless smile, but in his eyes she now recognized that special something that separated him from an ordinary ranch hand. *Power.* She wondered how she had missed it at their first meeting.

"I don't think there's much chance of that." He

paused and tugged at a loose lock of his hair before adding with irritating emphasis, "Ma'am. Nope, I don't think there's much chance of that at all."

Samantha was saved from coming up with a suitable rebuttal by Dan's reappearance. She began to spoon the stew into ceramic bowls, noting to her dismay that her hands were not altogether steady. This man was infuriating her with his arrogantly lazy confidence. I have never met a more irritating male, she thought. He thinks he can switch on that rugged cowboy charm and women will drop in droves at his feet. Well, maybe some do, but not this one.

"Okay, Sam?" Dan's voice shattered the electric silence.

"What? I'm sorry, I wasn't listening."

"You'll keep Jake company over lunch, won't you? I'll have mine in the living room with Sabrina."

She swore silently. "Of course," she answered with an impersonal smile.

Within a short time, Samantha found herself sitting across from the man she wanted most to avoid.

"You've a fine hand with dumplings, Sam." Her brows rose involuntarily at his easy use of her nickname, but she kept her voice even.

"Thank you, Mr. Tanner. It's just one of my many talents."

"I'm sure it is," he agreed with an inclination of his head.

"You haven't changed much from the girl in the picture in Sabrina's parlor." Samantha was astonished.

"You'd have been about fifteen," he continued. "A bit skinnier than you are now, but your hair was the same, not quite willing to stay bundled on top of your head."

Samantha's blank expression had turned to a frown at the word skinnier. She remembered the photo clearly.

"You'd just finished winning your second medal." She had indeed been fifteen. The picture had been snapped at the moment she had completed her floor routine. It had captured the look of stunned triumph, for she had known in that instant that a medal was hers.

"Sabrina's just about as proud of you as you are worried about her." Samantha said nothing, only staring into the lean, handsome features. His brows rose ever so slightly, a movement that would have gone unnoticed had she not been so intent on his face. For a moment, she forgot the thread of the conversation, caught up suddenly in a series of small, irrelevant details: the curling gold which spilled over his brow, the tiny white scar on his jawline, the thickness of his long lashes. Confused, she dropped her eyes to her bowl and struggled to bring her thoughts to order.

"I'd forgotten Bree had that picture," she said. "It was a long time ago."

"So now you teach. You don't look like any gym teacher I ever knew."

"Oh, really?"

"No, ma'am." He shook his head slowly and considered her through another mouthful of stew. "Don't look strong enough or old enough."

"I assure you, Jake, I'm both strong enough and old enough for my profession."

"What made you become a gym teacher?" His sudden question caught her off balance, and she stared at him.

"Well, I..." Her shoulders moved restlessly. "Our mother was a fanatic on lessons when Bree and I were growing up." She smiled in spite of herself. "We took lessons in everything, Mom's theory on being well-rounded. Anyway, Bree found her talent in music and I developed a knack for the physical. For a while, I focused on gymnastics, then, when the time came to work, it seemed natural. Bree taught little people to play the classics, and I teach bigger people to tumble."

"Do you like your work? Are you happy with it?"

"As a matter of fact, I do," she retorted. "I like the activity, I like being involved in a physical type of work. It can be frustrating at times, of course. Some of the girls I teach would rather be flirting with their boyfriends than learning gymnastics, I suspect."

"And you yourself are more interested in calisthenics than men?" The question was delivered with a broad masculine smile.

"That's hardly relevant," she snapped, annoyed that she had lowered her guard.

"You don't think so?"

Samantha scraped back her chair and moved to the stove. "Coffee?"

"Yes, ma'am, black." It was unnecessary to turn around; she felt the slow grin crease his face as clearly as if she had witnessed it with her eyes. She set the cup down on the table with a bang. Before she could spin back to pour her own, her hand was captured in a firm grip. There was nothing soft about the hand. It was hard and masculine.

Completely outmatched in the short battle that ensued, Samantha discovered that under the lean, lanky exterior lay an amazing strength. Deciding that it was undignified to grapple in her sister's kitchen, she allowed her hand to rest quietly in his, meeting his laughing eyes with a resentful glare. Her heart began to pound uncomfortably against her ribs.

"What do you want?" Her voice came out in a husky whisper. His eyes left hers to travel slowly down to the generous curve of her mouth, lingering until she could taste the heat on her lips, as real as a kiss. Taking his time, he moved his gaze back to her eyes.

"You're jumpy." His observation was laconic, as if none of the heat had touched him, though she herself was beginning to suffocate. "Powerful strong for such a little bit of a thing."

"I'm not little," she retorted. "You're just so big." She began to tug at her hand again, feeling a near desperate urgency to shake off the contact that was infusing her with an unexplained weakness around the knees.

"Your eyes are fabulous when you're angry, Sam." His tone was conversational. "Temper agrees with you. You grow beautiful with it." He laughed and pulled her closer.

"You're insufferable," she said, still struggling to escape his grasp.

"For telling you you're beautiful? I was just stating the obvious. I'm sure it's been mentioned to you once or twice before."

"You men are all the same." She ceased her struggles long enough to aim a lethal glare. "Always grabbing and groping."

"I don't grope, Samantha." His drawl was feather-soft. For an instant, the cocky cowboy vanished, and she glimpsed the man, shrewd and ruthless, beneath. Here was a man who not only expected to have his own way, but would. "And the next time I grab you, it won't only be to hold your hand." Releasing her, he leaned back in his chair. "You have been warned."

Later, as Sabrina napped and the house grew still around her, Samantha found herself staring blankly at the pages of a novel. Scowling, she tossed it aside and rose from the sofa to pace to the window. What an infuriating man. Obviously, he considers himself irresistible. She began to wander the room, attempting to block out the effect his blatant virility had had on her.

It was too bad, she decided on her fourth circle, that all those good looks, all that strength and appeal, had to belong to such a rude, arrogant man.

Deciding that a brisk walk was just what she needed to get Jake Tanner out of her mind, she stopped her pacing and grabbed a warm jacket. Moments later she was out the door, gazing around her in delight at the beauty of the starlit Wyoming night. Her breath puffed out in thin white mists as she moved. The air, tinged with frost, carried the aroma of pine, and she drank it in greedily, enjoying the mixed scent of hay and horses and aged wood. She could hear the lonely sound of a coyote calling to the full silver moon. And suddenly she realized that she had fallen in love with Wyoming. The spell of the mountains and plains was on her, and she was inexplicably glad she had come.

"Goodness, you were out a long time," her sister commented as Samantha plopped down in a wingback chair in front of the fire a few minutes later. "You must be frozen."

"No." Samantha stretched out her legs and sighed. "I love it out there. It's fantastic! I never realized how big the sky was before, and I don't think I'll ever get used to the space, the openness."

She turned her attention to the powerfully built man sitting next to her sister on the sofa. "I wonder if you appreciate it, Dan, living here all of your life. Even your letters, Bree, didn't do justice to that world out there." Running her fingers through her hair, she made a small sound of pleasure. "To someone used to traffic-choked streets and huge buildings, all this…" Her hands moved in an inadequate gesture.

"You haven't had much of a chance to see anything since you've been here," Dan observed. "You've been with us a month and you haven't gone a quarter mile away from the house. And that's been mostly to fetch the mail in the mornings."

"I'll have plenty of time to explore later. I'll be around through the summer."

"Just the same, we're not having you tied to the house while you're here, Sam," Dan announced, and sat back against the cushions. "Even the most devoted sister is entitled to a day off."

"Don't be silly. You make it sound as though I were slaving from dawn to dusk. Half the time I'm not doing anything."

"We know how hard you're working, Sam," Sabrina said quietly, glancing up at Dan before returning her gaze to her twin. "And I know the lack of activity is harder on you than the work. I also know how you disrupted your life to come out here and take care of me."

"Oh, Bree, for heaven's sake," Samantha began, shifting uncomfortably. "I never would have found out how much I love Wyoming if I hadn't come."

"Don't try to shrug if off, Sam." Dan grinned at the

embarrassed motion of her shoulders. "We're grateful, and you'll just have to get used to us telling you so. But tomorrow, we're going to show we're grateful instead of just talking about it. We're kicking you out for the day."

"Huh?" Blankly, Sam blinked at the bland smile before shifting her gaze to Sabrina's serene one.

"That's right." His grin widened as she drew her brows together. "Tomorrow's Sunday, and I'm staying home with my wife. And you…" He pointed a warning finger at his sister-in-law. "You're going to have your pick of the horses and take off."

Samantha sprung up from her slouched position. "Do you mean it?" Her face was glowing with pleasure, and Dan's smile warmed with affection.

"Yes, little sister, I mean it. It should be more."

"The dapple-gray gelding," she began in a rush, ignoring the last part of his comment. "Can I take him?"

"Already inspected the stock, and it appears you know your horses." Dan chuckled and shook his head. "Spook's a good mount. A little frisky, but from what Sabrina's told me, you can handle him."

"Oh, I can, and I promise I'll be careful with him." She sprang from her chair and crossed the room, flinging her arms around his neck. "Thanks, Dan. You are absolutely my favorite brother-in-law, bar none."

"I think she likes the idea, Sabrina," Dan commented as he met his wife's eyes over Samantha's head. "In fact, I'd say she's downright pleased about it."

"And I thought I hid my emotions so effectively." She gave his cheek a loud, smacking kiss.

"You be ready to start out about nine." He patted Samantha's slim shoulder. "Jake'll be around, then."

"Jake?" Samantha repeated. Her smile froze.

"Yeah, he'll be riding out with you. Actually," Dan continued, "he suggested the idea this afternoon. He thought it would do you good to get out of the house for a while." He sighed and scratched his dark head, managing to appear sheepish, for all his size. "I'm ashamed I didn't think of it first. I guess I've been a bit preoccupied and didn't notice you were looking a littled tired and hemmed in."

"I'm not tired," she denied automatically.

"Hemmed in?" Sabrina offered with a knowing smile.

"A little, maybe, but I'm hardly in the last stages of cabin fever. I'm sure it's very kind of Mr. Tanner to be so concerned about my welfare." She managed to say his name in a normal voice. "But there's certainly no need for him to go with me. I know he has hundreds of more important things to do with his Sunday."

"Well, now, he didn't seem to think so," Dan said. "It was his suggestion, and he seemed keen on the idea, too."

"I don't know why he would be," she muttered. "Besides, I don't want to impose on him. We're practically strangers. I can just go by myself."

"Nonsense." Dan's refusal was good-natured but firm. "I couldn't possibly let you ride out by yourself just yet, no matter how good you are on a horse. You don't know the country, and it's easy to get lost. There's always the possibility of an accident. Besides," he added, and his grin was expansive, "you're part of the family, and I grew up with Jake, so you're not strangers. If anyone knows his way around this part of Wyoming, he does." He shrugged and rested his back against the cushions. "He owns half of it, anyway." Samantha glanced at her sister for help. Sabrina, however, appeared to be engrossed in her needlepoint.

Frowning at the lack of support, Samantha stewed over her predicament. If she refused Jake's company, she would not only forfeit the opportunity to ride the Wyoming countryside, but she would spoil Sabrina and Dan's plans for a day alone together. She shrugged in resignation and offered a smile.

"I'll be ready at nine." She added to herself, If Jake Tanner can stand a day in my company, I guess I can stand a day in his.

Chapter 3

Sunday dawned with a sky as cold and clear as sapphire. The sun offered thin light and little warmth. To her annoyance, Samantha had overslept. Hurriedly, she showered and dressed in forest-green cords and a chunky beige pullover.

Her riding boots clattered on the parquet floor as she hurried from her room and down the hall to the kitchen. She frowned as she reached the doorway. Jake was sitting at the table, enjoying a cup of coffee with the air of one very much at home.

He was, she noted with illogical irritation, every bit as attractive as she remembered.

"Oh, you're here." Her greeting was hardly welcoming, but he returned it with his slow smile.

"Morning, ma'am."

"Don't start ma'aming me again," she said.

He remained silent as she clattered the cups in the cupboard and filled one with the steaming liquid from the pot on the stove.

"Sorry." She popped a piece of bread in the toaster and turned to offer a peace-offering smile. "My! I overslept. I hope you haven't been waiting long."

"I've got all day," he answered, leaning back in his chair as if to emphasize his words.

She drew a slab of bacon and a carton of eggs from the refrigerator. "Have you eaten?" she asked in invitation.

"Yeah, thanks." He rose, poured himself another cup of coffee and resumed his position at the table. "Dan's already seen to breakfast for himself and Sabrina. They're having it in their room."

"Oh." She replaced the items and pulled out the butter.

"Aren't you going to eat?"

"Toast and coffee. I'm not much on breakfast."

"If you always eat like that," he observed over the rim of his cup, "it's no wonder you never grew any bigger."

"For goodness' sake." She whirled around, brandishing the butter knife. "I'm hardly a midget. I'm five-four, that's tall enough for anybody."

He held up his hands in mock surrender. "I never argue with an armed woman.

"Ready?" He rose when she had finished both the toast and another cup of coffee.

When she mumbled her assent, he plucked her jacket from its hook, holding it out so that she had no choice but to allow him to help her into it. She stiffened as his hands touched her shoulders and turned her to face him. Her pulses responded immediately. As if he were aware of her reaction, he began to do up her leather buttons with slow care. She jerked back, but his hold on the front of her coat prevented her from a clean escape.

"You're a pretty little thing," he drawled, completing his task with his eyes directly on hers. "Can't have you catching cold." He reached out and plucked Sabrina's dark wide-brimmed hat from a peg and placed it neatly on her head. "This'll keep your head warm."

"Thanks." She pushed the hat firmly in place.

"Anytime, Sam." His face was unperturbed as he pulled his own sheepskin jacket over his flannel shirt and jeans.

On the way to the stables, Samantha increased her pace to a trot to keep up with Jake's long, careless stride. Despite herself, she admired the confident, loose-limbed grace of his movement. He took his time, she noted, deciding he probably did nothing quickly, and more than likely still finished ahead of everyone else.

The dapple gray had been saddled and led outside by a smiling ranch hand.

"Howdy, ma'am. Dan said to have Spook ready for you."

"Thanks." She returned his friendly smile and patted the gelding's neck. "But I could have done it. I don't like to give you extra work."

"No trouble, ma'am. Dan said you weren't to do a lick of work today. You just go and have yourself a good time, and I'll rub old Spook down when you get back."

Samantha vaulted easily onto the horse's back, happy to feel a mount beneath her again. Riding was an old pleasure, to be enjoyed only when finances allowed.

"Now, you take good care of Miss Evans, Jake," the

cowboy admonished with a conspirator's wink Samantha failed to catch. "Dan sets great store by this little lady."

Little again, Samantha thought.

"Don't you worry about Miss Evans, Lon." Jake mounted his stallion with a fluid motion. Again Samantha noticed that he wasted no time on superfluous movement. "I intend to keep a close eye on her."

Samantha acknowledged Jake's statement with a wrinkled nose, then, following the direction his hand indicated, set off in a brisk canter.

As the neat cluster of ranch buildings was left behind, her irritation vanished. The rushing air was exciting, filling her lungs and whipping roses into her cheeks. She had almost forgotten the sense of liberation riding gave her. It was the same sensation that she had experienced many times when flying from top to bottom or springing high in a double twist.

They rode in silence for a quarter of an hour. Jake allowed her to fill her being with the thrill of movement and the beauty of the countryside. Wild peaks jutted arrogantly into the sky. The rolling plains below were yellow-green with winter. They rode by Herefords, white-faced and sleek, who noted their passing with a lazy turn of the head before resuming their grazing.

A shape darted across an open field, and Samantha slowed her horse to a walk and pointed. "What's that?"

"Antelope," Jake answered, narrowing his eyes against the sun.

"Oh!" She halted her mount and watched the animal's graceful, bounding progress until it streaked over a hill and out of her view. "It must be marvelous to run like that, graceful and free." She turned her unguarded face to the man beside her and found him regarding her intently. His eyes held an expression she did not understand. A strange tingling raced along her spine, like warm fingers on cold skin. The tingling increased, the sensation spreading to settle somewhere in her stomach. Suddenly, his expression changed. The shadows of his face shifted as his lips moved into a smile.

"Someday you will be caught, little antelope."

She blinked at him, totally disoriented, trying to remember what they had been talking about. His grin increased. He pointed to a large, bare-limbed tree a quarter of a mile away.

"Race you." There was challenge under the lazy dare.

Her eyes brightened with excitement. "Fine chance I'd have against a horse like that. What handicap do I get?"

Jake pushed his hat back as if to view her more completely. "From the look of you, I'd say you've got a good fifty-pound advantage. That should balance the odds some."

"No head start?"

"No, ma'am."

She pouted for a moment, then grinned. "All right, Jake Tanner, I'll give you a run for your money."

"Whenever you say, Sam." He pulled the brim of his hat low over his forehead.

"Now!"

She met the gelding's sides with her heels and spurted forward in a gallop. The quiet morning air vibrated with the thunder of hooves. Samantha, her hair flowing behind her, gave herself over to the thrill of the race. She reached the finish just ahead of her competitor and reined in, filling the morning with dusty, breathless laughter.

"Oh, that was wonderful, absolutely wonderful."

"Anytime you want to give up teaching, Sam, you can work for me. I can use a hand who rides like you."

"I'll keep that in mind, even though I know you let me beat you."

"Now, what makes you think that?" He leaned his arm on the horn of his saddle and watched her thoughtfully.

"I'm not stupid." Her grin was good-natured and friendly. "I couldn't beat that Arabian in a million years. You, maybe," she added with a touch of arrogance, "but not that horse."

"Pretty sharp, aren't you?" he returned, answering her grin.

"As a tack," she agreed. "And," she continued, brushing her hair from her shoulders, "I am not a weak female who needs to be placated. With my background, I know how to compete, I know how to lose, and—" she grinned and lifted her brows "—I know how to win."

"Point taken." He tilted his head as if to view her from a different angle. "From now on, Sam, we play head-to-head." He smiled, and she was no longer sure they were talking about the same thing. "I know how to win, too," he added slowly. They continued at a leisurely pace for a time, crossing a narrow branch of the Medicine Bow River. They paused there for the horses to quench their thirst in the icy water that forced its way over shining rocks with hisses and whispers. At Samantha's request, Jake began to identify the surrounding mountains.

Pointing to the long fingers of peaks at the south, the Laramie Range, he told her they extended from eastern Colorado. The middle section was the Medicine Bow

Range, and the Sierra Madre loomed to the west. The vast ranges were separated by broad tongues of the Wyoming Basin. Silver-blue, they gleamed in the sunlight, lacings of snow trembling from their summits.

She had reined in without being aware of her action. "I can never look at them long enough. I suppose you're used to them."

"No." There was no laughter or mockery in his tone. "You never get used to them."

She smiled a bit uncertainly, not at all sure she could deal with this side of him.

"Are there bears up there?" she asked.

He glanced up at the mountains, smiled, then looked back at her. "Black bear and grizzly," he informed her. "Elk, coyotes, mountain lions…"

"Mountain lions?" she repeated, a little nervously.

"You're not likely to run into one down here," he returned with an indulgent smile.

She ignored the mockery in his voice and looked around her, again awed by the miles of open space. "I wonder if this looked the same a century ago."

"Some of it. Those don't change much." He indicated the Rockies with an inclination of his head. "The Indians are gone," he continued, as if thinking aloud. "There were Arapaho, Sioux, Cheyenne, Crow, Shoshone, all roaming free over the state before the first white man set foot here. Then trappers came, trading with Indians, dressing like them, living like them, and the beaver was nearly driven into extinction." He turned back to her, as if suddenly remembering she was there. "You're the teacher." His smile appeared. "You should be telling me."

Samantha shook her head in mock despair. "My

knowledge of Wyoming's history is limited to late-night Westerns." They were walking their horses slowly, side by side. She had completely forgotten her aversion to the man beside her. "It's impossible to believe the killing and cruelty that must have gone on here. It's so serene, and so vast. It seems there would have been room enough for everyone."

This time it was Jake who shook his head. "In 1841 more than a hundred and fifty thousand people crossed the South Pass going west, and a few years later, fifty thousand more came through on their way to California looking for gold. This was Indian land, had been Indian land for generations. Game disappeared, and when people get hungry, they fight. Treaties were signed, promises made by both sides, broken by both sides." He shrugged.

"In the 1860s, they tried to open the Bozeman Pass from Fort Laramie to Montana, and open war broke out. The trail ran through the Sioux hunting ground. The fighting was of the worst kind, massacres, indiscriminate killing of women and children, butcheries by both white and Indian. More treaties were signed, more misunderstandings, more killing, until the whites outnumbered the Indians, drove them away or put them on reservations."

"It doesn't seem fair," Samantha whispered, feeling a wave of sadness wash over her.

"No, it doesn't." He heard the wistful note in her voice and turned to regard her. "Life isn't always fair, though, is it, Samantha?"

"I suppose not." She sighed. "You seem to know quite a bit about what happened here. You must have had a good history teacher."

"I did." He held her curious look with a teasing half smile on his lips. "My great-grandmother lived to be ninety-eight. She was Sioux."

Samantha lifted her brows in surprised interest. "Oh, I'd love to have met her. The things she must have seen, the changes in nearly a century of living."

"She was quite a woman." His smile faded a moment. "She taught me a lot. Among other things, she told me that the land goes on no matter who walks on it, that life moves on whether you fight against it or flow with it, that when you want something, you go after it until it's yours."

Suddenly, she felt he was leading her out of her depth, reaching for something she was not sure she possessed. She turned from the directness of his eyes to search the land.

"I'd like to have seen all this before there were any fences, before there was any fighting."

Jake pointed skyward. Glancing up, Samantha watched the graceful flight of an eagle. For a timeless moment, it soared overhead, the undisputed sovereign of the skies. They moved off again, in companionable silence. "I hope you're getting some fun out of this trip, some compensation for taking care of your sister," Jake said at last.

"I don't need any compensation for taking care of Bree, she's my sister, my…"

"Responsibility?"

"Well…yes. I've always looked out for Bree, she's more delicate, more…dependent than I am." She shrugged and felt uncomfortable without knowing why. "Dad always joked that I took my share of strength and half of Bree's while we were still in the womb. She needs me," she added, feeling compelled to defend what she had always taken for granted.

"She has Dan," Jake reminded her. "And she's a grown woman now—just as you are. Did it ever occur to you that you have your own life to lead now that Sabrina has a husband to care for her?"

"I'm not trying to take over for Dan," she said quickly. "Perhaps you can figure out how he could see to her needs and tend to the house and the ranch all at the same time, but I can't." She glared at him, half in anger, half in exasperation. "What do you expect me to do? Sit up in Philadelphia teaching kids to jump on a tramp while my sister needs help?"

"No, Samantha." He met her eyes with a quiet patience that was more disturbing than angry words and shouts. "What you're doing is very kind and unselfish."

"There's nothing kind or unselfish about it," she interrupted, shrugging the words away. "We're sisters. More than that, we're twins. We shared life from its beginning. You can't understand the kind of bond that creates. I'd give up a hundred jobs to help Bree if she needed me."

"No one's condemning your loyalty, Samantha. It's an admirable trait." He gave her a long, level look. "Just a word of advice. Don't become so involved that you forget who Samantha Evans is, and that she just might have the right to her own woman's life."

Samantha drew herself up to her full height in the saddle. "I hardly need your advice on how to run my life. I've been managing nicely for some time now."

His face creased in a lazy smile. "Yes, ma'am, I'm sure you have."

Chapter 4

Samantha had been riding the dapple gray in stubborn silence for nearly thirty minutes when she noticed more cattle. Her guide seemed unperturbed by her silence and slowed his Arabian's gait to the gelding's meandering walk. She would never have admitted to the man at her side that his words had disturbed her peace of mind.

What business was it of his how she chose to run her life? What gave Jake Tanner the right to question her relationship with Sabrina? No one asked him for his advice. And why in heaven's name should anything he said matter in the first place?

They were approaching a large ranch house. A red-wood porch skirted the building's front, graced by evergreen shrubs. A gray wisp of smoke rose in a welcoming spire from the chimney. Ranch buildings sat neat and unobtrusive in the background.

"Welcome to the Double T, ma'am."

Jake drew her eyes with the uncharacteristic formality in his tone. She turned to see him smile and touch the brim of his well-worn Stetson.

"Thank you, Mr. Tanner. I can honestly say your ranch is spectacular. But what, may I ask, are we doing here?"

"Well, now…" Jake shifted in the saddle to face her directly. "I don't know about you, but nearly three hours in the saddle gives me a powerful appetite. I figured here we might do a bit better than beef jerky."

"Three hours?" Samantha repeated, and pushed Sabrina's hat from her head so it lay against her back. "Has it really been that long?"

The angles of his face moved slowly with his grin, and she found herself once more intrigued by the process. "I'll take that to mean you were so delighted with my company, time stood still."

She answered with a toss of her head. "I hate to tread on your ego, Jake, but the credit goes to Wyoming."

"Close enough for now." Reaching over, he plopped the brimmed hat back in place on Samantha's head and urged his mount into a canter.

Samantha stared after him in exasperation, watching the confidence with which he rode the Arabian. They moved like one form rather than horse and man. Scowling, she pressed her heels to the gelding's side and raced forward to join him.

As she reached his side, he skirted the ranch house and rode toward the buildings in the rear, following the left fork on a long, hard-packed road. A large, sleepy-eyed Saint Bernard rose from his siesta and romped forward to greet them. A deep, hoarse bark emitted from his throat. Jake halted in front of the stables. He slid off the Arabian's back, running his hand through the dog's thick fur as he hit the ground.

"Wolfgang's harmless." He acknowledged the loving, wet kisses with another brief caress and moved to the gelding's side. "He's just a puppy."

"A puppy," Samantha repeated. "You don't see many hundred-and-fifty-pound puppies." Tilting her head, she gave the overgrown baby a thorough examination before she brought her leg over the saddle to dismount.

Jake gripped her waist as she made her descent, holding her off the ground a moment as if she were weightless. As her boots touched earth, she was turned around and drawn against a hard chest. She tilted her head to inform him that his assistance was unnecessary, but saw only a brief blur of his face before his lips captured hers.

Her mind whirled with the touch and scent of him. She felt as though she were falling into a deep well and her heart began to beat a mad tempo against her ribs. She clutched at his jacket in defense. Perhaps the kiss was brief. It could have lasted no more than a portion of a minute, but it felt like forever. She knew his mouth was warm and sure on hers while decades flew into centuries.

The strange sensations of timelessness and loss of control frightened her. She stiffened and began to struggle against his grasp. He released her immediately, staring down at her clouded blue eyes with a satisfied smile. The smile transformed terror into fury.

"How dare you?"

"Just testing, ma'am." His answer was complacent, as though the kiss had been no more than that, a traditional touching of lips.

"Testing?" she repeated, running an agitated hand through her hair. "Testing what?"

"I've always wanted to kiss a teacher." Grinning, he gave her a friendly pat on the cheek. "I think there're some holes in your education."

"I'll show you holes, you conceited, high-handed—" her mind searched for something appropriately derogatory and settled on a generality "—*man*. If I didn't consider that kiss so insignificant, you'd be lying on your back checking out the sky."

He surveyed her as she trembled with a mixture of fury and wounded pride. He rubbed his chin thoughtfully. "You know, Sam, I almost believe you could do it."

"You can bank on it," she confirmed with an arrogant toss of her head. "And the next time you..." Feeling her arm sharply pulled, she glanced down to see the sleeve of her jacket captured in the awesome jaws of the Saint Bernard. "What'd you do, teach him to eat unwilling females?"

"He just wants to make your acquaintance," Jake laughed, as he led the horses to the stable to turn them over to one of his men.

Samantha was not normally timid, and her pride refused to allow her to call Jake to untangle her from the teeth of his puppy. She swallowed and spoke to her canine captor.

"Hello...Wolfgang, wasn't it?" she muttered. "I'm Sam. You, ah, wouldn't consider letting go of my jacket, would you?" The dog continued to stare with droopy, innocent eyes. "Well, that's all right," she said, trying out magnanimity. "It's just an old one, anyway. I'm very fond of dogs, you know." Tentatively, she brought her free hand up to touch the fur on his huge head. "Well, actually, I have a cat," she admitted in apology, "but I have absolutely no prejudices."

Though his expression did not alter, she decided it was prudent to give him time for consideration. Her patience was rewarded when he released her sleeve and bathed her hand with his enormous tongue.

"Well, I see you two have made friends," Jake drawled, coming up behind her.

"No thanks to you," she said. "He might have eaten me alive."

"Not you, Sam," Jake disagreed, taking her hand and striding toward the house. "Too tough for Wolfgang's taste."

Jake led her to the back entrance through a paneled, tiled-floor mudroom and into the kitchen. A large square room, it was bright and cheery with tangerine curtains framing the wide windows. The pleasant-looking woman who stood by the sink smiled at Samantha. "Jake, you scoundrel, have you had this poor little lady out in the cold all this time?" Samantha met the warm brown eyes with a returning smile.

Jake grinned, unabashed. "Samantha Evans, meet Annie Holloway, my cook, housekeeper and best girl."

"Don't you try soft soaping me, you young devil." She brushed off his words with indulgent affection, but pleased color rose to her pudgy cheeks. "Thinks he can get around me with sweet talk. Pleased to meet you, Miss Evans." Samantha found her hand enclosed in a firm grip.

"Hello, Miss Holloway, I hope I'm not putting you out."

"Putting me out?" Annie let out a rich, full laugh,

her ample bust heaving with the sound. "Isn't she the sweet one? Don't you be silly, now, and you just call me Annie like everyone else."

"Thank you, Annie." Samantha's smile warmed. "Everyone calls me Sam."

"Now, that's a pretty thing," Annie commented, peering candidly into Samantha's face. "Yes, sir, a right pretty thing. You two run along," she commanded with an attempt at sternness. "Out of my kitchen. Lunch will be along, and I'll bring you in some tea to warm you up. Not you," she said with a scowl as Jake grimaced. "For the little lady. You don't need any warming up."

"Annie runs things," Jake explained as he led Samantha down a wide hall into the living room.

"I can see she does, even when she's securely wrapped around your little finger."

For a moment, his smile was so boyish and full of mischief, she nearly gave in to the urge to brush the curls from his forehead.

The paneling in the living room was light. The expanse of wood was broken by a large stone fireplace and wide windows framed with cinnamon-colored sheers. The dark gleaming furniture had been upholstered in gold, burnt sienna and rich browns. There was a comfortable hodgepodge of Hepplewhites and Chippendales with piecrust tilt-top tables and Pembrokes, ladder-back chairs and candlestands. In the center of the hardwood floor lay a wide rug of Indian design, so obviously old and handworked, that Samantha wondered if it had been his great-grandmother's fingers that had hooked it perhaps nearly a century ago. The room reflected a quiet, understated wealth, a wealth she somehow did not associate with the rangy, brash cowboy side of Jake.

A Charles Russell painting caught her eye. She turned to study it, attempting to sort out her new impressions of this complex man. Turning back, she found him watching her reaction with unconcealed amusement.

"I have a feeling you were expecting bearskins and oilcloth."

Samantha focused her attention on the inviting fire. "I never know what to expect from you," she muttered.

"No?" He dropped his lanky form into a wingback chair and pulled out a long, thin cigar. "I thought you were pretty bright."

Samantha seated herself in the chair across from him, keeping the warmth and hiss of the fire between them. "This is a lovely room, very appealing and very warm."

"I'm glad you like it." If he noticed her blatant change of subject, he gave no sign. Lighting his cigar, he stretched out his legs and looked totally relaxed and content.

"I have a weakness for antiques," she continued, deciding the topic was safe and impersonal.

He smiled, the smoke curling lazily above his head. "There's a piece in one of the bedrooms you might like to see. A blanket chest in walnut that was brought over from the East in the 1860s."

"I'd like that very much." She returned his smile and settled back as Annie wheeled a small tea cart into the room.

"I brought you coffee," she said to Jake, and passed him a cup. "I know you won't take tea unless you douse it with bourbon. Something not quite decent about doing that to a good cup of tea."

"Tea is an old ladies' drink," he stated, ignoring her rapidly clucking tongue.

"How do you think Sabrina looks?" Samantha asked him when Annie had bustled back to the kitchen.

"I think you worry too much about her."

She bristled instinctively before replying. "Perhaps you're right," she surprised herself by admitting. "Our mother always said Bree and I were mirror images, meaning, I discovered after a while, opposites."

"Right down to Sabrina being right-handed, and you being left."

"Why, yes." She looked at him in faint surprise. "You don't miss much, do you?" He merely shook his head and gave her an enigmatic smile. "Well," she plunged on, not sure she liked his expression, a bit like a cat who already had the mouse between his paws. "I suppose the summary of my discrepancies was that I could never keep the hem in my white organdy party dress. You'd have to know my mother to understand that. She would have Bree and me all decked out in these frilly white organdy dresses and send us off to a party. Bree would come back spotless, pure and angelic. I'd come back with dirt on my frills, bloody knees and a trailing hem."

During her story, Jake's smile had widened. The coffee in his cup cooled, unattended as he watched her. "There're doers and there're watchers, Samantha. I imagine you had fun scraping up your knees."

As ridiculous as it seemed, she felt she'd just been complimented, and was both pleased and faintly embarrassed.

"I suppose you're a doer, too." She dropped her eyes. "You couldn't run a ranch like this and not be. Cattle ranching sounds romantic, but I imagine it's long hours, hot summers and cold winters. I don't suppose it's really all that different from the way it used to be a hundred years ago."

"The range isn't open anymore," he corrected. "You don't find cowboys going off to Texas to punch cattle with a ten-dollar horse and a forty-dollar saddle." He shrugged and set his empty cup on the table beside him. "But some change slow, and I'm one who likes to take my time."

She was frowning into his smile when Annie announced lunch. It was not until they were settled in the dining room that she spoke directly to him again, pressing him for more details on how the ranch was run.

He explained how roundups, which had once been accomplished on the vast open range with only men and horses, were now aided by fences and technology. But it was still men and ponies who moved the cattle into corrals. Over a few states there were still strongholds of riders and ropers, men who cultivated the old technique and blended it with the new. On the Double T, Jake employed the best of both.

"If roundups aren't what they once were, they still accomplish the same end. Getting the cattle together and branding them."

"Branding?" Samantha interrupted, and shuddered.

"Your Philadelphia's showing, Sam." He grinned. "Take my word for it, branding is a good deal more unpleasant for the branders than the brandees."

She decided to ignore his comments and changed the subject abruptly. "Bree told me your ranch borders Dan's. This place must be huge for it to have taken us three hours to get here."

Jake's deep, rich laughter filled the room, and she

decided unwillingly that she liked the sound very much. "It's a pretty big spread, Sam, but if you take the straight road north for the Lazy L, you can be here in twenty minutes on horseback. I took you on a big circle today," he explained. "Just a small taste of our part of the Laramie Basin."

They lingered over coffee, relaxed in each other's company.

"We'd better get started back," Jake said after a while. He rose and extended his hand. Her own slipped without hesitation into it as he pulled her to her feet. When she looked up at him, her smile was warm and spontaneous.

"Annie was right, that's a pretty thing." He lifted his hand and traced his fingers over the curve of her mouth. She started. "Now, don't go skittish on me, Sam, I'm not going to use spurs and a whip."

His mouth lowered, gentle and persuasive. One hand held hers while the other circled the back of her neck to soothe with coaxing fingers. She had only to sway forward to feel his body against hers, had only to lift her hand to bring his mouth firmer and warmer on hers. Before the choice could be made, he drew her away and the decision was taken out of her hands.

"Sam." He shook his head as if exasperated and lightly amused. "You're enough to try a man's patience."

With this, he pulled her through to the kitchen.

"Well, so you're off again." Annie wiped one hand on her apron and wagged the other at Jake. "And don't be keeping her out in that cold too long."

"No, ma'am," Jake returned with suspicious respect.

"Thank you, Annie," Samantha broke in. "Lunch was wonderful."

"Well, now, that's fine, then." She gave Samantha a friendly pat on the cheek. "You just come back real soon, and you say hi to Sabrina for me, and that young rascal Dan, too. As soon as she's fit again, I'll be coming by to see her. Oh, Jake, I clean forgot." Annie turned to him and sighed at her absentmindedness. "Lesley Marshall called earlier, something about dinner tonight. I told her you'd give her a call, then it went straight out of my mind."

"No problem," Jake said easily. "I'll get back to her later. Ready, Sam?"

"Yes, I'm ready." She kept her smile in place, though a large black cloud seemed to have suddenly smothered the sunshine.

Lesley Marshall, she mused, automatically going through the motions of securing her hat and coat. That was the woman Bree had predicted would marry Jake when he decided to settle down. *Why should it matter to me?* She straightened her spine and accompanied Jake to the waiting horses. *I have absolutely no interest in Jake Tanner's affairs.*

He's probably had dozens of girlfriends. Well, it's no concern of mine. Vaulting into the saddle, she followed as he set off down the hard-packed road.

They spoke little on the return journey. Samantha pretended an engrossment with the scenery that she was far from feeling. Unhappily, she realized Wyoming's magic was not quite enough to lift her flagging spirits. Snowcapped peaks glistened just as brightly in the late-afternoon sun, and the land still spread and beckoned, but as she surveyed them now she felt strangely depressed.

It had been an unusual day, she concluded. Jake had

annoyed her, charmed her, angered her and delighted her, all in a handful of hours. His kiss had aroused excitement and a deeper feeling she could not explain.

The knowledge that he was dining with another woman that evening depressed her beyond belief. She stole a sidelong look at his lean, tanned features.

He was undeniably attractive, she admitted, pulling her eyes away from him before he could sense her study. There was a powerful aura of virility about him, which alternately intrigued her and made her wary. Perhaps it would be wise to avoid his company. He confused her, and Samantha liked to know precisely where she stood with a man. She wanted to call the shots, and she realized that this man would never allow anyone to call the shots but himself.

She would keep her distance from now on. Let him spread his charm over this Lesley Marshall, or any of the other women who were undoubtedly thirsting for his attention. Samantha Evans could get along very easily without him. As the Lazy L grew closer, she resolved to be polite and casually friendly to her escort. After all, she reflected, there was no reason to be rude. He was perfectly free to dine with whomever he chose; his life was most assuredly his own. Besides, she added to herself, if she had anything to say about it, they would be seeing very little of each other in the future.

When they reached the ranch, she dismounted, handing Spook's reins to a waiting cowboy. "I had a wonderful time, Jake." Samantha's smile was faultless in its social politeness as he walked her toward the ranch house, leading his stallion behind him. "I appreciate your time and hospitality."

Jake's mouth lifted at one corner. "It was my pleasure, ma'am."

If there was a mockery in his tone, Samantha chose to ignore it. Reaching the back door, she turned to smile at him again as he stood, tall and lean, beside the gleaming chestnut.

"Would you like some coffee before you go?" she invited, determined to be polite.

"No, thanks, Sam." He continued to watch her, his eyes shaded by the brim of his hat. "I'd best be getting along."

"Well." She breathed a small sigh of relief when her hand touched the doorknob and safety was in easy reach. "Thanks again."

"Sure." He nodded briefly and turned to his horse, paused and turned back to look at her with a penetrating intensity that turned her legs to water. When he spoke, it was soft and final. "I mean to have you, you know."

Several moments of silence passed before she could summon up an answer.

"D-do you?" Her voice was a shaky whisper, unlike the coolly flippant tone she would have wished for.

"Yes, ma'am." He vaulted onto the chestnut's back and pushed the Stetson back on his head so that she had a disturbingly clear view of his eyes. "I do," he confirmed, turning his mount and galloping away.

Chapter 5

Often over the next few days, Samantha told herself that her reaction to Jake's kiss had been merely a passing physical attraction. She was a normal woman, wasn't she? So why feel guilty about it?

Jake Tanner *was* a very attractive man. *Too attractive,* she added to herself. And he knew too much about charming women. The fact that Jake was abrasive, smug and irritating had nothing to do with the way she had acted. It had just been a passing fancy. *And would certainly not occur again.*

Finally Sabrina was allowed up from the confinement of her bed. Samantha decided it was safe to leave her sister for a few hours. With a light heart, she saddled Spook and set off from the ranch at a brisk canter. For a while she enjoyed the feeling of Spook's hooves pounding the hard road. The sky hung low above her, and heavy, leaden gray clouds draped the distant mountains in mysterious gloom. There was a stillness, a waiting in the air, unnoticed by Samantha in her eagerness to escape the close confines of the house.

She rode swiftly past the bored, white-faced cattle and the stretches of barbed wire, eager to explore new territory, tasting the joy of motion and freedom. The mountains, grim sentinels above her, stood stone-gray under the unbroken sky. Remembering Dan's instructions, Samantha took care to mark her route, choosing a clump of rocks, a cottonwood tree with a broken limb, and a gnarled stump as landmarks for her return trip.

She led her mount to a crest of a hill, watching as a jackrabbit, startled by her intrusion, darted across the road and out of sight.

Nearly an hour passed before the first flakes began to drift lazily from sky to earth. She stopped and watched their progress in fascination. The snow fell slowly. Lifting her face, she let it caress her cheeks and closed lids. The air was moist, coming to life around her, and she stirred herself out of her dream.

"Well, Spook, this is my first Wyoming snow. I'd like to stay here all day and watch it fall, but duty calls. We'd better head back." Patting the horse's neck, she turned back toward the ranch.

They rode slowly. Samantha was enchanted with the fairyland that was forming around her. Cottonwoods and aspens were draped in white, their branches a stark contrast to the brilliant etchings of snow. The ground was cloaked quickly. Though the beauty was breathtaking, Samantha began to feel uncomfortably alone.

She took Spook into a canter. The sound of his

hooves was soft and muffled. The quiet surrounding her was unearthly, almost as though the world had ceased to breathe. She shivered, suddenly cold in the warm confines of her jacket. To her annoyance, she saw that in her preoccupation with the landscape she had taken a wrong turn, and she began to backtrack, berating herself for carelessness.

The snow increased, plunging down from a sky she could no longer see. She cursed herself for having come so far, fighting down a sudden surge of panic. "Don't be silly, Sam," she spoke aloud, wanting the reassurance of her own voice. "A little snow won't hurt you."

The cold became more intense, piercing the layers of her skin. Samantha tried to concentrate on steaming coffee and a blazing fire as she looked around for a familiar landmark. Nothing was the same as it had been. She clamped her lips tight to still the chattering of her teeth, telling herself that it was impossible that she could be lost. But it was a lie. The trees and hills around her were strangers blanketed in white.

The snow fell thickly, a blinding white wall blocking her vision. A wind had sprung up, breaking the silence with its moans and tossing snow, hard and bitter, into her face. She was forced to slow the gelding to a walk, afraid of tangling with the sharp teeth of barbed wire she was unable to see. Her teeth savaged her lips in an effort to control a growing terror.

It's so cold, she thought as she began to shiver convulsively, so unbelievably cold.

The snow had soaked through the wool of her slacks and slipped mercilessly down the neck of her coat. She hunched her shoulders against the driving wind. Snow was everywhere, blocking her in and seeping into her clothing.

She let the reins hang limp, praying that the horse's instinct would guide him back to the warm shelter of his stables. They trudged on, the vortex of white that had begun so innocently now whirling around her. Time and direction had lost all meaning, and though she tried calling out, her voice was soundless against the fierce breath of the wind.

Now she felt the cold. Her body was numbed into submission. Her mind was following suit. The swirling snow was hypnotic, and a growing lethargy was creeping over her. In a small part of her mind, she knew her survival depended on remaining alert.

Horse and rider plodded on. There was no time, no world beyond the unbroken curtain of white. Samantha felt her eyelids growing heavy, but she willed them open with all her strength. The snow piled onto her back, weighing her down until she slumped onto the gelding's mane and clung to him. Staring down at the gelding's front hoof, she began to count each drudging step that Spook took as he continued his slow progress through the blinding storm.

Samantha's concentration on the horse's halting steps began to fade.

If I close my eyes, she thought dimly, I won't see all that white and I can sleep. Oh, how I want to sleep....

The snow was talking, she mused deliriously. Well, why not? It's alive. Why should it sound like Jake? Helplessly, she began to giggle. Well, why shouldn't it? *They both play to win.*

"Samantha!" The snow was shouting at her. "Open

your eyes. Stop that insane laughing and open your eyes!"

Wearily, she forced herself to obey the command. Dimly she saw the blur of Jake's features through the flurries of snow. "You would be the last thing I see before I die." With a moan, she closed her eyes again and sought the silence.

"Tell Dan we've found her," Jake shouted against the howl of the wind. "I'm taking her back to the Double T."

The darkness was comforting. Samantha gave herself over to it, feeling herself falling slowly into a hole with no bottom. She burrowed deeper into it. Her consciousness swam to the surface.

Bemused, she looked around a dimly lit room. The snow that pooled around her was not snow at all, but a bed with a thick, warm quilt. She allowed her heavy lids to close again.

"Oh, no, you don't." The lids opened fractionally, and Samantha saw Jake standing in the open doorway.

"Hello."

His mouth thinned as he advanced to the bed to tower over her. It seeped through the misty reaches of her brain that he was angry. She stared at him with lazy fascination.

"What in heaven's name were you doing out in such a storm? I've seen some dumb stunts, but taking a joyride in the middle of a blizzard tops them all."

She wanted to ask him to stop shouting at her, but lacked the energy. "Where am I?" was all she could find to say.

Sitting on the edge of the bed, he drew her head from

the pillow, then held a cup to her lips. "Here, drink this first, then we'll talk."

The brandy was warm and strong, and she sputtered and gasped as he poured it down her throat. Its power spread through her, pushing back the mists of unconsciousness.

"Now, to answer your question, you're at the Double T." Jake set the empty cup aside, and laid her head back on the mound of pillows.

"Oh."

"Is that all you can say?" He was shouting again. He took her shoulders as if to shake her. "Just 'Oh'? What in heaven's name were you doing out there?"

"It seems so long ago." She frowned in concentration, closing her eyes with the effort. "It wasn't snowing when I left," she said in weak defense.

"Wasn't snowing?" Jake repeated, incredulous. "Samantha, didn't you see the sky? Where are your brains?"

"There's no excuse for insults," she retorted with a small flash of spirit.

"No excuse for insults? Are you stark raving mad? Do you realize what nearly happened to you?" His hands retreated to his pockets, as though he could barely prevent them from throttling her. "Out here in the middle of a blizzard, half-frozen and helplessly lost! It was a miracle we found you. A little longer, and you'd be lying somewhere buried in it, and no one would have found what was left until spring. Dan was half out of his mind when he got through to me and told me you'd gone out in this."

"Bree?"

"Knew nothing." He whirled to face her again. "She

was taking a nap. It never occurred to her that you had gone out with a storm brewing." He laughed harshly.

The memory of the snow and the terror washed over her, and she began to shake. "I'm sorry," she managed through the tears that threatened to flow. With a brief oath, Jake ran a hand through his hair. He closed the distance between them and gathered her in his arms. "Samantha," he murmured against her hair. "What hell you put us all through."

"I'm sorry," she repeated, and she began to sob in earnest. "I was so scared, so cold."

He rocked and murmured words she could not understand, his lips brushing through her hair and over her damp cheeks until they met hers. The kiss mingled with the salt of her tears. "I've gotten your shirt all wet," she murmured after a while.

He let out a deep breath. She saw his smile begin to spread before he rested his brow against hers. "That is without doubt the worst calamity of the day."

"It's dark," she said with sudden realization. "How long…?"

"Too long. What you need now is rest."

"Spook?" she began as he lay her down on the pillows.

"Is sleeping off his adventure in the stables. He looks a lot better than you, I might add."

"I want to thank you for everything." Samantha reached for his hand. In that instant, she discovered there was nothing covering her save sheets and blankets. "M-my clothes," she stammered, drawing the quilt higher in a purely feminine gesture that caused Jake's mouth to twitch.

"Soaked through, Sam." Rising, he stood, rocking

gently on his heels. "It was necessary to get you warm and dry."

"Did Annie?" she managed a smile at the thought of the matronly presence of Jake's housekeeper. "I seem to have put everyone to a lot of trouble. Will you thank her for me?"

"Well, Sam, I'd like to oblige you, but Annie left yesterday for Colorado to spend a week with her nephew." Jake's grin broadened.

"Then who—?" The question caught in her throat, and her eyes became round and impossibly dark. "Oh, no," she whispered, closing her eyes in humiliation.

"No need to be embarrassed, Sam, you have a beautiful body."

"Oh, no." With a moan, she squeezed her eyes tighter.

"Now, don't you fret." His tone took on the light insolence of the cowboy she'd met a month before in the cold March sunset. "When I took off your clothes and rubbed you down, it was strictly medical. I'd do as much for any stray." He patted her hand, and her eyes opened warily at his touch.

"Yes, of course." Moistening her lips, she attempted to see the practical side. "I, well…thank you."

"'S all right, don't give it a thought." He moved toward the door, then paused and turned back. "Now, the next time I get your clothes off, my purpose'll be completely different."

He strolled casually from the room, leaving a speechless Samantha.

Chapter 6

Samantha looked around her. She remembered with a shock that she was in Jake's house—and, worse yet, *naked* in bed. She was debating the wisdom of wrapping the quilt around her and searching for more appropriate attire when footsteps sounded down the hall outside her room. She pulled the covers to her chin as Jake strode through the open door.

"So, you're awake. How do you feel?"

"Fine." Her respiratory system behaved erratically as he continued toward her and dropped onto the bed. "I'm just fine," she repeated, then added unnecessarily, "It's still snowing."

"So it is," he agreed without taking his eyes from her face. "Slowing down, though."

"Is it?" She forced herself to look out the window.

"The worst'll be over by midday." He reached up and pried one of her hands loose from the death grip on the blankets. "Calm down, Sam, I'm not going to ravish you, I'm going to check your pulse."

"I'm fine," she repeated again.

"Far from fine, Samantha," he corrected. His fingers brushed against her cheek, as if to test its substance. "The first thing is to get some food into you." Rising, he held out a large flannel robe that he had dropped at the foot of the bed. "You'd probably feel better if you had something on." His smile was gently mocking. "Can you manage to get into this by yourself?"

"Of course." Plucking it from him, she kept a cautious grip on the blankets. "I'm not an invalid."

"You best think like one. Put that on, then get back in bed. I'll bring you some breakfast."

"I don't..."

"Don't argue." The two words were swift and final. He was gone before she could say another word.

He had shut the door, however, and grateful for the concession, Samantha tossed back the covers and slipped her arm into the robe. When she stood, the room swayed and spun around her. She sank back onto the bed and slipped her other arm into its sleeve, pulling the robe around her before attempting to stand again. Her limbs felt heavy and weak, and she noted with puzzlement that her ankle was throbbing lightly. Gripping one poster of the bed until the room steadied, she rolled up the sleeves of the robe several times until her hands became visible, then moved to the bathroom to study herself in the mirror.

The sight of her own face caught at her breath. Her skin seemed nearly transparent, her eyes darker and larger in contrast. The breath of color that resulted when she pinched her cheeks faded instantly. She ran a hand through her hair falling on the shoulders of the dark green robe.

It must be his, she realized, looking down at the sleeves, which swallowed her arms, and the hem, which fell nearly to her ankles. A strange sensation flowed over her as she felt the material on her skin. Turning away from the mirror, she studied the bed.

"I'm not getting in there again," she muttered, and with a small gesture of defiance belted the robe more securely. "I can eat at the table like a normal person."

After a moment, her progress down the hall seemed more of a crawl than a walk. Her legs were heavy with a weakness, which infuriated her. The stillness of the house vibrated around her, playing havoc with her nerves, and the need to hear the natural, everyday movements of another human being became increasingly important. She cursed the waves of giddiness that swam around in her head, forcing her to stop time after time to rest her hand against the wall.

"This is ridiculous."

"You're right."

The harsh agreement came from behind as Jake's hands gripped her shoulders.

"What are you doing out of bed?"

"I'm all right." She swayed against his chest. He gripped her waist to support her, and she rested her hands on his arms.

"I'm just a bit wobbly, and I'm having some trouble with my ankle."

He let his gaze travel down to rest on her bare feet. "Probably turned it when you fell off the horse."

"I fell off Spook?" Her expression was incredulous.

"You were unconscious at the time. Now, get back

in bed and stay there." Effortlessly, he swept her into his arms, and she laid her head against his shoulder.

"Jake, don't make me go back to bed. It's so quiet in there, and I don't feel like being alone now."

He bent and brushed lips that parted in confusion. "If you think you can sit in a chair without sliding on your face, you can come in the kitchen."

She nodded, sighed and closed her eyes. "I hate being so much trouble."

She felt him shift her in his arms before he began the journey down the hall. "I knew you were trouble the minute I set eyes on you."

"Don't tease, Jake, I'm trying to thank you."

"What for?"

She lifted a hand to his cheek, turning his face so that he would look at her. "For my life."

"Then take better care of it in the future," he suggested.

"Jake, please, I'm serious. I owe you…"

"Nothing, you owe me nothing." His voice had hardened with annoyance. "I don't want your gratitude." They had reached the kitchen, and he placed her in a chair at the table. "Which ankle did you hurt?" He crouched down by her feet.

"The left one. Jake, I— Ouch!"

"Sorry." He grinned up at her, then rested his hand with friendly ease on her knee. "It's not swollen."

"It still hurts," she said stubbornly.

"Keep off it, then," he advised with simple logic, and turned away to finish breakfast.

"You've got some bedside manners, Dr. Tanner," she observed sharply.

"Yes, ma'am, so I've been told." When he turned

to face her, his smile was bland. "Tell me, Sam, does Sabrina have a mole on her left hip, too?"

Color flooded her face. "You…you…" she faltered, and clutched the robe tight at her throat.

"Around here, we call that locking the barn door after the cow's got loose. Have some coffee," he invited with sudden graciousness, pouring a cup and setting it on the table. "Start on this bacon," he ordered, sliding a plate in front of her. "That color didn't last long, you're pale as a ghost again. When did you eat last?"

"I…at breakfast yesterday, I guess."

"Toast and coffee, I imagine," he said disgustedly. "It's a wonder you can manage to sit up at all. Eat." He plucked a piece of bacon from the plate and held it out to her. "I'll have some eggs ready in a minute."

Obediently, she accepted the bacon and took a bite. "Are you going to have something?"

"In a minute," he answered absently, involved with breaking and beating eggs in a bowl.

With the first bite of bacon, Samantha realized she was ravenous. Through her preoccupation with food, she watched Jake cook with a deftness that amused and surprised her.

In a moment, he sat across from her, his plate piled high. She wondered how he could eat with such abandon and remain hard and lean.

She watched him under the cover of her lashes, and the thought came unbidden into her mind that never before had she shared the breakfast table with a man. The intimacy of their situation washed over her; the scent of bacon and coffee drifting through the air, the house quiet and empty around them, the soft flannel of his robe against her skin, the faint masculine scent of him clinging to it. It was as if they were lovers, she thought suddenly, as if they had shared the night, and now they were sharing the morning. Her face grew warm.

"I don't know what thought put roses back in those cheeks, Sam, but keep it up."

Her eyes lifted to his, and she had the uncomfortable feeling that he knew very well what road her thoughts had taken. She dropped her eyes to her plate. "I should call Bree and let her know I'm all right."

"Phones are out," he said simply, and her eyes flew back to his.

"The phones are out?" she repeated.

No telephone, her mind said again. Without a telephone, they might as well be on an island a thousand miles from anyone. Their isolation was complete, and the snow was still falling as though it would never stop.

"With a storm like this, it's not surprising to lose the phones. Power's out, too. We're on generator. Don't worry about Sabrina, she knows you're with me." His words did nothing to erase her tension.

"When…when do you think I'll be able to get back?"

"Couple of days," he returned with an easy shrug, and sipped his coffee. "The roads'll have to be cleared after the storm lets up, and you're not in any shape to travel through a mess like that yet. In a day or two, you'll be more up to it."

"A couple of days?"

He leaned back comfortably in his chair, his voice smooth as a quiet river. "Of course, by then you'll be hopelessly compromised, not a scrap of your sterling reputation left. Alone with me for two or three days, without Annie to add a thread of decency to the situation." His eyes traveled down her slim figure. "Wearing my bathrobe, too." He shook his head. "Not too many years back, I'd have had to marry you."

"Thank goodness for progress," she retorted smartly.

"Oh, I don't know, Sam." His sigh was convincing. "I'm an old-fashioned sort of man."

"It's only a matter of circumstance that we're alone here in the first place." With great dignity, she folded her arms. "And I've hardly been compromised, as you so quaintly put it."

"No?" He watched her through lazily narrowed eyes. "So far, I've undressed you, tucked you in and fixed your breakfast. Who knows what that might lead to?"

His smile might have been lazy, but it was full of meaning. Suddenly Samantha found it difficult to swallow.

"Relax, Sam." His laugh was full of arrogant enjoyment. "I told you I mean to have you, but it's not in my plans to take on a pale child who barely has the strength to stand." He paused, lit one of his long, thin cigars and blew smoke at the ceiling. "When I make love to you, I want you to have your wits about you. I don't want you passing out in my arms."

The man's arrogance was amazing! "You conceited mule," she began. "How dare you sit there and tell me you're going to make love to me? You seem to think you're irresistible! Well, you have another think coming—"

"I'm going to remind you of that one day, Sam," Jake said mildly as he crushed out his cigar. "Now, I think you better lie down again. You're not quite up to sparring with me yet."

"I do not have to lie down. And I certainly don't need you carting me around. I can manage." She stood up, then was forced to grasp the table as the room revolved around her.

"You don't look ready to turn cartwheels, teacher," Jake observed as he took her arm.

"I'm all right." Her hand, which she had lifted to push him away, lay weakly on his chest for support. He tilted her chin, and he was no longer smiling. "Samantha, sometimes you have to be strong enough to let someone else take care of things. You're going to have to hand over the reins to me for a couple of days. If you fight it, you're only going to make it harder on yourself."

With a sigh, she allowed her head to fall against his chest, not protesting as his arms encircled her. "Do I have to like it?"

"Not necessarily." He gave a short laugh and lifted her easily and carried her back to bed.

Her small spurt of energy deserted her. With an odd feeling of contentment, she settled down under the covers. She was asleep even before his lips had lightly touched her forehead in a farewell kiss…

"I was beginning to think you'd sleep through the night."

She turned her head quickly. Jake was sitting across the room, the smoke of his cigar spiraling upward, the flickering lights from the fire shooting specks of gold into his eyes. Samantha brushed the tousled hair from her face and struggled into a sitting position.

"It's dark," she said. "What time is it?"

He glanced at the gold watch on his wrist and took a slow drag from his cigar. "It's a bit past six."

"Six? I've slept for hours. I feel as if I've slept for weeks."

"You needed it." Tossing the stub of his cigar into the mouth of the fire, Jake rose and moved toward her. His concerned eyes roamed over her sleep-flushed cheeks and heavy eyes. Gradually, his expression lightened, the angles of his face moving into a satisfied smile. "Your color's coming back." He took her wrist, and her eyes dropped from his to study the dancing flames of the fire. "Pulse's a bit jumpy." The smile reflected in his voice. "Strong though. Hungry?"

"I shouldn't be." She forced her eyes to meet his. "I've done nothing but lie around all day, but I'm starved."

He smiled again, lifting her without comment. She felt small and vulnerable in his arms, a sensation that was both pleasant and disturbing. She found it difficult to resist the impulse to rest her head against the strong curve of his shoulder. Instead, she concentrated on the sharp, clean lines of his profile.

"I'm sure I can walk. I really feel fine."

"I doubt it." She could feel his warm breath on her face. "Besides, you seem to fit in my arms pretty well."

Finding no quick comeback to this comment, she took the journey to the kitchen in silence.

Leaning back in her chair, replete and content, Samantha sipped the cool white wine in her glass and gave Jake a nod of approval.

"You're going to make some woman a terrific husband. You're an outstanding cook."

"I think so." He nodded smugly. "My wife wouldn't have to be a gourmet cook," he added with casual consideration. "I'd demand other qualities."

"Adoration," Samantha suggested. "Obedience, unswerving loyalty, solicitude."

"That's all right for a start."

"Poor woman."

"Of course, I don't want her to be a doormat. Let's say I like a woman who knows how to think, one who doesn't pretend to be anything but who she is. Of course," he added, finishing off his wine, "I'm also partial to good looks."

"Well, so far it doesn't sound as though you're asking for much." Samantha giggled. "Just perfection."

"The woman I have in mind can handle it." He smiled broadly as he rose to pour coffee. Samantha stared at his back, feeling as though her heart had been dropped into a deep hole. *Lesley Marshall.* Her mind flashed the name like a neon sign in bright red letters.

Jake squelched her offer to do the dishes and swooped her from her chair and deposited her on the living room sofa.

"I feel useless," she muttered, helplessly cocooned by blankets and pillows. "I'm not made for lying around. I'm never sick." She gave Jake a sulky glare as if the entire matter was his fault. "I don't know how Bree coped with this sort of thing for a month."

"Could be you got her share of strength, and she got your share of patience," he considered, then shrugged. "Of course, I could be wrong." She heard his chuckle and the quiet click of his lighter as he lit a cigar.

Well, Samantha, she chided herself, you've really done it this time. Not only are you isolated with a man who constantly confuses you, but you can't even stand on your own feet. They say people learn about each other quickly when they live together, but I think it's going to take much more than one day to learn what this man is all about. *Living together,* she repeated, finding herself more amused than embarrassed. If Momma could see me now, we'd need a gallon of smelling salts.

Chapter 7

Dawn was breaking. Pink and gold streaks split the hazy blue of the sky, and light tumbled through to rest on Samantha's closed lids.

Morning? Sitting up with a start, she shook her head vigorously to dispel the last remnants of sleep. Pulling on the borrowed robe, she set her feet on the floor, took three deep breaths and stood. When both the room and her head remained stable, she let out a long sigh of relief. Her legs were weak, but they no longer felt as if they would melt from under her, and the stiffness in her ankle had disappeared.

Mobility, she thought with arrogant glee. I've never truly appreciated it until now. Coffee. One thought followed swiftly on the trail of the other, and she deserted the room with the intention of making fantasy fact. A door opened as she passed it, and with a cry of surprise, she fell against the opposite wall.

Jake stood in the doorway, rubbing a towel briskly through his damp hair, a terry-cloth robe tied loosely around his waist. "Morning, ma'am."

"You startled me." She swallowed, overpowered by the lean, bronzed maleness that the terry cloth did little to hide. He took a step toward her, and her breath caught instinctively. "I—I'm much better." She began to babble, unconsciously cowering against the smooth paneling. "I can actually walk a straight line."

Her voice died to a whisper as he stood directly in front of her. Her eyes were on a line with the tanned column of throat revealed by the open neck of the robe. His hand lifted her chin, and she trembled.

"Relax, Sam." His laughter sounded deep in his throat. "I just want to look you over. You must have the constitution of an elephant," he concluded with unflattering candor. "You look as though you've been on vacation instead of battling blizzards. One day's rest after nearly freezing to death. Most women would have been stretched out for a week."

"I'm not most women." She pushed his hand away from her face. "I'm not fragile and delicate, and I'm not going back to bed. I'm going to fix breakfast." She nudged him out of her path and started down the hall.

"Coffee's already on," he called after her.

Samantha had breakfast under way by the time Jake joined her. Clad in the less disturbing attire of corded jeans and flannel shirt, he watched her prepare the meal as he silently sipped at his coffee at the kitchen table.

"I'm getting used to having a pretty face across from me at breakfast," he commented when she sat down to join him.

"I'm sure I'm not the first," she commented with

studied indifference. Nor, she added to herself, will I be the last.

"Nope," he agreed easily, "but there's something to be said for big blue eyes first thing in the morning."

"Blue eyes are common enough," she muttered, and lowered them to the contents of her plate. "Besides, this is hardly a long-term arrangement." He did not speak for a moment, and her fork moved restlessly among her eggs.

"We should have the road clear enough sometime tomorrow."

"Tomorrow?" she repeated. A hollow feeling spread through her stomach.

"There's a lot of snow out there, some of the drifts are small mountains. It's going to take a little time to move it."

"I see."

"Do you think you could manage on your own for a while today?"

"What? Oh, sure, I'll be fine."

"There's a lot I should see to. My foreman was in charge yesterday, but the men need all the help they can get." He was frowning. "Cattle need hay brought out to them. They haven't the sense to dig through to the grass. They'll just stand there and starve to death."

"I suppose the storm did a lot of damage."

"It's only minor from the reports I've gotten. We were hit worse a couple years ago."

"Reports?"

"One of my men came by yesterday afternoon to fill me in." Pouring more coffee in his cup, he reached for the cream. "You were asleep."

"Oh." Strange, she thought, there had been a ripple in their isolation and she had been totally unaware of it.

Lifting his cup, he studied her over the rim. "I don't like leaving you alone, especially with the phones out."

Her shoulders moved. "Don't worry about me, I'll be fine." Glancing up, she met his speculative gaze.

"I don't know how long I'll be gone."

"Jake, stop fussing. I feel fine."

He tilted his head to the side, his eyes still narrowed. "Stand up. I want to see how you feel for myself."

Before she realized his intent, his arms were around her, and his mouth was on hers. Her legs buckled.

His mouth was light, teasing, his teeth nibbling at the fullness of her bottom lip until she moaned from the exquisite agony. She gripped his shoulders as a dim light of control seeped into the darkness. Pulling away she shook her head in refusal.

"Now, Sam…" His voice was soft and persuasive, but the hands that descended to her hips were firm. "You wouldn't send a man out in the cold without something warm to remember, would you?"

Insistently, he brought her closer, molding her hips, exploring the soft roundness until she was pressed against him with exciting intimacy. His mouth closed over her protest, his tongue moving with slow devastation to tease hers until she felt the room spinning as wildly as it had the day before. Slowly, his hands ascended, his thumbs circling the sides of her breasts while his mouth and tongue destroyed all resistance. She was straining against him, moving against him, reason forgotten. Her body heated urgently at his touch. Her sigh was a moan as his mouth descended to her throat. His lips tasted, lingered, traveled to new territories, the tip of his tongue moist and warm against her skin, erotic and devastating against her ear, until her mouth was desperate for its return to hers.

Her mouth was to go unsatisfied. He pulled her away with the same arrogance as he had pulled her to him. Dazed and limp, she could do no more than stare up at him as her body throbbed with a myriad of newly discovered desires.

"You're learning fast, Sam. That was enough to keep any man moving through a six-foot snowdrift."

Furious, and humiliated by her own response, she drew back her hand.

"Now, Sam." He caught her wrist easily, holding it aloft, ignoring her efforts to escape. "You're not strong enough yet for wrestling. Give yourself a couple more days." Turning her hand over, his lips brushed her palm, causing her struggles to cease abruptly. "I'm going to bring in Wolfgang to keep an eye on you. Take it easy today, and try to remember, you're not as tough as you'd like to think."

Ruffling her hair as though she were a child, he disappeared into the adjoing mudroom.

Later Samantha indulged in a hot, steaming shower, attempting to forget, as she soaped her skin, the feel of Jake's hands running over her. In the bedroom, she noticed her clothes piled neatly on the spoon-back chair. She slipped them on and wandered through the house in aimless exploration, the Saint Bernard lumbering at her heels.

The house abounded in small, delightful treasures, an oak rolltop desk, a wall box with Friesian carving, a Windsor cradle. With a small sigh, she wondered if the latter had rocked the baby Jake. Opening yet another door, she found Jake's library.

It smelled of leather and age, and her fingers ran over volume after volume. She pulled out a small volume of love poetry and opened the cover. Light, feminine handwriting adorned the top corner, and her mouth turned down at the inscription.

Darling Jake... To remind you.
                                    Love, Lesley

Shutting the book with a snap, Samantha held it for one heat-blinded movement over the wastebasket, then, grinding her teeth, stuck it firmly back in place.

"It makes no difference to me," she informed Wolfgang. "She can give him a hundred books of poetry, she can give him a thousand books of poetry. It's her privilege."

She nudged the big dog with her toe. "Come on, Wolfgang, let's get moving."

She returned to the living room and built up the fire, which had burned down to a hissing pile of embers. She curled up beside it.

One hour slipped into two, two slipped into three. Surely, Jake should be home by now, she told the silent clock as the hands crept past six. It was getting dark. Rising, Samantha stared out into the diminishing light.

What if something had happened to Jake? Her throat went dry, fear creeping along her skin. Nothing could happen to him, she told herself, running her hands over her arms to combat the sudden chill. He's strong and self-reliant.

But why am I so worried about him?

"Because," she said aloud, slowly, *"I love him. I've lost my mind and fallen in love with him."* Her hands lifted to cover her eyes as the weight of the knowledge crushed down on her. "Oh, how could I be so stupid? Of all the men in the world, I had to fall in love with this one."

A man, she remembered, *who had chosen Lesley Marshall to be his wife.* Is that why I've felt pulled in two? Is that why I responded to him when I've never responded to anyone else? Looking out into the darkness, she shuddered. I might as well admit that I don't care about anything except his getting home....

When finally the sound of the outside door slamming reached her ears, she ran into the mudroom and threw herself at an astonished, snow-covered Jake.

"Sam, what's going on?" He tried to pull her away from his cold, wet jacket.

"I was afraid something had happened to you." Her voice was muffled against his chest, her cheek oblivious to the frigid dampness.

"Nothing's happened, except I'm half-frozen and soaked to the skin." Firmly now, he took her shoulders, disentangling himself from her arms. "You're getting covered with snow." His grip was gentle. She stared up at him with huge, swimming eyes. "I'm sorry I was gone so long, but things were piled up, and it's slow working in a mess like this."

Embarrassed by her outburst, she backed away. "You must be exhausted. I'm sorry, it was stupid to go on like that. It must come from being alone in the house all day." As she babbled, she was backing purposefully toward the door. "You probably want a shower and something hot to drink. I—I've got dinner on."

"Something smells good," he commented. His eyes roamed over her flushed face, and a smile spread over his features.

"S-spaghetti," she stammered and despised herself. "I'll go finish it up."

Retreating into the kitchen, Samantha kept her back toward him when he emerged and announced casually that he would have a hot shower before dinner. She mumbled a vague reply, pretending a complete involvement with her dinner preparation. Listening to his receding footsteps, she let out a long, pent-up breath.

"Oh, idiot that I am," she sighed, and pushed her hair from her face in an angry gesture. The type of behavior she had displayed in the mudroom would only lead to trouble. She took a solemn oath to keep her emotions on a tight leash as long as Jake Tanner was around.

Tomorrow, she remembered, with a mixture of relief and disappointment, she would be back with her sister, and avoiding Jake would be a great deal easier. She had only to get through one more evening without making a fool of herself, and then she would sort out her thinking.

She was setting the table when Jake returned.

"If that tastes as good as it smells, I'll die a happy man." He lifted the lid on the pot and gave a sigh of approval. Grinning, he disappeared for a moment, then returned with a bottle of wine just as she was placing the pot on the table.

"A nice burgundy," he said, opening the bottle and setting out two glasses.

"Samantha, this is fantastic." He broke off eating

long enough to give her a smile. "Where'd you learn to cook like this?"

"More of my mother's famous lessons."

"What else can you do?"

"Well, let's see. I do a rather superb swan dive, a very graceful arabesque, I can walk on my hands as easily as some walk on their feet, whip up an incredible quiche, and waltz without counting the time."

"I am suitably impressed. How did a woman of your talents spend the day?"

She sighed and grimaced and began to toy with her spaghetti. "Sleeping, mostly."

"Hmm." His cough did not quite cover his laugh.

After dinner, Samantha insisted on seeing to the washing up herself. She wanted to avoid the intimacy of working side by side with him in the confines of the kitchen.

When the last signs of the man had vanished, she walked down the hall to the living room. Jake was adding another log to the low, shifting blaze. As she entered, he turned to smile at her. "Want some brandy?"

"No, no, thank you." She took a deep breath and willed her legs to carry her to the sofa.

"Not in training, are you?" He moved from the hearth to join her on the sofa.

Smiling, she shook her head. "The fire's wonderful." Grasping the first topic that came to mind, she riveted her eyes on the flames. "I always wanted one in my apartment. We had one at home, and Bree and I used to pop corn over it. We'd always burn it, and…"

The rest of her rush of words was lost as Jake placed his finger under her chin and turned her face to his. His face moved closer, and when she jerked back in defense, his brow lifted in amusement. He bent toward her again, and again she started.

"I'm only going to kiss you, Samantha." His grip tightened on her chin. Sliding from her chin, his hand framed her face as his lips moved over hers, soft as a whisper. In spite of herself, she relaxed against him. Her lips parted, inviting him to explore, begging him to take.

"Samantha." Her name was a sigh.

"Kiss me again," she whispered slowly as she lifted her mouth to his.

With a low groan, he brought his lips down on hers. She clung to him, her body throbbing with heat, her heart desperate against his, while a part of her looked on, aghast, as she answered his kiss.

Her mouth clung, avid and sweet, to his. Dormant passion exploded into life until there remained only man and woman and the need, older than time, to love and be loved, to possess and be possessed.

He opened her shirt and claimed her breast. The first desperation mellowed into slow exploration as his fingers trailed lightly, drugging her with a new, delirious languor. His mouth moved to sample the taste of her neck, his face buried in the spreading lushness of her hair. She pressed against the rippling muscles of his back as his mouth and tongue and hands raged fire over her.

She felt rather than heard him say her name against her mouth, sensed rather than felt the tension enter his body before her lips were set free. Dimly, she heard the strident insistence of bells ringing as she groped to bring heaven back within reach.

"Hell of a time for them to fix the phones." She

opened her eyes, dark as sapphires, and stared without comprehension. "There's nothing I'd like more than to ignore it, Samantha, but it might be important." Her lids fluttered in confusion. She could feel the warm raggedness of his breath against her cheek. "The phones have been out for two days, and there's a lot of damage out there."

His body left hers and took the warmth with it. She struggled to sit up, pulling her shirt closed. The hands that worked at the buttons were unsteady and, rising on weak legs, she sought the warmth of the fire. Pushing at tumbled hair, she wrapped her arms around her body and closed her eyes.

What had she done, losing herself that way? Tossing away pride like damaged goods! What if the phone hadn't rung? Her arms closed tighter. Does love always hurt? Does it always make a fool of you?

"Samantha." She whirled at the sound of her name, her arms still tight in protection. "It's Sabrina." Dropping her eyes from his, she moved into the hall.

Samantha picked up the phone and swallowed. "Hi, Bree." Her voice sounded strangely high-pitched to her ears, and her fingers gripped hard on the receiver.

"Sam, how are you?"

Taking a deep breath, she answered. "Fine. How *you* are is more important."

"Stronger every minute. I'm so glad you had the sense to head for the Double T when the snow started. The thought of you getting caught in that blizzard makes my blood turn cold."

"That's me, a steady head in a crisis." Samantha nearly choked on a gurgle of hysterical laughter.

"Are you sure you're all right? You sound strange. You aren't coming down with a cold, are you?"

"It's probably the connection."

"I thought they'd never get the phones fixed! I guess I just couldn't really relax until I'd talked to you and made sure you were safe! Of course, I know Jake would take care of you, but it's not the same as hearing your voice. I won't keep you, Sam, we'll see you tomorrow. By the way, I think Shylock misses you."

"Probably indigestion. Tell him I'll see him tomorrow." After replacing the receiver, she stared at it for a full minute.

"Samantha." She whirled again at Jake's voice, finding him watching her from the living room archway.

"I…ah…Bree seems fine." She avoided his eyes and toyed with the ink pot by the phone. She took a step backward as Jake advanced. "She said she thought Shylock misses me. That's quite an accomplishment, he's so self-sufficient and aloof."

"Samantha. Come, sit down." He held out his hand for hers. She knew if he touched her, she would be lost.

"No, no, I think I'll go to bed, I'm still not quite myself." Her color had ebbed again, leaving pale cheeks and darkened eyes.

"Still running, Sam?" The anger in his tone was well controlled.

"No, no, I…"

"All right, then, for the moment we seem to be at a stalemate." He captured her chin before she could avoid the gesture. "But we haven't finished by a long shot. Do you understand?"

She nodded, then broke away to flee to the sanctuary of her room.

Chapter 8

As each day passed, Sabrina became more cheerful. Her features took on a roundness that gave her a contented appearance. And as Samantha watched her, she wondered if Sabrina possessed more strength than she had ever given her credit for. It was a sobering experience to see her usually dreamy sister grabbing life with determination and purpose while she herself couldn't seem to stop daydreaming. Jake Tanner, she had to admit, was disturbing her days and sneaking into her dreams.

Stuffing her hands in her pockets, she scowled and continued her morning trudge to the mailbox. He meant to have her, did he? Well, Samantha Evans had no intention of being had by anyone, especially some annoying cowboy with too much charm for his own good... and fascinating green eyes, and that beautiful mouth....

* * *

Now the days began to lengthen. The sun grew in strength. Spring began to drift over the basin, greening the grass and teasing the crocuses to push their heads from the earth.

Scurrying down the hall as the doorbell interrupted her latest project—painting the nursery—Samantha wiped a few streaks of canary yellow on her jeans and opened the door.

The woman in the doorway smiled, her almond-shaped dark eyes making a thorough survey. "Hello, you must be Samantha. I'm Lesley Marshall."

The introduction was unnecessary, for with an instinct she had been unaware of possessing, Samantha had recognized the woman instantly. "Please, come in. It's still rather cold, isn't it?" She smiled, refusing to acknowledge the effort it cost her, and shut the nippy May air outside.

"I'm so glad to meet you at last." The dark eyes swept down, then up Samantha briefly. "I've heard so much about you." There was light amusement in her voice.

"Oh, really? I'm afraid I can't say the same." Her smile was faintly apologetic. "But, of course, I've been rather busy."

"I would have been by sooner, but I wanted to wait until Sabrina was more up to company."

"Bree's feeling much better these days. I'm sure she'll be glad to see you. Let me take your coat." Samantha hung the soft fur in the hall closet. Turning back to her visitor, she needed all her willpower to keep the social smile in place. The oatmeal slacks accentuated Lesley's sleekness; the trim cerise blouse set off her delicately feathered ebony hair and the perfect ivory of her skin. Desperately, Samantha wished a miracle would transform her navy sweatshirt with its Wilson High School banner and her paint-streaked jeans into something smart and sophisticated. As usual, her hair was escaping from its pins. She resisted the urge to bring her hand up to it and jam them in tightly.

"Bree's in the living room," she announced, knowing the pale gray eyes had studied her and found her wanting. "I was just about to make some tea."

Sabrina appeared at that moment, and Samantha gladly relinquished the role of hostess and escaped to the kitchen.

"So, she's beautiful," she grumbled to an unconcerned Shylock as she set the kettle on to boil. "So, she's smooth and sophisticated and makes me feel like a pile of dirty laundry." Turning, she lowered her face to his and scowled. "Who cares?" Shylock scowled back and went to sleep. Her thoughts wandered on. "I don't imagine he's ever laughed at her and patted her head as though she were a slow-witted child," she muttered as she gathered up the tea tray.

"Sabrina, you look wonderful," Lesley commented sometime later, sipping from a dainty china cup. "I'm sure having your sister with you must be very good for you. I don't have to tell you how concerned everyone has been."

"No, and I appreciate it. Sam's made everything so easy. I didn't have anything to do but sit and heal." She shot her sister an affectionate glance. "I don't know what we would have done without her these past two months."

Lesley followed her gaze. "Jake was telling me that

you're a gym teacher, Samantha," she purred, managing to make this sound faintly disgusting.

"Physical education instructor," Samantha corrected, slipping into a vague Southern drawl.

"And you were in the Olympics, as well. I'm sure it must have been fascinating. You don't look the sturdy, athletic type." The shrug of her shoulders was elegant, as was the small gesture of her hand. "I suppose one can never tell." Samantha gritted her teeth against a biting retort and was vastly relieved when, glancing at a slender gold watch, Lesley suddenly rose from her chair. "I must run now, Sabrina, I have a dinner engagement." Turning to Samantha, she offered a small smile. "So happy to have met you. I'm sure we'll be seeing each other again soon."

She left amidst a swirl of fur and the drifting scent of roses. Samantha sat back in the cushioned chair, relaxing for the first time in more than an hour.

"Well, what did you think of Lesley?" Sabrina questioned, shifting into a more comfortable position on the sofa.

"Very sophisticated."

"Come on, Sam." Sabrina grinned, her hands folding across the mound of her belly. "This is Bree."

"I don't know why I should have to comment, since you seem to be reading me so well. But—" her mouth curved into a rueful smile "—I suppose she's a bit smooth for my taste, and I didn't much care for the way she looked down that aristocratic nose at me."

"Actually, you really don't appear very sturdy." The observation was made with wide-eyed innocence. Samantha grimaced, pulling pins from her hair with a sharp tug until a cascade of golden brown tumbled in confusion about her shoulders.

"She'd have gotten her own back on that one if you hadn't sent me that 'Don't make a scene' look."

"Oh, well, Lesley can be nice enough when it suits her. Her father spoils her dreadfully. Her mother died when she was barely into her teens, and he transferred all his attention to Lesley. An overabundance of clothes, the best horses, and, as she grew older, cars and European tours and so on. Whatever Lesley wants, Lesley gets."

"Poor thing." The sarcasm caused her to feel spiteful and unjust. She sighed. "I suppose too much is as bad as too little. It was nice of her to come and see how you were getting along."

Sabrina's laughter floated through the room. "Sam, darling, I've never known you to be so slow." At her sister's puzzled expression, she continued. "Lesley didn't come to see me, she came to get a look at you."

"At me?" Finely etched brows disappeared under a fringe of bangs. "What for? I wouldn't think a lowly gym teacher from Philadelphia would interest Lesley Marshall."

"Any teacher who caught Jake Tanner's attention the way you have would interest Lesley. He wouldn't have gone out of his way to show just anyone around the ranch, you know."

A light color rose in Samantha's cheeks. "I think Miss Marshall's mind was put to rest after she got a good look." Her hand moved expressively down her sweatshirt and jeans. "She'd hardly see any danger here."

"Don't underestimate yourself, Sam."

"No false modesty." Samantha's sigh came from nowhere. "If a man's attracted to silk and champagne, cotton and beer are no competition. I'm cotton and beer, Bree," she murmured. Her voice trailed away with her thoughts. "I couldn't be anything else if I wanted to."

The following day, Samantha's continuing battle with her paints and brushes was interrupted by a more welcome visitor. Annie Holloway arrived at the ranch's kitchen door with a beaming smile and a chocolate cake.

"Hi." Samantha opened the door wide in welcome. "It's nice to see you again, and bearing gifts, too."

"Never like to come empty-handed," Annie announced, handing the thickly frosted cake to Samantha. "Dan always had a partiality for chocolate cake."

"Me, too." She eyed the cake hungrily. "He's not here right now, and I was just going to make some coffee. Do you suppose we could start without him?"

"Good idea." Setting herself comfortably in a chair, Annie waved a wide-palmed hand. "I reckon it wouldn't hurt for us to have a slice or two."

"Bree's taking a nap," Samantha explained as she put down the mugs of steaming coffee. "The doctor says she still has to lie down every day, but she's beginning to grumble about it a bit. Very quietly, of course."

"You're keeping an eye on her." Annie nodded and added two generous spoons of sugar to her coffee. "Dan says she's up to company now."

"Oh, yes, people have been dropping by now and again. Ah…" Samantha added cream to her own cup. "Lesley Marshall was by yesterday."

"I wondered how long it would be before Lesley hauled herself over to get a look at you."

"You sound like Bree." Sipping her coffee, Samantha shook her head. "I don't know why Lesley Marshall would want to meet me."

"Easy. Lesley's a mite stingy with her possessions, and she'd like to group Jake among them. She hasn't figured out yet that Jake is his own man, and all her daddy's money can't buy him for her. When my Jake picks his woman, he'll decide the time and place. He's always been an independent rascal. He was barely twenty when he lost his folks, you know." Samantha lifted her eyes to the warm brown ones. "It wasn't an easy time for him, they'd been close. They were a pair, Jake's folks, always squabbling and loving. You're a bit like her when she was a young thing." Annie smiled, her head tilting with it as Samantha remained silent. "Nobody's going to ride roughshod over you, at least not for long. I saw that straight off. She was stubborn as a mule with two heads, and there's times, though it's been better than ten years, I still miss her."

"It must have been hard on Jake, losing his parents and having all the responsibility of the ranch when he was still so young," Samantha murmured.

"Seemed to change from boy to man overnight, just out of college and still green. 'Course," she continued, "he'd been in the saddle since childhood and what he hadn't learned about ranching from his father and that fancy college, he learned from doing. He picked up the reins of that ranch with both hands. There's not a man who works for him wouldn't wrestle a long-horned bull if he asked them to. He can fool you with that easygoing way of his, but nobody gets the better of Jake Tanner. He runs the ranch like his life, and Lesley's going to find him a hard steer to rope and brand."

"Maybe it's more the other way around," Samantha suggested. Annie's response was prevented by the appearance at the kitchen door of the man in question.

He entered with the easy familiarity of an old friend.

"Howdy, ma'am." He broke the silence with a cocky smile, removed his battered Stetson and glanced at her attire. "Been painting?"

"Obvious, isn't it?" Samantha said sharply.

"Nice colors." He helped himself to a cup of coffee. "Are you going to part with another piece of that cake?"

"Jake Tanner!" Annie exclaimed in disgust. "You should be ashamed, gobbling Dan's cake when you've got a perfectly good one of your own at home."

"Somebody else's always tastes better, Annie." He slipped off his jacket, tossing it over a hook, and grinned boyishly. "He won't miss it, anyway. I brought you and the cake over, didn't I? You're not going to begrudge me one little piece?"

"Don't waste those eyes on me, you young devil." Annie attempted to sniff and look indignant. "I'm not one of your fillies."

Jake's appearance had successfully shattered Samantha's peace of mind. After a reasonable period of politeness, she excused herself to Annie and Jake and went back to her job in the nursery.

Samantha's artistic talent was decidedly impressionistic. The floor, protected by plastic, was splotched and splattered, but the walls were coming to life with a joy of brilliant colors. Of the four walls, two were yellow and two were white, and each was trimmed with its opposite's color. On the one wall that was unbroken by door or windows, she had begun the construction of a wide, arching rainbow, carefully merging blues into pinks into greens.

Time passed, and in the quiet concentration of her work she forgot her preoccupation with Jake. Sitting on the ladder's top step, she paused, brushing the back of her hand across her cheek absently as she viewed the results.

"That's a mighty pretty sight."

She jolted, dropping the brush with a clatter, and would have fallen from the ladder had Jake's arms not gripped her waist and prevented the tumble.

"Sure spook easy," Jake commented, removing the dangerously sloshing paint bucket from her hand.

"You shouldn't come up behind a person like that," she complained. "I might have broken my neck." She wiped her hands on the legs of her jeans. "Where's Annie?"

"With your sister. She wanted to show Annie some things she's made for the baby." He set the bucket on the floor and straightened. "I didn't think they needed me."

"No, I'm sure they didn't. I need that paint, though, and the brush you made me drop." She glanced down, but his eyes remained on hers.

"I like the blue, especially that spot on your cheek," Jake said.

She rubbed at the offending area in annoyance. "If you'd just hand those things back to me, I could finish up."

"Green's nice, too," he said conversationally, and ran a finger over a long streak on her thigh. "Wilson High." His eyes lowered to the letters on her shirt. "Is that where you taught back East?"

"Yes." She shifted, uncomfortable that the name was

prominent over her breasts. "Are you going to hand me my things?"

"What are your plans for tonight?" he countered easily, ignoring her request. She stared, completely thrown off balance by his unexpected question.

"I, ah, I have a lot of things to do." She searched her mind for something vital in her schedule.

"Things?" he prompted. His smile grew as his finger began to twist through a stray curl that had escaped its confines.

"Yes, things," she retorted, abandoning the attempt to elaborate. "I'm going to be very busy, and I really want to finish this room."

"I suppose I could let you get by with that, even though we both know better. Well." He smiled and shrugged. "Come down and kiss me goodbye, then. I've got to get back to work."

"I will not kiss you goodbye…." she began, the words trailing off as he gripped her waist. Her hands automatically went to his arms, and he plucked her from her perch.

He lowered her slowly, his eyes never leaving hers, and her mouth was roughly claimed before her feet could reach the floor. His hands slipped under her shirt to roam the smooth skin of her back, pressing her closer as her body betrayed her and dissolved against his. Slowly he explored her soft, firm breasts, subtly rounded hips, lean thighs.

Every time, every time, her mind murmured. Every time he kisses me, I go under deeper, and one day I'll never find my way back. His teeth moved to nip at her ear and neck, searching and finding new vulnerabilities before returning to ravage her mouth again. Without will, without choice, she rested in his arms, surrendering to forces she could never defeat.

He drew her away, breaking the intimacy, but his mouth returned to hers to linger briefly before he spoke. "About tonight, Samantha."

"What?" she murmured as his tongue traced the softness of her lips.

"I want to see you tonight."

Jerking herself back into reality, she pressed her hands against his chest, but did not manage to break away. "No, no, I'm busy. I told you."

"So you did," he acknowledged, and his eyes narrowed in speculation.

His words were cut off by the sound of Sabrina's laughter drifting down the hall. Samantha wiggled against Jake's hold. "Let me go, will you?"

"Why?" He was grinning now, enjoying the flood of color in her cheeks.

"Because…"

"Don't ever play poker, Sam." The warning was curt. "You'd lose your shirt."

"I…I…"

"Sabrina's due in September, right?"

The sudden question caused her to blink in confusion. "Well, yes, she…"

"That gives you a little breathing space, Samantha." He leaned down, and his kiss was hard and brief and to the point. "After that, don't expect to get away so lightly."

"I don't know what…"

"You know exactly what I mean," he said interrupting. "I told you I meant to have you, and I always get what I want."

Her eyes flashed. "If you think I'm going to let you make love to me just because you say so, then you..."

The suggestion she would have made died as his mouth took hers again. She went rigid telling herself she would not amuse him with a response this time. As she told herself she would not, her arms circled his neck. Her body became pliant, her lips parted with the hunger she had lived with all through the past month. As he took, she offered more; as he demanded, she gave. Her own mouth was mobile, her own hands seeking, until it seemed the month of fasting had never been.

"I want you, I don't have to tell you that, do I?"

She shook her head, trying to steady her breathing as his eyes alone caused her pulse to triple its rate.

"We'll settle this in September, unless you decide to come to me sooner." She began to shake her head again, but the fingers on the back of her neck halted the movement. "If you don't come to me, I'll wait until after the baby's born and you've got that much off your mind. I'm a patient man, Sam, but..." He stopped talking as Annie and Sabrina stepped into the room.

"Well." Annie shook her head at the two of them. "I can see he's been giving you a hard time." She turned to Sabrina with a half-exasperated shrug. "He's always been fresh as a new-laid egg. This is going to be a beautiful room, Sam." She glanced around at Samantha's handiwork, nodding in approval. "Let go of the little lady now, Jake, and take me back home, I've got dinner to fix."

"Sure. I've already said what I came to say." He released Samantha with a last, penetrating look and strode from the room, calling a goodbye over his shoulder.

"Fresh as a new-laid egg," Annie reiterated, and echoing his goodbye, followed him.

When the guests had departed, Samantha began to gather up paint buckets and brushes.

"Sam." Walking over, Sabrina placed a hand on her sister's arm. "I had no idea."

"No idea about what?" Bending, she banged the lid securely on rose pink.

"That you were in love with Jake." The truth she had avoided for so long was out in the open now: She had fallen hopelessly, irrevocably in love with Jake Tanner! Standing, Samantha searched in vain for words of denial.

"We know each other too well, Sam," Sabrina said before she could answer. "How bad is it?"

Samantha lifted her hands and let them fall to her sides. "Terminal."

"Well, what are you going to do about it?"

"Do about it?" Samantha repeated. "What can I do about it? After the baby comes, I'll go back East and try to forget about him."

"I've never known you to give up without a fight," Sabrina spoke sharply. At the unexpected tone, Samantha's brows rose.

"I'd fight for something that belonged to me, Bree, but I don't move in on someone else's territory."

"Jake's not engaged to Lesley Marshall. Nothing's official."

"I'm not interested in semantics." Samantha began to fiddle with the paint cans. "Jake wants an affair with me, but he'll marry Lesley Marshall."

"Are you afraid to compete with Lesley?" Bree asked.

Samantha whirled around, eyes flashing. "I'm not

afraid of anyone," she stormed. Sabrina's lips curved in a smug smile. "Don't try your psychology on me, Sabrina! Lesley Marshall and I don't belong in the same league, but I'm not afraid of her. I *am* afraid of getting hurt, though." Her voice wavered and Sabrina's arm slipped over her shoulders.

"All right, Sam, we won't talk about it any more right now. Leave those brushes, I'll wash them out. Go take a ride. You know the only way to clear your head is to go off by yourself."

"I'm beginning to think you know me too well." With a wry smile, Samantha wiped her hands on her jeans.

"I know you, all right, Samantha." Sabrina patted her cheek and urged her from the room. "I just haven't always known what to do about you."

Chapter 9

During the months since their first meeting, Samantha had grown to know Jake Tanner, and to realize that when he wanted something, he made certain he got it. And she knew he wanted her.

If, when she rode out on horseback, she kept closer to the ranch than had been her habit, she told herself it was not fear of encountering Jake that prompted the action, but simply her desire to spend more of her free time with Sabrina. Now Sabrina was growing cumbersome in her pregnancy, there was a grain of truth to this, so Samantha found it easy to accept the half-truth.

Every day she fell more under the spell of Wyoming. Bare branches were now fully cloaked in green. The cattle grew sleek and fat. The land was fully awakened and rich.

"I think you may just have twins in there, Bree," Samantha commented as the two sisters took advantage of golden sun and fragrant warmth. Sabrina glanced down to where Samantha sat cross-legged on the wide front porch. "Dr. Gates thinks not." She patted the mound in question. "He says there's only one, and I'm just getting fat. One of us should have twins, though."

"I'm afraid that's going to be up to you, Bree. I think I'll revive the tradition of old-maid schoolteachers."

Sabrina was sensitive to the wistfulness in the words. "Oh, no, you'll have to get married, Sam. You can't let all those lessons go to waste."

This brought the light laugh it had intended. "I'm perfectly serious. Remember what Madame Dubois always said, 'Von must reach for ze stars.'"

"Oh, yes, Madame Dubois." Samantha smiled at the memory of their former ballet teacher. "You know, of course, that accent was a phony. She came from New Jersey."

"I'm suitably crushed. She did think she had a genuine protégé in you."

"Yes, I was magnificent." Samantha sighed with exaggerated pride.

"Let's see a few of your famous leaps now, Sam."

"Not on your life!"

"Come on, cutoffs are as good as a tutu any day. I'd join you in a pas de deux, but it would actually be a pas de trois."

Samantha rose reluctantly from her seat on the porch. "All right, I don't mind showing off a little."

With quiet dignity, Sabrina began to hum a movement from *Swan Lake,* and Samantha lowered into a purposefully dramatic body sweep before exploding with an energetic series of *grand jetés,* stage leaps and cabrioles. She concluded the performance with a group of pirouettes, ended by dropping in a dizzy heap on the grass.

"That's what you get," she said, closing her eyes and shaking her head at the giddiness, "when you forget to spot focus."

"Is this show open to the public?"

Samantha glanced sharply toward the sound of the all-too-familiar voice.

"Dan!" Sabrina exclaimed. "I didn't expect you back so early."

"Ran into Lesley and Jake out on the north boundary," he explained, striding over and planting a firm kiss. "I thought you and Sam might like some company."

"Hello, Lesley, Jake." Sabrina included them both in her smile. "Have a seat, I'll bring out something cool."

Samantha had been sitting, praying without result for the ground to open up and swallow her. "I'll do it, Bree." She jumped at the opportunity to escape. "Don't get up."

"I'm up," Sabrina pointed out, disappearing inside before Samantha could argue.

"Do you teach ballet as well, Samantha?" Lesley asked. She surveyed Samantha's outfit of semiragged cutoffs and T-shirt with dark, mocking eyes.

"No, no," Samantha muttered, feeling once more desperately at a disadvantage next to the slim woman in elegantly tailored breeches and silk shirt.

"I thought it was real nice," Dan commented, innocently turning the knife.

"Samantha's just full of surprises," Jake said.

Now that he had spoken again, Samantha was forced to give Jake a portion of her attention. He looked devastatingly male, the denim shirt rolled past his elbows to expose bronzed, corded arms, the low-slung belt in his jeans accentuating his leanness. She concentrated on a spot approximately six inches to the left of his face, in order to avoid the smile that had already mastered his face.

"Yeah," she returned. "I'm just a bushel of surprises."

"Anything you can't do, Sam?"

"A few things." She attempted a cool sophistication.

"You're so energetic," Lesley commented, slipping her hand through Jake's arm. "You must be horribly strong and full of bulging muscles."

For one heady moment, Samantha considered flight. She was opening her mouth to make her excuses when Dan effectively cut off all hope.

"Sit down, Sam, I want to talk over a little idea with you and Sabrina." Sinking down on the porch steps, Samantha avoided any glimpse of Jake's face. "Do you think Sabrina's up to a little party?" Samantha looked up at Dan's question and attempted to marshal her thoughts.

"A party?" she repeated, drawing her brows together in concentration. "I suppose so. Dr. Gates says she's doing very well, but you could always ask to be sure. Did you want to go to a party?"

"I was thinking of having one," he corrected with a grin. "There're these twins I know who have this birthday in a couple of weeks." Bending over, he tugged at Samantha's loosened locks. "Seems like a good excuse for having a party."

"Oh, our birthday." Samantha's response was vague. The impending anniversary had slipped her mind.

"Did I hear someone say party?" Sabrina emerged through the screen door with a tray of iced tea.

Samantha sipped the cool, sweet tea her sister handed her and watched Sabrina's face light up with anticipation.

"A birthday party, Sam." She turned to her sister, eyes shining with excitement. "When's the last time we had one?"

"When we were twelve and Billy Darcy got sick all over Mom's new carpet." Leaning back against the porch rail, Samantha unwittingly lifted her face to Jake's.

"Well, then, it's high time for another," Dan said. "What do you say, Sam? I know it means extra work for you."

"Huh." Tearing her eyes from Jake's smile, she endeavored to pick up the threads of the conversation. "What? Oh, no, it's no trouble. It'll be fun." Concentrating on Dan's face, she blocked out the sight of Lesley lounging intimately against Jake. "How many people did you have in mind?"

"Just neighbors and friends." He reached up to rub his chin. "About thirty or forty, I'd say. What do you think, Lesley?"

The full mouth pouted a moment in thought. "If you want to keep it small, Dan," she agreed after a short deliberation. Samantha's eyes grew wide. These people definitely had a different idea of small than she did.

"Oh, Lesley, come take a look at this punch bowl I've got, see if you think we should use it." Rising, Sabrina took Dan's hand. "Come, get it down for me, Dan." Throwing her sister an innocent smile, Sabrina disappeared inside and left her alone with Jake.

"How's the painting coming?" Jake stretched both arms over the back of the swing.

"Painting? Oh, the nursery. It's finished."

That, she recalled with a frown, was just one of many times he had come upon her in a ridiculous situation. Sleeping on stumps, covered with paint, and now leaping across the lawn like some crazed ballerina. Samantha, she told herself, you have class.

"What do you want for your birthday, Sam?" He prodded her with the toe of his boot and earned a scowl.

Blowing a wisp of hair from her eyes, she moved her shoulders. "Fur, diamonds."

"No, you're not the type for furs." Taking out a cigar, he lit it and blew a lazy stream of smoke. "You'd be thinking about all the little minks that were scalped to make it. And diamonds wouldn't suit you."

"I suppose I'm more the quartz type." She rose, irritated.

"No, I was thinking more of sapphires." He caught her wrist. "To go with your eyes, or maybe rubies to go with your temper."

"I'll be sure to put both on my list. Now, if you'll excuse me." She glanced at her captured hand, then back at him. "I've got to go feed my cat." She gestured to where Shylock lay on the far side of the porch.

"He doesn't look very hungry."

"He's pretending to be dead," she muttered. "Shylock, let's eat."

Amber eyes opened and blinked. Then, to her pleasure, Shylock rose and padded toward her. However, upon reaching his mistress, he gave her a disinterested stare, leaped into Jake's lap and began to purr with wicked enjoyment.

"No, ma'am." Jake glanced down at the contented cat. "He doesn't look hungry at all."

With a final glare, Samantha turned, stalked to the door and slammed the screen smartly behind her.

The sun shone warm and friendly on the morning of the twins' birthday. Samantha carried a large parcel into the kitchen. Dumping her burden on the table where her sister was enjoying a cup of tea, she nudged Shylock away with her foot. She had not yet decided to forgive him for his treacherous advances to Jake.

"This just came, it's from the folks."

"Open it, Sam." Sabrina poked an experimental finger at the package. "Dan refuses to give me my present yet, and I've searched everywhere I can think of."

"I bet it's six books on child rearing for you, and six on etiquette for me."

"A present's a present," Sabrina stated, and tore the mailing paper from the box.

"Here's a note." After breaking the seal, Samantha produced a sheet of paper and read aloud.

"To Samantha and Sabrina:
A very happy birthday and our love to you both. Sabrina, I do hope you are taking good care of yourself. As you know, proper diet and rest are essential. I'm sure having Samantha with you during the last weeks of your confinement is a great comfort. Samantha, do look after your sister and see that she takes the necessary precautions. However, I hope you're not overlooking your own social life. As your mother, it is my duty to remind you that you are long past the marriageable age.

Your father and I are looking forward to seeing you and our first grandchild in a few weeks. We will be in Wyoming the first part of September, if Dad's schedule holds true.

> With love,
> Mom and Dad

"There's a postscript for you, Bree.

"Sabrina, doesn't Daniel know any suitable men for your sister?"

With a sigh, Samantha folded the letter and dropped it on the table. "She never changes." Dipping into the box, Samantha plucked out a smaller one with Sabrina's name on it and handed it to her. "Marriageable age," she muttered, and shook her head.

"Did you peek in here before?" Sabrina accused, dumping out volumes on infant and child care.

"No," Samantha denied with a superior smirk. "I just know Mom." Drawing out her own package, she ripped off the concealing paper. "Good grief." She let the box drop to the table and held up a brief black lace negligee.

"I thought I knew Mom." Both sisters burst into laughter. "She must be getting desperate," Samantha concluded, holding the negligee in front of her.

"Now, that's a pretty thing," Jake observed as he and Dan entered the kitchen. "But it's even prettier with something in it." Samantha bundled the garment behind her and flushed scarlet.

"Presents from Mom and Dad," Sabrina explained, indicating her stack of books.

"Very suitable." Dan grinned as he glanced through the volumes.

"Doesn't look like Sam feels the same about hers." Jake smiled. Samantha felt her already alarming color deepen. "Let's see it again."

"Don't tease, Jake." Sabrina turned to her husband. "Mom says they'll be here the first part of September."

"I'll put this stuff away." Samantha tossed the gown into the box and began to bury it under books.

"Leave that till later." Dan took her hand and pulled her away. "I need you outside for a minute."

She went willingly. Escape was escape. Imagining it had something to do with Sabrina's gift, she was surprised when Dan slowed his pace and allowed his wife to join them in their walk toward the ranch buildings. He kept her involved in a running conversation about the party until they came to a halt at the paddock fence.

"Happy birthday, Sam." Sabrina kissed her sister's cheek as Samantha's eyes focused on the golden Arabian mare.

"Oh." She could manage no more.

"She's from a good line," Dan informed her, his arm slipping around Sabrina's shoulders. "She's out of the Double T stock, no finer in Wyoming."

"But I..." Words faltered, and she swallowed and tried to begin again.

"What do you give someone who packs their own life away for six months without hesitation, without asking for anything in return?" Dan's free arm slipped around Samantha and pulled her to his side.

"We figured if you insisted on going back East, we'd always have a hold on you. You'd have to come visit us to ride your mare."

"I don't know how to thank you."

"Then don't," Dan ordered. "Go try her out."

"Now?"

"Now's as good a time as any." Not needing a second urging, Samantha was over the fence, stroking the mare and murmuring.

"We may convince her to stay yet," Dan commented, watching as she slipped into the saddle and took the mare around the paddock. "I could have a word with Jake."

Sabrina shook her head. "No, Sam would be furious if we interfered. She'd bolt back to Philadelphia before we could take a breath. For now, we'd better keep out of it." She lowered her voice as a beaming Samantha trotted around to them and slipped off the little mare.

"She's a real beauty," she sighed. "I don't know how I can ever bear to leave her..."

Sabrina's eyes met her husband's in silent satisfaction. Perhaps it will not be necessary, their unspoken message said.

"Come, little sister," Dan said. "If you can tear yourself away from your new friend, I sure could use a cup of coffee now."

As the trio trooped back toward the house, Jake swung through the back door. "Delivery just came. It's in the living room."

"Oh," Dan murmured, looking entirely too innocent. "Come on, Sabrina, we'd best see what it is."

"Is it the piano?" Sam asked Jake, as Dan and Sabrina disappeared inside.

"Looked like one to me. I guess that's another present that'll go over big. Walk to the truck with me," Jake commanded, and captured her hand before she could protest.

"Really, Jake, I have a million things to do." She trotted to keep pace with his loose, lanky stride.

"I know, you're indispensable." Stopping by his truck, he reached in the cab and produced a package. "But this seems to be the time for gift giving. I thought I'd let you have your present now."

"You didn't have to get me anything."

"Samantha." His drawl was lazy, but his eyes narrowed in annoyance. "I never do anything unless I want to." Taking her hand from behind her back, he placed the box in it. "Open it."

Lifting the statue from its tissue bedding, she examined it in silent amazement. The alabaster was smooth and cool in her hands, carved into the shape of a horse and rider in full gallop. The artist had captured the fluid grace, the freedom of motion. She ran a hesitant finger over the delicate features.

"It looks like me." She lifted her eyes to Jake's.

"And so it should," he answered easily. "It's supposed to be you."

"But how?" She shook her head, torn between pleasure and confusion.

"A man I know does this kind of thing. I described you to him."

For the second time that day, Samantha found herself at a loss for words.

"Why?" The question was out before she could swallow it.

Slowly, a smile drifted across his face. He pushed back his hat. "Because it suits you better than furs and diamonds."

She braced herself to meet his eyes again. "Thank you."

He nodded, his face solemn. He took the box from her hands and placed it on the hood of the truck. "I think a birthday kiss is traditional."

Swallowing, she took an instinctive step in retreat, but he gripped her arms and held her still. She offered her cheek, and his laughter broke out, full and rich on the summer air. "Sam—" he turned her face to his, and his eyes sparkled with humor "—you're incredible."

His lips met hers. His hands moved from her arms to her hips, drawing her firmly against the hard lines of his body. She submitted to the embrace, as long as his arms held her, as long as they were mouth to mouth, as long as the heat from his body infused hers, he owned her, and she could not run.

Finally he drew her away, bringing his hands to her shoulders while hers rested on his chest for support.

"Happy birthday, Sam."

"Thank you," she managed, still breathless from the impact of his embrace.

He lifted the box from the hood of the truck and placed it in her hands before sliding into the cab. "See you tonight." With a salute, he started the engine. The truck moved down the road, leaving her staring after it.

Chapter 10

Party sounds filled the house. Laughter and voices and music mingled and drifted through open windows to float on the night air.

On this evening, the twins were dramatically different in their appearance. Sabrina's pale blue gown floated around her, cunningly disguising her pregnancy. Her hair was a glinting halo around rose-tinted cheeks. Samantha's black-striped satin clung to her body, her halter neckline plunging deep to a wide, gathered waist. Her hair was free and thick around her shoulders.

As she moved and mingled with the crowd, Samantha searched for a tall, lanky form, noting with increasing despair and a gnawing jealousy that a slim, dark woman had also as yet failed to put in an appearance.

Cornered by an enthusiastic young cowboy, Samantha was feeling her attention begin to wander from a detailed account of horse breeding when her eyes met dark jade across the room.

He was standing with two men she did not recognize, and Lesley Marshall stood beside him. She was elegant in an oyster-white gown. Her fine-boned ivory hand was placed from time to time on Jake's arm, as if, Samantha thought grimly, she were flaunting her possession.

Furious with the sudden feeling of inadequacy, Samantha turned to her companion with a dazzling smile. He stammered over his lecture, his words grinding to a halt. She tucked her arm in his and used her eyes without shame.

"Howdy, Tim." Jake appeared from nowhere and placed a hand on the young man's shoulder. "I'm going to steal this little lady for a moment." He paused and smiled easily into Samantha's mutinous face. "There's a couple of people she hasn't met yet."

Without waiting for an assent, he had her unwilling hand in his, propelling her through the crowd. "Tim won't be the same for weeks," he whispered close to her ear. "A woman could get run out of town for using her eyes that way on susceptible young boys," he warned, pulling her through the sea of people.

"You don't have to drag me."

"I know a stubborn mule when I see one," he countered, without bothering to lower his voice. Her furious retort was swallowed as Jake presented her to the two men who flanked Lesley.

"Sam, I'd like you to meet George Marshall, Lesley's father." Samantha's hand was enveloped in a hearty grip. "And Jim Bailey," he continued, nodding toward the second man.

"Jim only works with cattle on paper. He's a lawyer."

"My, this is a mighty pretty girl!" George Marshall boomed. Giving Jake a sly wink, he patted his daughter's shoulder.

"You always manage to rope in the pick of the herd, don't you, Jake?"

Jake slipped his hands easily into his pockets. "I do my best. But then, roping them's one thing, getting them's another."

"Well, now, little lady," George's genial voice continued, "Les tells me you're a gym teacher."

"That's right, Mr. Marshall."

"Now, you just call me George," he instructed, squeezing her shoulder with a genial affection. "Tell me, why isn't a pretty little thing like you married and settled down instead of running around some gymnasium?"

Jake was grinning with obvious enjoyment. Samantha tossed her hair behind her back, but before she could think of a suitable answer, George's laughter boomed through the room.

"I like this girl," George announced to the group. "Looks like she has spirit. You come over to our ranch anytime, little lady, anytime at all."

In spite of herself, Samantha found herself liking his expansive hospitality. "If you'll excuse me now, I've got…got to get a tray out of the kitchen." She gave the group an all-encompassing smile and melted into the crowd.

In the kitchen, she pulled a tray from the refrigerator to give her excuse credibility and was glad she had when Jake followed her in a moment later.

"George is a good man. He has the right ideas when it

comes to women." Smiling knowingly at her, he leaned against the door watching her every move.

"That's your opinion," she returned tartly, bustling around the kitchen in an attempt to ignore him.

"Sit down a minute, Sam."

She glanced up, immediately wary, then lifted the tray as a defense. "No, I've got to get back."

"Please."

Despite herself, she lowered the tray to the table and herself into a chair.

"I ran into Jack Abbot, the school principal, the other day."

"Oh?"

"He told me the girls' phys ed instructor isn't coming back next term." Leaning back in his chair, Jake studied her. "He's going to offer you the job."

"Oh," she repeated before she could stop herself.

"He wants you pretty bad. He really needs someone this fall. I told him I'd be seeing you, and that I'd mention it. He's going to call you officially, of course."

How simple, Samantha thought.

How simple it would all be if I didn't love this man. I could stay where I want to stay, work where I want to work. But now, I've got to refuse, I've got to go away.

"I appreciate your telling me, and I appreciate Mr. Abbot wanting me, but…"

"Don't appreciate it, Samantha, think about it."

"You don't know what you're asking me to do."

He rose to pace the room, his hands seeking the depths of his pockets. "I'm just asking you to think about it. You like it here. You've made friends. You like being near your sister. You'd still have the satisfaction of doing what you feel you're suited for. Is it so much to ask that you consider it?"

"Yes, it's quite a lot. Jake, I don't want to argue with you. There are things I have to do, the same way there are things you have to do."

"All right." He nodded, then repeated slowly, as if coming to a decision. "All right, there *are* things I have to do." Moving over, he captured her chin between his thumb and fingers.

His arms slipped around her waist to bring her close, his mouth lowering to brush her cheeks and the corners of her lips. "Come home with me now, Samantha. We can be alone there." His voice had become low and seductive, as his fingers trailed over the bare skin of her back.

"No, please don't." She turned her face away.

"I want to make love to you. I want to feel your skin under my hands, all of you. I want to hear you sigh when I touch you."

"Jake, please." She dropped her head to his chest. "It's unfair, here, like this."

"Then come home with me."

"No, I can't." She shook her head without raising it. "I won't."

"All right, Samantha." He framed her face and brought it up to his. "I said I'd give you until the baby was born. We'll stick to that. We won't argue tonight. Let's call it a truce for your birthday. Agreed?"

He kissed her once, briefly, and turned to lift the tray. "Then we'll both do what we have to do when the time comes."

Leaving her confused, Jake moved through the doorway.

Rejoining the festivities, Samantha moved from group to group, but her thoughts were only about Jake. Why was he so interested in her career choices? Why did he want her to take the job in Wyoming? *Maybe he cared for her.* For a brief moment, she allowed hope to shimmer. Her eyes swept the room to find him. Finally she spotted him. He was dancing with Lesley. The shining cap of her raven hair brushing his cheek, the ivory of her hand entwined with the bronze of his. Samantha winced as he threw back his head and laughed at something Lesley had said for his ears alone.

Care for me? her mind repeated in a scathing whisper. Grow up, Samantha, *caring* and *wanting* don't always mean the same thing. In a few weeks, she comforted herself, she would no longer be subjected to this constant pain. When the ache had eased, she could visit Bree again. Jake would probably be too busy with his wife to spare time for visits to the Lazy L. Samantha felt her heart contract with pain.

She turned away and bumped solidly into Jim Bailey.

"Sorry." He took her shoulders to steady her. "I didn't see you."

"It's all right," she returned, offering a smile. "Besides, I think I ran into you."

"Well, no harm done either way." She watched his eyes slide past her and focus on Jake and Lesley. "They look nice together, don't they?"

Embarrassed that he must have seen her staring at them, Samantha nodded, and looked down at her empty glass. "Come on, we better get you a refill."

A few moments later, they joined the group around the piano as Sabrina played.

"So, you're a lawyer." She smiled at Jim. "I don't think I've ever met a lawyer before."

Jim returned her smile. "And you're a gymnast."

"No, actually, I'm a gym teacher now."

He lifted his glass in a toast and drank. "I remember you. I've always been an avid fan of the Olympics. I thought you were fabulous."

"Well, that's nice to hear after a decade."

He tapped his glass to hers. "Well, Olympic star, would you like to dance?"

"I'd love to."

Samantha enjoyed Jim Bailey's easy conversation. She learned during their two dances that he was interested in getting into politics. His dark good looks and ready wit would certainly be assets, she decided.

"Sam." Sabrina motioned to her as they moved back toward the piano. "It's your turn. Union rules."

"Okay," Samantha agreed, sliding onto the bench.

She played with practiced ease, moving from one song to the next. Time slipped through her fingers. As in a dream, she was aware of the voices behind her, the faint, drifting breeze of Wyoming through the open windows.

Someone sat beside her. Recognizing the lean fingers that lifted to turn the page of her sheet music, she faltered and missed a note.

"You and Jim seem to have hit it off." Samantha heard the click of his lighter over the sounds of the party.

"He's a very nice man. Have you known him long?"

"Oh, only since we were about eight and I gave him a black eye and he loosened a few of my teeth."

"Sounds like a loving friendship."

Jake again turned the page before she could do so herself. "Well, after that we sort of stuck together." He pushed the curtain of hair behind her shoulder, and Samantha struggled not to break the thread of the melody. "The two of you seemed to have a lot to talk about."

"He's very charming, and we have a few mutual interests."

"Hmm." Jake shifted slightly in his seat. His thigh brushed hers, and her fingers responded by hitting three wrong notes.

"You play very well."

Was he being ironic? She turned to look at him, but found no mockery in his jade eyes.

"Pleasantly," she corrected. "I get the general melody, but the details are a bit fuzzy."

"I've noticed that you have a tendency to shrug off your own capabilities. Are you aware of that?"

"That's not true. I just know what I do well and what I don't."

"You're a very tough critic, and you're inclined to underestimate."

"Honesty," she countered, finishing the song with a flourish. "I am a totally honest person."

"Are you, Samantha?" he said softly. "That's what I plan to find out."

Chapter 11

The days grew hot and sultry. The skies were improbably blue, rarely softened by clouds.

Long hours in the sun had deepened the honey of Samantha's skin, teasing out the gold in her hair. As long as she was occupied, she had no time for soul-searching. She could enjoy the long summer days without thinking of the fall. As Sabrina wilted like a thirsty rose in the searing heat, Samantha confined her own activities to the early-morning hours. In the long, hot haze of the afternoon, Sabrina moved slowly through the house, her body clumsy. Samantha did not dare leave her. The baby was due in two weeks, and Samantha wanted to remain within calling distance of her sister as much as possible.

One particularly humid afternoon, the two women were sitting idly in the living room. Sabrina got up heavily from her chair to look out the window. "Sam," she said, "before Dan left for town, he said a storm was brewing. From the looks of the sky, I'd say he was right."

Before Samantha could answer, there was a sudden flash of lightning. A blast of thunder rolled in on the wind, and the rain began to fall in sheets.

"It's coming down fast," Samantha agreed. "It should cool us off a bit." She looked sympathetically at her sister's bulky form.

The storm built in power. Jagged flashes of lightning illuminated the room and an angry wind hurled the rain against the windows. The two women watched in fascination as the storm exhausted itself. Soon rain dripped tentatively from the eaves and the thunder was a mere grumble in the distance.

The sun struggled to reappear, breaking through the gloom with a hazy promise of light.

"That," Sabrina commented with an enormous sigh, "was a mean one."

Samantha turned from her place by the window and again slumped into a chair. "Remember when you used to hide in the closet whenever we had a thunderstorm?"

"All too well." She gave her sister a pained smile. "And you used to stand on the porch, loving every minute of it, until Mom dragged you in, soaking wet. On that note from the past," Sabrina announced, "I'm going to take a nap, Sam." She turned at the doorway and studied the woman slouched in the chair, bare legs and feet stretched out in unconscious grace. "I love you."

With a rather puzzled smile, Samantha watched her walk away.

Wandering out to the porch, Samantha drank in the

rain-fresh air. Everything sparkled. Raindrops clung like jewels to blossoms and leaves. Though the flowers had drooped with the weight of the storm, their colors had been washed into brilliant life. A bird, flying by on a shaft of light, trilled above her. She could hear the steady dripping of the rain off the eaves above the whisper of the dying wind. Satisfied, she curled up on a porch rocker and instantly fell asleep.

She had no idea how long she had drifted in the soft twilight world when, with reluctance, she woke at the touch of a hand on her shoulder. She looked up drowsily and yawned. "Oh, Bree, I must have fallen asleep. It's so wonderfully cool out here."

"Sam, I think the baby's decided to put in an unscheduled appearance."

"Huh? Oh!" Springing to her feet, she was instantly awake. "Right now? Dan's not here, and it's not time yet. Sit down, sit," she ordered, running agitated fingers through her hair.

"I think the first thing to do is to calm down," Sabrina suggested.

"You're right. I'm not going to fall apart, it was just a shock. I wasn't expecting this for another week or two."

"Neither was I." Sabrina's smile was half amused, half apologetic.

"All right, how long have you been having contractions, and how far apart are they?"

"Only for an hour or so."

"That should give us plenty of time." Samantha patted Sabrina's hand.

"But they've been getting awfully strong, and…" Breaking off, she closed her eyes and began to breathe in a deep, methodical rhythm. "And," she continued, after a final long breath, "awfully close together."

"How close?" Samantha asked, feeling new tension at the base of her neck.

"Ten minutes."

"Ten minutes," Samantha repeated. "I'd better get you to the hospital. I'll bring the car around. Stay put," she told her sister, and raced to the garage.

Upon reaching Sabrina's compact and sliding behind the wheel, Samantha was horrified to find the engine unresponsive to the turn of the key. The little car sputtered, emitted an apologetic groan and died.

"You can't," she insisted, and smacked the steering wheel. "We just had you fixed."

There was no use wasting more time trying to figure out what was wrong with the car. It was clearly not going to start, and Samantha hadn't the first idea of where to look for the problem.

Rushing back to the house, she picked up the phone in the kitchen. At least she could call Dr. Gates. A groan of despair was wrenched from her when she heard the dead silence on the line. Oh, no, the storm must have knocked out the phones!

Forcing herself to appear calm, she returned to the living room where Sabrina was waiting for her.

Reaching her sister again, Samantha knelt down so their eyes were level. "Bree, the car won't start. All the trucks and jeeps are out with the men, and the storm must have knocked down the phone lines."

"Looks like we've got a few problems." Sabrina took a deep breath.

"It's going to be all right." Samantha took her hand in reassurance. "I'll help you get into bed, and then I'll

take a horse and ride toward the Double T. If I don't
see any of the men on the way, I'll get a truck there and
bring it back. Most of them have radios, and I can call
ahead to the doctor."

"Sam, it's going to take time for you to get there,
and to get back. I don't think I'll make it in time to get
to the hospital after that. You'll have to have the doctor come here."

"Here?" Samantha repeated. Her throat closed on the
word. Sabrina nodded. "All right. Don't worry, I won't
be long. I'll be back as soon as I can." Samantha raced
off to the stables, and without wasting the time for a
saddle, she leaped on her mare's back.

The familiar landscape was a blur, as she urged
more speed out of the powerful horse. The sound of
her own breath was masked by the sound of thudding
hooves. Every minute she took was a minute longer that
Sabrina was alone. She crouched lower on the horse
and dug in bare heels.

When Samantha spotted the men on horseback, she
spurred the Arabian over the fence in a fluid leap. As
her hooves touched earth, she met the horse's sides
again. They streaked across the field, scattering annoyed cattle.

When she reached the group, she reined in sharply.
The mare reared, nearly unseating her. Her breath came
in gasps as she struggled to keep her seat.

"What are you trying to do, break your neck?" Furi-
ously Jake snatched the reins from her hands. "If you're
stupid enough not to care about yourself, think of your
horse. What do you mean riding like a fool and jump-
ing fences? Where's your saddle? Have you lost your
mind?"

"Bree," she managed at last between giant gulps of air. "The baby's coming, and the phone's out. The car wouldn't start, and there's nobody around. Dan's in town. Bree says there's no time to get her to the hospital now, and I have to call the doctor." She felt tears of fear burning at her eyes and bit her lip.

"All right, take it easy." Twisting in the saddle, Jake called out to one of his men. "Get back to the ranch and get hold of Dr. Gates on the CB radio. Tell him Sabrina Lomax is in labor and to get to the Lazy L in a hurry." Turning back, he handed the reins to Samantha. "Let's go."

"Are you coming back with me?" Flooded with relief, she gripped tight on the leather.

"What do you think?"

Together, they sprang forward in a gallop.

Speed and thundering hooves were all Samantha ever remembered of the ride back. There was no time for conversation, no time for thought. She was sliding to the ground before she came to a full stop and Jake once more secured her reins.

"Keep your head, Samantha," he ordered, watching her bound up the steps and through the front door.

The house was silent. Her stomach tightened as she rushed to the master bedroom. Sabrina sat up in bed, propped by a mound of pillows and greeted her with a cheerful smile.

"That was quick, did you fly?"

"Just about," Samantha returned, faint with relief.

"We've sent for the doctor. Everything's under control." She sat down on the bed, taking her sister's hand. "How are you doing?"

"Not too bad." Her hand closed over Samantha's,

as much to reassure as seeking reassurance. "I'm glad you're back. Here comes another one."

Samantha looked on with unfamiliar helplessness. Her fingers grew tighter over her twin's, as if to steal some of her pain.

"We can thank Mom for that book on natural childbirth." Sabrina gave a long, shaky sigh and relaxed against the pillows.

"Don't look so worried, I'm doing fine. Oh, hello, Jake." Glancing at the doorway, Sabrina greeted him with friendly cheerfulness. "I didn't know you were here. Come in. It's not contagious."

He advanced into the room, looking tall, male and out of place. His hands retreated to his pockets. "How're you doing?"

"Oh, well, you've seen a cow in labor before, I don't imagine there's much difference." The small hand tightened on Samantha's. "Here we go again."

Samantha lifted the hand to her cheek. *Where was the doctor?* Sabrina should be in the hospital, surrounded by experts.

"This baby's in a big hurry," Sabrina announced with a small moan. "I'm sorry, Sam, it's not going to wait much longer."

I don't know anything about childbirth, Samantha thought in a moment of terror. *What am I going to do? What do I do first?*

Standing, she turned to Jake. "Go sterilize some towels, lots of them, and some string and scissors."

"All right." His hand rested on her shoulder a moment. "If you need me, give a call."

Nodding, she moved into the adjoining bath and scrubbed her hands and arms until they hurt.

"You're going to be fine," she stated as she reentered the bedroom.

"Yes, I am." Sabrina lay back on the pillows and closed her eyes. "I'm going to have this baby, Sam, and I'm going to do a good job of it. You can't do this for me, I have to be strong."

"You are strong." Brushing away the hair from Sabrina's cheeks, she realized with a sudden jolt that it was true. "You're stronger than I ever knew."

Her calm had returned, and she took over the duties of midwifery with an instinct as old as time. She wiped moisture from her sister's face, working with her, breathing with her, uttering soothing encouragements. Sabrina had not gone through all she had to lose now, and Samantha would not allow anything to go wrong.

"All right." Wiping beads of sweat from her own brow, Samantha straightened. "I think she's going to come this time, it's almost over. You have to help."

Sabrina nodded, her face pale and composed. Her hair had darkened with dampness. She shuddered and moaned with the final pang of childbirth. A thin, shrill cry pierced the stillness of the room. Samantha held new life in her hands.

"Oh, Bree." She stared down at the tiny, wriggling form.

Dan burst into the room two steps ahead of the doctor.

Suddenly, it was all so simple, Dan standing by Sabrina's side, his large hand clutching hers, the small, fresh form swaddled in the curve of her mother's arms.

"Only one." Sabrina sighed, her eyes luminous. "You'll have to handle the twins, Sam. One at a time is enough for me."

* * *

Sometime later, Samantha shut the door behind her and walked toward the kitchen. Jake looked up at her approach.

"A girl." She lowered herself into a chair. "The doctor says she's perfect, almost seven pounds. Bree's fine." She pushed at her tumbled hair and ran a hand across her brow. "I want to thank you."

"I didn't do anything."

"You were here." She lifted her eyes, and they were young and vulnerable. "I needed to know you were here."

"Samantha." He smiled and shook his head. "You sure find a man's weak points. I'll get you a drink."

He was back in a moment with a decanter of brandy and two snifters. Sitting across from her, he filled both generously. "It's not champagne, but it'll do." Lifting his glass, he touched it solemnly to hers. "To mother and child, and to Samantha Evans." He paused, his smile fading into seriousness. "She's one hell of a woman."

Samantha folded her arms on the table, laid her head on them and burst into tears.

"I was so scared." She found her voice muffled against his shoulder as he brought her against him. "I've never been so scared. I thought I would lose them both."

He tilted her chin as one hand rubbed the small of her back. "You're a survivor, Sam, and too stubborn to let anything happen to Sabrina or the baby."

Her forehead dropped to his chest as she struggled to stem the flow of tears.

"I always seem to fall apart in front of you."

"Don't much care for that, do you?" She felt his lips descend to her hair and allowed herself the joy of being cradled in his arms. "Most people don't look for perfection, Sam, they find it boring. You," he said, framing her face with his hands, "are never boring."

She sniffed and smiled. "I guess that was a compliment." Giving in to impulse, she leaned over and rested her cheek against his. "I don't think you're boring, either."

"Well." He stroked her hair a moment, and his voice was curiously soft. "That's about the nicest thing you've ever said to me.

"Now, drink some of that." He pushed her gently away and handed her the brandy.

Obeying, she allowed the warm strength to seep into her veins and relaxed with a sigh. "Bree certainly came through this better than I did." She drank again. Jake straddled a chair, leaning his arms on the back. "When I left her, she was lying there with the baby, looking like she'd just finished having a picnic. Dan looked like he was about to keel over, I was ready for someone to cart me away. Yet Bree lies there, glowing like a rose."

"Your sister's quite a woman."

"I know." Her eyes dropped to the surface of the table. "She said she has someone to depend on her now. I guess the time's come to stop playing big sister. She doesn't need that anymore."

"So, what will you do now?" His voice was casual.

"I'll stay around a couple of weeks, then I'll go on." She struggled, seeing only a void.

"To what?"

Her fingers tightened on her glass. "To my work, to my life." She drank, and the brandy was bitter.

"Still set on leaving?" He lifted his own glass, swirling the liquid. Amber danced under the kitchen light. "You haven't seen Wyoming in the autumn."

"No, I haven't," she answered, evading his prior question. "Maybe I'll come back next year." She stared down at her hands, knowing she never would.

"She's hungry!" Dan charged into the kitchen, his grin threatening to split his face. "Just had a baby, and she says she's hungry. Sam, I love you." Plucking her from her chair, Dan tossed her into the air. Her laughter ended on a shriek as she clutched at him on her journey down. The shriek was strangled as she was smothered by a bear hug. "I swear, if bigamy wasn't against the law, I'd marry you."

"If I was still all in one piece," she managed, turning her face and gulping for air.

"I ask you, Jake." He consulted the other man as his arms threatened to destroy the alignment of Samantha's rib cage. "Have you ever known another like this one?"

"Can't say that I have." She heard the smile in his voice, though it was impossible in her position to see his face. "I'd say Samantha is unique. One of a kind."

Rising, he lifted his brandy and toasted them both.

Chapter 12

"Sam, you're going to spoil her."

"Impossible." Sitting in the front porch rocker with the week-old Jennifer, Samantha smiled at her sister. "She's much too intelligent to be spoiled. Anyway, it's an aunt's privilege."

As she continued to rock, her lips strayed to Jennifer's soft tuft of dark hair. *I won't be able to do this much longer.* She looked to the massive peaks gleaming silver-blue in the afternoon sun. A light breeze stirred the air, bringing the sweet scent of freshly mowed grass. She breathed it in, and the soft scent of Jennifer's talc mingled with it. A sigh escaped.

She had not realized such a small creature could wrap her way around the heart so completely. Another love to leave behind. *In just a week, I'll have to say goodbye to all the things that matter: Bree, Dan, Wyoming, and now Jennifer.*

Dents and bruises, she thought again, but not the open wound that comes from leaving the man. Arrogant and gentle, demanding and kind, hot-tempered and easy; the parts that made up Jake Tanner were complicated and many, but to Samantha, it was a simple equation of love.

Blast you, Jake Tanner, if it weren't for you, I could stay. I belong here. I felt it from the first time I saw the mountains. There's nothing for me in Philadelphia. You've left me without anything to go back to.

"Looks like Lesley's coming to pay a visit," Sabrina observed. Samantha jerked back to the present with a snap.

She watched the late-model compact winding down the drive. Ignoring the flare of impossible jealousy, she set her features in casual lines.

"Sabrina, how well you look." Lesley's greeting was obviously tinged by surprise. "It's only been a week, and you look positively…" She hesitated, searching for a word.

"Radiant?" Sabrina suggested, and laughed. "I just had a baby, Lesley, not open-heart surgery."

"But to go through all that here, and without a doctor." She turned to Samantha. "I heard from Jake that you were marvelous and handled everything."

Samantha shrugged, uncomfortable at hearing Jake's praise from Lesley's lips. "It was nice of him to say so, but Sabrina did all the work."

"Well, having a baby is not a prospect I look forward to." Lesley shivered delicately. "I certainly intend to put it off as long as possible." Gliding over, she bent her head over the sleeping infant. "She is quite lovely, Sabrina. Very sweet."

"Would you like to hold her?" Samantha offered.

"Oh, no." Lesley stepped back. "I'm afraid I'm not very good with babies."

As she moved, Samantha caught the glint of the large square-cut diamond on her left hand. Lesley followed her gaze, and held out her hand. "You didn't know I was engaged, did you, Sabrina?"

"No." Sabrina cast a quick glance at her sister. "We hadn't heard."

"Well, you have been rather busy." She moved her fingers, enjoying the changing lights. "And we haven't made any formal announcement yet. We're planning a bit of a party for next week. As a matter of fact, I'm just on my way into town to begin shopping for my trousseau. Of course, I'll have to make a trip into New York for some proper clothes, but I'll just have to make do locally for the time being. We've set the wedding for the end of September." She smoothed her perfectly groomed hair with a well-manicured hand. "I could have done with a bit more time, but men have no idea how difficult things are to arrange properly." She smiled again. "Well, I must fly. I have so much to do. I do hope you'll be able to make it to the wedding, Samantha."

Sabrina glanced again at her sister. "Sam won't be here in September, Lesley."

"Oh, too bad." The regret in Lesley's voice was mild. Her mind had already run ahead to her wardrobe. She opened the door of the compact and slid behind the wheel. Lifting a slim arm in farewell, she drove away.

Rising, Sabrina took the sleeping Jennifer from her sister's arms and went into the house. When she returned, she sat on the arm of the rocker and laid her hand on Samantha's shoulder.

"I knew it was going to happen," Samantha murmured. "I just didn't want to be here when it did. I didn't think it would hurt this much. Oh, Bree." She looked up at her twin with helpless, swimming eyes. "What am I going to do?"

For the first time in their relationship, their situations were reversed, and Samantha was vulnerable, seeking comfort and advice.

"Sam, you can't go on like this. Why don't you talk to him?" Sabrina stroked the thick fall of her sister's hair. "Something is wrong here, and the two of you have to talk things out."

"No. I won't give him the opportunity to feel sorry for me."

"Pride can be a very cold companion," Sabrina murmured.

Samantha stood up. "I'm going back early, Bree. I can have everything arranged by the day after tomorrow, maybe even by tomorrow night."

"Sam, you can't run away from this."

"Just watch me."

"Mom and Dad won't be here for a few more days. They'll be disappointed."

"I'm sorry, I hate to miss them, but I can't handle this." Pausing, she repeated, the admission surprising her, "I *really* can't handle this."

"But, Sam…" Sabrina joined her at the porch rail. "You should at least talk to Jake. Don't you want to know how he feels? You can't just go flying off without speaking to him, without saying goodbye. Something's not right about all this. I've thought about the two of you. I've seen the way he looks at you."

Shaking her head, Samantha moved toward the door.

"No, he hasn't shown his face since the baby was born, and Lesley Marshall has his ring on her finger. A diamond. He has what he wants."

Samantha spent the evening packing, while Shylock watched her in silent accusation from his habitual place in the center of her bed.

Once in bed, she spent most of the night staring at a moon-washed ceiling. When the first pale light of dawn crept into the room, she rose. The mauve shadows under her eyes were a sad tribute to the restless hours.

The house slept on, and she deserted it, making her way to the stables. She saddled her mount with quick, deft movements, then galloped over the faint mist of morning.

As the sky lightened, the air came to life with the sweet song of birds. Sadly, she listened to the song of the west, for she knew that the melody would linger forever in her heart. She watched the mountains transformed by the dawn. Ribbons of rose and gold melted into blue until the peaks were no longer silhouettes, but stood proud in the full glory of the sun. She stayed for a last look at the white-faced Herefords grazing on the short, coarse grass. She knew now that her love for this wild, free country was forever bound up with her love for Jake. In saying goodbye to one, she was saying goodbye to the other. Straightening her shoulders, she turned the little mare back to the Lazy L.

When she returned to the house, she greeted her sister with bright chatter, the meaningless words no disguise for sleep-starved eyes. Sabrina made no comment, and shortly disappeared into the bedroom to tend to the baby.

Alone, Samantha wandered aimlessly from window to window. Tonight, she thought, slipping her hands into the pockets of her jeans, I'll be on a plane. And tomorrow morning, all this will just be a dream.

"Morning, ma'am."

She whirled, nearly upsetting a vase of roses with the movement. Jake leaned against the door frame, legs crossed at the ankles, as if he had been watching for some time.

"What are you doing here?"

He took a few strides into the room. "Well, now, I came to fetch you." This information was imparted in an irritatingly slow drawl.

"Fetch me? What are you talking about? I'm not a dog or a maverick calf to be fetched."

"Maverick calf sounds pretty close. You're always running off in the wrong direction." Reaching out, he took her arm. "Come on, we're going for a ride." His voice was pleasant, but the steel was there. She jerked away, angry with his arrogance, wary of his tone.

"I have no intention of going anywhere with you. Why don't you just go away and leave me alone?"

"Now, I can't do that, Sam," he returned in a reasonable tone. "We have some unfinished business to attend to. Your time's up."

The fire in her eyes flickered and died. "You can't be serious."

"I'm dead serious."

"What...what about Lesley?"

"She's not invited," he returned simply.

"I'm not going with you," she said, somewhere between terror and fury. "You can't make me."

Stopping, he looked down at her from his overpowering height. "Sure I can," he corrected with easy confidence. With a swift movement, he swung her over his shoulder. "See?" He walked effortlessly down the hall. "Nothing to it."

"Let me down!" Furious fists beat against his back. "This is crazy, it's illegal. I'll have you thrown in jail!"

"No kidding? Sam, you're scaring me to death."

He continued easily down the hall, as if he carried an empty sack, rather than an irate woman who was thumping against his back. Pausing, he touched the brim of his hat as Sabrina appeared in the bedroom doorway, the baby in her arms.

"Morning, Sabrina." His greeting was genial, and he cocked his head to get a better view of Jennifer. "She's a real beauty."

"Thank you, Jake. We certainly think so." She shifted the baby and smiled. "Are you two going out?"

"Thought we'd go for a little ride," Jake informed her. "We may be gone some time."

"It's a fine day for it, hardly a cloud in the sky."

"Bree." Samantha's voice was desperate. "Don't just stand there, *do* something." She pushed at the hair that hung over her face. "Don't you see what he's doing? He's kidnapping me. Call the police, call Dan." She continued to plead as Jake touched the brim of his hat once more and moved down the hall. "Bree, say something."

"Have a good time" was her sister's surprising response.

Samantha's mouth fell open in dumb astonishment. A stream of imaginative curses was hurled on Jake's unperturbed head as he took the reins of his mount from a grinning cowboy.

"Looks like you got yourself a real handful there, Jake."

"No more than I can handle," he countered, swinging into the saddle with Samantha still held over his shoulder. With a speed that defied his easygoing manner, he had her in front of him in the saddle, spurring the horse into a gallop, before she could think of escape.

"You're going to pay for this," Samantha promised, clutching the saddle horn to keep her balance. "You can't just run off with me this way!"

"I didn't see anybody try to stop me," Jake pointed out.

He followed the road for some time without decreasing his pace, then cut across an open field. At a small grove of trees, he reined in, gripping Samantha around the waist when she attempted to wiggle down.

"Now, don't do that, Sam," he warned in a friendly voice. "I'd just have to catch you, and I throw a mean lasso."

He slid from the chestnut, and before her feet could touch the ground, she was back over his shoulder. Without ceremony, she was dumped under the fragile, bending leaves of a willow while he towered over her, grinning with obvious enjoyment.

"You're going to be sorry," she predicted, smoldering with fury. "I'm going to..." The rest of her words slipped back down her throat as he dropped down next to her. "You—you can't do this, Jake. You're not the kind of man who forces himself on a woman."

"Who says?" Pushing her back on the soft grass, he covered her body with his.

Her body betrayed her with instant response. Her skin tingled as his mouth brushed over it. "You're not really going to do this."

"I told you once—" his mouth moved to her ear, and his words were warm and soft against it "—not to forget your own words. There are some things you just have to do."

His kiss was long and lingering.

When her mouth was free, she drew in a deep breath and spit out with all her strength, "What kind of man are you, to make love to one woman and plan to marry another?"

His eyes lazily narrowed. He propped himself on one elbow, his other arm pinning her down. Lifting his head from his elbow, he undid the top button of her blouse. "Suppose," he continued, moving down to the next button, "you tell me whom I'm supposed to marry."

His fingers trailed a slow line from her throat, down the smooth skin her open blouse revealed, and rested on the next button. The blood began to pound in her ears. His eyes alone held her still as he spread her blouse apart. Slowly, his fingers roamed up the warmth of her skin, moving with casual possession over her. Her eyes clouded with growing need as he explored.

"Tell me who I'm going to marry, Samantha." His body shifted again, molding to hers. His shirt was warm against her naked flesh.

"L-Lesley," she stammered.

"No." His mouth lowered to the curve of her throat, his tongue teasing the vulnerable skin.

She felt the waist of her jeans loosen under his hand. His finger pushed away the material and moved along her hip. With her last claim to lucidity, she pushed against his chest.

"Please stop."

"Now, I just can't do that, Sam." His hands teased the curve of her hip, trailing back up to the side of her breast. "I've waited a good long time to get you where I want you."

"I'm not staying… Did you say you weren't marrying Lesley?"

He frowned down in consideration, winding her hair around his finger. "Seems to me I did mention that. I don't know why you're always piling your hair on top of your head when it looks so good spread all over."

"But she was wearing your ring."

"Not mine," Jake corrected, still concentrating on the hair around his finger. "Your hair's gotten lighter these past few weeks, you haven't been wearing a hat. Les has a diamond, doesn't she? I told you once diamonds don't suit you. They're cold, and they don't have much imagination. But that's Les." He shrugged and began to move his mouth over her face again. "It doesn't seem to matter to Jim."

Valiantly, Samantha attempted to follow his words. Her head shook with the effort.

"Les is engaged to Jim Bailey. I'm sure you remember Jim Bailey, you spent enough time with him at the party."

"Yes, but…"

"No buts," he interrupted. "Les likes to have a couple of fish on the line, and when she got it through her head I wasn't in season, she netted Jim without a struggle."

"But I thought…"

"I know what you thought." He cut her off again and smiled. "Running away a few days early, weren't you?"

"I wasn't running. How did you know I was leaving?"

"Sabrina told me."

"Bree?" Samantha whispered. Bree did that?

"Yeah, yesterday. She came to see me while you were packing. I like this spot right here," he stated, planting his lips against the hollow of her throat. "I've had a devil of a time putting things in order since then, so I could take time for a honeymoon. Busy time of year for a cattleman."

"Honeymoon?" Her skin was trembling where his lips continued to taste.

"I've got a good foreman," he continued, as if thinking aloud. "I reckon he can manage things for a while. I could use another day or two. I had a nice long honeymoon in mind, someplace quiet." He brought his attention back to her stunned face. "You've never been to Bora-Bora, have you?"

"Are you talking about getting your ranch in order so you can take time off to marry me?" She attempted to speak slowly and clearly while her emotions whirled like a summer tornado.

"Just being practical," he explained with a bland smile.

"Why you conceited, overbearing... Just what makes you think I'll marry you? You sit back and make all these plans and expect me to run off to Bora-Bora with you like a passive little puppy. Of all the chauvinist—"

"How about Antarctica?" he suggested, willing to be reasonable. "Not too many people there, either."

"You're crazy. I never said I'd marry you. What

makes you think…" Her tirade was cut off effectively as his mouth coaxed her silence. When he let her breathe, her voice had lost its strength. "That's not going to help you. I'm not in love with you."

"Seems to me I recall someone telling me she was a totally honest person." His gaze was disconcertingly direct. He held her chin, preventing her face from turning away. "You want to look at me and tell me that again? You've been fighting me all along, and I think I've just about used up my patience." His lips were teasing hers again, and his hands moved over her with more urgency. "Mmm, but you have a nice body. I can't take much more of this waiting around. Six months is a long time, Sam. I've wanted you from the minute you stood there ordering Dan to have his man tend to the horses."

"Yes, you let me know very early what you wanted." She no longer struggled, but lay passive in his arms.

"Gave you something to think about. Of course, you didn't know I wanted you to be my wife, too. It was easy to tell you I wanted you, but a bit difficult to tell you I loved you. Sam, look at me." She shook her head, but the fingers on her chin tightened in authority. "Look at me." She obeyed, her lids opening to reveal eyes veiled with tears. "You stubborn little idiot. Listen carefully, I've never said this to another woman, and I've had to wait too long to say it to you. If you don't marry me soon, I'm going to lose my mind." His mouth took hers, spinning the world into nothing. Her arms flew around him as pain evaporated into unspeakable joy. "Samantha." He buried his face in the lushness of her hair. "It's been quite a race."

"I don't understand." She brought his face back to

hers, needing to see the truth in his eyes. "Why didn't you tell me before?"

"I didn't think you'd believe that a man had nearly been knocked off his feet by a picture of a girl less than half his age, then had completely lost his balance when he saw the woman she'd become. If you hadn't been so wrapped up in Sabrina those first few minutes, you'd have seen how a man looks when he gets hit by lightning."

"Just like that?" Stunned, she traced the angles of his face to assure herself she was not dreaming.

"Just like that," he agreed, bringing her palm to his lips. "Then, after I'd recovered a bit, I knew I had to work around your dedication to Sabrina until you'd figured out there was room in your life for someone else. Then you stood there telling me you were going back home as soon as the baby was born. I nearly strangled you." His fingers tightened on her hand as he brought his eyes back to hers. "How was I supposed to tell you that I loved you, that I wanted to marry you, wanted you to stay in Wyoming? The night of the party, in the kitchen, I made up my mind I wasn't letting you go, no matter what I had to do to keep you."

"But I never wanted to leave." She shook her head in brisk denial, as if he should have realized it all along. "It was just that I couldn't bear to see you married to Lesley."

"You know, things might have gotten even more complicated if Sabrina hadn't come by and laid things out for me. She's got a bit more of you in her than I had thought." Laughing, he lifted his face from hers. "She told me to sit down and listen. She'd never seen two people run around in circles so long and get nowhere."

"It's not like Bree to interfere."

"She interfered beautifully. First thing she did was ask me what business I had getting engaged to Lesley. I must have stared at her like she'd lost her mind. After I managed to tell her I was definitely not engaged to Lesley, she let me have it with both barrels. Mixed with the buckshot was the information that you were miserable about going home, and that I was a fool for not seeing it myself. Then she folded her arms, stuck out her chin exactly like someone else has a habit of doing and asked me what the devil I intended to do about it."

Samantha stared up at him and shook her head in astonishment. "I wish I could have seen that."

He smiled and lowered his mouth. "Just look in the mirror sometime." Flesh met flesh with no barriers, and with a small sound of desperation he savaged her mouth. The hard lines of his chest pressed into her breasts. "Let me hear you say it, Samantha," he murmured, unable to resist the curve of her neck. "I need to hear you say it."

"I love you." Her mouth searched for his, her arms urging him closer. "I love you. I love you." Her lips found their objective, and her silence told him again.

"I need you, Samantha." His mouth and hands continued to seek, growing wilder, possessive, demanding. "I never knew I could need anyone the way I need you. I want you for myself for a while, no distractions, no complications, just you. We've got six months of loving to make up for. I'm going to keep you fully occupied for a very long time." Lifting his face, he smiled down at her, running his hand through the hair spread over the grass. "A very long time."

She smiled back, running her hands up his chest to circle his neck. "I intend to keep you occupied, as well.

Your cows are going to get very lonely." Removing his
hat, she tossed it carelessly aside, then turned back to
him with raised brows. "Okay, cowboy." Her arms lifted
to lock around his neck, fingers tangling possessively
in his hair. "Start occupying."

"Yes, ma'am." With a polite nod, he lowered his
mouth and followed orders.

* * * * *

UNFINISHED BUSINESS

For Laura Sparrow—
old friends are the best friends.

Chapter 1

What am I doing here?

The question rolled around in Vanessa's mind as she drove down Main Street. The sleepy town of Hyattown had changed very little in twelve years. It was still tucked in the foothills of Maryland's Blue Ridge Mountains, surrounded by rolling farmland and thick woods. Apple orchards and dairy cows encroached as close as the town limits, and here, inside those limits, there were no stoplights, no office buildings, no hum of traffic.

Here there were sturdy old houses and unfenced yards, children playing and laundry flapping on lines. It was, Vanessa thought with both relief and surprise, exactly as she had left it. The sidewalks were still bumpy and cracked, the concrete undermined by the roots of towering oaks that were just beginning to green. Forsythia were spilling their yellow blooms, and azaleas held just the hint of the riotous color to come. Crocuses, those vanguards of spring, had been overshadowed by spears of daffodils and early tulips. People continued, as they had in her childhood, to fuss with their lawns and gardens on a Saturday afternoon.

Some glanced up, perhaps surprised and vaguely interested to see an unfamiliar car drive by. Occasionally someone waved—out of habit, not because they recognized her. Then they bent to their planting or mowing again. Through her open window Vanessa caught the scent of freshly cut grass, of hyacinths and earth newly turned. She could hear the buzzing of power mowers, the barking of a dog, the shouts and laughter of children at play.

Two old men in fielders' caps, checked shirts and work pants stood in front of the town bank gossiping. A pack of young boys puffed up the slope of the road on their bikes. Probably on their way to Lester's Store for cold drinks or candy. She'd strained up that same hill to that same destination countless times. A hundred years ago, she thought, and felt the all-too-familiar clutching in her stomach.

What am I doing here? she thought again, reaching for the roll of antacids in her purse. Unlike the town, she had changed. Sometimes she hardly recognized herself.

She wanted to believe she was doing the right thing. Coming back. Not home, she mused. She had no idea if this was home. Or even if she wanted it to be.

She'd been barely sixteen when she'd left—when her father had taken her from these quiet streets on an odyssey of cities, practice sessions and performances. New York, Chicago, Los Angeles and London, Paris,

Bonn, Madrid. It had been exciting, a roller coaster of sights and sounds. And, most of all, music.

By the age of twenty, through her father's drive and her talent, she had become one of the youngest and most successful concert pianists in the country. She had won the prestigious Van Cliburn Competition at the tender age of eighteen, over competitors ten years her senior. She had played for royalty and dined with presidents. She had, in her single-minded pursuit of her career, earned a reputation as a brilliant and temperamental artist. The coolly sexy, passionately driven Vanessa Sexton.

Now, at twenty-eight, she was coming back to the home of her childhood, and to the mother she hadn't seen in twelve years.

The burning in her stomach as she pulled up to the curb was so familiar she barely noticed it. Like the town that surrounded it, the home of her youth was much the same as when she'd left it. The sturdy brick had weathered well, and the shutters were freshly painted a deep, warm blue. Along the stone wall that rose above the sidewalk were bushy peonies that would wait another month or more to bloom. Azaleas, in bud, were grouped around the foundation.

Vanessa sat, hands clutching the wheel, fighting off a desperate need to drive on. Drive away. She had already done too much on impulse. She'd bought the Mercedes convertible, driven up from her last booking in D.C., refused dozens of offers for engagements. All on impulse. Throughout her adult life, her time had been meticulously scheduled, her actions carefully executed, and only after all consequences had been considered. Though impulsive by nature, she had learned the importance of an ordered life. Coming here, awakening old hurts and old memories, wasn't part of that order.

Yet if she turned away now, ran away now, she would never have the answers to her questions, questions even she didn't understand.

Deliberately not giving herself any more time to think, she got out of the car and went to the trunk for her suitcases. She didn't have to stay if she was uncomfortable, she reminded herself. She was free to go anywhere. She was an adult, a well-traveled one who was financially secure. Her home, if she chose to make one, could be anywhere in the world. Since her father's death six months before, she'd had no ties.

Yet it was here she had come. And it was here she needed to be—at least until her questions were answered.

She crossed the sidewalk and climbed the five concrete steps. Despite the trip-hammer beating of her heart, she held herself straight. Her father had never permitted slumped shoulders. The presentation of self was as important as the presentation of music. Chin up, shoulders straight, she started up the walk.

When the door opened, she stopped, as if her feet were rooted in the ground. She stood frozen as her mother stepped onto the porch.

Images, dozens of them, raced into her mind. Of herself on the first day of school, rushing up those steps full of pride, to see her mother standing at the door. Sniffling as she limped up the walk after falling off her bike, her mother there to clean up the scrapes and kiss away the hurt. All but dancing onto the porch after her first kiss. And her mother, a woman's knowledge in her eyes, struggling not to ask any questions.

Then there had been the very last time she had stood here. But she had been walking away from the house, not toward it. And her mother hadn't been on the porch waving goodbye.

"Vanessa."

Loretta Sexton stood twisting her hands. There was no gray in her dark chestnut hair. It was shorter than Vanessa remembered, and fluffed around a face that showed very few lines. A rounder face, softer, than Vanessa recalled. She seemed smaller somehow. Not shrunken, but more compact, fitter, younger. Vanessa had a flash of her father. Thin, too thin, pale, old.

Loretta wanted to run to her daughter, but she couldn't. The woman standing on the walk wasn't the girl she had lost and longed for. She looks like me, she thought, battling back tears. Stronger, more sure, but so much like me.

Bracing herself, as she had countless times before stepping onto a stage, Vanessa continued up the walk, up the creaking wooden steps, to stand in front of her mother. They were nearly the same height. That was something that jolted them both. Their eyes, the same misty shade of green, held steady.

They stood, only a foot apart. But there was no embrace.

"I appreciate you letting me come." Vanessa hated the stiffness she heard in her own voice.

"You're always welcome here." Loretta cleared her throat, cleared it of the rush of emotional words. "I was sorry to hear about your father."

"Thank you. I'm glad to see you're looking well."

"I…" What could she say? What could she possibly say that could make up for twelve lost years? "Did you…run into much traffic on the way up?"

"No. Not after I got out of Washington. It was a pleasant ride."

"Still, you must be tired after the drive. Come in and sit down."

She had remodeled, Vanessa thought foolishly as she followed her mother inside. The rooms were lighter, airier, than she remembered. The imposing home she remembered had become cozy. Dark, formal wallpaper had been replaced by warm pastels. Carpeting had been ripped up to reveal buffed pine floors that were accented by colorful area rugs. There were antiques, lovingly restored, and there was the scent of fresh flowers. It was the home of a woman, she realized. A woman of taste and means.

"You'd probably like to go upstairs first and unpack." Loretta stopped at the stairs, clutching the newel. "Unless you're hungry."

"No, I'm not hungry."

With a nod, Loretta started up the stairs. "I thought you'd like your old room." She pressed her lips together as she reached the landing. "I've redecorated a bit."

"So I see." Vanessa's voice was carefully neutral.

"You still have a view of the backyard."

"I'm sure it's fine."

Loretta opened a door, and Vanessa followed her inside.

There were no fussily dressed dolls or grinning stuffed animals. There were no posters tacked on the walls, no carefully framed awards and certificates. Gone was the narrow bed she had once dreamed in, and the desk where she had fretted over French verbs and geometry. It was no longer a room for a girl. It was a room for a guest.

The walls were ivory, trimmed in warm green. Pretty priscillas hung over the windows. There was a four-poster bed, draped with a watercolor quilt and plumped with pillows. A glass vase of freesias sat on an elegant Queen Anne desk. The scent of potpourri wafted from a bowl on the bureau.

Nervous, Loretta walked through the room, twitching at the quilt, brushing imaginary dust from the dresser. "I hope you're comfortable here. If there's anything you need, you just have to ask."

Vanessa felt as if she were checking into an elegant and exclusive hotel. "It's a lovely room. I'll be fine, thank you."

"Good." Loretta clasped her hands together again. How she longed to touch. To hold. "Would you like me to help you unpack?"

"No." The refusal came too quickly. Vanessa struggled with a smile. "I can manage."

"All right. The bath is just—"

"I remember."

Loretta stopped short, looked helplessly out the window. "Of course. I'll be downstairs if you want anything." Giving in to her need, she cupped Vanessa's face in her hands. "Welcome home." She left quickly, shutting the door behind her.

Alone, Vanessa sat on the bed. Her stomach muscles were like hot, knotted ropes. She pressed a hand against her midsection, studying this room that had once been hers. How could the town have seemed so unchanged, and this room, her room, be so different? Perhaps it was the same with people. They might look familiar on the outside, but inside they were strangers.

As she was.

How different was she from the girl who had once lived here? Would she recognize herself? Would she want to?

She rose to stand in front of the cheval glass in the corner. The face and form were familiar. She had examined herself carefully before each concert to be certain her appearance was perfect. That was expected. Her hair was to be groomed—swept up or back, never loose— her face made up for the stage, but never heavily, her costume subtle and elegant. That was the image of Vanessa Sexton.

Her hair was a bit windblown now, but there was no one to see or judge. It was the same deep chestnut as her mother's. Longer, though, sweeping her shoulders from a side part, it could catch fire from the sun or gleam deep and rich in moonlight. There was some fatigue around her eyes, but there was nothing unusual in that. She'd been very careful with her makeup that morning, so there was subtle color along her high cheekbones, a hint of it over her full, serious mouth. She wore a suit in icy pink with a short, snug jacket and a full skirt. The waistband was a bit loose, but then, her appetite hadn't been good.

And all this was still just image, she thought. The confident, poised and assured adult. She wished she could turn back the clock so that she could see herself as she'd been at sixteen. Full of hope, despite the strain that had clouded the household. Full of dreams and music.

With a sigh, she turned away to unpack.

* * *

When she was a child, it had seemed natural to use her room as a sanctuary. After rearranging her clothes for the third time, Vanessa reminded herself that she was no longer a child. Hadn't she come to find the bond she had lost with her mother? She couldn't find it if she sat alone in her room and brooded.

As she came downstairs, Vanessa heard the low sound of a radio coming from the back of the house. From the kitchen, she remembered. Her mother had always preferred popular music to the classics, and that had always irritated Vanessa's father. It was an old Presley ballad now—rich and lonely. Moving toward the sound, she stopped in the doorway of what had always been the music room.

The old grand piano that had been crowded in there was gone. So was the huge, heavy cabinet that had held reams and reams of sheet music. Now there were small, fragile-looking chairs with needlepoint cushions. A beautiful old tea caddy sat in a corner. On it was a bowl filled with some thriving leafy green plant. There were watercolors in narrow frames on the walls, and there was a curvy Victorian sofa in front of the twin windows.

All had been arranged around a trim, exquisite rosewood spinet. Unable to resist, Vanessa crossed to it. Lightly, quietly, only for herself, she played the first few chords of a Chopin étude. The action was so stiff that she understood the piano was new. Had her mother bought it after she'd received the letter telling her that her daughter was coming back? Was this a gesture, an attempt to reach across the gap of twelve years?

It couldn't be so simple, Vanessa thought, rubbing

at the beginnings of a headache behind her eyes. They both had to know that.

She turned her back on the piano and walked to the kitchen.

Loretta was there, putting the finishing touches on a salad she'd arranged in a pale green bowl. Her mother had always liked pretty things, Vanessa remembered. Delicate, fragile things. Those leanings showed now in the lacy place mats on the table, the pale rose sugar bowl, the collection of Depression glass on an open shelf. She had opened the window, and a fragrant spring breeze ruffled the sheer curtains over the sink.

When she turned, Vanessa saw that her eyes were red, but she smiled, and her voice was clear. "I know you said you weren't hungry, but I thought you might like a little salad and some iced tea."

Vanessa managed an answering smile. "Thank you. The house looks lovely. It seems bigger somehow. I'd always heard that things shrunk as you got older."

Loretta turned off the radio. Vanessa regretted the gesture, as it meant they were left with only themselves to fill the silence. "There were too many dark colors before," Loretta told her. "And too much heavy furniture. At times I used to feel as though the furniture was lurking over me, waiting to push me out of a room." She caught herself, uneasy and embarrassed. "I saved some of the pieces, a few that were your grandmother's. They're stored in the attic. I thought someday you might want them."

"Maybe someday," Vanessa said, because it was easier. She sat down as her mother served the colorful salad. "What did you do with the piano?"

"I sold it." Loretta reached for the pitcher of tea.

"Years ago. It seemed foolish to keep it when there was no one to play it. And I'd always hated it." She caught herself again, set the pitcher down. "I'm sorry."

"No need. I understand."

"No, I don't think you do." Loretta gave her a long, searching look. "I don't think you can."

Vanessa wasn't ready to dig too deep. She picked up her fork and said nothing.

"I hope the spinet is all right. I don't know very much about instruments."

"It's a beautiful instrument."

"The man who sold it to me told me it was top-of-the-line. I know you need to practice, so I thought... In any case, if it doesn't suit, you've only to—"

"It's fine." They ate in silence until Vanessa fell back on manners. "The town looks very much the same," she began, in a light, polite voice. "Does Mrs. Gaynor still live on the corner?"

"Oh yes." Relieved, Loretta began to chatter. "She's nearly eighty now, and still walks every day, rain or shine, to the post office to get her mail. The Breckenridges moved away, oh, about five years ago. Went south. A nice family bought their house. Three children. The youngest just started school this year. He's a pistol. And the Hawbaker boy, Rick, you remember? You used to babysit for him."

"I remember being paid a dollar an hour to be driven crazy by a little monster with buckteeth and a slingshot."

"That's the one." Loretta laughed. It was a sound, Vanessa realized, that she'd remembered all through the years. "He's in college now, on a scholarship."

"Hard to believe."

"He came to see me when he was home last Christmas. Asked about you." She fumbled again, cleared her throat. "Joanie's still here."

"Joanie Tucker?"

"It's Joanie Knight now," Loretta told her. "She married young Jack Knight three years ago. They have a beautiful baby."

"Joanie," Vanessa murmured. Joanie Tucker, who had been her best friend since her earliest memory, her confidante, wailing wall and partner in crime. "She has a child."

"A little girl. Lara. They have a farm outside of town. I know she'd want to see you."

"Yes." For the first time all day, Vanessa felt something click. "Yes, I want to see her. Her parents, are they well?"

"Emily died almost eight years ago."

"Oh." Vanessa reached out instinctively to touch her mother's hand. As Joanie had been her closest friend, so had Emily Tucker been her mother's. "I'm so sorry."

Loretta looked down at their joined hands, and her eyes filled. "I still miss her."

"She was the kindest woman I've ever known. I wish I had—" But it was too late for regrets. "Dr. Tucker, is he all right?"

"Ham is fine." Loretta blinked back tears, and tried not to be hurt when Vanessa removed her hand. "He grieved hard, but his family and his work got him through. He'll be so pleased to see you, Van."

No one had called Vanessa by her nickname in more years than she could count. Hearing it now touched her.

"Does he still have his office in his house?"

"Of course. You're not eating. Would you like something else?"

"No, this is fine." Dutifully she ate a forkful of salad.

"Don't you want to know about Brady?"

"No." Vanessa took another bite. "Not particularly."

There was something of the daughter she remembered in that look. The slight pout, the faint line between the brows. It warmed Loretta's heart, as the polite stranger had not. "Brady Tucker followed in his father's footsteps."

Vanessa almost choked. "He's a doctor?"

"That's right. Had himself a fine, important position with some hospital in New York. Chief resident, I think Ham told me."

"I always thought Brady would end up pitching for the Orioles or going to jail."

Loretta laughed again, warmly. "So did most of us. But he turned into quite a respectable young man. Of course, he was always too handsome for his own good."

"Or anyone else's," Vanessa muttered, and her mother smiled again.

"It's always hard for a woman to resist the tall, dark and handsome kind, especially if he's a rogue, as well."

"I think *hood* was the word."

"He never did anything really bad," Loretta pointed out. "Not that he didn't give Emily and Ham a few headaches. Well, a lot of headaches." She laughed. "But the boy always looked out for his sister. I liked him for that. And he was taken with you."

Vanessa sniffed. "Brady Tucker was taken with anything in skirts."

"He was young." They had all been young once, Loretta thought, looking at the lovely, composed stranger who was her daughter. "Emily told me he mooned around the house for weeks after you…after you and your father went to Europe."

"It was a long time ago." Vanessa rose, dismissing the subject.

"I'll get the dishes." Loretta began stacking them quickly. "It's your first day back. I thought maybe you'd like to try out the piano. I'd like to hear you play in this house again."

"All right." She turned toward the door.

"Van?"

"Yes?"

Would she ever call her "Mom" again? "I want you to know how proud I am of all you've accomplished."

"Are you?"

"Yes." Loretta studied her daughter, wishing she had the courage to open her arms for an embrace. "I just wish you looked happier."

"I'm happy enough."

"Would you tell me if you weren't?"

"I don't know. We don't really know each other anymore."

At least that was honest, Loretta thought. Painful, but honest. "I hope you'll stay until we do."

"I'm here because I need answers. But I'm not ready to ask the questions yet."

"Give it time, Van. Give yourself time. And believe me when I say all I ever wanted was what was best for you."

"My father always said the same thing," she said quietly. "Funny, isn't it, that now that I'm a grown woman I have no idea what that is."

She walked down the hall to the music room. There

was a gnawing, aching pain just under her breastbone. Out of habit, she popped a pill out of the roll in her skirt pocket before she sat at the piano.

She started with Beethoven's "Moonlight" sonata, playing from memory and from the heart, letting the music soothe her. She could remember playing this piece, and countless others, in this same room. Hour after hour, day after day. For the love of it, yes, but often—too often—because it was expected, even demanded.

Her feelings for music had always been mixed. There was her strong, passionate love for it, the driving need to create it with the skill she'd been given. But there had always also been the equally desperate need to please her father, to reach that point of perfection he had expected. That unattainable point, she thought now.

He had never understood that music was a love for her, not a vocation. It had been a comfort, a means of expression, but never an ambition. On the few occasions she had tried to explain it, he had become so enraged or impatient that she had silenced herself. She, who was known for her passion and temper, had been a cringing child around one man. In all her life, she had never been able to defy him.

She switched to Bach, closed her eyes and let herself drift. For more than an hour she played, lost in the beauty, the gentleness and the genius, of the compositions. This was what her father had never understood. That she could play for her own pleasure and be content, and that she had hated, always hated, sitting on a stage ringed by a spotlight and playing for thousands.

As her emotions began to flow again, she switched to Mozart, something that required more passion and speed. Vivid, almost furious, the music sang through her. When the last chord echoed, she felt a satisfaction she had nearly forgotten.

The quiet applause behind her had her spinning around. Seated on one of the elegant little chairs was a man. Though the sun was in her eyes and twelve years had passed, she recognized him.

"Incredible." Brady Tucker rose and crossed to her. His long, wiry frame blocked out the sun for an instant, and the light glowed like a nimbus around him. "Absolutely incredible." As she stared at him, he held out a hand and smiled. "Welcome home, Van."

She rose to face him. "Brady," she murmured, then rammed her fist solidly into his stomach. "You creep."

He sat down hard as the air exploded out of his lungs. The sound of it was every bit as sweet to her as the music had been. Wincing, he looked up at her. "Nice to see you, too."

"What the hell are you doing here?"

"Your mother let me in." After a couple of testing breaths, he rose. She had to tilt her head back to keep her eyes on his. Those same fabulous blue eyes, in a face that had aged much too well. "I didn't want to disturb you while you were playing, so I just sat down. I didn't expect to be sucker punched."

"You should have." She was delighted to have caught him off guard, and to have given him back a small portion of the pain he'd given her. His voice was the same, she thought, deep and seductive. She wanted to hit him again just for that. "She didn't mention that you were in town."

"I live here. Moved back almost a year ago." She had that same sexy pout. He fervently wished that at least that much could have changed. "Can I tell you that you look terrific, or should I put up my guard?"

How to remain composed under stress was something she'd learned very well. She sat, carefully smoothing her skirts. "No, you can tell me."

"Okay. You look terrific. A little thin, maybe."

The pout became more pronounced. "Is that your medical opinion, Dr. Tucker?"

"Actually, yes." He took a chance and sat beside her on the piano stool. Her scent was as subtle and alluring as moonlight. He felt a tug, not so much unexpected as frustrating. Though she sat beside him, he knew she was as distant as she had been when there had been an ocean between them.

"You're looking well," she said, and wished it wasn't so true. He still had the lean, athletic body of his youth. His face wasn't as smooth, and the ruggedness maturity had brought to it only made it more attractive. His hair was still a rich, deep black, and his lashes were just as long and thick as ever. And his hands were as strong and beautiful as they had been the first time they had touched her. A lifetime ago, she reminded herself, and settled her own hands in her lap.

"My mother told me you had a position in New York."

"I did." He was feeling as awkward as a schoolboy. No, he realized, much more awkward. Twelve years before, he'd known exactly how to handle her. Or he'd thought he did. "I came back to help my father with his practice. He'd like to retire in a year or two."

"I can't imagine it. You back here," she elaborated. "Or Doc Tucker retiring."

"Times change."

"Yes, they do." She couldn't sit beside him. Just a residual of those girlish feelings, she thought, but she rose anyway. "It's equally hard to picture you as a doctor."

"I felt the same way when I was slogging through medical school."

She frowned. He was wearing jeans and a sweatshirt and running shoes—exactly the kind of attire he'd worn in high school. "You don't look like a doctor."

"Want to see my stethoscope?"

"No." She stuck her hands in her pockets. "I heard Joanie was married."

"Yeah—to Jack Knight, of all people. Remember him?"

"I don't think so."

"He was a year ahead of me in high school. Football star. Went pro a couple of years, then bunged up his knee."

"Is that the medical term?"

"Close enough." He grinned at her. There was still a little chip in his front tooth that she had always found endearing. "She'll be crazy to see you again, Van."

"I want to see her, too."

"I've got a couple of patients coming in, but I should be done by six. Why don't we have some dinner, and I can drive you out to the farm?"

"I don't think so."

"Why not?"

"Because the last time I was supposed to have dinner with you—dinner and the senior prom—you stood me up."

He tucked his hands in his pockets. "You hold a grudge a long time."

"Yes."

"I was eighteen years old, Van, and there were reasons."

"Reasons that hardly matter now." Her stomach was beginning to burn. "The point is, I don't want to pick up where we left off."

He gave her a considering look. "That wasn't the idea."

"Good." That was just one more thing she could damn him for. "We both have our separate lives, Brady. Let's keep it that way."

He nodded, slowly. "You've changed more than I'd thought."

"Yes, I have." She started out, stopped, then looked over her shoulder. "We both have. But I imagine you still know your way out."

"Yeah," he said to himself when she left him alone. He knew his way out. What he hadn't known was that she could still turn him inside out with one of those pouty looks.

Chapter 2

The Knight farm was rolling hills and patches of brown and green field. The hay was well up, she noted, and the corn was tender green shoots. A gray barn stood behind a trio of square paddocks. Nearby, chickens fussed and pecked at the ground. Plump spotted cows lolled on a hillside, too lazy to glance over at the sound of an approaching car, but geese rushed along the bank of the creek, excited and annoyed by the disturbance.

A bumpy gravel lane led to the farmhouse. At the end of it, Vanessa stopped her car, then slowly alighted. She could hear the distant putting of a tractor and the occasional yip-yipping of a cheerful dog. Closer was the chatter of birds, a musical exchange that always reminded her of neighbors gossiping over a fence.

Perhaps it was foolish to feel nervous, but she couldn't shake it. Here in this rambling three-story house, with its leaning chimneys and swaying porches, lived her oldest and closest friend—someone with whom she had shared every thought, every feeling, every wish and every disappointment.

But those friends had been children—girls on the threshold of womanhood, where everything is at its most intense and emotional. They hadn't been given the chance to grow apart. Their friendship had been severed quickly and completely. Between that moment and this, so much—too much—had happened to both of them. To expect to renew those ties and feelings was both naive and overly optimistic.

Vanessa reminded herself of that, bracing herself for disappointment, as she started up the cracked wooden steps to the front porch.

The door swung open. The woman who stepped out released a flood of stored memories. Unlike the moment when she had started up her own walk and seen her mother, Vanessa felt none of the confusion and grief.

She looks the same, was all Vanessa could think. Joanie was still sturdily built, with the curves Vanessa had envied throughout adolescence. Her hair was still worn short and tousled around a pretty face. Black hair and blue eyes like her brother, but with softer features and a neat Cupid's-bow mouth that had driven the teenage boys wild.

Vanessa started to speak, searched for something to say. Then she heard Joanie let out a yelp. They were hugging, arms clasped hard, bodies swaying. The laughter and tears and broken sentences melted away the years.

"I can't believe—you're here."

"I've missed you. You look... I'm sorry."

"When I heard you—" Shaking her head, Joanie

pulled back, then smiled. "Oh, God, it's good to see you, Van."

"I was almost afraid to come." Vanessa wiped her cheek with her knuckles.

"Why?"

"I thought you might be polite and offer me some tea and wonder what we were supposed to talk about."

Joanie took a rumpled tissue out of her pocket and blew her nose. "And I thought you might be wearing a mink and diamonds and stop by out of a sense of duty."

Vanessa gave a watery laugh. "My mink's in storage."

Joanie grabbed her hand and pulled her through the door. "Come in. I might just put that tea on, after all."

The entryway was bright and tidy. Joanie led Vanessa into a living room of faded sofas and glossy mahogany, of chintz curtains and rag rugs. Evidence that there was a baby in the house was found in teething rings, rattles and stuffed bears. Unable to resist, Vanessa picked up a pink-and-white rattle.

"You have a little girl."

"Lara." Joanie beamed. "She's wonderful. She'll be up from her morning nap soon. I can't wait for you to see her."

"It's hard to imagine." Vanessa gave the rattle a shake before setting it down again. It made a pretty, musical sound that had her smiling. "You're a mother."

"I'm almost used to it." She took Vanessa's hand again as they sat on the sofa. "I still can't believe you're here. Vanessa Sexton, concert pianist, musical luminary and globe-trotter."

Vanessa winced. "Oh, please, not her. I left her in D.C."

"Just let me gloat a minute." She was still smiling,

but her eyes, eyes that were so like her brother's, were searching Vanessa's face. "We're so proud of you. The whole town. There would be something in the paper or a magazine, something on the news—or an event like that PBS special last year. No one would talk about anything else for days. You're Hyattown's link to fame and fortune."

"A weak link," Vanessa murmured, but she smiled. "Your farm, Joanie—it's wonderful."

"Can you believe it? I always thought I'd be living in one of those New York lofts, planning business lunches and fighting for a cab during rush hour."

"This is better." Vanessa settled back against the sofa cushions. "Much better."

Joanie toed off her shoes, then tucked her stockinged feet under her. "It has been for me. Do you remember Jack?"

"I don't think so. I can't remember you ever talking about anyone named Jack."

"I didn't know him in high school. He was a senior when we were just getting started. I remember seeing him in the halls now and then. Those big shoulders, and that awful buzz haircut during the football season." She laughed and settled comfortably. "Then, about four years ago, I was giving Dad a hand in the office. I was doing time as a paralegal in Hagerstown."

"A paralegal?"

"A former life," Joanie said with a wave of her hand. "Anyway, it was during Dad's Saturday office hours, and Millie was sick— You remember Millie?"

"Oh, yes." Vanessa grinned at the memory of Abraham Tucker's no-nonsense nurse.

"Well, I jumped into the breach for the weekend appointments, and in walks Jack Knight, all six foot three, two hundred and fifty pounds of him. He had laryngitis." A self-satisfied sigh escaped her. "There was this big, handsome hulk trying to tell me, in cowboy-and-Indian sign language, that no, he didn't have an appointment, but he wanted to see the doctor. I squeezed him in between a chicken pox and an earache. Dad examined him and gave him a prescription. A couple hours later he was back, with these raggedy-looking violets and a note asking me to the movies. How could I resist?"

Vanessa laughed. "You always were a soft touch."

Joanie rolled her big blue eyes. "Tell me about it. Before I knew it, I was shopping for a wedding dress and learning about fertilizer. It's been the best four years of my life." She shook her head. "But tell me about you. I want to hear everything."

Vanessa shrugged. "Practice, playing, traveling."

"Jetting off to Rome, Madrid, Mozambique—"

"Sitting on runways and in hotel rooms," Vanessa finished for her. "It isn't nearly as glamorous as it might look."

"No, I guess partying with famous actors, giving concerts for the queen of England and sharing midnight schmoozes with millionaires gets pretty boring."

"Schmoozes?" Vanessa had to laugh. "I don't think I ever schmoozed with anyone."

"Don't burst my bubble, Van." Joanie leaned over to brush a hand down Vanessa's arm. All the Tuckers were touchers, Vanessa thought. She'd missed that. "For years I've had this image of you glittering among the glittery. Celebing among the celebrities, hoitying among the toity."

"I guess I've done my share of hoitying. But mostly I've played the piano and caught planes."

"It's kept you in shape," Joanie said, sensing Vanessa's reluctance to talk about it. "I bet you're still a damn size four."

"Small bones."

"Wait until Brady gets a load of you."

Her chin lifted a fraction. "I saw him yesterday."

"Really? And the rat didn't call me." Joanie tapped a finger against her lips. There was laughter just beneath them. "So, how did it go?"

"I hit him."

"You—" Joanie choked, coughed, recovered. "You hit him? Why?"

"For standing me up for his senior prom."

"For—" Joanie broke off when Vanessa sprang to her feet and began pacing.

"I've never been so angry. I don't care how stupid it sounds. That night was so important to me. I thought it would be the most wonderful, the most romantic night of my life. You know how long we shopped for the perfect dress."

"Yes," Joanie murmured. "I know."

"I'd been looking forward to that night for weeks and weeks." On a roll now, she swirled around the room. "I'd just gotten my license, and I drove all the way into Frederick to get my hair done. I had this little sprig of baby's breath behind my ear." She touched the spot now, but there was no sentiment in the gesture. "Oh, I knew he was unreliable and reckless. I can't count the number of times my father told me. But I never expected him to dump me like that."

"But, Van—"

"I didn't even leave the house for two days after. I was so sick with embarrassment, so hurt. And then, with my parents fighting. It was—oh, it was so ugly. Then my father took me to Europe, and that was that."

Joanie bit her lip as she considered. There were explanations she could offer, but this was something Brady should straighten out himself. "There might be more to it than you think" was all she said.

Recovered now, Vanessa sat again. "It doesn't matter. It was a long time ago." Then she smiled. "Besides, I think I got the venom out when I punched him in the stomach."

Joanie's lips twitched in sisterly glee. "I'd like to have seen that."

"It's hard to believe he's a doctor."

"I don't think anyone was more surprised than Brady."

"It's odd he's never married…" She frowned. "Or anything."

"I won't touch 'anything,' but he's never married. There are a number of women in town who've developed chronic medical problems since he's come back."

"I'll bet," Vanessa muttered.

"Anyway, my father's in heaven. Have you had a chance to see him yet?"

"No, I wanted to see you first." She took Joanie's hands. "I'm so sorry about your mother. I didn't know until yesterday."

"It was a rough couple of years. Dad was so lost. I guess we all were." Her fingers tightened, taking comfort and giving it. "I know you lost your father. I understand how hard it must have been for you."

"He hadn't been well for a long time. I didn't know

how serious it was until, well…until it was almost over." She rubbed a hand over her stomach as it spasmed. "It helped to finish out the engagements. That would have been important to him."

"I know." She was starting to speak again when the intercom on the table crackled. There was a whimper, a gurgle, followed by a stream of infant jabbering. "She's up and ready to roll." Joanie rose quickly. "I'll just be a minute."

Alone, Vanessa stood and began to wander the room. It was filled with so many little, comforting things. Books on agriculture and child-rearing, wedding pictures and baby pictures. There was an old porcelain vase she remembered seeing in the Tucker household as a child. Through the window she could see the barn, and the cows drowsing in the midday sun.

Like something out of a book, she thought. Her own faded wish book.

"Van?"

She turned to see Joanie in the doorway, a round, dark-haired baby on her hip. The baby swung her feet, setting off the bells tied to her shoelaces.

"Oh, Joanie. She's gorgeous."

"Yeah." Joanie kissed Lara's head. "She is. Would you like to hold her?"

"Are you kidding?" Van came across the room to take the baby. After a long suspicious look, Lara smiled and began to kick her feet again. "Aren't you pretty?" Van murmured. Unable to resist, she lifted the baby over her head and turned in a circle while Lara giggled. "Aren't you just wonderful?"

"She likes you, too." Joanie gave a satisfied nod.

"I kept telling her she'd meet her godmother sooner or later."

"Her godmother?" Confused, Vanessa settled the baby on her hip again.

"Sure." Joanie smoothed Lara's hair. "I sent you a note right after she was born. I knew you couldn't make it back for the christening, so we had a proxy. But I wanted you and Brady to be her godparents." Joanie frowned at Vanessa's blank look. "You got the note, didn't you?"

"No." Vanessa rested her cheek against Lara's. "No, I didn't. I had no idea you were even married until my mother told me yesterday."

"But the wedding invitation—" Joanie shrugged. "I guess it could have gotten lost. You were always traveling around so much."

"Yes." She smiled again while Lara tugged at her hair. "If I'd known… I'd have found a way to be here if I'd known."

"You're here now."

"Yes." Vanessa nuzzled Lara's neck. "I'm here now. Oh, God, I envy you, Joanie."

"Me?"

"This beautiful child, this place, the look in your eyes when you talk about Jack. I feel like I've spent twelve years in a daze, while you've made a family and a home and a life."

"We've both made a life," Joanie said. "They're just different ones. You have so much talent, Van. Even as a kid I was awed by it. I wanted so badly to play like you." She laughed and enveloped them both in a hug. "As patient as you were, you could barely get me through 'Chopsticks.'"

"You were hopeless but determined. And I'm so glad you're still my friend."

"You're going to make me cry again." After a sniffle, Joanie shook her head. "Tell you what, you play with Lara for a few minutes and I'll go fix us some lemonade. Then we can be catty and gossip about how fat Julie Newton got."

"Did she?"

"And how Tommy McDonald is losing his hair." Joanie hooked an arm through Vanessa's. "Better yet, come in the kitchen with me. I'll fill you in on Betty Jean Baumgartner's third husband."

"Third?"

"And counting."

There was so much to think about. Not just the funny stories Joanie had shared with her that day, Vanessa thought as she strolled around the backyard at dusk. She needed to think about her life and what she wanted to do with it. Where she belonged. Where she wanted to belong.

For over a decade she'd had little or no choice. Or had lacked the courage to make one, she thought. She had done what her father wanted. He and her music had been the only constants. His drive and his needs had been so much more passionate than hers. And she hadn't wanted to disappoint him.

Hadn't dared, a small voice echoed, but she blocked it off.

She owed him everything. He had dedicated his life to her career. While her mother had shirked the responsibility, he had taken her, he had molded her, he had taught her. Every hour she had worked, he had worked. Even when he had become desperately ill, he had pushed himself, managing her career as meticulously as ever. No detail had ever escaped his notice— just as no flawed note had escaped his highly critical ear. He had taken her to the top of her career, and he had been content to bask in the reflected glory.

It couldn't have been easy for him, she thought now. His own career as a concert pianist had stalled before he'd hit thirty. He had never achieved the pinnacle he'd so desperately strived for. For him, music had been everything. Finally he'd been able to see those ambitions and needs realized in his only child.

Now she was on the brink of turning her back on everything he had wanted for her, everything he had worked toward. He would never have been able to understand her desire to give up a glowing career. Just as he had never been able to understand, or tolerate, her constant terror of performing.

She could remember it even now, even here in the sheltered quiet of the yard. The gripping sensation in her stomach, the wave of nausea she always battled back, the throbbing behind her eyes as she stood in the wings.

Stage fright, her father had told her. She would outgrow it. It was the one thing she had never been able to accomplish for him.

Yet, despite it, she knew she could go back to the concert stage. She could endure. She could rise even higher if she focused herself. If only she knew it was what she wanted.

Perhaps she just needed to rest. She sat on the lawn glider and sent it gently into motion. A few weeks or a few months of quiet, and then she might yearn for the life she had left behind. But for now she wanted nothing more than to enjoy the purple twilight.

From the glider she could see the lights glowing inside the house, and the neighboring houses. She had shared a meal with her mother in the kitchen—or had tried to. Loretta had seemed hurt when Vanessa only picked at her food. How could she explain that nothing seemed to settle well these days? This empty, gnawing feeling in her stomach simply wouldn't abate.

A little more time, Vanessa thought, and it would ease. It was only because she wasn't busy, as she should be. Certainly she hadn't practiced enough that day, or the day before. Even if she decided to cut back professionally, she had no business neglecting her practice.

Tomorrow, she thought, closing her eyes. Tomorrow was soon enough to start a routine. Lulled by the motion of the glider, she gathered her jacket closer. She'd forgotten how quickly the temperature could dip once the sun had fallen behind the mountains.

She heard the whoosh of a car as it cruised by on the road in front of the house. Then the sound of a door closing. From somewhere nearby, a mother called her child in from play. Another light blinked on in a window. A baby cried. Vanessa smiled, wishing she could dig out the old tent she and Joanie had used and pitch it in the backyard. She could sleep there, just listening to the town.

She turned at the sound of a dog barking, then saw the bright fur of a huge golden retriever. It dashed across the neighboring lawn, over the bed where her mother had already planted her pansies and marigolds. Tongue lolling, it lunged at the glider. Before Vanessa could decide whether to be alarmed or amused, it plopped both front paws in her lap and grinned a dog's grin.

"Well, hello there." She ruffled his ears. "Where did you come from?"

"From two blocks down, at a dead run." Panting, Brady walked out of the shadows. "I made the mistake of taking him to the office today. When I went to put him in the car, he decided to take a hike." He paused in front of the glider. "Are you going to punch me again, or can I sit down?"

Vanessa continued to pet the dog. "I probably won't hit you again."

"That'll have to do." He dropped down on the glider and stretched out his legs. The dog immediately tried to climb in his lap. "Don't try to make up," Brady said, pushing the dog off again.

"He's a pretty dog."

"Don't flatter him. He's already got an inflated ego."

"They say people and their pets develop similarities," she commented. "What's his name?"

"Kong. He was the biggest in his litter." Hearing his name, Kong barked twice, then raced off to chase the shadows. "I spoiled him when he was a puppy, and now I'm paying the price." Spreading his arms over the back of the glider, he let his fingers toy with the ends of her hair. "Joanie tells me you drove out to the farm today."

"Yes." Vanessa knocked his hand away. "She looks wonderful. And so happy."

"She is happy." Undaunted, he picked up her hand to play with her fingers. It was an old, familiar gesture. "You got to meet our godchild."

"Yes." Vanessa tugged her hand free. "Lara's gorgeous."

"Yeah." He went back to her hair. "She looks like me."

The laugh came too quickly to stop. "You're still conceited. And will you keep your hands off me?"

"I never was able to." He sighed, but shifted away an inch. "We used to sit here a lot, remember?"

"I remember."

"I think the first time I kissed you, we were sitting here, just like this."

"No." She folded her arms across her chest.

"You're right." As he knew very well. "The first time was up at the park. You came to watch me shoot baskets."

She brushed casually at the knee of her slacks. "I just happened to be walking through."

"You came because I used to shoot without a shirt and you wanted to see my sweaty chest."

She laughed again, because it was absolutely true. She turned to look at him in the shadowy light. He was smiling, relaxed. He'd always been able to relax, she remembered. And he'd always been able to make her laugh.

"It—meaning your sweaty chest—wasn't such a big deal."

"I've filled out some," he said easily. "And I still shoot hoops." This time she didn't seem to notice when he stroked her hair. "I remember that day. It was at the end of the summer, before my senior year. In three months you'd gone from being that pesty little Sexton kid to Sexy Sexton with a yard of the most incredible chestnut hair, and these great-looking legs you used to show off in teeny little shorts. You were such a brat. And you made my mouth water."

"You were always looking at Julie Newton."

"No, I was pretending to look at Julie Newton while I looked at you. Then you just happened to stroll by the court that day. You'd been to Lester's Store, because you had a bottle of soda. Grape soda."

She lifted a brow. "That's quite a memory you've got."

"Hey, these are the turning points in our lives. You said, 'Hi, Brady. You look awful hot. Want a sip?'" He grinned again. "I almost took a bite out of my basketball. Then you flirted with me."

"I did not."

"You batted your eyes."

She struggled with a giggle. "I've never batted my eyes."

"You batted them then." He sighed at the memory. "It was great."

"As I remember it, you were showing off, doing layups and hook shots or whatever. Macho stuff. Then you grabbed me."

"I remember grabbing. You liked it."

"You smelled like a gym locker."

"I guess I did. It was still my most memorable first kiss."

And hers, Vanessa thought. She hadn't realized she was leaning back against his shoulder and smiling. "We were so young. Everything was so intense, and so uncomplicated."

"Some things don't have to be complicated." But sitting there with her head feeling just right on his shoulder, he wasn't so sure. "Friends?"

"I guess."

"I haven't had a chance to ask you how long you're staying."

"I haven't had a chance to decide."

"Your schedule must be packed."

"I've taken a few months." She moved restlessly. "I may go to Paris for a few weeks."

He picked up her hand again, turning it over. Her hands had always fascinated him. Those long, tapering fingers, the baby-smooth palms, the short, practical nails. She wore no rings. He had given her one once—spent the money he'd earned mowing grass all summer on a gold ring with an incredibly small emerald. She'd kissed him senseless when he'd given it to her, and she'd sworn never to take it off.

Childhood promises were carelessly broken by adults. It was foolish to wish he could see it on her finger again.

"You know, I managed to see you play at Carnegie Hall a couple of years ago. It was overwhelming. You were overwhelming." He surprised them both by bringing her fingers to his lips. Then hastily dropped them. "I'd hoped to see you while we were both in New York, but I guess you were busy."

The jolt from her fingertips was still vibrating in her toes. "If you had called, I'd have managed it."

"I did call." His eyes remained on hers, searching, even as he shrugged it off. "It was then I fully realized how big you'd become. I never got past the first line of defense."

"I'm sorry. Really."

"It's no big deal."

"No, I would have liked to have seen you. Sometimes the people around me are too protective."

"I think you're right." He put a hand under her chin. She was more beautiful than his memory of her, and more fragile. If he had met her in New York, in less sentimental surroundings, would he have felt so drawn to her? He wasn't sure he wanted to know.

Friends was what he'd asked of her. He struggled to want no more.

"You look very tired, Van. Your color could be better."

"It's been a hectic year."

"Are you sleeping all right?"

Half-amused, she brushed his hand aside. "Don't start playing doctor with me, Brady."

"At the moment I can't think of anything I'd enjoy more, but I'm serious. You're run-down."

"I'm not run-down, just a little tired. Which is why I'm taking a break."

But he wasn't satisfied. "Why don't you come into the office for a physical?"

"Is that your new line? It used to be 'Let's go parking down at Molly's Hole.'"

"I'll get to that. Dad can take a look at you."

"I don't need a doctor." Kong came lumbering back, and she reached down for him. "I'm never sick. In almost ten years of concerts, I've never had to cancel one for health reasons." She buried her face in the dog's fur when her stomach clenched. "I'm not going to say it hasn't been a strain coming back here, but I'm dealing with it."

She'd always been hardheaded, he thought. Maybe it would be best if he simply kept an eye—a medical eye—on her for a few days. "Dad would still like to see you—personally, if not professionally."

"I'm going to drop by." Still bent over the dog, she turned her head. In the growing dark, he caught the familiar gleam in her eye. "Joanie says you've got your hands full with women patients. I imagine the same holds true of your father, if he's as handsome as I remember."

"He's had a few...interesting offers. But they've eased off since he and your mother hooked up."

Dumbfounded, Vanessa sat up straight. "Hooked up? My mother? Your father?"

"It's the hottest romance in town." He flicked her hair behind her shoulder. "So far."

"My mother?" she repeated.

"She's an attractive woman in her prime, Van. Why shouldn't she enjoy herself?"

Pressing a hand against her stomach, she rose. "I'm going in."

"What's the problem?"

"No problem. I'm going in. I'm cold."

He took her by the shoulders. It was another gesture that brought a flood of memories. "Why don't you give her a break?" Brady asked. "God knows she's been punished enough."

"You don't know anything about it."

"More than you think." He gave her a quick, impatient shake. "Let go, Van. These old resentments are going to eat you from the inside out."

"It's easy for you." The bitterness poured out before she could control it. "It's always been easy for you, with your nice happy family. You always knew they loved you, no matter what you did or didn't do. No one ever sent you away."

"She didn't send you away, Van."

"She let me go," she said quietly. "What's the difference?"

"Why don't you ask her?"

With a shake of her head, she pulled away. "I stopped being her little girl twelve years ago. I stopped being a lot of things." She turned and walked into the house.

Chapter 3

Vanessa had slept only in snatches. There had been pain. But she was used to pain. She masked it by coating her stomach with liquid antacids, by downing the pills that had been prescribed for her occasional blinding headaches. But most of all, she masked it by using her will to ignore.

Twice she had nearly walked down the hall to her mother's room. A third time she had gotten as far as her mother's door, with her hand raised to knock, before she had retreated to her own room and her own thoughts.

She had no right to resent the fact that her mother had a relationship with another man. Yet she did. In all the years Vanessa had spent with her father, he had never turned to another woman. Or, if he had, he had been much too discreet for her to notice.

And what did it matter? she asked herself as she

dressed the next morning. They had always lived their own lives, separate, despite the fact that they shared a house.

But it did matter. It mattered that her mother had been content all these years to live in this same house without contact with her only child. It mattered that she had been able to start a life, a new life, that had no place for her own daughter.

It was time, Vanessa told herself. It was time to ask why.

She caught the scent of coffee and fragrant bread as she reached the bottom landing. In the kitchen she saw her mother standing by the sink, rinsing a cup. Loretta was dressed in a pretty blue suit, pearls at her ears and around her throat. The radio was on low, and she was humming even as she turned and saw her daughter.

"Oh, you're up." Loretta smiled, hoping it didn't look forced. "I wasn't sure I'd see you this morning before I left."

"Left?"

"I have to go to work. There're some muffins, and the coffee's still hot."

"To work?" Vanessa repeated. "Where?"

"At the shop." To busy her nervous hands, she poured Vanessa a cup of coffee. "The antique shop. I bought it about six years ago. The Hopkinses' place, you might remember. I went to work for them when—some time ago. When they decided to retire, I bought them out."

Vanessa shook her head to clear it of the grogginess. "You run an antique shop?"

"Just a small one." She set the coffee on the table. The moment they were free, her hands began to tug at her pearl necklace. "I call it Loretta's Attic. Silly, I suppose, but it does nicely. I closed it for a couple of days, but… I can keep it closed another day or so if you'd like."

Vanessa studied her mother thoughtfully, trying to imagine her owning a business, worrying about inventory and bookkeeping. Antiques? Had she ever mentioned an interest in them?

"No." It seemed that talk would have to wait. "Go ahead."

"If you like, you can run down later and take a look." Loretta began to fiddle with a button on her jacket. "It's small, but I have a lot of interesting pieces."

"We'll see."

"Are you sure you'll be all right here alone?"

"I've been all right alone for a long time."

Loretta's gaze dropped. Her hands fell to her sides. "Yes, of course you have. I'm usually home by six-thirty."

"All right. I'll see you this evening, then." She walked to the sink to turn on the faucet. She wanted water, cold and clear.

"Van."

"Yes?"

"I know I have years to make up for." Loretta was standing in the doorway when Vanessa turned. "I hope you'll give me a chance."

"I want to." She spread her hands. "I don't know where either of us is supposed to start."

"Neither do I." Loretta's smile was hesitant, but less strained. "Maybe that's its own start. I love you. I'll be happy if I can make you believe that." She turned quickly and left.

"Oh, Mom," Vanessa said to the empty house. "I don't know what to do."

* * *

"Mrs. Driscoll." Brady patted the eighty-three-year-old matron on her knobby knee. "You've got the heart of a twenty-year-old gymnast."

She cackled, as he'd known she would. "It's not my heart I'm worried about, Brady. It's my bones. They ache like the devil."

"Maybe if you'd let one of your great-grandchildren weed that garden of yours."

"I've been doing my own patch for sixty years—"

"And you'll do it another sixty," he finished for her, setting the blood pressure cuff aside. "Nobody in the county grows better tomatoes, but if you don't ease up, your bones are going to ache." He picked up her hands. Her fingers were wiry, not yet touched by arthritis. But it was in her shoulders, in her knees, and there was little he could do to stop its march.

He completed the exam, listening to her tell stories about her family. She'd been his second-grade teacher, and he'd thought then she was the oldest woman alive. After nearly twenty-five years, the gap had closed considerably. Though he knew she still considered him the little troublemaker who had knocked over the goldfish bowl just to see the fish flop on the floor.

"I saw you coming out of the post office a couple of days ago, Mrs. Driscoll." He made a notation on her chart. "You weren't using your cane."

She snorted. "Canes are for old people."

He lowered the chart, lifted a brow. "It's my considered medical opinion, Mrs. Driscoll, that you *are* old."

She cackled and batted a hand at him. "You always had a smart mouth, Brady Tucker."

"Yeah, but now I've got a medical degree to go with

it." He took her hand to help her off the examining table. "And I want you to use that cane—even if it's only to give John Hardesty a good rap when he flirts with you."

"The old goat," she muttered. "And I'd look like an old goat, too, hobbling around on a cane."

"Isn't vanity one of the seven deadly sins?"

"It's not worth sinning if it isn't deadly. Get out of here, boy, so I can dress."

"Yes, ma'am." He left her, shaking his head. He could hound her from here to the moon and she wouldn't use that damn cane. She was one of the few patients he couldn't bully or intimidate.

After two more hours of morning appointments, he spent his lunch hour driving to Washington County Hospital to check on two patients. An apple and a handful of peanut butter crackers got him through the afternoon. More than one of his patients mentioned the fact that Vanessa Sexton was back in town. This information was usually accompanied by smirks, winks and leers. He'd had his stomach gouged several times by teasing elbows.

Small towns, he thought as he took five minutes in his office between appointments. The people in them knew everything about everyone. And they remembered it. Forever. Vanessa and he had been together, briefly, twelve years before, but it might as well have been written in concrete, not just carved in one of the trees in Hyattown Park.

He'd forgotten about her—almost. Except when he'd seen her name or picture in the paper. Or when he'd listened to one of her albums, which he'd bought strictly for old times' sake. Or when he'd seen a woman tilt her head to the side and smile in a way similar to the way Van had smiled.

But when he had remembered, they'd been memories of childhood. Those were the sweetest and most poignant. They had been little more than children, rushing toward adulthood with a reckless and terrifying speed. But what had happened between them had remained beautifully innocent. Long, slow kisses in the shadows, passionate promises, a few forbidden caresses.

Thinking of them now, of her, shouldn't make him ache. And yet he rubbed a hand over his heart.

It had seemed too intense at the time, because they had faced such total opposition from her father. The more Julius Sexton had railed against their blossoming relationship, the closer they had become. That was the way of youth, Brady thought now. And he had played the angry young man to perfection, he remembered with a smirk. Defying her father, giving his own a lifetime of headaches. Making threats and promises as only an eighteen-year-old could.

If the road had run smoothly, they would probably have forgotten each other within weeks.

Liar, he thought with a laugh. He had never been so in love as he had been that year with Vanessa. That heady, frantic year, when he had turned eighteen and anything and everything had seemed possible.

They had never made love. He had bitterly regretted that after she had been swept out of his life. Now, with the gift of hindsight, he realized that it had been for the best. If they had been lovers, how much more difficult it would be for them to be friends as adults.

That was what he wanted, all he wanted, he assured

himself. He had no intention of breaking his heart over her a second time.

Maybe for a moment, when he had first seen her at the piano, his breath had backed up in his lungs and his pulse had scrambled. That was a natural enough reaction. She was a beautiful woman, and she had once been his. And if he had felt a yearning the night before, as they had sat on the glider in the growing dusk, well, he was human. But he wasn't stupid.

Vanessa Sexton wasn't his girl anymore. And he didn't want her for his woman.

"Dr. Tucker." One of the nurses poked a head in the door. "Your next patient is here."

"Be right there."

"Oh, and your father said to stop by before you leave for the day."

"Thanks." Brady headed for examining room 2, wondering if Vanessa would be sitting out on the glider that evening.

Vanessa knocked on the door of the Tucker house and waited. She'd always liked the Main Street feeling of the home, with its painted porch and its window boxes. There were geraniums in them now, already blooming hardily. The screens were in the open windows. As a girl, she had often seen Brady and his father removing the storms and putting in the screens—a sure sign that winter was over.

There were two rockers sitting on the porch. She knew Dr. Tucker would often sit there on a summer evening. People strolling by would stop to pass the time or to relay a list of symptoms and complaints.

And every year, over the Memorial Day weekend, the

Tuckers would throw a backyard barbecue. Everyone in town came by to eat hamburgers and potato salad, to sit under the shade of the big walnut tree, to play croquet.

He was a generous man, Dr. Tucker, Vanessa remembered. With his time, with his skill. She could still remember his laugh, full and rich, and how gentle his hands were during an examination.

But what could she say to him now? This man who had been such a larger-than-life figure during her childhood? This man who had once comforted her when she'd wept over her parents' crumbling marriage? This man who was now involved with her mother?

He opened the door himself, and stood there studying her. He was tall, as she remembered. Like Brady, he had a wiry, athletic build. Though his dark hair had turned a steely gray, he looked no older to her. There were lines fanning out around his dark blue eyes. They deepened as he smiled.

Unsure of herself, she started to offer him a hand. Before she could speak, she was caught up in a crushing bear hug. He smelled of Old Spice and peppermint, she thought, and nearly wept. Even that hadn't changed.

"Little Vanessa." His powerful voice rolled over her as he squeezed. "It's good to have you home."

"It's good to be home." Held against him, she believed it. "I've missed you." It came with a rush of feeling. "I've really missed you."

"Let me have a look at you." Still standing in the doorway, he held her at arm's length. "My, my, my..." he murmured. "Emily always said you'd be a beauty."

"Oh, Dr. Tucker, I'm so sorry about Mrs. Tucker."

"We all were." He rubbed her hands briskly up and down her arms. "She always kept track of you in the papers and magazines, you know. Had her heart set on you for a daughter-in-law. More than once she said to me, 'Ham, that's the girl for Brady. She'll straighten him out.'"

"It looks like he's straightened himself out."

"Mostly." Draping an arm over her shoulder, he led her inside. "How about a nice cup of tea and a piece of pie?"

"I'd love it."

She sat at the kitchen table while he brewed and served. The house hadn't changed on the inside, either. It was still neat as a pin. It was polished and scrubbed, with Emily's collection of knickknacks on every flat surface.

The sunny kitchen looked out over the backyard, with its big trees leafing and its spring bulbs blooming. To the right was the door that led to the offices. The only change she saw was the addition of a complicated phone and intercom system.

"Mrs. Leary still makes the best pies in town." He cut thick slabs of chocolate meringue.

"And she still pays you in baked goods."

"Worth their weight in gold." With a contented sigh, he sat across from her. "I guess I don't have to tell you how proud we all are of you."

She shook her head. "I wish I could have gotten back sooner. I didn't even know Joanie was married. And the baby." She lifted her teacup, fully comfortable for the first time since her return. "Lara's beautiful."

"Smart, too." He winked. "Of course, I might be a

tad prejudiced, but I can't remember a smarter child. And I've seen my share of them."

"I hope to see a lot of her while I'm here. Of all of you."

"We're hoping you'll stay a good long time."

"I don't know." She looked down at her tea. "I haven't thought about it."

"Your mother hasn't been able to talk about anything else for weeks."

Vanessa took a smidgen of the fluffy meringue. "She seems well."

"She is well. Loretta's a strong woman. She's had to be."

Vanessa looked up again. Because her stomach had begun to jump, she spoke carefully. "I know she's running an antique shop. It's hard to imagine her as a businesswoman."

"It was hard for her to imagine, but she's doing a good job of it. I know you lost your father a few months ago."

"Cancer. It was very difficult for him."

"And for you."

She moved her shoulders. "There was little I could do…little he would allow me to do. Basically he refused to admit he was ill. He hated weaknesses."

"I know." He laid a hand on hers. "I hope you've learned to be more tolerant of them."

He didn't have to explain. "I don't hate my mother," she said with a sigh. "I just don't know her."

It was a good answer. One he appreciated. "I do. She's had a hard life, Van. Any mistakes she made, she's paid for more times than any one person should have to. She loves you. She always has."

"Then why did she let me go?"

His heart went out to her, as it always had. "That's a question you'll have to ask her yourself. And one she needs to answer."

With a little sigh, Vanessa sat back. "I always did come to cry on your shoulder."

"That's what shoulders are for. Mostly I was vain enough to think I had two daughters."

"You did." She blinked the tears away and took a soothing drink of tea. "Dr. Tucker, are you in love with my mother?"

"Yes. Does that upset you?"

"It shouldn't."

"But?"

"It's just that it's difficult for me to accept. I've always had such a clear picture of you and Mrs. Tucker as a set. It was one of my constants. My parents…as unhappy as they were together, for as long as I can remember…"

"Were your parents," he said quietly. "Another permanent set."

"Yes." She relaxed a little, grateful that he understood. "I know that's not reasonable. It's not even reality. But…"

"It should be," he finished for her. "My dear child, there is far too much in life that's unfair. I had twenty-eight years with Emily, and had planned for twenty-eight more. It wasn't to be. During the time I had with her, I loved her absolutely. We were lucky enough to grow into people each of us could continue to love. When she died, I thought that a part of my life was over. Your mother was Emily's closest and dearest friend, and that was how I continued to look at Loretta, for several years. Then she became mine—my closest and dearest friend. I think Emily would have been pleased."

"You make me feel like a child."

"You're always a child when it comes to your parents." He glanced down at her plate. "Have you lost your sweet tooth?"

"No." She laughed a little. "My appetite."

"I didn't want to sound like an old fogy and tell you you're too thin. But you are, a bit. Loretta mentioned you weren't eating well. Or sleeping well."

Vanessa raised a brow. She hadn't realized her mother had noticed. "I suppose I'm keyed up. The last couple of years have been pretty hectic."

"When's the last time you had a physical?"

Now she did laugh. "You sound like Brady. I'm fine, Dr. Tucker. Concert tours makes you tough. It's just nerves."

He nodded, but promised himself that he'd keep an eye on her. "I hope you'll play for me soon."

"I'm already breaking in the new piano. In fact, I should get back. I've been skimping on my practice time lately."

As she rose, Brady came through the connecting door. It annoyed him to see her there. It wasn't bad enough that she'd been in his head all day. Now she was in his kitchen. He nodded to her, then glanced down at the pie.

"The dependable Mrs. Leary." He grinned at his father. "Were you going to leave any for me?"

"She's my patient."

"He always hoards the goodies," Brady said to Vanessa, dipping a finger in the meringue on her plate. "You wanted to see me before I left?"

"You wanted me to look over the Crampton file." Ham tapped a finger on a folder on the counter. "I made some notes."

"Thanks."

"I've got some things to tie up." He took Vanessa by the shoulders and kissed her soundly. "Come back soon."

"I will." She'd never been able to stay away.

"The barbecue's in two weeks. I expect you to be here."

"I wouldn't miss it."

"Brady," he said as he left, "behave yourself with that girl."

Brady grinned as the door closed. "He still figures I'm going to talk you into the backseat of my car."

"You did talk me into the backseat of your car."

"Yeah." The memory made him restless. "Any coffee?"

"Tea," she said. "With lemon verbena."

With a grunt, he turned and took a carton of milk from the refrigerator. "I'm glad you stopped by to see him. He's crazy about you."

"The feeling's mutual."

"You going to eat that pie?"

"No, I was just—" he sat down and dug in "—leaving."

"What's your hurry?" he asked over a forkful.

"I'm not in a hurry, I just—"

"Sit down." He poured an enormous glass of milk.

"Your appetite's as healthy as ever, I see."

"Clean living."

She should go, really. But he looked so relaxed, and relaxing, sitting at the table shoveling in pie. Friends, he'd said. Maybe they *could* be friends. She leaned back against the counter.

"Where's the dog?"

"Left him home. Dad caught him digging in the tulips yesterday, so he's banished."

"You don't live here anymore?"

"No." He looked up and nearly groaned. She was leaning on the counter in front of the window, the light in her hair. There was the faintest of smiles playing on that full, serious mouth of hers. The severe tailoring of her slacks and shirt made her seem that much softer and feminine. "I, ah…" He reached for the milk. "I bought some land outside of town. The house is going up slow, but it's got a roof."

"You're building your own house?"

"I'm not doing that much. I can't get away from here long enough to do much more than stick up a couple of two-by-fours. I've got a couple of guys hammering it together." He looked at her again, considering. "I'll drive you out some time so you can take a look."

"Maybe."

"How about now?" He rose to put his dishes in the sink.

"Oh, well…I really have to get back…."

"For what?"

"To practice."

He turned. Their shoulders brushed. "Practice later."

It was a challenge. They both knew it, both understood it. They were both determined to prove that they could be in each other's company without stirring up old yearnings.

"All right. I'll follow you out, though. That way you won't have to come back into town."

"Fine." He took her arm and led her out the back door.

He'd had a secondhand Chevy sedan when she'd left town. Now he drove a sporty four-wheel drive. Three miles out of town, when they came to the steep, narrow lane, she saw the wisdom of it.

It would be all but impassable in the winter, she thought as her Mercedes jolted up the graveled incline. Though the leaves were little more than tender shoots, the woods were thick. She could see the wild dogwoods blooming white. She narrowly avoided a rut. Gravel spit out from under her wheels as she negotiated the last sweeping turn and came to a halt behind Brady.

The dog came racing, barking, his tail fanning in the breeze.

The shell of the house was up. He wasn't contenting himself with a cabin in the woods, she noted. It was a huge, spreading two-story place. The windows that were in place were tall, with half-moon arches over them. What appeared to be the skeleton of a gable rose up from the second story. It would command a majestic view of the distant Blue Mountains.

The grounds, covered with the rubble of construction, sloped down to a murmuring creek. Rain would turn the site into a mud pit, she thought as she stepped from her car. But, oh, when it was terraced and planted, it would be spectacular.

"It's fabulous." She pushed back her hair as the early evening breeze stirred it. "What a perfect spot."

"I thought so." He caught Kong by the collar before he could leap on her.

"He's all right." She laughed as she bent down to rub

him. "Hello, fella. Hello, big boy. You've got plenty of room to run around here, don't you?"

"Twelve acres." He was getting that ache again, just under his heart, watching her play with his dog. "I'm going to leave most of it alone."

"I'm glad." She turned a full circle. "I'd hate to see you manicure the woods. I'd nearly forgotten how wonderful they are. How quiet."

"Come on." He took her hand, held it. "I'll give you the tour."

"How long have you had the land?"

"Almost a year." They walked across a little wooden bridge, over the creek. "Watch your step. The ground's a mess." He looked down at her elegant Italian flats. "Here." He hoisted her up and over the rubble. She felt the bunching of his arm muscles, he the firm length of her legs.

"You don't have to—" He set her down, hastily, in front of a pair of atrium doors. "Still Mr. Smooth, aren't you?"

"You bet."

Inside there was subflooring and drywall. She saw power tools, sawhorses and piles of lumber. A huge stone fireplace was already built into the north wall. Temporary stairs led to the second level. The scent of sawdust was everywhere.

"The living room," he explained. "I wanted plenty of light. The kitchen's over there."

He indicated a generous space that curved off the main room. There was a bay window over the sink that looked out into the woods. A stove and refrigerator were nestled between unfinished counters.

"We'll have an archway to keep in tune with the windows," he went on. "Then another will lead around to the dining room."

She looked up at the sky through a trio of skylights. "It seems very ambitious."

"I only intend to do it once." Taking her hand again, he led her around the first floor. "Powder room. Your mother found me this great pedestal sink. The porcelain's in perfect shape. And this is a kind of a den, I guess. Stereo equipment, books." When he narrowed his eyes, he could see the finished product perfectly. And oddly, so could she. "Do you remember Josh McKenna?"

"Yes. He was your partner in crime."

"Now he's a partner in a construction firm. He's doing all these built-ins himself."

"Josh?" She ran a hand over a shelf. The workmanship was beautiful.

"He designed the kitchen cabinets, too. They're going to be something. Let's go up. The stairs are narrow, but they're sturdy."

Despite his assurances, she kept one hand pressed against the wall as they climbed. There were more skylights, more arches. The eyebrow windows, as he called them, would go over the bed in the master suite, which included an oversize bathroom with a tiled sunken tub. Though there were a mattress and a dresser in the bedroom, the bath was the only finished room. Vanessa stepped off subflooring onto ceramic.

He'd chosen cool pastels with an occasional vivid slash of navy. The huge tub was encircled by a tiled ledge that sat flush against another trio of windows. Vanessa imagined soaking there with a view of the screening woods.

"You've pulled out all the stops," she commented.

"When I decided to move back, I decided to do it right." They continued down the hall, between the studded walls. "There are two more bedrooms on this floor, and another bath. I'm going to use glass brick in that one. The deck will run all around, then drop down to the second level on the west side for sunset." He took her up another flight of splattered steps into the gable. "I'm thinking about putting my office up here."

It was like a fairy tale, Vanessa thought, circular in shape, with more arching windows. Everywhere you stood there was a lofty view of the woods and the mountains beyond.

"I could live right here," she said, "and feel like Rapunzel."

"Your hair's the wrong color." He lifted a handful. "I'm glad you never cut it. I used to dream about this hair." His gaze shifted to hers. "About you. For years after you left, I used to dream about you. I could never figure it out."

She turned away quickly and walked to one of the windows. "When do you think you'll have it finished?"

"We're shooting for September." He frowned at her back. He hadn't thought of her when he'd designed the house, when he'd chosen the wood, the tiles, the colors. Why was it that now that she was here it was as if the house had been waiting for her? As if he'd been waiting for her? "Van?"

"Yes," she answered, keeping her back to him. Her stomach was in knots, her fingers were twisted. When he said nothing else, she forced herself to turn, made her lips curve. "It's a fabulous place, Brady. I'm glad you showed it to me. I hope I get the chance to see it when it's done."

He wasn't going to ask her if she was going to stay. He didn't want to know. He couldn't let it matter. But he knew that there was unfinished business between them, and he had to settle it, at least in his own mind.

He crossed to her slowly. He saw the awareness come into her eyes with his first step. She would have backed away if there had been anywhere to go.

"Don't," she said when he took her arms.

"This is going to hurt me as much as it does you."

He touched his lips to hers, testing. And felt her shudder. Her taste, just that brief taste, made him burn. Again he kissed her, lingering over it only seconds longer. This time he heard her moan. His hands slid up her arms to cup her face. When his mouth took hers again, the testing was over.

It did hurt. She felt the ache through every bone and muscle. And damn him, she felt the pleasure. A pleasure she had lived without for too long. Greedy for it, she pulled him closer and let the war rage frantically inside her.

She was no longer kissing a boy, however clever and passionate that boy had been. She wasn't kissing a memory, no matter how rich and clear that memory had been. It was a man she held now. A strong, hungry man who knew her much too well.

When her lips parted for his, she knew what he would taste like. As her hands dug into his shoulders, she knew the feel of those muscles. With the scent of sawdust around them, and the light gentle through the glass, she felt herself rocked back and forth between the past and present.

She was all he remembered, and more. He had always been generous, always passionate, but there seemed to be more innocence now than there had been before. It was there, sweet, beneath the simmer of desire. Her body trembled even as it strained against his.

The dreams he thought he had forgotten flooded back. And with them the needs, the frustrations, the hopes, of his youth.

It was her. It had always been her. And yet it had never been.

Shaken, he pulled back and held her at arm's length. The color had risen over her cheekbones. Her eyes had darkened, clouded, in that way that had always made him churn. Her lips were parted, soft, unpainted. His hands were lost, as they had been countless times before, in her hair.

And the feeling was the same. He could have murdered her for it. Twelve years hadn't diluted the emotion she could pull out of him with a look.

"I was afraid of that," he murmured. He needed to keep sane, he told himself. He needed to think. "You always could stop my heart, Vanessa."

"This is stupid." Breathless, she stepped back. "We're not children anymore."

He dipped his hands in his pockets. "Exactly."

She ran an unsteady hand through her hair. "Brady, this was over a long time ago."

"Apparently not. Could be we just have to get it out of our systems."

"My system's just fine," she told him. It was a lie. "You'll have to worry about your own. I'm not interested in climbing into the backseat with you again."

"That might be interesting." He surprised himself by

smiling, and meaning it. "But I had more comfortable surroundings in mind."

"Whatever the surroundings, the answer's still no."

She started toward the steps, and he took her by the arm. "You were sixteen the last time you said no." Slowly, though impatience simmered through him, he turned her to face him. "As much as I regret it, I have to say you were right. Times have changed, and we're all grown up now."

Her heart was beating too fast, she thought. His fault. He had always been able to tie her into knots. "Just because we're adults doesn't mean I'll jump in your bed."

"It does mean that I'll take the time and make the effort to change your mind."

"You are still an egotistical idiot, Brady."

"And you still call me names when you know I'm right." He pulled her close for a hard, brief kiss. "I still want you, Van. And this time, by God, I'm going to have you."

She saw the truth of it in his eyes before she jerked away. She felt the truth of it inside herself. "Go to hell."

She turned and rushed down the stairs.

He watched from the window as she raced across the bridge to her car. Even with the distance, he heard her slam the door. It made him grin. She'd always had a devil of a temper. He was glad to see it still held true.

Chapter 4

She pounded the keys. Tchaikovsky. The first piano concerto. The first movement. Hers was a violently passionate interpretation of the romantic theme. She wanted the violence, wanted to let it pour out from inside her and into the music.

He'd had no right. No right to bring everything back. To force her to face feelings she'd wanted to forget. Feelings she'd forgotten. Worse, he'd shown her how much deeper, how much more raw and intense, those feelings could be now that she was a woman.

He meant nothing to her. Could be nothing more to her than an old acquaintance, a friend of her childhood. She would not be hurt by him again. And she would never—never—allow anyone to have the kind of power over her that Brady had once had.

The feelings would pass, because she would make

them pass. If there was one thing she had learned through all these years of work and travel, it was that she and she alone was responsible for her emotions.

She stopped playing, letting her fingers rest on the keys. While she might not have been able to claim serenity, she was grateful that she had been able to exorcise most of the anger and frustration through her music.

"Vanessa?"

She turned her head to see her mother standing in the doorway. "I didn't know you were home."

"I came in while you were playing." Loretta took a step forward. She was dressed as she had been that morning, in her sleek suit and pearls, but her face showed a hesitant concern. "Are you all right?"

"Yes, I'm fine." Vanessa lifted a hand to push back her hair. Looking at her mother, she felt flushed, untidy and vulnerable. Automatically, defensively, she straightened her shoulders. "I'm sorry. I guess I lost track of the time."

"It doesn't matter." Loretta blocked off the urge to move closer and smooth her daughter's hair herself. "Mrs. Driscoll stopped by the shop before I closed. She mentioned that she saw you going into Ham Tucker's house."

"She still has an eagle eye, I see."

"And a big nose." Loretta's smile was hesitant. "You saw Ham, then."

"Yes." Vanessa turned on the stool, but didn't rise. "He looks wonderful, almost unchanged. We had some pie and tea in the kitchen."

"I'm glad you had a chance to visit with him. He's always been so fond of you."

"I know." She took a bracing breath. "Why didn't you tell me you were involved with him?"

Loretta lifted a hand to her pearls and twisted the strand nervously. "I suppose I wasn't sure how to bring it up. To explain. I thought you might be…might feel awkward about seeing him again if you knew we were…" She let her words trail off, certain the word *dating* would be out of place at her age.

Vanessa merely lifted a brow. "Maybe you thought it was none of my business."

"No." Her hand fell to her side. "Oh, Van…"

"Well, it isn't, after all." Slowly, deliberately, Vanessa patched up the cracks in her shield. "You and my father had been divorced for years before he died. You're certainly free to choose your own companions."

The censure in her daughter's voice had Loretta's spine straightening. There were many things, many, that she regretted, that had caused her shame. Her relationship with Abraham Tucker wasn't one of them.

"You're absolutely right," she said, her voice cool. "I'm not embarrassed, and I certainly don't feel guilty, about seeing Ham. We're adults, and both of us are free." The tilt of her chin as she spoke was very like her daughter's. "Perhaps I felt odd about what started between us, because of Emily. She had been my oldest and dearest friend. But Emily was gone, and both Ham and I were alone. And maybe the fact that we both had loved Emily had something to do with our growing closer. I'm very proud that he cares for me," she said, color dotting her cheeks. "In the past few years, he's given me something I've never had from another man. Understanding."

She turned and hurried up the stairs. She was standing in front of her dresser, removing her jewelry, when Vanessa came in.

"I apologize if I seemed too critical."

Loretta slapped the pearls down on the wood. "I don't want you to apologize like some polite stranger, Vanessa. You're my daughter. I'd rather you shouted at me. I'd rather you slammed doors or stormed into your room the way you used to."

"I nearly did." She walked farther into the room, running a hand over the back of a small, tufted chair. Even that was new, she thought—the little blue lady's chair that so suited the woman who was her mother. Calmer now, and more than a little ashamed, she chose her next words carefully. "I don't resent your relationship with Dr. Tucker. Really. It surprised me, certainly. And what I said before is true. It's none of my business."

"Van—"

"No, please." Vanessa held up a hand. "When I first drove into town, I thought nothing had changed. But I was wrong. It's difficult to accept that. It's difficult to accept that you moved on so easily."

"Moved on, yes," Loretta said. "But not easily."

Vanessa looked up, passion in her eyes. "Why did you let me go?"

"I had no choice," Loretta said simply. "And at the time I tried to believe it was what was best for you. What you wanted."

"What I wanted?" The anger she wanted so badly to control seeped out as bitterness. "Did anyone ever ask me what I wanted?"

"I tried. In every letter I wrote you, I begged you to tell me if you were happy, if you wanted to come home. When you sent them back unopened, I knew I had my answer."

The color ran into and then out of Vanessa's face as she stared at Loretta. "You never wrote me."

"I wrote you for years, hoping that you might find the compassion to open at least one."

"There were no letters," Vanessa said, very deliberately, her hands clenching and unclenching.

Without a word, Loretta went over to an enameled trunk at the foot of her bed. She drew out a deep box and removed the lid. "I kept them," she said.

Vanessa looked in and saw dozens of letters, addressed to her at hotels throughout Europe and the States. Her stomach convulsing, she took careful breaths and sat on the edge of the bed.

"You never saw them, did you?" Loretta murmured. Vanessa could only shake her head. "He would deny me even such a little thing as a letter." With a sigh, Loretta set the box back in the trunk.

"Why?" Vanessa's throat was raw. "Why did he stop me from seeing your letters?"

"Maybe he thought I would interfere with your career." After a moment's hesitation, Loretta touched her shoulder. "He was wrong. I would never have stopped you from reaching for something you wanted and deserved so much. He was, in his way, protecting you and punishing me."

"For what?"

Loretta turned and walked to the window.

"Damn it, I have a right to know." Fury had her on her feet and taking a step forward. Then, with an involuntary gasp, she was clutching her stomach.

"Van?" Loretta took her shoulders, moving her gently back to the bed. "What is it?"

"It's nothing." She gritted her teeth against the grinding pain. It infuriated her that it could incapacitate her, even for a moment, in front of someone else. "Just a spasm."

"I'm going to call Ham."

"No." Vanessa grabbed her arm. Her long musician's fingers were strong and firm. "I don't need a doctor. It's just stress." She kept one hand balled at her side and struggled to get past the pain. "And I stood up too fast." Very carefully, she relaxed her hand.

"Then it won't hurt to have him look at you." Loretta draped an arm over her shoulders. "Van, you're so thin."

"I've had a lot to deal with in the last year." Vanessa kept her words measured. "A lot of tension. Which is why I've decided to take a few months off."

"Yes, but—"

"I know how I feel. And I'm fine."

Loretta removed her arm when she heard Vanessa's dismissive tone. "All right, then. You're not a child anymore."

"No, I'm not." She folded her hands in her lap as Loretta rose. "I'd like an answer. What was my father punishing you for?"

Loretta seemed to brace herself, but her voice was calm and strong when she spoke. "For betraying him with another man."

For a moment, Vanessa could only stare. Here was her mother, her face pale but set, confessing to adultery. "You had an affair?" Vanessa asked at length.

"Yes." Shame rushed through her. But she knew she could deal with it. She'd lived with shame for years.

"There was someone… It hardly matters now who it was. I was involved with him for almost a year before you went to Europe."

"I see."

Loretta gave a short, brittle laugh. "Oh, I'm sure you do. So I won't bother to offer you any excuses or explanations. I broke my vows, and I've been paying for it for twelve years."

Vanessa lifted her head, torn between wanting to understand and wanting to condemn. "Did you love him?"

"I needed him. There's a world of difference."

"You didn't marry again."

"No." Loretta felt no regret at that, just a vague ache, as from an old scar that had been bumped once too often. "Marriage wasn't something either of us wanted at the time."

"Then it was just for sex." Vanessa pressed her fingers against her eyes. "You cheated on your husband just for sex."

A flurry of emotions raced over Loretta's face before she calmed it again. "That's the least common denominator. Maybe, now that you're a woman, you'll understand, even if you can't forgive."

"I don't understand anything." Vanessa stood. It was foolish to want to weep for something that was over and done. "I need to think. I'm going for a drive."

Alone, Loretta sat on the edge of the bed and let her own tears fall.

She drove for hours, aimlessly. She spent most of the time negotiating curving back roads lined with budding wildflowers and arching trees. Some of the old farms had been sold and subdivided since she'd been here last.

Houses and yards crisscrossed over what had once been sprawling corn or barley fields. She felt a pang of loss on seeing them. The same kind of pang she felt when she thought of her family.

She wondered if she would have been able to understand the lack of fidelity if it had been some other woman. Would she have been able to give a sophisticated little shrug and agree that the odd affair was just a part of life? She wasn't sure. She hadn't been raised to see a sanctified state. And it wasn't some other woman. It was her mother.

It was late when she found herself turning into Brady's lane. She didn't know why she'd come here, come to him, of all people. But she needed someone to listen. Someone who cared.

The lights were on. She could hear the dog barking from inside the house at the sound of her car. Slowly she retraced the steps she had taken that evening. When she had run from him, and from her own feelings. Before she could knock, Brady was at the door. He took a long look at her through the glass before pulling it open.

"Hi."

"I was out driving." She felt so completely stupid that she took a step back. "I'm sorry. It's late."

"Come on in, Van." He took her hand. The dog sniffed at her slacks, wagging his tail. "Want a drink?"

"No." She had no idea what she wanted. She looked around, aware that she'd interrupted him. There was a stepladder against a wall, and a portable stereo set too loud. Rock echoed to the ceiling. She noted there was a fine coat of white dust on his hands and forearms, even in his hair. She fought a ridiculous urge to brush it out for him. "You're busy."

"Just sanding drywall." He walked over to turn off the music. The sudden silence made her edgy. "It's amazingly therapeutic." He picked up a sheet of sandpaper. "Want to try it?"

She managed to smile. "Maybe later."

He stopped by the refrigerator to pull out a beer. He gestured with it. "Sure?"

"Yes. I'm driving, and I can't stay long."

He popped the top and took a long drink. The cold beer eased through the dust in his throat—and through the knot that had lodged there when he saw her walking to his door. "I guess you decided not to be mad at me anymore."

"I don't know." Hugging her arms, Vanessa walked to the far window. She wished she could see the moon, but it was hiding behind a bank of clouds. "I don't know what I feel about anything."

He knew that look, that set of her shoulders, that tone of voice. It had been the same years before, when she would escape from one of the miserable arguments between her parents. "Why don't you tell me about it?"

Of course he would say that, she thought. Hadn't she known he would? And he would listen. He always had. "I shouldn't have come here," she said with a sigh. "It's like falling back into an old rut."

"Or slipping into a comfortable pair of shoes." He winced a little at his own words. "I don't think I like that much better. Look, do you want to sit down? I can dust off a sawhorse, or turn over a can of drywall compound."

"No. No, I couldn't sit." She continued to stare out the window. All she could see was her own pale reflection ghosted on the glass. "My mother told me she'd

had an affair before my father took me to Europe."
When he didn't respond, she turned to study his face.
"You knew."

"Not at the time." The hurt and bewilderment on her
face had him crossing to her to brush at her hair. "Not
long after you were gone, it came out." He shrugged.
"Small towns."

"My father knew," Vanessa said carefully. "My
mother said as much. That must have been why he took
me away the way he did. And why she didn't come
with us."

"I can't comment on what went on between your
parents, Van. If there are things you need to know, you
should hear them from Loretta."

"I don't know what to say to her. I don't know what
to ask." She turned away again. "In all those years, my
father never said a thing about it."

That didn't surprise him, but he doubted Julius's mo-
tives had been altruistic. "What else did she tell you?"

"What else is there to tell?" Vanessa countered.

Brady was silent for a moment. "Did you ask her
why?"

"I didn't have to." She rubbed a chill from her arms.
"She told me she didn't even love the man. It was just
physical. Just sex."

He contemplated his beer. "Well, I guess we should
drag her out in the street and shoot her."

"It's not a joke," Vanessa said, whirling around. "She
deceived her husband. She cheated on him while they
were living together, while she was pretending to be
part of a family."

"That's all true. Considering the kind of woman Loretta is, it seems to me she must have had some very

strong reasons." His eyes stayed on hers, calm and searching. "I'm surprised it didn't occur to you."

"How can you justify adultery?"

"I'm not. But there are very few situations that are simple black and white. I think once you get over the shock and the anger, you'll ask her about those gray areas."

"How would you feel if it was one of your parents?"

"Lousy." He set the beer aside. "Want a hug?"

She felt the tears rise to burn the backs of her eyes. "Yes," she managed, and went gratefully into his arms.

He held her, his arms gentle, his hands easy as they stroked along her back. She needed him now, he thought. And the need was for friendship. However tangled his emotions were, he could never refuse her that. He brushed his lips over her hair, enchanted by the texture, the scent, the warm, deep color. Her arms were tight around him. Her head was nestled just beneath his.

She still fitted, he thought. She was still a perfect fit.

He seemed so solid. She wondered how such a reckless boy could have become such a solid, dependable man. He was giving her, without her even having asked, exactly what she needed. Nothing more, nothing less.

Her eyes closed, she thought how easy, how terrifyingly easy, it would be to fall in love with him all over again.

"Feeling any better?"

She didn't know about better, but she was definitely feeling. The hypnotic stroke of his hands up and down her spine, the steady rhythm of his heart against hers.

She lifted her head, just enough to see his eyes. There was understanding in them, and a strength that had developed during the time she had been without him.

"I can't make up my mind whether you've changed or whether you're the same."

"Some of both." Her scent was waltzing through his system. "I'm glad you came back."

"I didn't mean to." She sighed again. "I wasn't going to get near you again. When I was here before, I was angry because you made me remember—and what I remembered was that I'd never really forgotten."

If she looked at him that way five more seconds, he knew, he'd forget she'd come looking for a friend. "Van…you should probably try to straighten this out with your mother. Why don't I drive you home?"

"I don't want to go home tonight." Her words echoed in her head. She had to press her lips tightly together before she could form the next words. "Let me stay here with you."

The somewhat pleasant ache that had coursed through him as he'd held her turned sharp and deadly. With his movements slow and deliberate, he put his hands on her shoulders and stepped back.

"That's not a good idea." When her mouth turned into a pout, he nearly groaned.

"A few hours ago, you seemed to think it was a very good idea." She shrugged his hands off her shoulders before she turned. "Apparently you're still a lot of talk and no action."

He spun her around quickly, threats hovering on his tongue. As she watched, the livid fury in his eyes died to a smolder. "You still know what buttons to push."

She tilted her head. "And you don't."

He slipped a hand around her throat. "You're such a brat." When she tossed back her head, he was tempted to give her throat just one quick squeeze. He reminded himself that he was a doctor. "It would serve you right if I dragged you upstairs and made love to you until you were deaf, dumb and blind."

She felt a thrill of excitement mixed with alarm. What would it be like? Hadn't she wondered since the first moment she'd seen him again? Maybe it was time to be reckless.

"I'd like to see you try."

Desire seared through him as he looked at her, her head thrown back, her eyes hooded, her mouth soft and sulky. He knew what it would be like. Damn her. He'd spent hours trying not to imagine what now came all too clearly to his mind. In defense he took a step backward.

"Don't push it, Van."

"If you don't want me, why—?"

"You know I do," he shouted at her as he spun away. "Damn it, you know I always have. You make me feel like I'm eighteen and itchy again." When she took a step forward, he threw up a hand. "Just stay away from me." He snatched up his beer and took a long, greedy swallow. "You can take the bed," he said more calmly. "I've got a sleeping bag I can use down here."

"Why?"

"The timing stinks." He drained the beer and tossed the empty bottle into a five-gallon drum. It shattered. "By God, if we're going to have another shot at this, we're going to do it right. Tonight you're upset and confused and unhappy. You're angry with your mother, and you're not going to hate me for taking advantage of all of that."

She looked down at her hands and spread them. He was right. That was the hell of it. "The timing's never been right for us, has it?"

"It will be." He put a hand on either side of her face. "You can count on it. You'd better go up." He dropped his hands again. "Being noble makes me cranky."

With a nod, she started toward the stairs. At the base, she stopped and turned. "Brady, I'm really sorry you're such a nice guy."

He rubbed at the tension at the back of his neck. "Me, too."

She smiled a little. "No, not because of tonight. You're right about tonight. I'm sorry because it reminds me how crazy I was about you. And why."

Pressing a hand to the ache in his gut, he watched her go upstairs. "Thanks a lot," he said to himself. "That's just what I needed to hear to make sure I don't sleep at all tonight."

Vanessa lay in Brady's bed, tangled in Brady's sheets. The dog had deserted him to sleep at her feet. She could hear the soft canine snoring as she stared into the deep, deep country dark.

Would she—could she—have gone through with her invitation to come to this bed with him? A part of her yearned to. A part of her that had waited all these years to feel as only he could make her feel.

Yet, when she had offered herself to him, she had done so recklessly, heedlessly, and in direct opposition to her own instinct for survival.

She had walked away from him just this evening, angry, even insulted, at his cocky insistence that they would become lovers. What kind of sense did it make for her to have come back to him in emotional turmoil and rashly ask to do just that?

It made no sense at all.

He had always confused her, she thought as she turned restlessly in his bed. He had always been able to make her ignore her own common sense. Now that she was sleeping—or trying to—alone, her frustration was tempered by gratitude that he understood her better than she understood herself.

In all the years she had been away, in all the cities where she had traveled, not one of the men who had escorted her had tempted her to open the locks she had so firmly bolted on her emotions.

Only Brady. And what, for God's sake, was she going to do about it?

She was sure—nearly sure—that if things stayed as they were she would be able to leave painlessly when the time came. If she could think of him as a friend, a sometimes maddening friend, she could fly off to pick up her career when she was ready. But if he became her lover, her first and only lover, the memory might haunt her like a restless ghost throughout her life.

And there was more, she admitted with a sigh. She didn't want to hurt him. No matter how angry he could make her, no matter how deeply he had, and could, hurt her, she didn't want to cause him any real pain.

She knew what it was like to live with that kind of pain, the kind that spread and throbbed, the kind that came when you knew someone didn't care enough. Someone didn't want you enough.

She wouldn't do to Brady what had been done to her.

If he had been kind enough to allow her to hide in his home for a few hours, she would be kind enough to repay the favor by making sure they kept a reasonable distance between them.

No, she thought grimly, she would not be his lover.

Or any man's. She had her mother's example before her. When her mother had taken a lover, it had ruined three lives. Vanessa knew her father had never been happy. Driven, yes. Obsessed with his daughter's career. And bitter, Vanessa thought now. Oh, so bitter. He had never forgiven his wife for her betrayal. Why else had he blocked the letters she had sent to her daughter? Why else had he never, never spoken her name?

As the gnawing in her stomach grew sharper, she curled up tight. Somehow she would try to accept what her mother had done, and what she hadn't done.

Closing her eyes, she listened to the call of an owl in the woods, and the distant rumble of thunder on the mountain.

She awoke at first light to the patter of rain on the roof. It sent music playing in her head as she shifted. Though she felt heavy with fatigue, she sat up, hugging her knees as she blinked at the gloom.

The dog was gone, but the sheets at her feet were still warm from him. It was time for her to go, as well.

The big tiled tub was tempting, but she reminded herself to be practical and turned instead to the glassed-in corner shower. In ten minutes she was walking quietly downstairs.

Brady was flat on his stomach in his twisted sleeping bag, his face buried in a ridiculously small pillow. With his dog sitting patiently beside him, he made a picture that turned her heart upside down.

Kong grinned and thumped his tail as she came to the bottom of the steps. She put a warning finger to her lips. Kong obviously wasn't up on sign language, as he let out two sharp, happy barks, then turned to lick Brady's face wherever he could reach.

Swearing, Brady shoved the dog's face away from his. "Let yourself out, damn it. Don't you know a dead man when you see one?"

Undaunted, Kong sat on him.

"Here, boy." Vanessa walked to the door and opened it. Delighted to have his needs understood, Kong bounded outside into the pattering rain. When she looked back, Brady was sitting up, the sleeping bag pooled around his waist. Bleary-eyed, he scowled at her.

"How come you look so damn good?"

The same could be said about him, she thought. As he'd claimed, he'd filled out a bit. His naked chest looked rock-firm, his shoulders leanly muscled. Because her nerves were beginning to jump, she concentrated on his face.

Why was it he looked all the more attractive with a night's stubble and a surly set to his mouth?

"I used your shower. I hope you don't mind." When he just grunted, she worked up a smile. If she felt this awkward now, she wondered, how would she have felt if he'd joined her in the bed? "I appreciate the night's sanctuary, Brady. Really. Why don't I pay you back by making some coffee?"

"How fast can you make it?"

"Faster than room service." She slipped past him to the adjoining kitchen. "I learned to keep a travel pot with me in hotels." She found a glass pot and a plastic cone filter. "But I think this is a little out of my league."

"Put some water in the kettle. I'll walk you through it."

Grateful for the occupation, she turned on the tap.

"I'm sorry about all this," she said. "I know I dumped on you last night, and you were very…" She turned, and her words trailed off. He was standing now, tugging jeans over his hips. Her mouth went bone-dry.

"Stupid," he finished for her. Metal rasped on metal as he pulled up the zipper. "Insane."

"Understanding," she managed. He started toward her. Her feet knocked up against the unfinished counter as she took a hasty step in retreat.

"Don't mention it," he said. "And I do mean don't mention it. I've had an entire sleepless night to regret it."

She lifted a hand to his cheek, then hastily dropped it when she saw his eyes darken. "You should have told me to go home. It was childish of me not to. I'm sure my mother was worried."

"I called her after you went up."

She looked down at the floor. "You're much kinder than I am."

He didn't want her gratitude, he thought. Or her embarrassment. Annoyed, he passed her a paper filter. "You put this in the cone and put the cone on the glass pot. Six scoops of coffee in the filter, then pour the hot water through. Got it?"

"Yes." There was no need for him to be so snotty when she was trying to thank him.

"Terrific. I'll be back in a minute."

She set her hands on her hips as he padded upstairs. An exasperating man, she thought. Sweet and compassionate one minute, surly and rude the next. With a half laugh, she turned back to scowl at the teakettle. And wasn't that just the combination that had always fascinated her? At least she was no longer a naive girl certain he would turn into a prince.

Determined to finish what she had started, she measured out the coffee. She loved the rich morning aroma of it, and wished she hadn't had to stop drinking it. Caffeine, she thought with a wistful sigh. It no longer seemed to agree with her.

She was pouring the boiling water over the coffee when Brady came back. His hair was damp, she noted. And there was the lingering scent of soap around him. Because her mind was set to be friendly, she smiled at him.

"That had to be the quickest shower on record."

"I learned to be quick when I was an intern." He took a long, deep sniff of the coffee. It was his bad luck that he could also smell his shampoo on her hair. "I'm going to feed Kong," he said abruptly, and left her alone again.

When he returned, she was smiling at the coffee, which had nearly dripped through. "I remember one of these in your kitchen on Main Street."

"My mother always made drip coffee. The best."

"Brady, I haven't told you how sorry I am. I know how close you were."

"She never gave up on me. Probably should have more than once, but she never did." His eyes met Vanessa's. "I guess mothers don't."

Uncomfortable, Vanessa turned away. "I think it's ready." When he reached for two mugs, she shook her head. "No, I don't want any, thanks. I've given it up."

"As a doctor, I can tell you that's commendable." He poured a full mug. "As a human being, I have to ask how you function."

She smiled. "You just start a little slower, that's all. I have to go."

He simply put a hand on the counter and blocked her

way. There was rain on his hair now, and his eyes were very clear. "You didn't sleep well."

"I'd say that makes two of us."

He took a casual sip of his coffee as he completed a thorough study of her face. The fatigue he saw was due to more than one restless night. "I want you to do something for me."

"If I can."

"Go home, pull the covers over your head, and tune out until noon."

Her lips curved. "I might just do that."

"If those shadows under your eyes aren't gone in forty-eight hours, I'm going to sic my father on you."

"Big talk."

"Yeah." He set the mug aside and then, leaning his other hand on the counter, effectively caged her. "I seem to remember a comment last night about no action."

Since she couldn't back up, she held her ground. "I was trying to make you mad."

"You did." He leaned closer until their thighs met.

"Brady, I don't have the time or patience for this. I have to go."

"Okay. Kiss me goodbye."

Her chin tilted. "I don't want to."

"Sure you do." His mouth whispered over hers before she could jerk her head back. "You're just afraid to."

"I've never been afraid of you."

"No." He smiled an infuriating smile. "But you've learned to be afraid of yourself."

"That's ridiculous."

"Prove it."

Seething, she leaned forward, intent on giving him a brief, soulless kiss. But her heart was in her throat almost instantly. He used no pressure, only soft, soft persuasion. His lips were warm and mobile against hers, his tongue cleverly tracing the shape of her mouth before dipping inside to tease and tempt.

On a breathless murmur, she took her hands up and over his naked chest to his shoulders. His skin was damp and cool.

He nipped gently at her lips, drowning in the taste of her. Using all his control, he kept his tensed hands on the counter. He knew that if he touched her now, even once, he wouldn't stop.

She would come to him. He had promised himself that as he'd sweated through the night. She would come to him, and not because of a memory, not because of grief. Because of need.

Slowly, while he still had some control, he lifted his head and backed away. "I want to see you tonight, Van."

"I don't know." She put a hand to her spinning head.

"Then you think about it." He picked up his mug again, surprised the handle didn't shatter in his grip. "You can call me when you make up your mind."

Her confusion died away, to be replaced by anger. "I'm not playing games."

"Then what the hell are you doing?"

"I'm just trying to survive." She snatched up her purse and ran out into the rain.

Chapter 5

Bed sounded like a wonderful idea, Vanessa decided as she pulled up in front of the house. Maybe if she drew down the shades, put the music on low and willed herself to relax, she would find the sleep she had lost the night before. When she felt more rested, she might have a clearer idea of what to say to her mother.

She wondered if a few hours' sleep would help her resolve her feelings about Brady.

It was worth a shot.

She stepped out of the car and rounded the hood to the sidewalk. When she heard her name called, she turned. Mrs. Driscoll was lumbering toward her, clutching her purse and a stack of mail. A huge, wood-handled black umbrella was tight in her fist. Vanessa's smile came naturally as she moved forward to greet her.

"Mrs. Driscoll. It's good to see you again."

Only a little winded, Mrs. Driscoll peered out of sharp little eyes. "Heard you were back. Too skinny."

With a laugh, Vanessa bent to kiss her leathery cheek. As always, her former teacher smelled of lavender sachet. "You look wonderful."

"Take care of yourself." She sniffed. "That snippy Brady tells me I need a cane. He thinks he's a doctor. Hold on to this." Bossy by nature, she shoved the umbrella into Vanessa's hand. She opened her purse to stuff her mail inside, stubbornly keeping her balance. The rain made her bones ache all the more, but she had always loved to walk in it. "It's about time you came home. You staying?"

"Well, I haven't—"

"About time you gave your mother some attention," she interrupted, leaving Vanessa with nothing to say. "I heard you playing when I walked to the bank yesterday, but I couldn't stop."

Vanessa struggled with the heavy umbrella, and with her manners. "Would you like to come in, have some tea?"

"Too much to do. You still play real nice, Vanessa."

"Thank you."

When Mrs. Driscoll took the umbrella back, Vanessa thought the little visit was over. She should have known better. "I've got a grandniece. She's been taking piano lessons in Hagerstown. Puts a strain on her ma, having to haul her all that way. Figured now that you're back, you could take over."

"Oh, but I—"

"She's been taking them nigh on a year, an hour once a week. She played 'Jingle Bells' real well at Christmas. Did a fair turn on 'Go Tell Aunt Rhody,' too."

"That's very nice," Vanessa managed, beginning to feel desperate, as well as wet. "But since she's already got a teacher, I wouldn't want to interfere."

"Lives right across from Lester's. Could walk to your place. Give her ma a breather. Lucy—that's my niece, my younger brother's second girl—she's expecting another next month. Hoping for a boy this time, since they've got the two girls. Girls just seem to run in the family."

"Ah..."

"It's hard on her driving clear up to Hagerstown."

"I'm sure it is, but—"

"You have a free hour once a week, don't you?"

Exasperated, Vanessa dragged a hand through her rapidly dampening hair. "I suppose I do, but—"

Violet Driscoll knew when to spring. "How about today? The school bus drops her off just after three-thirty. She can be here at four."

She had to be firm, Vanessa told herself. "Mrs. Driscoll, I'd love to help you out, but I've never given instruction."

Mrs. Driscoll merely blinked her little black eyes. "You know how to play the thing, don't you?"

"Well, yes, but—"

"Then you ought to be able to show somebody else how. Unless they're like Dory—that's my oldest girl. Never could teach her how to crochet. Clumsy hands. Annie's got good hands. That's my grandniece. Smart, too. You won't have any trouble with her."

"I'm sure I won't—I mean, I'm sure she is. It's just that—"

"Give you ten dollars a lesson." A smug smile creased Mrs. Driscoll's face as Vanessa rattled her brain for excuses. "You were always quick in school, Vanessa. Quick and well behaved. Never gave me any grief like Brady. That boy was trouble from the get-go. Couldn't help but like him for it. I'll see that Annie's here at four."

She trundled off, sheltered under the enormous umbrella, leaving Vanessa with the sensation of having been flattened by an antique but very sturdy steamroller.

Piano lessons, she thought on a little groan. How had it happened? She watched the umbrella disappear around the corner. It had happened the same way she had "volunteered" to clean the blackboard after school.

Dragging a hand through her hair, she walked to the house. It was empty and quiet, but she'd already given up on the idea of going back to bed. If she was going to be stuck running scales with a fledgling virtuoso, then she'd better prepare for it. At least it would keep her mind occupied.

In the music room, she went to the gracefully curved new cabinet. She could only hope that her mother had saved some of her old lesson books. The first drawer contained sheet music she considered too advanced for a first-year student. But her own fingers itched to play as she skimmed the sheets.

She found what she was looking for in the bottom drawer. There they were, a bit dog-eared, but neatly stacked. All of her lesson books, from primer to level six. Struck by nostalgia, she sat cross-legged on the floor and began to pore through them.

How well she remembered those first heady days of lessons. Finger exercises, scales, drills, those first simple melodies. She felt an echo of that rush of emotion that had come when she had learned that she had the power to turn those printed notes into music.

More than twenty years had passed since that first day, that first lesson. Her father had been her teacher then, and though he had been a hard taskmaster, she had been a willing student. How proud she had been the first time he had told her she'd done well. Those small and rare words of praise had driven her to work all the harder.

With a sigh, she dipped into the drawer for more books. If young Annie had been taking lessons for a year, she should have advanced beyond the primary level. It was then that she found the thick scrapbook, the one she knew her mother had started years before. With a smile, she opened the first page.

There were pictures of her at the piano. It made her laugh to see herself in pigtails and neat white ankle socks. Sentimentally she paged through photos of her first recital, her early certificates of accomplishment. And here were the awards that had once hung on her walls, the newspaper clippings from when she had won her first regional competition, her first national.

How terrified she'd been. Sweaty hands, buzzing ears, curdling stomach. She'd begged her father to let her withdraw. He'd refused to listen to her fears. And she'd won, Vanessa mused.

It surprised her that the clippings continued. Here was an article from the London *Times,* written a full year after she had left Hyattown. And here a picture of her in Fort Worth after she'd won the Van Cliburn.

There were dozens—no, hundreds—Vanessa realized. Hundreds of pictures, snippets of news, pieces of gossip, magazine articles—many she had never seen herself. It seemed that everything that had ever been printed about her was here, carefully preserved. Everything, Vanessa thought, down to the last interview she had granted before her concerts in D.C.

First the letters, she thought, the book weighing heavily on her thighs, and now this. What was she supposed to think? What was she supposed to feel? The mother she had believed had forgotten her had written her religiously, even when there had been no answer. Had followed every step of her career, though she'd been allowed no part in it.

And, Vanessa added with a sigh, had opened the door to her daughter again without question.

But it didn't explain why Loretta had let her go without a murmur. It didn't explain the years away.

I had no choice.

She remembered her mother's words. But what had she meant? An affair would have destroyed her marriage. There was no doubt of that. Vanessa's father would never have forgiven her. But why had it severed her relationship with her daughter?

She had to know. She would know. Vanessa rose and left the books scattered on the rug. She would know today.

The rain had stopped, and the watery sunlight was already struggling through the clouds. Birdsong competed with the sound of a children's television show that chirped through the window of the house next door. Though it was only a few blocks away, she drove to the antique shop. Under other circumstances she would have enjoyed the walk, but she wanted no interruptions from old friends and acquaintances. The old two-story house was just on the edge of town. The sign that read Loretta's Attic was a graceful arch over the front door.

There was an old-fashioned sleigh in the yard, its metal fittings polished to a gleam. A scarred whiskey barrel was filled to overflowing with petunias, their purple-and-white petals drenched with rain. On either side of the entrance, well-groomed beds spilled over with spring color. A beribboned grapevine wreath hung on the door. When she pushed it open, bells jingled.

"It's circa 1860," she heard her mother say. "One of my finest sets. I had it refinished locally by a man who does a great deal of work for me. You can see what a wonderful job he does. The finish is like glass."

Vanessa half listened to the exchange coming from the next room. Though she was frustrated to find her mother with a customer, the shop itself was a revelation.

No dusty, cramped antique shop this. Exquisite glass-fronted cabinets displayed china, statuettes, ornate perfume bottles and slender goblets. Wood gleamed on each individual piece. Brass shone. Crystal sparkled. Though every inch of space was utilized, it was more like a cozy family home than a place of business. The scent of rose-and-spice potpourri wafted from a simmer pot.

"You're going to be very happy with that set," Loretta was saying as she walked back into the main room. "If you find it doesn't suit after you get it home, I'll be more than willing to buy it back from you. Oh, Vanessa." After fumbling a moment, she turned to the young executive type beside her. "This is my daughter. Vanessa, this is Mr. Peterson. He's from Montgomery County."

"Damascus," he explained. He looked like a cat who'd been given a whole pitcher of cream. "My wife and I just bought an old farmhouse. We saw that dining room set here a few weeks ago. My wife hasn't been able to talk about anything else. Thought I'd surprise her."

"I'm sure she'll be thrilled."

Vanessa watched as her mother accepted his credit card and went briskly about completing the transaction.

"You've got a terrific place here, Mrs. Sexton," he went on. "If you came over the county line, you'd have to beat off customers."

"I like it here." She handed him his receipt. "I've lived here all my life."

"Cute town." He pocketed the receipt. "After our first dinner party, I can guarantee you some new customers."

"And I can guarantee I won't beat them off." She smiled at him. "Will you need some help Saturday when you pick it up?"

"No, I'll drag a few friends with me." He shook her hand. "Thanks, Mrs. Sexton."

"Just enjoy it."

"We will." He turned to smile at Vanessa. "Nice meeting you. You've got a terrific mother."

"Thank you."

"Well, I'll be on my way." He stopped halfway to the door. "Vanessa Sexton." He turned back. "The pianist. I'll be damned. I just saw your concert in D.C. last week. You were great."

"I'm glad you enjoyed it."

"I didn't expect to," he admitted. "My wife's the classical nut. I figured I'd catch a nap, but, man, you just blew me away."

She had to laugh. "I'll take that as a compliment."

"No, really. I don't know Mozart from Muzak, but I was—well, I guess enthralled's a good word. My wife'll just about die when I tell her I met you." He pulled out a leather-bound appointment book. "Would you sign this for her? Her name's Melissa."

"I'd be glad to."

"Who'd have expected to find someone like you in a little place like this?" He shook his head as she handed the book back to him.

"I grew up here."

"I can guarantee my wife'll be back." He winked at Loretta. "Thanks again, Mrs. Sexton."

"You're welcome. Drive carefully." She laughed a little after the bells had jingled at his exit. "It's an amazing thing, watching your own child sign an autograph."

"It's the first one I've signed in my hometown." She took a deep breath. "This is a beautiful place. You must work very hard."

"I enjoy it. I'm sorry I wasn't there this morning. I had an early delivery coming."

"It's all right."

Loretta picked up a soft rag, then set it down again. "Would you like to see the rest of the shop?"

"Yes. Yes, I would."

Loretta led the way into the adjoining room. "This is the set your admirer just bought." She ran a fingertip over the top of a gleaming mahogany table. "It has three leaves and will sit twelve comfortably when extended. There's some beautiful carving on the chairs. The buffet and server go with it."

"They're beautiful."

"I bought them at an estate sale a few months ago. They'd been in the same family for over a hundred years. It's sad." She touched one of the glass knobs on the server. "That's why I'm so happy when I can sell something like this to people who will care for it."

She moved to a curved glass china cabinet and opened the door. "I found this cobalt glass at a flea market, buried in a box. Now, the cranberry I got at auction, and paid too much. I couldn't resist it. These saltcellars are French, and I'll have to wait for a collector to take them off my hands."

"How do you know about all of this?" Vanessa asked.

"I learned a lot by working here before I bought it. From reading, from haunting other shops and auctions." She laughed a little as she closed the cabinet door. "And through trial and error. I've made some costly mistakes, but I've also wangled some real bargains."

"You have so many beautiful things. Oh, look at this." Almost reverently, she picked up a Limoges ring box. It was perhaps six inches high and fashioned in the shape of a young girl in a blue bonnet and blue checkered dress. There was a look of smug pleasure on her glossy face. "This is charming."

"I always try to keep in a few Limoges pieces. Whether they're antique or new."

"I have a small collection myself. It's difficult to travel with fragile things, but they always make hotel suites more like home."

"I'd like you to have it."

"I couldn't."

"Please," Loretta said before Vanessa could set it down again. "I've missed a number of birthdays. It would give me a great deal of pleasure if you'd accept it."

Vanessa looked up. They had to turn at least the first corner, she told herself. "Thank you. I'll treasure it."

"I'll get a box for it. Oh, there's the door. I get a lot of browsers on weekday mornings. You can take a look upstairs if you like."

Vanessa kept the little box cupped in her hands. "No, I'll wait for you." Loretta gave her a pleased look before she walked away to greet her customer. When she heard Dr. Tucker's voice join her mother's, Vanessa hesitated, then went in to meet him.

"Well, Van, getting a look at your mother at work?"

"Yes."

He had his arm around her mother's shoulders. Loretta's color had risen. He's just kissed her, Vanessa realized, trying to analyze her feelings. "It's a wonderful place."

"Keeps her off the streets. Of course, I'm going to be doing that myself from now on."

"Ham!"

"Don't tell me you haven't told the child yet." He gave her a quick, impatient squeeze. "Good grief, Loretta, you've had all morning."

"Tell me what?"

With these two, Ham thought, a man had to take the bull by the horns. "It's taken me two years to wear her down, but she finally gave me a yes."

"A yes?" Vanessa repeated.

"Don't tell me you're as thickheaded as your mother?" He kissed the top of Loretta's head and grinned like a boy. "We're getting married."

"Oh." Vanessa stared blankly. "Oh."

"Is that the best you can do?" he demanded. "Why don't you say congratulations and give me a kiss?"

"Congratulations," she said mechanically, and walked over to peck his cheek.

"I said a kiss." He swung his free arm around her and squeezed. Vanessa found herself hugging him back.

"I hope you'll be happy," she managed, and discovered she meant it.

"Of course I will. I'm getting two beauties for the price of one."

"Quite a bargain," Vanessa said with a smile. "When's the big day?"

"As soon as I can pin her down." It hadn't escaped him that Vanessa and Loretta hadn't exchanged a word or an embrace. "Joanie's fixing dinner for all of us tonight," he decided on the spot. "To celebrate."

"I'll be there."

When she stepped back, he grinned wickedly. "After the piano lesson."

Vanessa rolled her eyes. "News travels fast."

"Piano lesson?" Loretta repeated.

"Annie Crampton, Violet Driscoll's grandniece." He gave a hearty laugh as Vanessa wrinkled her nose. "Violet snagged Vanessa this morning."

Loretta smiled. "What time's the lesson?"

"Four. She made me feel like I was the second-grade milk monitor again."

"I can speak to Annie's mother if you'd like," Loretta said.

"No, it's all right. It's only an hour a week while I'm here. But I'd better get back." This was not the time for questions and demands. "I have to put some kind of program together. Thank you again for the box."

"But I haven't wrapped it."

"It's all right. I'll see you at Joanie's, Dr. Tucker."

"Maybe you could call me Ham now. We're family."

"Yes. Yes, I guess we are." It was less effort than

she had expected to kiss her mother's cheek. "You're a very lucky woman."

"I know." Loretta's fingers dug into Ham's.

When the bells jingled behind Vanessa, Ham took out a handkerchief.

"I'm sorry," Loretta said as she sniffled into it.

"You're entitled to shed a few. I told you she'd come around."

"She has every reason to hate me."

"You're too hard on yourself, Loretta, and I won't have it."

She merely shook her head as she balled the handkerchief in her hand. "Oh, the choices we make in this life, Ham. And the mistakes. I'd give anything in the world to have another chance with her."

"Time's all you need to give." He tilted her chin up and kissed her. "Just give her time."

Vanessa listened to the monotonous plunk of the keys as Annie ground out "Twinkle, Twinkle, Little Star." She might have good hands, but so far Vanessa hadn't seen her put them to good use.

She was a skinny girl with pale flyaway hair, a sulky disposition and knobby knees. But her twelve-year old hands were wide-palmed. Her fingers weren't elegant, but they were as sturdy as little trees.

Potential, Vanessa thought as she tried to smile her encouragement. Surely there was some potential buried there somewhere.

"How many hours a week do you practice, Annie?" Vanessa asked when the child had mercifully finished.

"I don't know."

"Do you do your finger exercises every day?"

"I don't know."

Vanessa gritted her teeth. She had already learned this was Annie's standard answer for all questions. "You've been taking lessons regularly for nearly a year."

"I don't—"

Vanessa put up a hand. "Why don't we make this easy? What do you know?"

Annie just shrugged and swung her feet.

Giving up, Vanessa sat beside her on the stool. "Annie—and give me a real answer—do you want to take piano lessons?"

Annie knocked the heels of her orange sneakers together. "I guess."

"Is it because your mother wants you to?"

"I asked if I could." She stared sulkily down at the keys. "I thought I would like it."

"But you don't."

"I kinda do. Sometimes. But I just get to play baby songs."

"Mmm." Sympathetic, Vanessa stroked her hair. "And what do you want to play?"

"Stuff like Madonna sings. You know, good stuff. Stuff like you hear on the radio." She slanted Vanessa a look. "My other teacher said that's not real music."

"All music is real music. We could make a deal."

Suspicion lighted in Annie's pale eyes. "What kind of deal?"

"You practice an hour every day on your finger exercises and the lesson I give you." She ignored Annie's moan. "And I'll buy some sheet music. One of Madonna's songs. I'll teach you to play it."

Annie's sulky mouth fell open. "For real?"

"For real. But only if you practice every day, so that when you come next week I see an improvement."

"All right!" For the first time in nearly an hour, she grinned, nearly blinding Vanessa with her braces. "Wait till I tell Mary Ellen. She's my best friend."

"You've got another fifteen minutes before you can tell her." Vanessa rose, inordinately pleased with herself. "Now, why don't you try that number again?"

Her face screwed up with concentration, Annie began to play. A little incentive, Vanessa thought with a lifted brow, went a long way.

An hour later, she was still congratulating herself. Tutoring the girl might be fun, after all. And she could indulge her own affection for popular music.

Later in her room, Vanessa ran a finger down the Limoges box her mother had given her. Things were changing for her, faster than she had expected. Her mother wasn't the woman she had thought she would find. She was much more human. Her home was still her home. Her friends still her friends.

And Brady was still Brady.

She wanted to be with him, to have her name linked with his as it once had been. At sixteen she had been so sure. Now, as a woman she was afraid, afraid of making a mistake, of being hurt, of losing.

People couldn't just pick up where they had left off. And she could hardly start a new beginning when she had yet to resolve the past.

She took her time dressing for the family dinner. It was to be a festive occasion, and she was determined to be a part of it. Her deep blue dress was cut slimly, with a splash of multicolored beadwork along one shoulder.

She left her hair loose, and added braided earrings studded with sapphires.

Before she closed her jewelry box, she took out a ring with a tiny emerald. Unable to resist, she slipped it on. It still fit, she thought, and smiled at the way it looked on her finger. With a shake of her head, she pulled it off again. That was just the sort of sentiment she had to learn to avoid. Particularly if she was going to get through an evening in Brady's company.

They were going to be friends, she reminded herself. Just friends. It had been a long time since she had been able to indulge in the luxury of a friendship. And if she was still attracted to him—well, that would just add a touch of spice, a little excitement. She wouldn't risk her heart, or his, on anything more.

She pressed a hand to her stomach, swearing at the discomfort. Out of her drawer she took an extra roll of antacids. Festive the evening might be, she thought as she took a pill. But it would still be stressful.

It was time she learned to deal with stress better, she told herself as she stared at her reflection. It was time she refused to allow her body to revolt every time she had to deal with something uncomfortable or unpleasant. She was a grown woman, after all, and a disciplined one. If she could learn to tolerate emotional distress, she could certainly overcome the physical.

After checking her watch, she started downstairs. Vanessa Sexton was never late for a performance.

"Well, well." Brady was lounging at the base of the steps. "You're still Sexy Sexton."

Just what she needed, she thought, her stomach muscles knotting. Did he have to look so gorgeous? She glanced at the front door that he'd left open behind him, then back at him.

"You're wearing a suit."

He glanced down at the gray tweed. "Looks like."

"I've never seen you in a suit," she said foolishly. She stopped a step above him. Eye-to-eye. "Why aren't you at Joanie's?"

"Because I'm taking you to Joanie's."

"That's silly. I have my own—"

"Shut up." Taking her shoulders, he hauled her against him for a kiss. "Every time I do that, you taste better."

She had to wait for her heart to flutter back into place. "Look, Brady, we're going to have to set up some ground rules."

"I hate rules." He kissed her again, lingering over it this time. "I'm going to get a real kick out of being related to you." He drew back, grinning. "Sis."

"You're not acting very brotherly," she murmured.

"I'll boss you around later. How do you feel about it?"

"I've always loved your father."

"And?"

"And I hope I'm not hard-hearted enough to begrudge my mother any happiness she might have with him."

"That'll do for now." He narrowed his eyes as she rubbed her temple. "Headache?"

She dropped her hand quickly. "Just a little one."

"Take anything?"

"No, it'll pass. Shouldn't we go?"

"All right." He took her hand to lead her out. "I was

thinking...why don't we drop by Molly's Hole on the way home?"

She couldn't help but laugh. "You still have a one-track mind."

He opened the car door for her. "Is that a yes?"

She tilted her head, slanted him a look. "That's an I'll-think-about-it."

"Brat," he muttered as he closed the door.

Ten minutes later, Joanie was bursting through her front door to greet them. "Isn't it great? I can hardly stand it!" She grabbed Vanessa to swing her around. "We're really going to be sisters now. I'm so happy for them, for us!" She gave Vanessa another crushing hug.

"Hey, how about me?" Brady demanded. "Don't I even get a hello?"

"Oh, hi, Brady." At his disgusted look, she laughed and launched herself at him. "Wow! You wore a suit and everything!"

"So I'm told. Dad said we had to dress up."

"And did you ever." She pulled back. "Both of you. Lord, Van, where did you get that dress? Fabulous," she said, before Vanessa could answer. "I'd kill to be able to squeeze my hips into that. Well, don't just stand out here, come on in. We've got a ton of food, champagne, the works."

"Hell of a hostess, isn't she?" Brady commented as Joanie rushed inside, shouting for her husband.

Joanie hadn't exaggerated about the food. There was a huge glazed ham, with a mountain of whipped potatoes, an array of vegetables, fluffy homemade biscuits. The scent of cooling apple pies wafted in from the kitchen. The home's festive air was accented by candles and the glint of crystal wineglasses.

The conversation was loud and disjointed, punctuated by Lara's cheerful banging of her spoon against the tray of her high chair.

Vanessa heard her mother laughing, more freely, more openly, than she could ever remember. And she looked lovely, Vanessa thought, smiling at Ham, leaning over to stroke Lara. It was happiness, she realized. True happiness. In all her memories, she could pull out no picture of her mother's face when it had been truly happy.

As the meal wore on, she nibbled lightly, certain that no one would notice her lack of appetite in the confusion. But when she saw Brady watching her, she forced herself to take another bite, to sip at the iced champagne, to laugh at one of Jack's jokes.

"I think this occasion calls for a toast." Brady rose. He shot Lara a look as she squealed. "You have to wait your turn," he told her, hefting his glass. "To my father, who turned out to be smarter than I always figured. And to his beautiful bride-to-be, who used to look the other way when I'd sneak into the backyard to neck with her daughter." Over the ensuing laughter, glasses were clinked.

Vanessa drank the bubbly wine and hoped she wouldn't pay for it later.

"Anyone for dessert?" Joanie's question was answered by communal moans. "Okay, we'll hold off on that. Jack, you help me clear the table. Absolutely not," she said when Loretta stood to stack plates. "The guest of honor does not do dishes."

"Don't be silly—"

"I mean it."

"All right, then I'll just clean Lara up."

"Fine, then you and Dad can spoil her until we're done here. Not you, either," she added when Vanessa began to clear the table. "You're not doing dishes on your first dinner in my home."

"She's always been bossy," Brady commented when his sister disappeared into the kitchen. "Would you like to go into the living room? We can put on some music."

"No, actually, I'd like some air."

"Good. There's nothing I like better than walking in the twilight with a beautiful woman." He gave her a cocky grin and held out a hand.

Chapter 6

The evening was soft and smelled of rain. There were lilacs blooming, their scent an elegant whisper on the air. She remembered they had been Joanie's favorite. To the west, the sun was sinking below the mountains in a blaze of red. Cows stood slack-hipped in the fading light. They walked around the side of the house toward a field thick with hay.

"I hear you've taken on a student."

"Mrs. Driscoll gets around."

"Actually, I heard it from John Cory while I was giving him a tetanus shot. He heard it from Bill Crampton—that's Annie's father's brother. He runs a repair shop out of his garage. All the men hang around over there to tell lies and complain about their wives."

Despite her dragging discomfort, Vanessa had to laugh. "At least it's reassuring to know the grapevine still works."

"So how'd the lesson go?"

"She has...possibilities."

"How does it feel to be on the other end?"

"Odd. I promised I'd teach her how to play rock."

"You?"

Vanessa bristled. "Music," she said primly, "is music."

"Right." He put a fingertip behind her earlobe so that he could watch the jewels she wore there catch the last light of the setting sun. And so that he could touch her. "I can see it now, Vanessa Sexton on keyboards with a heavy metal band." He considered a minute. "Do you think you could wear one of those metal corsets, or whatever they're called?"

"No, I couldn't, no matter what they're called. And if you're only along to make fun of me, I can walk by myself."

"Touchy." He draped an arm around her shoulders. He was glad the scent of his shampoo was still in her hair. He wondered if any of the men he'd seen her linked with in magazines and newspapers had felt the same way.

"I like Jack," she said.

"So do I." They walked along a fence thick with honeysuckle.

"Joanie seems so happy here, on the farm, with her family. I often wondered about her."

"Did you ever think about me? After you'd left, after you'd hit it so big, did you ever think about me?"

She looked out over the fields. "I suppose I did."

"I kept thinking you would write."

Too much, she thought. Too often. "Time passed, Brady. And at first I was too angry and hurt. At you and at my mother." Because she wanted to lighten the mood, she smiled. "It took me years to forgive you for dumping me the night of the prom."

"I didn't." He swore and stuck his hands in his pockets. "Look, it's a stupid thing and long over, but I'm tired of taking the rap."

"What are you talking about?"

"I didn't dump you, damn it. I'd rented my first tux, bought my first corsage. Pink and yellow roses." Now that he had brought it up, he felt like a total fool. "I guess I was probably as excited about that night as you were."

"Then why did I sit in my room wearing my new dress for two and a half hours?"

He blew out a long breath. "I got arrested that night."

"What?"

"It was a mistake," he said carefully. "But by the time it was straightened out, it was too late to explain. The charges were pretty thin, to say the least, but I hadn't exactly been a Boy Scout up until then."

"But what were you arrested for?"

"Statutory rape." At her astonished look, he shrugged. "I was over eighteen. You weren't."

It took almost a full minute before it could sink in, before she could find her voice. "But that's ridiculous. We never…"

"Yeah." To his undying regret. "We never."

She pulled both hands through her hair as she tried to reason it out. "Brady, it's almost too ludicrous to believe. Even if we had been intimate, it wouldn't have had anything to do with rape. You were only two years older than I was, and we loved each other."

"That was the problem."

She put a hand on her stomach, kneading a deep

ache. "I'm sorry, so sorry. How miserable you must have been. And your parents. Oh, God. What a horrible thing for anyone to go through. But who in the world would have had you arrested? Who would have—" She saw his face, and her answer. "Oh, no!" she moaned, turning away. "Oh, God!"

"He was dead sure I'd taken advantage of you. And he was dead sure I would ruin your life." And maybe, Brady thought as he stared out over the fields, he wouldn't have been far off. "The way he put it, he was going to see I paid for the first, and he was going to do what needed to be done to prevent the second."

"He could have asked me," she whispered. "For once in my life, he could have asked me." She shivered against a quick chill. "It's my fault."

"That's a stupid response."

"No," she said quietly. "It's my fault, because I could never make him understand how I felt. Not about you, not about anything." She took a long breath before she looked at Brady again. "There's nothing I can say that can make up for what he did."

"There's nothing you have to say." He put his hands on her shoulders, and would have drawn her back against him if she hadn't held herself so stiff. Instead, he massaged her knotted muscles, patiently, with his competent physician's hands. "You were as innocent as I was, Van. We never straightened it out, because for the first few days I was too mad to try and you were too mad to ask. Then you were gone."

Her vision blurred before she blinked back the tears. She could picture him all too easily—young, rebellious, angry. Afraid. "I don't know what to say. You must have been terrified."

"Some," he admitted. "I was never formally charged, just held for questioning. You remember old Sheriff Grody—he was a hard-edged, potbellied bully. And he didn't like me one little bit. Later I realized he was just taking the opportunity to make me sweat. Someone else might have handled it differently."

There was no use bringing up the way he'd sat in the cell, bone-scared, helplessly angry, waiting to be allowed his phone call, while the sheriff and Sexton consulted in the next room.

"There was something else that happened that night. Maybe it balanced the scales some. My father stood up for me. I'd never known he would stand up for me that way, no questions, no doubts, just total support. I guess it changed my life."

"My father," Vanessa said. "He knew how much that night meant to me. How much you meant to me. All my life I did what he wanted—except for you. He made sure he had his way even there."

"It's a long way behind us, Van."

"I don't think I can—" She broke off on a muffled gasp of pain.

He turned her quickly. "Vanessa?"

"It's nothing. I just—" But the second wave came too sharp, too fast, doubling her over. Moving fast, he scooped her up and headed back for the house. "No, don't. I'm all right. It was just a twinge."

"Breathe slow."

"Damn it, I said it's nothing." Her head fell back as the burning increased. "You're not going to cause a scene," she said between shallow breaths.

"If you've got what I think you've got, you're going to see one hell of a scene."

The kitchen was empty as he came in, so he took the back stairs. At least she'd stopped arguing, Brady thought as he laid her on Joanie's bed. When he switched on the lamp, he could see that her skin was white and clammy.

"I want you to try to relax, Van."

"I'm fine." But the burning hadn't stopped. "It's just stress, maybe a little indigestion."

"That's what we're going to find out." He eased down beside her. "I want you to tell me when I hurt you." Very gently, he pressed on her lower abdomen. "Have you ever had your appendix out?"

"No."

"Any abdominal surgery?"

"No, nothing."

He kept his eyes on her face as he continued the examination. When he pressed just under her breastbone, he saw the flare of pain in her eyes before she cried out. Though his face was grim, he took her hand soothingly.

"Van, how long have you been having pain?"

She was ashamed to have cried out. "Everyone has pain."

"Answer the question."

"I don't know."

He struggled for patience. "How does it feel now?"

"It's fine. I just want—"

"Don't lie to me." He wanted to curse her as pungently as he was cursing himself. He'd known she wasn't well, almost from the moment he'd seen her again. "Is there a burning sensation?"

Because she saw no choice, she relented. "Some."

It had been just about an hour since they'd eaten, he

thought. The timing was right. "Have you had this happen before, after you've had alcohol?"

"I don't really drink anymore."

"Because you get this reaction?"

She closed her eyes. Why didn't he just go and leave her alone? "I suppose."

"Do you get gnawing aches, here, under the breastbone?"

"Sometimes."

"And in your stomach?"

"It's more of a grinding, I guess."

"Like acute hunger pangs."

"Yes." The accuracy of his description made her frown. "It passes."

"What are you taking for it?"

"Just over-the-counter stuff." And enough was enough. "Brady, becoming a doctor's obviously gone to your head. You're making a case out of nothing. I'll take a couple of antacids and be fine."

"You don't treat an ulcer with antacids."

"I don't have an ulcer. That's ridiculous. I'm never sick."

"You listen to me." He propped a hand on either side of her head. "You're going into the hospital for tests—X-rays, an upper G.I. And you're going to do what I tell you."

"I'm not going to the hospital." The very idea of it made her remember the horror of her father's last days. "You're not my doctor."

He swore at her richly.

"Nice bedside manner. Now get out of my way."

"You stay right here. And I mean right here."

She obeyed, only because she didn't know if she

could manage to stand. Why now? she wondered as she fought against the pain. Why here? She'd had nasty attacks like this before, but she'd always been alone, and she'd always been able to weather them. And she would weather it this time. Just as she was struggling to sit up, Brady came back with his father.

"Now, what's all this?" Ham said.

"Brady overreacting." She managed to smile, and would have swung her legs off the bed if Brady hadn't stopped her.

"She doubled up with pain when we were outside. There's burning in the abdomen, acute tenderness under the breastbone."

Ham sat on the bed and began his own gentle probing. His questions ran along the same lines as Brady's, and his face became more and more sober at her answers. At last he sat back.

"Now what's a young girl like you doing with an ulcer?"

"I don't have an ulcer."

"You've got two doctors telling you different. I assume that's your diagnosis, Brady."

"It is."

"Well, you're both wrong." Vanessa struggled to push herself up. Ham merely shifted the pillows behind her and eased her back. With a nod, he looked back at his son.

"Of course, we'll confirm it with X-rays and tests."

"I'm not going in the hospital." She was desperately hanging on to one small bit of control. "Ulcers are for Wall Street brokers and CEOs. I'm a musician, for God's sake. I'm not a compulsive worrier, or someone who lets tension rule my life."

"I'll tell you what you are," Brady said, anger shimmering in his voice. "You're a woman who hasn't bothered to take care of herself, who's too damn stubborn to sit back and admit when she's taken on too much. And you're going to the hospital if I have to hog-tie you."

"Easy there, Dr. Tucker," Ham said mildly. "Van, have you had any vomiting, any traces of blood?"

"No, of course not. It's just a little stress, maybe a little overwork—"

"A little ulcer," he told her firmly. "But I think we can treat it with medication if you're going to hang tough about the hospital."

"I am. And I don't see that I need medication, or two doctors hovering over me."

"Testy," Ham commented. "You'll have medication or the hospital, young lady. Remember, I'm the one who treated you for damn near everything, starting with diaper rash. I think a cimetidine might clear this up," he said to Brady. "As long as she stays away from spicy food and alcohol for the length of the treatment."

"I'd like it better if she had the tests."

"So would I," he agreed. "But short of dosing her with morphine and dragging her in, I think this is the cleanest way to treat it."

"Let me think about the morphine," Brady grumbled, and made his father chuckle.

"I'm going to write you a prescription," he told Vanessa. "You get it filled tonight. You have twenty minutes before the pharmacy in Boonsboro closes."

"I'm not sick," she said, pouting.

"Just humor your soon-to-be-stepfather. I've got my bag downstairs. Brady, why don't you come along with me?"

Outside the door, Ham took his son's arm and pulled him to the head of the stairs. "If the medication doesn't clear it up within three or four days, we'll put some pressure on her to have the tests. Meanwhile, I think the less stress the better."

"I want to know what caused it." Fury vibrated through his voice as he stared at the closed bedroom door.

"So do I. She'll talk to you," Ham said quietly. "Just give her some room. I'm going to tell Loretta. Vanessa won't like that, but I'm going to do it. See that she gets the first dose in her tonight."

"I will. Dad, I'm going to take care of her."

"You always meant to." Ham put a hand on Brady's shoulder. "Just don't push too hard too fast. She's like her mother in that way, tends to pull back when you get close." He hesitated, and though he reminded himself that his son was a grown man, he could only think that the grown man was his son. "Are you still in love with her?"

"I don't know. But this time I'm not going to let her get away until I do."

"Just remember, when a man holds on to something too tight, it slips right through his fingers." He gave Brady's shoulder a final squeeze. "I'll go write that prescription."

When Brady walked back into the bedroom, Vanessa was sitting on the edge of the bed, embarrassed, humiliated, furious.

"Come on." His voice was brisk and unsympathetic. "We can just get to the pharmacy before it closes."

"I don't want your damn pills."

Because he was tempted to throttle her, he dipped

his hands into his pockets. "Do you want me to carry you out of here, or do you want to walk?"

She wanted to cry. Instead, she rose stiffly. "I'll walk, thank you."

"Fine. We'll take the back stairs."

She didn't want to be grateful that he was sparing her the explanations and sympathy. She walked with her chin up and her shoulders squared. He didn't speak until he slammed the car door.

"Somebody ought to give you a swift right hook." His engine roared into life. Gravel spit from under the tires.

"I wish you'd just leave me alone."

"So do I," he said fervently. He turned off the lane onto asphalt. By the time he'd hit fifth gear, he was calmer. "Are you still having pain?"

"No."

"Don't lie to me, Van. If you can't think of me as a friend, think of me as a doctor."

She turned to stare out the darkened window. "I've never seen your degree."

He wanted to gather her close then, rest her head on his shoulder. "I'll show it to you tomorrow." He slowed as they came to the next town. He said nothing until they pulled up at the pharmacy. "You can wait in the car. It won't take long."

She sat, watching him stride under the lights through the big glass windows of the pharmacy. They were having a special on a popular brand of soft drink. There was a tower of two-liter bottles near the window. There were a few stragglers left inside, most of whom obviously knew Brady, as they stopped to chat while he stood by the drug counter. She hated the feeling of being trapped inside the car with the pain gnawing inside her.

An ulcer, she thought. It wasn't possible. She wasn't a workaholic, a worrier, a power-mad executive. And yet, even as she denied it, the grinding ache dragged through her, mocking her.

She just wanted to go home to lie down, to will the pain away into sleep. Oblivion. It would all be gone tomorrow. Hadn't she been telling herself that for months and months?

When he came back, he set the small white bag in her lap before he started the car. He said nothing as she sat back in the seat with her eyes closed. It gave him time to think.

It didn't do any good to snap at her. It did even less good to be angry with her for being sick. But it hurt and infuriated him that she hadn't trusted him enough to tell him she was in trouble. That she hadn't trusted herself enough to admit it and get help.

He was going to see that she got that help now, whether she wanted it or not. As a doctor, he would do the same for a stranger. How much more would he do for the only woman he had ever loved?

Had loved, he reminded himself. In this case, the past tense was vital. And because he had once loved her with all the passion and purity of youth, he wouldn't see her go through this alone.

At the curb in the front of her house, he parked, then walked around the car to open her door. Vanessa climbed out and began the speech she'd carefully planned on the drive.

"I'm sorry if I acted childishly before. And ungrateful. I know you and your father only want to help. I'll take the medication."

"Damn right you will." He took her arm.

"You don't have to come in."

"I'm coming in," he said as he pulled her up the walk. "I'm watching you take the first dose, and then I'm putting you to bed."

"Brady, I'm not an invalid."

"That's right, and if I have anything to say about it, you won't become one."

He pushed open the door—it was never locked— and hauled her directly upstairs. He filled a glass in the bathroom, handed it to her, then opened the bottle of medication and shook out a pill himself.

"Swallow."

She took a moment to scowl at him before she obeyed. "Are you going to charge me for a house call?"

"The first one's for old times' sake." Gripping her arm again, he pulled her into the bedroom. "Now take off your clothes."

Pain or no pain, she tossed back her head. "Aren't you supposed to be wearing a lab coat and a stethoscope when you say that?"

He didn't even bother to swear. Turning, he yanked open a drawer and searched until he found a nightshirt. She would wear silk to bed, he thought, clenching his teeth. Of course she would. After tossing it on the bed, he pushed her around and dragged down her zipper.

"When I undress you for personal reasons, you'll know it."

"Cut it out." Shocked, she caught the dress as it pooled at her waist. He merely tugged the nightshirt over her head.

"I can control my animal lust by thinking of your stomach lining."

"That's disgusting."

"Exactly." He tugged the dress over her hips. The nightshirt drifted down to replace it. "Stockings?"

Unsure if she should be mortified or infuriated, she unrolled them down the length of her legs. Brady gritted his teeth again. No amount of hours in anatomy class could have prepared him for the sight of Vanessa slowly removing sheer stockings in lamplight.

He was a doctor, he reminded himself, and tried to recite the first line of the Hippocratic oath.

"Now get in bed." He pulled down the quilt, then carefully tucked it up to her chin after she climbed in. Suddenly she looked sixteen again. He clung to his professionalism, setting the bottle of pills on her nightstand. "I want you to follow the directions."

"I can read."

"No drinking." A doctor, he repeated to himself. He was a doctor, and she was a patient. A beautiful patient with sinfully soft skin and big green eyes. "We don't use bland diets so much anymore, just common sense. Stay away from spicy foods. You're going to get some relief fairly quickly. In all probability you won't even remember you had an ulcer in a few days."

"I don't have one now."

"Vanessa." With a sigh, he brushed back her hair. "Do you want anything?"

"No." Her hand groped for his before he could rise. "Can you—? Do you have to go?"

He kissed her fingers. "Not for a while."

Satisfied, she settled back. "I was never supposed to let you come up here when we were teenagers."

"Nope. Remember the night I climbed in the window?"

"And we sat on the floor and talked until four in the morning. If my father had known, he would have—" She broke off, remembering.

"Now isn't the time to worry about all that."

"It isn't a matter of worry, really, but of wondering. I loved you, Brady. It was innocent, and it was sweet. Why did he have to spoil that?"

"You were meant for big things, Van. He knew it. I was in the way."

"Would you have asked me to stay?" She hadn't thought she would ask, but she had always wanted to know. "If you had known about his plans to take me to Europe, would you have asked me to stay?"

"Yes. I was eighteen and selfish. And if you had stayed, you wouldn't be what you are. And I wouldn't be what I am."

"You haven't asked me if I would have stayed."

"I know you would have."

She sighed. "I guess you only love that intensely once. Maybe it's best to have it over and done with while you're young."

"Maybe."

She closed her eyes, drifting. "I used to dream that you would come and take me away. Especially before a performance, when I stood in the wings, hating it."

His brows drew together. "Hating what?"

"The lights, the people, the stage. I would wish so hard that you would come and we would go away together. Then I knew you wouldn't. And I stopped wishing. I'm so tired."

He kissed her fingers again. "Go to sleep."

"I'm tired of being alone," she murmured before she drifted off.

He sat, watching her, trying to separate his feelings for what had been from what was. And that was the problem, he realized. The longer he was with her, the more the edges between the past and present blurred.

There was one and only one thing that was clear. He had never stopped loving her.

After touching his lips to hers, he turned off the bedside light and left her to sleep.

Chapter 7

Bundled in her ratty blue terry-cloth robe, her hair tousled and her disposition grim, Vanessa trudged downstairs. Because she'd been hounded, she'd been taking the medication Ham Tucker had prescribed for two days. She felt better. It annoyed her to have to admit it, but she was a long way from ready to concede that she'd needed it.

More, she was embarrassed that it was Brady who had supervised her first dose and tucked her into bed. It hadn't been so bad when they'd been sniping at each other, but when she'd weakened and asked him to stay with her, he'd been kind. Doctor to patient, she reminded herself. But she had never been able to resist Brady when he was kind.

The morning suited her mood. Thick gray clouds, thick gray rain. It was, she thought, a perfect day to sit alone in the house and brood. In fact, it was something to look forward to. Rain, depression, and a private pity party. At least solitary sulking would be a change. She'd had little time to be alone since the night of Joanie's dinner party.

Her mother tended to hover, finding excuses to come home two or three times each workday. Dr. Tucker checked in on her twice a day, no matter how much Vanessa protested. Even Joanie had come by, to cluck and fuss, bringing armfuls of lilacs and bowls of chicken soup. Neighbors peeped in from time to time to measure her progress. There were no secrets in Hyattown. Vanessa was certain she'd had good wishes and advice from all two hundred and thirty-three residents of the town.

Except one.

Not that she cared that Brady hadn't found time to come by. She scowled and tugged at the belt of her robe. In fact, she told herself as her fingers trailed over the newel post, she was glad he had been conspicuously absent. The last thing she wanted was Brady Tucker—Hyattown's own Dr. Kildare—looming over her, poking at her and shaking his head in his best I-told-you-so manner. She didn't want to see him. And she certainly didn't need to.

She hated making a fool of herself, she thought as she scuffed barefoot down the hallway to the kitchen. And what other term was there for all but keeling over in Joanie's backyard? Then being carried to bed and having Brady treat her like some whining patient.

An ulcer. That was ridiculous, of course. She was strong, competent and self-sufficient—hardly ulcer material. But she unconsciously pressed a hand to her stomach.

The gnawing ache she'd lived with longer than she could remember was all but gone. Her nights hadn't been disturbed by the slow, insidious burning that had so often kept her awake and miserable. In fact, she'd slept like a baby for two nights running.

A coincidence, Vanessa assured herself. All she'd needed was rest. Rest and a little solitude. The grueling schedule she'd maintained the past few years was bound to wear even the strongest person down a bit.

So she'd give herself another month—maybe two— of Hyattown's version of peace, quiet and restoration before making any firm career decisions.

At the kitchen doorway, she came to an abrupt halt. She hadn't expected to find Loretta there. In fact, she had purposely waited to come down until after she'd heard the front door open and close.

"Good morning." Loretta, dressed in one of her tidy suits, hair and pearls in place, beamed a smile.

"I thought you'd gone."

"No, I ran up to Lester's for a paper." She gestured toward the newspaper folded neatly beside the single place setting. "I thought you might want to see what's happening in the world."

"Thank you." Exasperated, Vanessa stood where she was. She hated the fact that she still fumbled whenever Loretta made a gentle maternal gesture. She was grateful for the consideration, but she realized it was the gratitude of a guest for a hostess's generosity. And so it left her feeling guilty and disheartened. "You didn't have to bother."

"No bother. Why don't you sit down, dear? I'll fix

you some tea. Mrs. Hawbaker sent some of her own chamomile over from her herb garden."

"Really, you don't have to—" Vanessa broke off at the sound of a knock on the back door. "I'll get it."

She opened the door, telling herself she didn't want it to be Brady. She didn't care if it was Brady. Then she told herself she wasn't the least bit disappointed when the visitor turned out to be female.

"Vanessa." A brunette who huddled under a dripping umbrella was smiling at her. "You probably don't remember me. I'm Nancy Snooks—used to be Nancy McKenna, Josh McKenna's sister."

"Well, I—"

"Nancy, come in." Loretta hurried to the door. "Lord, it's really coming down, isn't it?"

"Doesn't look like we'll have to worry about a drought this year. I can't stay." She remained on the stoop, shifting from foot to foot. "It's just that I heard Vanessa was back and giving piano lessons. My boy Scott's eight now."

Vanessa saw the blow coming and braced herself. "Oh, well, I'm not really—"

"Annie Crampton's just crazy about you," Nancy said quickly. "Her mama's my second cousin, you know. And when I was talking it over with Bill—Bill's my husband—we agreed that piano lessons would be real good for Scott. Mondays right after school would work out best for us—if you don't have another student then."

"No, I don't, because—"

"Great. Aunt Violet said ten dollars is what you're charging for Annie. Right?"

"Yes, but—"

"We can swing that. I'm working part-time over to

the feed and grain. Scott'll be here sharp at four. Sure is nice to have you back, Vanessa. I gotta go. I'll be late for work."

"You be careful driving in this rain," Loretta put in.

"I will. Oh, and congratulations, Mrs. Sexton. Doc Tucker's the best."

"Yes, he is." Loretta managed to smile without laughing out loud as she shut the door on a whoosh of rain. "Nice girl," she commented. "Takes after her aunt Violet."

"Apparently."

"I should warn you." Loretta walked over to set a cup of tea on the table. "Scott Snooks is a terror."

"It figures." It was too early in the morning to think, Vanessa decided. She sat, dropped her heavy head in her hands. "She wouldn't have trapped me if I'd been awake."

"Of course not. How about some nice French toast?"

"You don't have to fix me breakfast." Vanessa's voice was muffled by her hands.

"No trouble at all." Loretta was humming as she poured milk into a bowl. She'd been cheated out of being a mother for twelve years. There was nothing she'd rather do than pamper her daughter with a hot breakfast.

Vanessa scowled down at her tea. "I don't want to keep you. Don't you have to open the shop?"

Still humming, Loretta broke an egg into the bowl. "The beauty of having your own place is calling your own hours." She added touches of cinnamon, sugar and vanilla. "And you need a good breakfast. Ham says you're on the mend, but he wants you to put on ten pounds."

"Ten?" Vanessa nearly choked on her tea. "I don't need—" She bit off an oath as another knock sounded.

"I'll get it this time," Loretta announced. "If it's another hopeful parent, I'll shoo them away."

But it was Brady who stood dripping on the back stoop this time. Without the shelter of an umbrella, he grinned at Vanessa while rain streamed from his dark hair. Instant pleasure turned to instant annoyance the moment he opened his mouth.

"Morning, Loretta." He winked at Vanessa. "Hi, gorgeous."

With something close to a snarl, Vanessa huddled over her steaming tea.

"Brady, what a nice surprise." After accepting his kiss on the cheek, Loretta closed the door on the rain. "Have you had breakfast?" she asked as she went back to the stove to soak the bread.

"No, ma'am." He took an appreciative sniff and hoped he was about to. "Is that French toast?"

"It will be in just a minute. You sit down and I'll fix you a plate."

He didn't have to be asked twice. After dragging his hands through his dripping hair and scattering rain all over creation, he joined Vanessa at the table. He flashed her a smile, a cheerful, friendly look that neatly disguised the fact that he was studying her color. The lack of shadows under her eyes gratified him as much as the mutinous expression in them.

"Beautiful day," he said.

Vanessa lifted her gaze to the rain-lashed windows. "Right."

Undaunted by her grudging response, he shifted in

his chair to chat with Loretta as she flipped the brown-ing bread in the skillet.

Not a peep from him in two days, Vanessa thought, and now he pops up on the doorstep, big as life and twice as irritating. He hadn't even asked her how she was feeling—not that she wanted to be fussed over, she reminded herself. But he was a doctor—and he was the one who'd come up with that ridiculous diagnosis.

"Ah, Loretta." Brady all but drooled when she set a heaping plate of fragrant bread in front of him. "My father's a lucky man."

"I suppose cooking's the first priority when a Tucker goes looking for a wife," Vanessa said, feeling nasty.

Brady only smiled as he glopped on maple syrup. "It couldn't hurt."

Vanessa felt her temper rise. Not because she couldn't cook. Certainly not. It was the narrow-minded, sexist idea that infuriated her. Before she could think of a suit-ably withering reply, Loretta set a plate in front of her.

"I can't eat all of this."

"I can," Brady said as he started on his own meal. "I'll finish up what you don't."

"If you two are set, I'd best go open the shop. Van, there's plenty of that chicken soup left that Joanie brought over yesterday. It'll heat up fine in the micro-wave for lunch. If this rain keeps up, I'll probably be home early. Good luck with Scott."

"Thanks."

"Scott?" Brady asked, as Loretta went out.

Vanessa merely propped her elbows on the table. "Don't ask."

Brady waited until Loretta had left them alone

before rising to help himself to coffee. "I wanted to talk to you about the wedding."

"The wedding?" She looked over. "Oh, the wedding. Yes, what about it?"

"Dad's been applying a little Tucker pressure. He thinks he's got Loretta convinced to take the plunge over the Memorial Day weekend."

"Memorial Day? But that's next week."

"Why wait?" Brady said after a sip, echoing his father's sentiments. "That way they can use the annual picnic as a kind of town wedding reception."

"I see." But it was so soon, Vanessa thought frantically. She hadn't even adjusted to being with her mother again, to living in the same house with her, and now… But it wasn't her decision, she reminded herself. "I suppose they'll move into your father's house."

"I think that's the plan." He sat again. "They've been kicking around the idea of renting this one eventually. Does that bother you?"

She concentrated on cutting a neat slice of the bread. How could she know? She hadn't had time to find out if it was home or not. "No, I suppose not. They can hardly live in two houses at once."

Brady thought he understood. "I can't see Loretta selling this place. It's been in your family for years."

"I often wondered why she kept it."

"She grew up here, just as you did." He picked up his coffee again. "Why don't you ask her what she plans to do about it?"

"I might." She moved her shoulders restlessly. "There's no hurry."

Because he knew her, he let it go at that. "What I really wanted to talk to you about was a wedding present. Obviously they won't need a toaster or a set of china."

"No." Vanessa frowned down at her plate. "I suppose not."

"I was thinking—I ran it by Joanie and she likes the idea. Why don't we pool our resources and give them a honeymoon? A couple weeks in Cancún. You know, a suite overlooking the Caribbean, tropical nights, the works. Neither one of them has ever been to Mexico. I think they'd get a charge out of it."

Vanessa looked up at him again. It was a lovely idea, she decided. And it was typical of him to have thought of it. "As a surprise?"

"I think we can pull it off. Dad's been trying to juggle his schedule to get a week free. I can sabotage that so he'll think he can only manage a couple of days. Getting the tickets, making some reservations, that's the easy part. Then we have to pack their bags without getting caught."

Warming to the idea, she smiled. "If your father has the same stars in his eyes my mother does, I think we can manage that. We could give them the tickets at the picnic, then bundle them into a limo. Is there a limo service around here?"

"There's one in Frederick. I hadn't thought of that." He pulled out a pad to make a note.

"Get them the bridal suite," Vanessa said. When he looked up and grinned, she shrugged. "If we're going to do it, let's do it right."

"I like it. One limo, one bridal suite, two first-class tickets. Anything else?"

"Champagne. A bottle in the limo, and another in the room when they arrive. And flowers. Mom likes gardenias." She stopped abruptly as Brady continued to write. She'd called Loretta "Mom." It had come out naturally. It sounded natural. "She—she used to like gardenias."

"Terrific." He slipped the pad back in his jacket pocket. "You didn't leave me any."

Baffled, she followed his gaze to her own empty plate. "I...I guess I was hungrier than I thought."

"That's a good sign. Any burning?"

"No." Off balance, she rose to take her plate to the sink.

"Any pain?"

"No. I told you before, you're not my doctor."

"Um-hmm." He was standing behind her when she turned. "We'll just figure I'm taking Doc Tucker's appointments today. Let's have a little vertical examination." Before she could move aside, he pressed gentle fingers to her abdomen. "Hurt?"

"No, I told you I—"

He pressed firmly under her breastbone. She winced. "Still tender?"

"A little."

He nodded. When he'd touched that spot two days before, she'd nearly gone through the roof. "You're coming along nicely. Another few days and you can even indulge in a burrito."

"Why is it that everyone who comes in here is obsessed with what I eat?"

"Because you haven't been eating enough. Understandable, with an ulcer."

"I don't have an ulcer." But she was aching from his touch—for an entirely different reason. "And would you move?"

"Right after you pay your bill." Before she could object or respond, he pressed his lips to hers, firmly, possessively. Murmuring her name, he took her deeper, until she was clinging to him for balance. The floor seemed to drop away from her feet so that he, and only he, was touching her. His thighs against hers, his fingers knotted in her hair, his mouth, hungry and impatient, roaming her face.

She smelled of the morning, of the rain. He wondered what it would be like to love her in the gloomy light, her sigh whispering against his cheek. And he wondered how much longer he would have to wait.

He lifted his head, keeping his hands in her hair so that her face was tilted toward his. In the misty green of her eyes, he saw himself. Lost in her. Gently now, and with an infinite care that stilled her wildly beating heart, he touched his lips to hers again.

Her arms tightened around him, strengthening, even as every bone in her body seemed to melt. She tilted her head so that their lips met in perfect alignment, with equal demand.

"Vanessa—"

"Don't say anything, not yet." She pressed her mouth to his throat and just held on. She knew she would have to think, but for now, for just a moment, she wanted only to feel.

His pulse throbbed, strong and fast, against her lips. His body was firm and solid. Gradually his hands relaxed their desperate grip and stroked through her hair. She became aware of the hiss and patter of rain, of the cool tiles under her bare feet, of the morning scents of coffee and cinnamon.

But the driving need would not abate, nor would the confusion and fear that blossomed inside her.

"I don't know what to do," she said at length. "I haven't been able to think straight since I saw you again."

Her murmured statement set off dozens of new fires. His hands moved up to her shoulders and gripped harder than he had meant them to. "I want you, Van. You want me. We're not teenagers anymore."

She stepped back as far as his hands would allow. "It's not easy for me."

"No." He studied her as he struggled to examine his own emotions. "I'm not sure I'd want it to be. If you want promises—"

"No," she said quickly. "I don't want anything I can't give back."

He'd been about to make them, hundreds of them. With an effort, he swallowed them all, reminding himself that he'd always moved too fast when it involved Vanessa. "What can you give back?"

"I don't know." She lifted her hands to his and squeezed before she stepped away. "God, Brady, I feel as though I'm slipping in and out of the looking glass."

"This isn't an illusion, Van." It was a struggle to keep from reaching for her again. But he knew that what his father had told him was true. When you held too tight, what you wanted most slipped through your fingers. "This is just you and me."

She studied him, the eyes so blue against the dark lashes, the damp, untidy hair, the stubborn set of his jaw, the impossibly romantic shape of his mouth. It was so easy to remember why she had loved him. And so easy to be afraid she still did.

"I won't pretend I don't want to be with you. At the same time, I want to run the other way, as fast as I can." Her sigh was long and shaky. "And hope like hell you catch up with me. I realize my behavior's been erratic since I've come home, and a big part of that is because I never expected to find you here, or to have all these old feelings revived. And that's part of the problem. I don't know how much of what I feel for you is just an echo and how much is real."

He found himself in the frustrating position of competing with himself. "We're different people now, Van."

"Yes." She looked at him, her eyes level and almost calm. "When I was sixteen, I would have gone anywhere with you, Brady. I imagined us together forever, a house, a family."

"And now?" he said carefully.

"Now we both know things aren't that simple, or that easy. We're different people, Brady, with different lives, different dreams. I had problems before—we both did. I still have them." She lifted her hands, let them fall. "I'm not sure it's wise to begin a relationship with you, a physical relationship, until I resolve them."

"It's more than physical, Vanessa. It's always been more."

She nodded, taking a moment to calm a fresh flood of emotion. "All the more reason to take it slowly. I don't know what I'm going to do with my life, with my music. Having an affair will only make it that much more difficult for both of us when I leave."

Panic. He tasted it. When she left again, it would break his heart. He wasn't sure that particular organ would survive a second time. "If you're asking me to turn off my feelings and walk away, I won't." In one swift movement, he pulled her against him again. The hell with what was right. "And neither will you."

She felt the thrill race up her spine, those twin sprinters—excitement and alarm. The ghost of the boy she had known and loved was in his eyes, reckless, relentless. She'd never been able to resist him.

"I'm asking you to let me sort this through." If he wanted to use anger, then she would match him blow for blow. "The decision's mine, Brady," she said, jerking away. "I won't be pressured or threatened or seduced. Believe me, it's all been tried before."

It was the wrong switch to pull. His eyes, already hot, turned to blue fire. "I'm not one of your smooth, well-mannered lovers, Van. I won't pressure or threaten or seduce. When the time comes, I'll just take."

Challenged, she tossed her head back. "You won't take anything I don't give. No man does. Oh, I'd like to toss those smooth, well-mannered lovers in your face." She gave him a shove as she walked past him to the stove. "Just to see you squirm. But I'll do better than that." She whirled back, hair flying. "I'll tell you the truth. There haven't been any lovers. Because I haven't wanted there to be." Insolent and mocking, she leaned against the stove. "And if I decide I don't want you, you'll just have to join the ranks of the disappointed."

No one. There had been no one. Almost before he could absorb it, she was hurling her final insult. He bristled, took a step toward her, then managed to stop himself. If he touched her now, one of them would crawl. He didn't want it to be him. He stalked to the back door, and had wrenched it open before he got his temper under control enough to realize that his retreat was exactly what she'd wanted.

So he'd throw her a curve.

"How about going to the movies tonight?"

If he'd suggested a quick trip to the moon, she would have been no less surprised. "What?"

"The movies. Do you want to go to the movies?"

"Why?"

"Because I have a craving for popcorn," he snapped. "Do you want to go or not?"

"I... Yes," she heard herself say.

"Fine." He slammed the door behind him.

Life was a puzzle, Vanessa decided. And she was having a hard time fitting the pieces together. For a week she'd been whirled into wedding and picnic plans. Coleslaw and potato salad, long-stemmed roses and photographers. She was dead sure it was a mistake to try to coordinate a town picnic with an intimate family wedding. It was like trying to juggle bowling balls and feathers.

As the final week passed, she was too busy and too confused to notice that she felt better than she had in years. There was the secret honeymoon, and Joanie's enthusiastic bubbling over every aspect of the upcoming nuptials. There were flowers to be ordered and arranged—and a hundred hamburger patties to make.

She went out with Brady almost every night. To the movies, to dinner. To a concert. He was such an easy and amusing companion that she began to wonder if she had dreamed the passion and anger in the gloomy kitchen.

But each night when he walked her to the door, each night when he kissed her breathless, she realized he was indeed giving her time to think things through. Just as he was making certain she had plenty to think about.

The night before the wedding, she stayed at home. But she thought of him, even as she and Loretta and Joanie bustled around the kitchen putting last-minute touches on a mountain of food.

"I still think the guys should be here helping," Joanie muttered as she slapped a hamburger patty between her hands.

"They'd just be in the way." Loretta molded another hunk of meat into shape. "Besides, I'm too nervous to deal with Ham tonight."

Joanie laughed. "You're doing fine. Dad's a basket case. When he came by the farm today, he asked me three times for a cup of coffee. He had one in his hand the whole time."

Pleased, Loretta chuckled. "It's nice to know he's suffering, too." She looked at the kitchen clock for the fifth time in five minutes. Eight o'clock, she thought. In fourteen hours she would be married. "I hope it doesn't rain."

Vanessa, who'd been deemed an amateur, looked up from her task of arranging the patties in layers between waxed paper. "The forecast is sunny and high seventies."

"Oh, yes." Loretta managed a smile. "You told me that before, didn't you?"

"Only fifty or sixty times."

Her brows knitted, Loretta looked out the window. "Of course, if it did rain, we could move the wedding indoors. It would be a shame to have the picnic spoiled, though. Ham enjoys it so."

"It wouldn't dare rain," Joanie stated, taking the forgotten patty from the bride-to-be's hands. Unable to re-sist, she tucked her tongue in her cheek. "It's too bad you had to postpone your honeymoon."

"Oh, well." With a shrug, Loretta went back to work. She didn't want to show her disappointment. "Ham just couldn't manage to clear his schedule. I'll have to get used to that sort of thing, if I'm going to be a doctor's wife." She pressed a hand to her nervous stomach. "Is that rain? Did I hear rain?"

"No," Vanessa and Joanie said in unison.

With a weak laugh, Loretta washed her hands. "I must be hearing things. I've been so addled this past week. Just this morning I couldn't find my blue silk blouse—and I've misplaced the linen slacks I got on sale just last month. My new sandals, too, and my good black cocktail dress. I can't think where I might have put them."

Vanessa shot Joanie a warning look before her friend could chuckle. "They'll turn up."

"What? Oh, yes…yes, of course they will. Are you sure that's not rain?"

Exasperated, Vanessa put a hand on her hip. "Mom, for heaven's sake, it's not rain. There isn't going to be any rain. Go take a hot bath." When Loretta's eyes filled, Vanessa rolled her eyes. "I'm sorry. I didn't mean to snap at you."

"You called me 'Mom,'" Loretta said, her breath hitching. "I never thought you would again." As tears overflowed, she rushed from the room.

"Damn it." Vanessa leaned her hands on the counter. "I've been working overtime to keep the peace all week, and I blow it the night before the wedding."

"You didn't blow anything." Joanie put a hand on her

shoulder and rubbed. "I'm not going to say it's none of my business, because we're friends, and tomorrow we'll be family. I've watched you and Loretta walk around each other ever since you got back. And I've seen the way she looks at you when your back is turned, or when you leave a room."

"I don't know if I can give her what she wants."

"You're wrong," Joanie said quietly. "You can. In a lot of ways you already have. Why don't you go upstairs, make sure she's all right? I'll give Brady a call and have him help me load most of this food up and take it down to Dad's."

"All right."

Vanessa went upstairs quietly, slowly, trying to work out the right things to say. But when she saw Loretta sitting on the bed, nothing seemed right.

"I'm sorry." Loretta dabbed at her eyes with a tissue. "I guess I'm overly emotional tonight."

"You're entitled." Vanessa hesitated in the doorway. "Would you like to be alone?"

"No." Loretta held out a hand. "Would you sit awhile?"

Unable to refuse, Vanessa crossed the room to sit beside her mother.

"For some reason," Loretta began, "I've been thinking about what you were like as a baby. You were so pretty. I know all mothers say that, but you were. So bright and alert, and all that hair." She reached out to touch the tips of Vanessa's hair. "Sometimes I would just sit and watch you as you slept. I couldn't believe you were mine. As long as I can remember, I wanted to have a home and children. Oh, I wanted to fill a house with children. It was my only ambition." She looked down at the tissue she had shredded. "When I had you, it was the happiest day of my life. You'll understand that better when you have a baby of your own."

"I know you loved me." Vanessa chose her words carefully. "That's why the rest was so difficult. But I don't think this is the time for us to talk about it."

"Maybe not." Loretta wasn't sure it would ever be the time for a full explanation. One that might turn her daughter away again, just when she was beginning to open her heart. "I just want you to know that I understand you're trying to forgive, and to forgive without explanations. That means a great deal to me." She took a chance and gripped her daughter's hand. "I love you now even more than I did that first moment, when they put you into my arms. No matter where you go or what you do, I always will."

"I love you, too." Vanessa brought their joined hands to her cheek for a moment. "I always have." And that was what hurt the most. She rose and managed to smile. "I think you should get some sleep. You want to look your best tomorrow."

"Yes. Good night, Van."

"Good night." She closed the door quietly behind her.

Chapter 8

Vanessa heard the hiss at her window and blinked groggily awake. Rain? she thought, trying to remember why it was so important there be no rain that day.

The wedding, she thought with a start, and sat straight up. The sun was up, she realized as she shook herself. It was streaming through her half-opened window like pale gold fingers. But the hiss came again—and a rattle.

Not rain, she decided as she sprang out of bed. Pebbles. Rushing to the window, she threw it all the way up.

And there he was, standing in her backyard, dressed in ripped sweats and battered sneakers, his legs spread and planted, his head back and a fistful of pebbles in his hand.

"It's about time," Brady whispered up at her. "I've been throwing rocks at your window for ten minutes."

Vanessa leaned an elbow on the sill and rested her chin in her palm. "Why?"

"To wake you up."

"Ever hear of a telephone?"

"I didn't want to wake your mother."

She yawned. "What time is it?"

"It's after six." He glanced over to see Kong digging at the marigolds and whistled the dog to him. Now they both stood, looking up at her. "Well, are you coming down?"

She grinned. "I like the view from here."

"You've got ten minutes before I find out if I can still shimmy up a drainpipe."

"Tough choice." With a laugh, she shut the window. In less than ten minutes, she was creeping out the back door in her oldest jeans and baggiest sweater. Thoughts of a romantic assignation were dispelled when she saw Joanie, Jack and Lara.

"What's going on?" she demanded.

"We're decorating." Brady hefted a cardboard box and shoved it at her. "Crepe paper, balloons, wedding bells. The works. We thought we'd shoot for discreet and elegant here for the ceremony, then go all out down at Dad's for the picnic."

"More surprises." The box weighed a ton, and she shifted it. "Where do we start?"

They worked in whispers and muffled laughter, arguing about the proper way to drape crepe paper on a maple tree. Brady's idea of discreet was to hang half a dozen paper wedding bells from the branches and top it off with balloons. But it wasn't until they had carted everything down the block to the Tuckers that he really cut loose.

"It's a reception, not a circus," Vanessa reminded

him. He had climbed into the old sycamore and was gleefully shooting out strips of crepe paper.

"It's a celebration," he replied. "It reminds me of when we'd roll old Mr. Taggert's willow every Halloween. Hand me some more pink."

Despite her better judgment, Vanessa obeyed. "It looks like a five-year-old did it."

"Artistic expression."

With a muttered comment, Vanessa turned. She saw that Jack had climbed on the roof and was busily anchoring a line of balloons along the gutter. While Lara sat on a blanket with a pile of plastic blocks and Kong for company, Joanie tied the last of the wedding bells to the grape arbor. The result of their combined efforts wasn't elegant, and it certainly wasn't artistic. But it was terrific.

"You're all crazy," Vanessa decided when Brady jumped from the tree to land softly beside her. He smelled lightly of soap and sweat. "What's next? A calliope and a snake charmer?"

He reached into a box and drew out another roll of white and a roll of pink. "The mall was out of calliopes, but we've still got some of this left."

Vanessa thought a moment, then grinned. "Give me the tape." With it in her hand, she raced to the house. "Come on," she said, gesturing to Brady. "Give me a boost."

"A what?"

"I need to get up on your shoulders." She got behind him and leaped up nimbly to hook her legs around his waist. "Try to stand still," she muttered as she inched her way upward. He tried not to notice that her thighs were slender and only a thin layer of denim away. "Now I need both rolls."

They juggled the paper and tape between them.

"I like your knees," Brady commented, turning his head to nip at one.

"Just consider yourself a stepladder." She secured the tips of the streamers to the eaves of the house. "Move back, but slowly. I'll twist as you go."

"Go where?"

"To the back of the yard—to that monstrosity that used to be a sycamore tree."

Balancing her and craning his neck behind him to be sure he didn't step on an unwary dog—or his niece—or in a gopher hole, he walked backward. "What are you doing?"

"I'm decorating." She twisted the strips of pink and white together, letting the streamer droop a few inches above Brady's head. "Don't run into the tree." When they reached it, she hooked her feet around Brady's chest and leaned forward. "I just have to reach this branch. Got it."

"Now what?"

"Now we do another from the tree to the other side of the house. Balance," she said, leaning forward to look at him. "That's artistic."

When the deed was done, and the last scrap of colored paper used, she put her hands on her hips and studied the results. "Nice," she decided. "Very nice—except for the mess you made of the sycamore."

"The sycamore is a work of art," he told her. "It's riddled with symbolism."

"It looks like Mr. Taggert's willow on Halloween," Joanie chimed in as she plucked up Lara and settled her on her hip. "One look at that and he's going to know who rolled it in toilet paper every year." She grinned up at Vanessa, who was still perched on Brady's shoulders. "We'd better run. Only two hours until countdown." She poked a finger in Brady's chest. "You're in charge of Dad until we get back."

"He's not going anywhere."

"I'm not worried about that. He's so nervous he might tie his shoelaces together."

"Or forget to wear shoes at all," Jack put in, taking Joanie's arm to lead her away. "Or he could wear his shoes and forget his pants, all because you were standing here worrying about it so you didn't get home and change and get back in time to nag him."

"I don't nag," she said with a chuckle as he pulled her along. "And, Brady, don't forget to check with Mrs. Leary about the cake. Oh, and—" The rest was muffled when Jack clamped a hand over her mouth.

"And I used to put my hands over my ears," Brady murmured. He twisted his head to look up at Vanessa. "Want a ride home?"

"Sure."

He trooped off, still carrying her, through the neighboring yards. "Putting on weight?" He'd noticed she was filling out her jeans very nicely.

"Doctor's orders." She gave his hair an ungentle tug. "So watch your step."

"Purely a professional question. How about I give you an exam?" He turned his head to leer at her.

"Look out for the—" She ducked down so that the clotheslines skimmed over her head. "You might have walked around it."

"Yeah, but now I can smell your hair." He kissed her

before she could straighten up again. "Are you going to make me some breakfast?"

"No."

"Coffee?"

She chuckled as she started to squirm down his back. "No."

"Instant?"

"No." She was laughing when her feet hit the ground. "I'm going to take a long, hot shower, then spend an hour primping and admiring myself in the mirror."

He gathered her close, though the dog was trying to wiggle between them. "You look pretty good right now."

"I can look better."

"I'll let you know." He tipped her face up to his. "After the picnic, you want to come by, help me look at paint chips?"

She gave him a quick, impulsive kiss. "I'll let you know," she said before she dashed inside.

Loretta's nerves seemed to have transferred to her daughter. While the bride calmly dressed for her wedding day, Vanessa fussed with the flower arrangements, checked and rechecked the bottle of champagne that had been set aside for the first family toast, and paced from window to window looking for the photographer.

"He should have been here ten minutes ago," she said when she heard Loretta start downstairs. "I knew it was a mistake to hire Mrs. Driscoll's grandson's brother-in-law. I don't understand why—" She turned, breaking off when she saw her mother.

"Oh. You look beautiful."

Loretta had chosen a pale, pale green silk with only a touch of ecru lace along the tea-length hem. It was simple—simply cut, simply beautiful. On an impulse, she'd bought a matching picture hat, and she'd fluffed her hair under the brim.

"You don't think it's too much?" She reached up, her fingers skimming the hat. "It is just a small, informal wedding."

"It's perfect. Really perfect. I've never seen you look better."

"I feel perfect." She smiled. As a bride should, she was glowing. "I don't know what was wrong with me last night. Today I feel perfect. I'm so happy." She shook her head quickly. "I don't want to cry. I spent forever on my face."

"You're not going to cry," Vanessa said firmly. "The photographer— Oh, thank God, he's just pulling up outside. I'll— Oh, wait. Do you have everything?"

"Everything?"

"You know, something old, something new?"

"I forgot." Struck by bridal superstition, Loretta started a frantic mental search. "The dress is new. And these…" She touched a finger to her pearls. "These were my mother's—and her mother's, so they're old."

"Good start. Blue?"

Color rose in Loretta's cheeks. "Yes, actually, under the dress. I have, ah… My camisole has little blue ribbons down the front. I suppose you think I'm foolish buying fancy lingerie."

"No, I don't." Vanessa touched her mother's arm, and was surprised by the quick impulse she had to hug her. Instead, she stepped back. "That leaves borrowed."

"Well, I—"

"Here." Vanessa unclasped the thin gold braided bracelet she wore. "Take this, and you'll be all set."

She peeked out the window again. "Oh, here comes Doc Tucker and the rest of them." With a laugh, she waved. "They look like a parade. Go into the music room until I can hustle them outside."

"Van." Loretta was still standing, holding the bracelet in her hand. "Thank you."

Vanessa waited until her mother was out of sight before opening the door. Mass confusion entered. Joanie was arguing with Brady about the proper way to pin a boutonniere. Jack claimed his wife had tied his tie so tight that he couldn't breathe, much less talk. Ham paced the length of the house and back again before Vanessa could nudge him outside.

"You brought the dog," Vanessa said, staring at Kong, who had a red carnation pinned jauntily to his collar.

"He's family," Brady claimed. "I couldn't hurt his feelings."

"Maybe a leash?" she suggested.

"Don't be insulting."

"He's sniffing at Reverend Taylor's shoes."

"With any luck, that's all he'll do to Reverend Taylor's shoes." He turned back to her as she stifled a giggle. "You were right."

"About what?"

"You can look better."

She was wearing a thin, summery dress with yards of skirt in a bold floral print. Its snug contrasting bodice was a rich teal blue, with a bandeau collar that left the curve of her shoulders bare. The gold rope around her neck, and her braided earrings, matched the bracelet she had given Loretta.

"So can you." In a natural movement, she reached up

to straighten the knot in the dark blue tie he was wearing with an oyster-colored suit. "I guess we're all set."

"We're still missing something."

She looked around quickly. The baskets of flowers were in place. Joanie was brushing imaginary dust off her father's sleeve while Reverend Taylor cooed over Lara and tried to avoid Kong. The wedding bells were twirling slowly in the light breeze.

"What?"

"The bride."

"Oh, Lord. I forgot. I'll go get her." Turning, Vanessa raced into the house. She found Loretta in the music room, sitting on the piano stool taking long, deep breaths. "Are you ready?"

She took one more. "Yes." Rising, she walked through the house. But at the back door she paused and groped for Vanessa's hand. Together they crossed the lawn. With each step, Ham's smile grew wider, her mother's hand steadier. They stopped in front of the minister. Vanessa released her mother's hand, stepped back and took Brady's.

"Dearly beloved…" the minister began.

She watched her mother marry under the shade of the maple with paper wedding bells swaying.

"You may kiss the bride," the minister intoned. A cheer went up from neighboring yards where people had gathered. The camera clicked as Ham brought Loretta close for a long, full-bodied kiss that brought on more whistles and shouts.

"Nice job," Brady said as he embraced his father.

Vanessa put her confused emotions on hold and turned to hug her mother. "Best wishes, Mrs. Tucker."

"Oh, Van."

"No crying yet. We've still got lots of pictures to take."

With a squeal, Joanie launched herself at them both. "Oh, I'm so happy." She plucked Lara from Jack's arms. "Give your grandma a kiss."

"Grandma," Loretta whispered, and with a watery laugh she swung Lara into her arms. "Grandma."

Brady laid an arm over Vanessa's shoulders. "How do you feel, Aunt Van?"

"Amazed." She laughed up at him as Mrs. Driscoll's grandson's brother-in-law scurried around snapping pictures. "Let's go pour the champagne."

Two hours later, she was in the Tucker backyard, hauling a tray of hamburger patties to the grill.

"I thought your father always did the honors," she said to Brady.

"He passed his spatula down to me." He had his suit coat off now, his sleeves rolled up and his tie off. Smoke billowed up from the grill as meat sizzled. He flipped a patty expertly.

"You do that very well."

"You should see me with a scalpel."

"I'll pass, thanks." She shifted to avoid being mowed down by two running boys. "The picnic's just like I remember. Crowded, noisy and chaotic."

People milled around in the yard, in the house, even spilled out along the sidewalks. Some sat at the long picnic tables or on the grass. Babies were passed from hand to hand. The old sat in the shade waving at flies as they gossiped and reminisced. The young ran in the sunshine.

Someone had brought a huge portable stereo. Music

poured from the rear corner of the yard, where a group of teenagers had gathered to flirt.

"We'd have been there just a few years back," Brady commented.

"You mean you're too old to hang around a boom box now?"

"No. But they think I am. Now I'm Dr. Tucker—as opposed to my father, who's Doc Tucker—and that automatically labels me an adult." He skewered a hot dog. "It's hell growing up."

"Being dignified," she added as he popped it into a bun and slathered on mustard.

"Setting an example for the younger generation. Say 'ah,'" he told her, then shoved the hot dog in her mouth.

She chewed and swallowed in self-defense. "Maintaining a certain decorum."

"Yeah. You've got mustard on your mouth. Here." He grabbed her hand before she could wipe it off. "I'll take care of it." He leaned down and slid the tip of his tongue over the corner of her mouth. "Very tasty," he decided, then nipped lightly at her bottom lip.

"You're going to burn your burgers," she murmured.

"Quiet. I'm setting an example for the younger generation."

Even as she chuckled, he covered her mouth fully with his, lengthening the kiss, deepening it, drawing it out, until she forgot she was surrounded by people. And so did he.

When he released her, she lifted a hand to her spinning head and tried to find her voice.

"Just like old times," someone shouted.

"Better," Brady said quietly, and would have pulled her close again, but for a tap on his shoulder.

"Let that girl go and behave yourself, Brady Tucker." Violet Driscoll shook her head at the pair of them. "You've got hungry people here. If you want to smooch with your girl, you just wait till later."

"Yes, ma'am."

"Never had a lick of sense." She winked at Vanessa as she started back to the shade. "But he's a handsome so-and-so."

"She's right." Vanessa tossed back her hair.

"I'm a handsome so-and-so?"

"No, you've never had a lick of sense."

"Hey!" he called after her. "Where are you going?"

Vanessa shot him a long, teasing look over her shoulder and kept walking.

It was like old times, Vanessa thought as she stopped to talk to high school friends and watched children race and shout and gobble down food. Faces had aged, babies had been born, but the mood was the same. There was the smell of good food, the sounds of laughter and of a cranky baby being lulled to sleep. She heard arguments over the Orioles' chances for a pennant this year, talk about summer plans and gardening tips.

She could smell the early roses blooming and see the tangle of morning glories on the trellis next door.

When Brady found her again, she was sitting on the grass with Lara.

"What're you doing?"

"Playing with my niece." They both lifted their heads to smile at him.

Something shifted inside him. Something fast and unexpected. And something inevitable, he realized. Seeing her smiling up at him, a child's head on her shoulder, sunlight pouring over her skin. How could he have known he'd been waiting, almost his entire life, for a moment like this? But the child should be his, he thought. Vanessa and the child should be his.

"Is something wrong?" she asked.

"No." He brought himself back with a long, steadying breath. "Why?"

"The way you were staring at me."

He sat beside her, touched a hand to her hair. "I'm still in love with you, Vanessa. And I don't know what the hell to do about it."

She stared. Even if she could have latched on to the dozens of emotions swirling through her, she couldn't have put any into words. It wasn't a boy she was looking at now. He was a man, and what he had spoken had been said deliberately. Now he was waiting for her to move, toward him or away. But she couldn't move at all.

Lara bounced in her lap and squealed, shattering the silence. "Brady, I—"

"There you are." Joanie dropped down beside them. "Whoops," she said as the tension got through to her. "I'm sorry. I guess it's bad timing."

"Go away, Joanie," Brady told her. "Far away."

"I'd already be gone, since you've asked so nicely, but the limo's here. People are already heading around front to stare at it. I think it's time to see the newlyweds off."

"You're right." Almost using Lara as a shield, Vanessa scrambled to her feet. "We don't want them to miss their plane." She braced herself and looked at Brady again. "You've got the tickets?"

"Yeah, I got them." Before she could skirt around him, he cupped her chin in his hand. "We've still got unfinished business, Van."

"I know." She was grateful her voice could sound so calm when her insides were knotted. "Like Joanie said, it's bad timing." With Lara on her hip, she hurried off to find her mother.

"What's all this about a limo?" Ham demanded as Joanie began unrolling his pushed-up sleeves. "Did somebody die?"

"Nope." Joanie fastened the button on his cuff. "You and your new wife are going on a little trip."

"A trip?" Loretta repeated, as Vanessa handed her her purse.

"When newlyweds take a trip," Brady explained, "it's called a honeymoon."

"But I've got patients all next week."

"No, you don't." With Brady and Jack on either side of Ham, and Vanessa and Joanie flanking Loretta, they led the baffled bride and groom to the front of the house.

"Oh, my" was all Loretta could say as she spotted the gleaming white stretch limo.

"Your plane leaves at six." Brady took an envelope out of his pocket and handed it to his father. *"Vaya con Dios."*

"What is all this?" Ham demanded. Vanessa noted with a chuckle that old shoes and cans were already being tied to the bumper. "My schedule—"

"Is cleared." Brady gave Ham a slap on the back. "See you in a couple weeks."

"A couple weeks?" His eyebrows shot up. "Where the hell are we going?"

"South of the border," Joanie chimed in, and gave her father a hard, smacking kiss. "Don't drink the water."

"Mexico?" Loretta's eyes widened. "Are we going

to Mexico? But how can we— The shop. We haven't any luggage."

"The shop's closed," Vanessa told her. "And your luggage is in the trunk." She kissed Loretta on each cheek. "Have a good time."

"In the trunk?" Her baffled smile widened. "My blue silk blouse?"

"Among other things."

"You all did this." Despite the persistent photographer, Loretta began to cry. "All of you."

"Guilty." Brady gave her a huge hug. "Bye, Mom."

"You're a sneaky bunch." Ham had to take out his handkerchief. "Well, Loretta, I guess we've got ourselves a honeymoon."

"Not if you miss your plane." Joanie, always ready to worry, began to push them toward the limo. "Don't sit in the sun too long. It's much more intense down there. Oh, and whatever you buy, make sure you shop around and bargain first. You can change your money at the hotel—there's a phrase book in the carry-on. And if you need—"

"Say goodbye, Joanie," Jack told her.

"Oh, shoot." She rubbed her knuckles under her damp eyes. "Bye. Wave bye-bye, Lara."

"Oh, Ham. Gardenias." Loretta began to weep again.

With shouts and waves from the entire town, the limo began to cruise sedately down Main Street, followed by the clang and thump of cans and shoes, and an escort of running children.

"There they go," Joanie managed, burying her face in Jack's shoulder. He patted her hair.

"It's okay, honey. Kids have to leave home sometime.

Come on, I'll get you some potato salad." He grinned at Brady as he led her away.

Vanessa cleared the lump in her throat. "That was quite a send-off."

"I want to talk to you. We can go to your house or mine."

"I think we should wait until—"

"We've already waited too long."

Panicked, she looked around. How was it that they were alone again so quickly? "The party— You have guests."

"Nobody'll miss us." With a hand on her arm, he turned toward his car.

"Dr. Tucker, Dr. Tucker!" Annie Crampton was racing around the corner of the house. "Come quick! Something's wrong with my grandpa!"

He moved quickly. By the time Vanessa reached the backyard, he was already kneeling beside the old man, loosening his collar.

"Pain," the old man said. "In my chest…can't breathe."

"I got Dad's bag," Joanie said as she passed it to Brady. "Ambulance is coming."

Brady just nodded. "Take it easy, Mr. Benson." He took a small bottle and a syringe out of the bag. "I want you to stay calm." He continued to talk as he worked, calming and soothing with his voice. "Joanie, get his file," he murmured.

Feeling helpless, Vanessa put an arm around Annie's shoulders and drew her back. "Come on, Annie."

"Is Grandpa going to die?"

"Dr. Tucker's taking care of him. He's a very good doctor."

"He takes care of my mom." She sniffled and wiped

at her eyes. "He's going to deliver the baby and all, but Grandpa, he's real old. He fell down. He just got all funny-looking and fell down."

"Dr. Tucker was right here." She stroked Annie's flyaway hair. "If he was going to get sick, it was the best place for it. When he's better, you can play your new song for him."

"The Madonna song?"

"That's right." She heard the wail of an ambulance. "They're coming to take him to the hospital."

"Will Dr. Tucker go with him?"

"I'm sure he will." She watched as the attendants hurried out with a stretcher. Brady spoke to them briskly, giving instructions. She saw him put his hands on Annie's mother's shoulders, speaking slowly, calmly, while she looked up at him with trust and tears in her eyes. When Brady started after the stretcher, Vanessa gave Annie a last squeeze.

"Why don't you go sit with your mother for a minute? She'll be scared." How well she knew, Vanessa thought. She remembered the fear and despair she had felt when they had taken her own father. Turning, she rushed after Brady.

"Brady." She knew she couldn't waste his time. When he turned, she saw the concern, the concentration and the impatience in his eyes. "Please let me know how—what happens."

He nodded, then climbed in the rear of the ambulance with his patient.

It was nearly midnight when Brady pulled up in front of his house. There was a sliver of a moon, bone-white against a black sky studded with stars as clear as ice.

He sat where he was for a moment, letting his muscles relax one by one. With his windows down he could hear the wind sighing through the trees.

The fatigue of an eighteen-hour-day had finally caught up with him on the drive home. He was grateful Jack had brought his car to the hospital. Without it, he would have been tempted to stretch out in the lounge. Now all he wanted was to ease his tired body into a hot tub, turn on the jets and drink a cold beer.

The lights were on downstairs. He was glad he'd forgotten to turn them off. It was less depressing to come home to an empty house if the lights were on. He'd detoured into town on the way home and driven by Vanessa's. But her lights had been out.

Probably for the best, he thought now. He was tired and edgy. Hardly the mood for patient, sensible talk. Maybe there was an advantage to letting her stew over the fact that he was in love with her.

And maybe there wasn't. He hesitated, his hand on the door. What the hell was wrong with him, he wondered. He'd always been a decisive man. When he'd decided to become a doctor, he'd gone after his degree with a vengeance. When he'd decided to leave his hospital position in New York and come home to practice general medicine, he'd done so without a backward glance or a whisper of regret.

Life-altering decisions, certainly. So why the hell couldn't he decide what to do about Vanessa?

He was going back to town. If she didn't answer her door, he would climb up the damn rainspout and crawl in her bedroom window. One way or the other, they were going to straighten this mess out tonight.

He'd already turned away and started back to his car when the door to the house opened.

"Brady?" Vanessa stood in the doorway, the light at her back. "Aren't you coming in?"

He stopped dead and stared at her. In a gesture of pure frustration, he dragged a hand through his hair. Was it any wonder he couldn't decide what to do about her? She'd never been predictable. Kong raced out of the house, barking, and jumped on him.

"Jack and Joanie dropped us off." Vanessa stood, twisting the doorknob back and forth. "I hope you don't mind."

"No." With the dog racing in circles around him, he started back to the house. Vanessa stepped back, out of reach.

"I brought some leftovers from the picnic. I didn't know if you'd have a chance to get any dinner."

"No, I didn't."

"Mr. Benson?"

"Stabilized. It was shaky for a while, but he's tough."

"I'm glad. I'm so glad. Annie was frightened." She rubbed her hands on her thighs, linked her fingers together, pulled them apart, then stuck them in the pockets of her skirt. "You must be exhausted—and hungry. There's plenty of food in the fridge. The, ah, kitchen looks wonderful." She gestured vaguely. "The new cabinets, the counters, everything."

"It's coming along." But he made no move toward it. "How long have you been here?"

"Oh, just a couple of hours." Five, to be exact. "You had some books, so I've been reading."

"Why?"

"Well, to pass the time."

"Why are you here, Van?"

She bent to stroke the dog. "That unfinished business you mentioned. It's been a long day, and I've had plenty of time to think."

"And?"

Why didn't he just sweep her away, carry her upstairs? And shut her up. "And I... About what you said this afternoon."

"That I'm in love with you."

She cleared her throat as she straightened. "Yes, that. I'm not sure what I feel—how I feel. I'm not sure how you feel, either."

"I told you how I feel."

"Yes, but it's very possible that you think you feel that way because you used to—and because falling back into the same routine, the same relationship—with me—is familiar, and comfortable."

"The hell it is. I haven't had a comfortable moment since I saw you sitting at the piano."

"Familiar, then." She began to twist the necklace at her throat. "But I've changed, Brady. I'm not the same person I was when I left here. We'll never be able to pretend those years away. So, no matter how attracted we are to each other, it could be a mistake to take it any further."

He crossed to her, slowly, until they were eye to eye. He was ready to make a mistake. More than ready. "Is that what you were waiting here to tell me?"

She moistened his lips. "Partly."

"Then I'll have my say."

"I'd like to finish first." She kept her eyes level. "I came here tonight because I've never been able to get you completely out of my mind. Or my..." Heart. She wanted to say it, but couldn't. "My system," she finished. "I've never stopped caring about you, or wondering. Because of something we had no control over, we were cheated out of growing up enough to make the decision to move apart or to become lovers." She paused, but only for a moment. "I came here tonight because I realized I want what was taken away from us. I want you." She stepped closer and put her arms around him. "Is that clear enough?"

"Yeah." He kissed her gently. "That's clear enough."

She smiled at him. "Make love with me, Brady. I've always wanted you to."

With their hands joined, they walked upstairs together.

Chapter 9

She had already been upstairs while she had waited for him to come home—smoothing and straightening the covers on the bed, fluffing the pillows, standing and looking at the room and wondering what it would be like to walk into it with him.

He turned on the lamp beside the bed. It was a beautiful old rose-tinted globe that sat on a packing crate. The floors were unfinished, the walls spackled with drywall mud. The bed was only a mattress on the floor beneath the windows. It was the most beautiful room she'd ever seen.

He wished he could have given her candles and roses, a huge four-poster with satin sheets. All he could give her was himself.

And suddenly he was as nervous as a boy on his first date.

"The atmosphere's a little thin in here."

"It's perfect," she told him.

He took her hands and raised them to his lips. "I won't hurt you, Van."

"I know." She kissed his hands in turn. "This is going to sound stupid, but I don't know what to do."

He lowered his mouth to hers, testing, tempting. "You'll catch on."

Her lips curved as her hands slid up his back. "I think you're right." With an instinct that was every bit as potent as experience, she let her head fall back, let her hands glide and press and wander.

Her lips parted for his, and she tasted his little groan of pleasure. Then she shivered with pleasure of her own as his strong, clever hands skimmed down her body, his thumb brushing down the side of her breast, his fingers kneading at her waist, his palm cupping her hip, sliding down her thigh, before its upward journey.

She pressed against him, delighting in the shower of sensations. When his teeth scraped lightly down her throat, over her bare shoulder, she murmured his name. Like the wind through the trees, she sighed for him, and swayed. Pliant and willing, she waited to be molded.

Her absolute trust left him shaken. No matter how hot her passion, she was innocent. Her body might be that of a woman, but she was still as untouched as the girl he had once loved and lost. He wouldn't forget it. As the need flamed inside him, he banked it. This time it would be for her. All for her.

Compassion and tenderness were as much a part of his nature as his recklessness. He showed her only the gentle side now, as he eased the snug top down to her hips. He kissed her, soothing her with murmurs even as his hands set off millions of tiny explosions as they tugged her dress to the floor.

She wore a swatch of white lace that seemed to froth over the swell of her breasts before skimming down to nip at her waist. For his own pleasure, he held her at arm's length and just looked.

"You stop my heart," he told her.

With unsteady hands, she reached out to unbutton his shirt. Though her breath was already ragged, she kept her eyes on his as she slid the shirt from his shoulders and let it fall to join her dress on the floor. With her heart pounding wildly in her ears, she linked her arms around his neck.

"Touch me." She tilted her head back, offered her mouth. "Show me."

Though the kiss was hard, demanding, ruthless, he forced his hands to be gentle. Her own were racing over him, bringing a desperate edge to an already driving need. When he lowered her onto the bed, he watched her eyes close on a sigh, then open again, clouded with desire.

He dipped his head to absorb her taste on his tongue as it skimmed along the verge of lace, as it slid beneath to tease her taut nipples. Her hips ached and her fingers dug into his back as the pleasure rocketed through her.

With a flick of the wrist, he unsnapped her garters, then sent her churning as he slowly peeled down her stockings, blazing the newly bared flesh with his lips. It seemed he found every inch of her, every curve, fascinating. His gentle fingers played over her, everywhere, until the music roared in her head.

As patient as he was ruthless, he drove her closer and closer to the edge she'd never seen. Her body was like a furnace, pumping out heat, pulsing with needs as sharp as his. He drove himself mad watching her, seeing the way everything she felt, each new sensation he brought to her, raced over her face, into her eyes.

Desire. Passion. Pleasure. Excitement. They flowed from him to her, then back again. Familiar. Oh, yes. They recognized each other. That brought comfort. Yet it was new, unique, gloriously fresh. That was the adventure.

He reveled in the way her skin flowed through his hands, the way her body tensed and arched at his touch. The way the lamplight slanted over her, over his hands as he peeled the last barrier of lace away.

Naked, she reached for him, tugging frantically at his slacks. Because he knew his own needs were tearing his control to shreds, he cupped her in his hand and sent her flying over the last line.

She cried out, stunned, helpless, her eyes glazing over, as her hand slipped limply from his shoulder. Even as she shuddered, he eased into her, slowly, gently, murmuring her name again and again as the blood roared in his ears and pushed him to take his pleasure quickly. Love demanded gentleness.

She lost her innocence sweetly, painlessly, and with simple joy.

She lay in Brady's bed, tangled in Brady's sheets. A sparrow heralded the dawn. During the night, the dog had crept in to take his rightful place at the foot of the bed. Lazily Vanessa opened her eyes.

Brady's face was barely an inch from hers, and she had to ease back and blink to focus on him. He was deep in sleep, his arm heavy around her waist, his breathing slow and even. Now, completely relaxed and vulnerable, he looked more like the boy she remembered than the man she was beginning to know.

She loved. There was no doubt in her mind that she loved. Her heart nearly burst with it. But did she love the boy or the man?

Very gently, she brushed at the hair on his forehead. All she was really sure of was that she was happy. And, for now, it was enough.

More than enough, she thought as she slowly stretched. During the night he had shown her how beautiful making love could be when two people cared about each other. And how exciting it could be when needs were met and desires reached. Whatever happened tomorrow, or a year from tomorrow, she would never forget what they had shared.

Lightly, not wanting to wake him, she touched her lips to his. Even that quiet contact stirred her. Hesitant, curious, she trailed her fingertips over his shoulders, down the length of his back. The need grew and spread inside her.

As dreams went, Brady thought, this was one of the best. He was under a warm quilt in the first light of day. Vanessa was in bed beside him. Her body was pressed against his, shifting gently, arousing quickly. Those beautiful, talented fingers were stroking along his skin. That soft, sulky mouth was toying with his. When he reached for her, she sighed, arching under his hand.

Everywhere he touched she was warm and smooth. Her arms were around him, strong silken ropes that trapped him gloriously against her. When she said his name, once, then twice, the words slipped under the gauzy curtain of his fantasy. He opened his eyes and saw her.

This was no dream. She was smiling at him. Those misty green eyes were heavy with sleep and passion. Her body was slim and soft and curved against his.

"Good morning," she murmured. "I wasn't sure if you—"

He closed his mouth over hers. Dream and reality melded seductively as he slipped inside her.

The sunlight was stronger when she lay over him, her head on his heart, her body still pulsing.

"You were saying?"

"Hmm." The effort to open her eyes seemed wasted, so she kept them closed. "Was I?"

"You weren't sure if I what?"

She sifted through her thoughts. "Oh. I wasn't sure if you had any morning appointments."

He continued to comb his fingers through her hair. "It's Sunday," he reminded her. "Office is closed. But I have to run into the hospital and check on Mr. Benson and a couple of other patients. How about you?"

"Nothing much. Some lesson plans, now that I have ten students."

"Ten?" There was more snicker than surprise in his voice.

She shifted then, folding her arms over his chest and resting her chin on them. "I was ambushed at the picnic yesterday."

"Ten students." He grinned at her. "That's quite a commitment. Does that mean you're planning to settle in town again?"

"At least for the summer. I haven't decided whether I'll agree to a fall tour."

So he had the summer to convince her, he thought. "How about dinner?"

She narrowed her eyes. "We haven't even had breakfast yet."

"I mean tonight. We could have our own picnic with the leftovers. Just you and me."

Just you and me. "I'd like that."

"Good. Now why don't we start the day off right?"

After a chuckle, she pressed her lips to his chest. "I thought we already had."

"I meant you could wash my back." Grinning, he sat up and dragged her out of bed.

Vanessa discovered she didn't mind being alone in the house. After Brady dropped her off, she changed into jeans and a short-sleeved sweatshirt. She wanted to spend the day at the piano, planning the lessons, practicing and, if her current mood held, composing.

There had never been enough time for composing on tour, she thought as she tied her hair back. But now she had the summer. Even if ten hours a week would be taken up by lessons, and nearly that many again by planning them, she had plenty of time to indulge in her first love.

Her first love, she repeated with a smile. No, that wasn't composing. That was Brady. He had been her first love. Her first lover. And it was more than probable he would be her last.

He loved her. Or believed he did. He would never have used the words unless he believed it. Nor could she, Vanessa reflected. She had to be sure of what was best for herself, for him, for everyone, before she risked her heart with those three words.

Once she said them, he wouldn't let go again. However much he had mellowed over the years, however responsible he had become, there was still enough of that wild and willful boy in him to have him tossing her over his shoulder and carrying her off. While that fantasy might have its appeal, a daydream appeal, she was too sensible a woman to tolerate it in reality.

The past was done, she thought. Mistakes had been made. She wouldn't risk the future.

She didn't want to think about tomorrow. Not yet. She wanted only to think of, and enjoy, today.

As she started toward the music room, the phone rang. She debated just letting it ring—a habit she'd developed in hotel rooms when she hadn't wanted to be disturbed. On the fifth ring, she gave in and answered.

"Hello."

"Vanessa? Is that you?"

"Yes. Frank?" She recognized the voice of her father's nervous and devoted assistant.

"Yes. It's me—I," he corrected.

Vanessa could all but see him running a soothing hand over the wide bald spot on top of his head. "How are you, Frank?"

"Fine. Fine. Oh—how are you?"

"I'm fine, too." She had to smile. Though she knew her father had tolerated Frank Margoni only because the man would work an eighty-hour week without complaint, Vanessa was fond of him. "How's the new protégé?"

"Protégé—? Oh, you mean Francesco. He's brilliant, really brilliant. Temperamental, of course. Throws things. But then, he's an artist. He's going to be playing at the benefit in Cordina."

"Princess Gabriella's benefit? The Aid to Handicapped Children?"

"Yes."

"I'm sure he'll be wonderful."

"Oh, of course. No doubt. Certainly. But, you see, the princess…she's terribly disappointed that you won't perform. She asked me—" there was an audible gulp "—personally, if I would persuade you to reconsider."

"Frank—"

"You'd stay at the palace, of course. Incredible place."

"Yes, I know. Frank, I haven't decided if I'm going to perform again."

"You know you don't mean that, Vanessa. With your gift—"

"Yes, *my* gift," she said impatiently. "Isn't it about time I realized it is mine?"

He was silent a moment. "I know your father was often insensitive to your personal needs, but that was only because he was so aware of the depth of your talent."

"You don't have to explain him to me, Frank."

"No…no, of course I don't."

She let out a long sigh. It wasn't fair to take out her frustrations on the hapless Frank Margoni, as her father always had. "I understand the position you're in, Frank, but I've already sent my regrets, and a donation, to Princess Gabriella."

"I know. That's why she contacted me. She couldn't get ahold of you. Of course, I'm not officially your manager, but the princess knew our connection, so…"

"If I decide to tour again, Frank, I'll depend on you to manage me."

"I appreciate that, Vanessa." His glum voice brightened perceptibly. "And I realize that you've needed some time for yourself. The last few years—grueling, I know. But this benefit is important." He cleared his throat with three distinct clicks. "And the princess is very stubborn."

Reluctantly Vanessa smiled. "Yes, I know."

"It's only one performance," he continued, sensing a weak spot. "Not even a full concert. You'll have carte blanche on the material. They'd like you to play two pieces, but even one would make such a tremendous difference. Your name on the program would add so much." He paused only long enough to suck in a breath. "It's a very worthy cause."

"When is the benefit?"

"Next month."

She cast her eyes to the ceiling. "Next month. It's practically next month already, Frank."

"The third Saturday in June."

"Three weeks." She let out a long breath. "All right, I'll do it. For you, and for Princess Gabriella."

"Vanessa, I can't tell you how much I—"

"Please don't." She softened the order with a laugh. "It's only one night."

"You can stay in Cordina as long as you like."

"One night," she repeated. "Send me the particulars here. And give my best to Her Highness."

"I will, of course. She'll be thrilled. Everyone will be thrilled. Thank you, Vanessa."

"It's all right, Frank. I'll see you in a few weeks."

She hung up and stood silent and still. Odd, but she

didn't feel tensed and keyed up at the thought of a performance. And a huge one, she considered. The theater complex in Cordina was exquisite and enormous.

What would happen if she clutched in the wings this time? She would get through it somehow. She always had. Perhaps it was fate that she had been called now, when she was teetering on some invisible line. To go forward, or backward, or to stay.

She would have to make a decision soon, she thought as she walked to the piano. She prayed it would be the right one.

She was playing when Brady returned. He could hear the music, romantic and unfamiliar, flowing through the open windows. There was the hum of bees in the flowers, the purr of a lawn mower, and the music. The magic of it. He saw a woman and a young child standing on the sidewalk, listening.

She had left the door open for him. He had only to push the screen to be inside. He moved quietly. It seemed he was stepping through the liquid notes.

She didn't see him. Her eyes were half-closed. There was a smile on her face, a secret smile. As if whatever images she held in her mind were pouring out through her fingers and onto the keys.

The music was slow, dreamy, enriched by an underlying passion. He felt his throat tighten.

When she finished, she opened her eyes and looked at him. Somehow she had known he would be there when the last note died away.

"Hello."

He wasn't sure he could speak. He crossed to her and lifted her hands. "There's magic here. It astonishes me."

"Musician's hands," she said. "Yours are magic. They heal."

"There was a woman standing on the sidewalk with her little boy. I saw them when I drove up. She was listening to you play, and there were tears on her cheeks."

"There's no higher compliment. Did you like it?"

"Very much. What was it called?"

"I don't know. It's something I've been working on for a while. It never seemed right until today."

"You wrote it?" He looked at the music on the piano and saw the neatly written notes on the staff paper. "I didn't know you composed."

"I'm hoping to do more of it." She drew him down to sit beside her. "Aren't you going to kiss me hello?"

"At least." His lips were warm and firm on hers. "How long have you been writing?"

"For several years—when I've managed to sneak the time. Between traveling, rehearsals, practice and performances, it hasn't been much."

"But you've never recorded anything of your own."

"None of it's really finished. I—" She stopped, tilted her head. "How do you know?"

"I have everything you've ever recorded." At her smug smile, he continued. "Not that I actually play any of them." He gave an exaggerated yelp when her elbow connected with his ribs. "I suppose that's the sign of a temperamental artist."

"That's *artiste* to you, philistine."

"Why don't you tell this philistine about your composing?"

"What's to tell?"

"Do you like it?"

"I love it. It's what I like best."

He was playing with her fingers. "Then why haven't you finished anything?" He felt the tension the moment it entered her.

"I told you. There hasn't been time. Touring isn't all champagne and caviar, you know."

"Come on." Keeping her hands in his, he pulled her to her feet.

"Where are we going?"

"In here, where there's a comfortable couch. Sit." He eased her down, then put his hands on her shoulders. His eyes were dark and searching on her face. "Talk to me."

"About what?"

"I wanted to wait until you were recovered." He felt her stiffen, and shook his head. "Don't do that. As your friend, as a doctor, and as the man who loves you, I want to know what made you ill. I want to make sure it never happens again."

"You've already said I've recovered."

"Ulcers can reoccur."

"I didn't have an ulcer."

"Can it. You can deny it all you want—it won't change the facts. I want you to tell me what's been going on the last few years."

"I've been touring. Performing." Flustered, she shook her head. "How did we move from composing to all this?"

"Because one leads to the other, Van. Ulcers are often caused by emotion. By frustrations, angers, resentments that are bottled up to fester instead of being aired out."

"I'm not frustrated." She set her chin. "And you, of all people, should know I don't bottle things up. Ask around, Brady. My temper is renowned on three continents."

He nodded, slowly. "I don't doubt it. But I never once remember you arguing with your father."

She fell silent at that. It was nothing more than the truth.

"Did you want to compose, or did you want to perform?"

"It's possible to do both. It's simply a matter of discipline and priorities."

"And what was your priority?"

Uncomfortable, she shifted. "I think it's obvious it was performing."

"You said something to me before. You said you hated it."

"Hated what?"

"You tell me."

She pulled away to rise and pace the room. It hardly mattered now, she told herself. But he was sitting here, watching her, waiting. Past experience told her he would dig and dig until he uncovered whatever feelings she wanted to hide.

"All right. I was never happy performing."

"You didn't want to play?"

"No," she corrected. "I didn't want to perform. I have to play, just as I have to breathe, but..." She let her words trail off, feeling like an imbecile. "It's stage fright," she snapped. "It's stupid, it's childish, but I've never been able to overcome it."

"It's not stupid or childish." He rose, and would have gone to her, but she was already backing away. "If you hated performing, why did you keep going on? Of course," he said, before she could answer.

"It was important to him." She sat on the arm of a chair, then stood again, unable to settle. "He didn't understand. He'd put his whole life into my career. The idea that I couldn't perform, that it frightened me—"

"That it made you ill."

"I was never ill. I never missed one performance because of health."

"No, you performed despite your health. Damn it, Van, he had no right."

"He was my father. I know he was a difficult man, but I owed him something."

He was a selfish son of a bitch, Brady thought. But he kept his silence. "Did you ever consider therapy?"

Vanessa lifted her hands. "He opposed it. He was very intolerant of weakness. I suppose that was his weakness." She closed her eyes a moment. "You have to understand him, Brady. He was the kind of man who would refuse to believe what was inconvenient for him. And, as far as he was concerned, it just ceased to exist." *Like my mother,* she thought with a weary sigh. "I could never find the way to make him accept or even understand the degree of the phobia."

"I'd like to understand."

She cupped her hands over her mouth a moment, then let them fall. "Every time I would go to the theater, I would tell myself that this time, this time, it wouldn't happen. This time I wouldn't be afraid. Then I would stand in the wings, shaking and sick and miserable. My skin would be clammy, and the nausea would make me dizzy. Once I started playing, it would ease off. By the end I'd be fine, so I would tell myself that the next time…" She shrugged.

He understood, too well. And he hated the idea of

her, of anyone, suffering time after time, year after year. "Did you ever stop to think that he was living his life through you?"

"Yes." Her voice was dull. "He was all I had left. And, right or wrong, I was all he had. The last year, he was so ill, but he never let me stop, never let me care for him. In the end, because he had refused to listen, refused the treatments, he was in monstrous pain. You're a doctor—you know how horrible terminal cancer is. Those last weeks in the hospital were the worst. There was nothing they could do for him that time. So he died a little every day. I went on performing, because he insisted, then flying back to the hospital in Geneva every chance I had. I wasn't there when he died. I was in Madrid. I got a standing ovation."

"Can you blame yourself for that?"

"No. But I can regret." Her eyes were awash with it.

"What do you intend to do now?"

She looked down at her hands, spread her fingers, curled them into her palms. "When I came back here, I was tired. Just worn out, Brady. I needed time—I still do—to understand what I feel, what I want, where I'm going." She stepped toward him and lifted her hands to his face. "I didn't want to become involved with you, because I knew you'd be one more huge complication." Her lip curved a little. "And I was right. But when I woke up this morning in your bed, I was happy. I don't want to lose that."

He took her wrists. "I love you, Vanessa."

"Then let me work through this." She went easily into his arms. "And just be with me."

He pressed a kiss to her hair. "I'm not going anywhere."

Chapter 10

"That was the last patient, Dr. Tucker."

Distracted, Brady looked up from the file on his desk and focused on his nurse. "What?"

"That was the last patient." She was already swinging her purse over her shoulder and thinking about putting her feet up. "Do you want me to lock up?"

"Yeah. Thanks. See you tomorrow." He listened with half an ear to the clink of locks and the rattle of file drawers. The twelve-hour day was almost at an end. The fourth twelve-hour day of the week. Hyattown was a long way from New York, but as far as time served was concerned, Brady had found practicing general medicine in a small town as demanding as being chief resident in a major hospital. Along with the usual stream of patients, hospital rounds and paperwork, an outbreak of chicken pox and strep throat had kept him tied to his stethoscope for over a week.

Half the town was either scratching or croaking, he thought as he settled down to his paperwork. The waiting room had been packed since the end of the holiday weekend. As the only doctor in residence, he'd been taking office appointments, making house calls, doing rounds. And missing meals, he thought ruefully, wishing they still stocked lollipops, rather than balloons and plastic cars, for their younger patients.

He could get by with frozen microwave meals and coffee for a few days. He could even get by with only patches of sleep. But he couldn't get by without Vanessa. He'd barely seen her since the weekend of the wedding—since the weekend they had spent almost exclusively in bed. He'd been forced to cancel three dates. For some women, he thought, that alone would have been enough to have them stepping nimbly out of a relationship.

Better that she knew up front how bad it could get. Being married to a doctor was being married to inconvenience. Canceled dinners, postponed vacations, interrupted sleep.

Closing the file, he rubbed his tired eyes. She was going to marry him, he determined. He was going to see to that. If he ever wangled an hour free to set the stage and ask her.

He picked up the postcard on the corner of his desk. It had a brilliant view of the sun setting on the water, palm trees and sand—and a quickly scrawled note from his father on the back.

"You'd better be having a good time, Dad," Brady mused as he studied it. "Because when you get back, you're going to pay up."

He wondered if Vanessa would enjoy a tropical

honeymoon. Mexico, the Bahamas, Hawaii. Hot, lazy days. Hot, passionate nights. Moving too fast, he reminded himself. You couldn't have a honeymoon until you had a wedding. And you couldn't have a wedding until you'd convinced your woman she couldn't live without you.

He'd promised himself he would take it slowly with Vanessa. Give her all the romance they'd missed the first time around. Long walks in the moonlight. Champagne dinners. Evening drives and quiet talks. But the old impatience pulled at him. If they were married now, he could drag his weary bones home. She'd be there. Perhaps playing the piano. Or curled up in bed with a book. In the next room, there might be a child sleeping. Or two.

Much too fast, Brady warned himself. But he hadn't known, until he'd seen her again, how much he'd wanted that basic and traditional home. The woman he loved, and the children they made between them. Christmas mornings and Sunday afternoons.

Leaning back, he let his eyes close. He could picture it perfectly. Too perfectly, he admitted. He knew his vision left questions unanswered and problems unresolved. They were no longer children who could live on dreams. But he was too tired to be logical. Too needy to be sensible.

Vanessa stood in the doorway and watched him with a mixture of surprise and awe. This was Brady, she reminded herself. Her Brady. But he looked so different here, so professional, in his white lab coat with the framed diplomas and certificates surrounding him. There were files neatly stacked on his desk, and there was an ophthalmoscope in his pocket.

This wasn't the wild youth hell-bent on giving the world a left jab. This was a settled, responsible man who had hundreds of people depending on him. He had already made his niche.

And where was hers? she wondered. He had made his choices and found his place. She was still floundering. Yet, however much she flailed or stumbled, she was always drawn to him. Always back to him.

With a faint smile on her face, she stepped into the office. "You've got another appointment, Dr. Tucker."

"What?" His eyes snapped open. He stared at her as dream and reality merged. She was standing on the other side of his desk, her hair pulled back, in a breezy cotton blouse and slacks.

"I was going to say code blue, or red alert, one of those things you hear on TV, but I didn't know which would fit." She put the basket she carried on the desk.

"I'd settle for 'Hi.'"

"Hi." With a quick laugh, she looked around the office. "I almost didn't come in," she told him. "When I came to the door, you looked so...intimidating."

"Intimidating?"

"Like a doctor. A real doctor," she said on another laugh. "The kind who uses needles and makes terrifying noncommittal noises and scribbles things on charts."

"Hmm," Brady said. "Ah."

"Exactly."

"I can take off the lab coat."

"No, actually, I think I like it. As long as you promise not to whip out a tongue depressor. I saw your nurse as she was leaving. She said you were through for the day."

"Just." The rest of the paperwork would have to wait. "What's in the basket?"

"Dinner—of sorts. Since you wouldn't make a house call, I decided to see if you could fit me into your office schedule."

"It's an amazing coincidence, but I've just had a cancellation." The fatigue simply drained away as he looked at her. Her mouth was naked, and there was a dusting of freckles across the bridge of her nose. "Why don't you sit down and tell me what the problem is?"

"Well." Vanessa sat in the chair in front of the desk. "You see, doctor, I've been feeling kind of light-headed. And absentminded. I forget what I'm doing in the middle of doing it and catch myself staring off into space."

"Hmmm."

"Then there have been these aches. Here," she said, and put a hand on her heart.

"Ah."

"Like palpitations. And at night…" She caught her lower lip between her teeth. "I've had these dreams."

"Really?" He came around to sit on the corner of the desk. There was her scent, whispery light, to flirt with him. "What kind of dreams?"

"They're personal," she said primly.

"I'm a doctor."

"So you say." She grinned at him. "You haven't even asked me to take off my clothes."

"Good point." Rising, he took her hand. "Come with me."

"Where?"

"Your case warrants a full examination."

"Brady—"

"That's Dr. Brady to you." He hit the lights in examining room 1. "Now about that ache."

She gave him a slow, measured look. "Obviously you've been dipping into the rubbing alcohol."

He merely took her by the hips and boosted her onto the examining table. "Relax, sweetie. They don't call me Dr. Feelgood for nothing." He took out his ophthalmoscope and directed the light into her eyes. "Yes, they're definitely green."

"Well, that's a relief."

"You're telling me." He set the instrument aside. "Okay, lose the blouse and I'll test your reflexes."

"Well..." She ran her tongue over her teeth. "As long as I'm here." She let her fingers wander down the buttons, unfastening slowly. Under it she wore sheer blue silk. "I'm not going to have to wear one of those paper things, am I?"

He had to catch his breath as she peeled off the blouse. "I think we can dispense with that. You look to be in excellent health. In fact, I can say without reservation that you look absolutely perfect."

"But I have this ache." She took his hand and pressed it to her breast. "Right now my heart's racing. Feel it?"

"Yeah." Gently he absorbed the feeling of silk and flesh. Her flesh. "I think it's catching."

"My skin's hot," she murmured. "And my legs are weak."

"Definitely catching." With a fingertip he slid a thin silk strap from her shoulder. "You may just have to be quarantined."

"With you, I hope."

He unhooked her slacks. "That's the idea."

When she toed off her sandals, the other strap slithered down her shoulders. Her voice was husky now, and growing breathless. "Do you have a diagnosis?"

He eased the slacks down her hips. "Sounds like the rocking pneumonia and the boogie-woogie flu."

She'd arched up to help him remove her slacks, and now she just stared. "What?"

"Too much Mozart."

"Oh." She twined her arms around his shoulders. It seemed like years since she'd been able to hold him against her. When his lips found the little hollow near her collarbone, she smiled. "Can you help me, Doctor?"

"I'm about to do my damnedest."

His mouth slid over hers. It was like coming home. Her little sigh merged with his as she leaned into him. Dreamily she changed the angle of the kiss and let his taste pour into her. Whatever illness she had, he was exactly the right medicine.

"I feel better already." She nibbled on his lip. "More."

"Van?"

Her heavy eyes opened. While her fingers combed through his hair, she smiled. The light glowed in her eyes. Again he could see himself there, trapped in the misty green. Not lost this time. Found.

Everything he'd ever wanted, ever needed, ever dreamed of, was right here. He felt the teasing pleasure turn to grinding ache in the flash of an instant. With an oath, he dragged her mouth back to his and feasted.

No patience this time. Though the change surprised her, it didn't frighten her. He was her friend, her lover. Her only. There was a desperation and a fervency that thrilled, that demanded, that possessed. As the twin of his emotions rose in her, she pulled him closer.

More, she thought again, but frantically now. She could never get enough of being wanted this wildly. She dragged at his lab coat, even as her teeth scraped over his lip. Desire pumped through her like a drug and had her yanking at his T-shirt before the coat hit the floor. She wanted the feel of his flesh, the heat of it, under her hands. She wanted the taste of that flesh, the succulence of it, under her lips.

The loving he had shown her until now had been calm and sweet and lovely. This time she craved the fire, the dark, the madness.

Control broken, he pushed her back on the narrow padded table, tearing at the wisp of silk. He could tolerate nothing between them now—only flesh against flesh and heart against heart. She was a wonder of slender limbs and subtle curves, of pale skin and delicate bones. He wanted to taste, to touch, to savor every inch.

But her demands were as great as his. She pulled him to her, sliding agilely over him so that her lips could race from his to his throat, his chest, beyond. Rough and greedy, his hands streaked over her, exploiting everywhere, as her questing mouth drove him mad.

His taste. Hot and dark and male, it made her giddy. His form. Firm and hard and muscled, it made her weak. Already damp, his skin slid under her seeking fingers. And she played him deftly, as she would her most passionate concerto.

She feared her heart would burst from its pounding rhythm. Her head spun with it. Her body trembled. Yet there was a power here. Even through the dizziness she felt it swelling in her. How could she have known she could give so much—and take so much?

His pulse thundered under her fingertips. Between his frenzied murmurs, his breath was ragged. She saw the echo of her own passion in his eyes, tasted it when she crushed her mouth to his. For her, she thought as she let herself drown in the kiss. Only for her.

He grasped her hips, fingers digging in. With each breath he took, her scent slammed into his system, potent as any narcotic. Her hair curtained his face, blocking the light and letting him see only her. The faint smile of knowledge was in her eyes. With her every movement, she enticed.

"For God's sake, Van." Her name was part oath, part prayer. If he didn't have her now, he knew he would die from the need.

She shifted, arching back, as she took him into her. For an instant, time stopped, and with it his breath, his thoughts, his life. He saw only her, her hair streaming back like a wild red river, her body pale and gleaming in the harsh light, her face glowing with the power she had only just discovered.

Then it was all speed and sound as she drove them both.

This was glory. She gave herself to it, her arms reaching up before she lost her hands in her own hair. This was wonder. And delight. No symphony had ever been so rousing. No prelude so passionate. Even as sensation shuddered through her, she begged for more.

There was freedom in the greed. Ecstasy in the knowledge that she could take as much as she wanted. Excitement in understanding that she could give just as generously.

Her heart was roaring in her ears. When she groped for his hands, his fingers clamped on to hers. They held tight as they burst over the peak together.

She slid down to him, boneless, her head spinning and her heart racing still. His skin was damp, as hers was, his body as limp. When she pressed her lips to his throat, she could feel the frantic beating of his pulse.

She had done that, Vanessa realized, still dazed. She had taken control and given them both pleasure and passion. She hadn't even had to think, only to act, only to feel. Sailing on this new self-awareness, she propped herself up on an elbow and smiled down at him.

His eyes were closed, his face so completely relaxed that she knew he was next to sleep. His heartbeat, was settling down to a purr, as was hers. Through the contentment, she felt need bloom anew.

"Doctor," she murmured, nibbling at his ear.

"Hmm."

"I feel a lot better."

"Good." He drew in a deep breath, let it out. He figured that was the most exercise he would be able to handle for days. "Remember, your health is my business."

"I'm glad to hear that." She ran a fingertip down his chest experimentally. And felt muscles jump. "Because I think I'm going to need more treatments." She trailed the tip of her tongue down his throat. "I still have this ache."

"Take two aspirin and call me in an hour."

She laughed, a low, husky sound that had his blood humming again. "I thought you were dedicated." Slowly, seductively, she roamed his face with kisses. "God, you taste good." She lowered her mouth to his and sunk in.

"Vanessa." He could easily have floated off to sleep with her gentle stroking. But when her hand slid downward, contentment turned into something more demanding. He opened his eyes and saw that she was smiling at him. She was amused, he noted. And—pun intended—completely on top of things. "You're asking for trouble," he told her.

"Yeah." She lowered her head again to nip at his lip. "But am I going to get it?"

He answered the question to their mutual satisfaction.

"Good God," he said when he could breathe again. "I'm going to have this table bronzed."

"I think I'm cured." She pushed the hair from her face as she slid to the floor. "For now."

Groaning a little, he swung his legs off the table. "Wait till you get my bill."

"I'm looking forward to it." She handed him his pants, then slithered into her teddy. She didn't know about him, but she'd never think the same way about examining room 1 again. "And to think I came by to offer you some ham sandwiches."

"Ham?" His fingers paused on the snap of his jeans. "As in food? Like meat and bread?"

"And potato chips."

His mouth was already watering. "Consider yourself paid in full."

She shook back her hair, certain that if she felt any better she'd be breaking the law. "I take it to mean you're hungry."

"I haven't eaten since breakfast. Chicken pox," he explained as she pulled on her blouse. "If someone was to offer me a ham sandwich, I'd kiss her feet."

She wiggled her toes. "I like the sound of that. I'll go get the basket."

"Hold it." He took her arm. "If we stay in this room,

my nurse is going to get a shock when she opens up tomorrow."

"Okay." She picked up his T-shirt. "Why don't we take it back to my house?" She rubbed the soft cotton against her cheek before handing it to him. "And eat in bed."

"Good thinking."

An hour later, they were sprawled across Vanessa's bed as Brady poured the last drop from a bottle of chardonnay. Vanessa had scoured the house for candles. Now they were set throughout the room, flickering while Chopin played quietly on the bedside radio.

"That was the best picnic I've had since I was thirteen and raided the Girl Scout overnight jamboree."

She scrounged for the last potato chip, then broke it judiciously in half. "I heard about that." There hadn't been time for Girl Scouts with her training. "You were always rotten."

"Hey, I got to see Betty Jean Baumgartner naked. Well, almost naked," he corrected. "She had on a training bra and panties, but at thirteen that's pretty erotic stuff."

"A rotten creep."

"It was hormones." He sipped his wine. "Lucky for you, I've still got plenty." With a satisfied sigh, he leaned back against the pillow. "Even if they're aging."

Feeling foolish and romantic, she bent over to kiss his knee. "I've missed you, Brady."

He opened his eyes again. "I've missed you, too. I'm sorry this week's been so messed up."

"I understand."

He reached out to twine a lock of her hair around

his finger. "I hope you do. Office hours alone doubled this week."

"I know. Chicken pox. Two of my students are down with it. And I heard you delivered a baby—boy, seven pounds six ounces—took out a pair of tonsils… Is it pair or set?" she wondered. "Sewed up a gash in Jack's arm, and splinted a broken finger. All that being above and beyond the day-to-day sniffles, sneezes, aches and exams."

"How do you know?"

"I have my sources." She touched his cheek. "You must be tired."

"I was before I saw you. Anyway, it'll ease off when Dad gets back. Did you get a postcard?"

"Yes, just today." She settled back with her wine. "Palm trees and sand, mariachi players and sunsets. It sounds like they're having a wonderful time."

"I hope so, because I intend to switch places with them when they get back."

"Switch places?"

"I want to go away with you somewhere, Van." He took her hand, kissed it. "Anywhere you want."

"Away?" Her nerves began to jump. "Why?"

"Because I want to be alone with you, completely alone, as we've never had the chance to be."

She had to swallow. "We're alone now."

He set his wine aside, then hers. "Van, I want you to marry me."

She couldn't claim surprise. She had known, once he had used the word *love,* that marriage would follow. Neither did she feel fear, as she'd been certain she would. But she did feel confusion.

They had talked of marriage before, when they'd

been so young and marriage had seemed like such a beautiful dream. She knew better now. She knew marriage was work and commitment and a shared vision.

"Brady, I—"

"This isn't the way I planned it," he interrupted. "I'd wanted it to be very traditional—to have the ring and a nicely poetic speech. I don't have a ring, and all I can tell you is that I love you. I always have, I always will."

"Brady." She pressed his hand to her cheek. Nothing he could have said would have been more poetic. "I want to be able to say yes. I didn't realize until just this moment how much I want that."

"Then say it."

Her eyes were wide and wet when they lifted to his. "I can't. It's too soon. No," she said, before he could explode. "I know what you're going to say. We've known each other almost our whole lives. It's true. But in some ways it's just as true that we only met a few weeks ago."

"There was never anyone but you," he said slowly. "Every other woman I got close to was only a substitute. You were a ghost who haunted me everywhere I went, who faded away every time I tried to reach out and touch."

Nothing could have moved her or unnerved her more. "My life's turned upside down since I came back here. I never thought I would see you again—and I thought that if I did it wouldn't matter, that I wouldn't feel. But it does matter, and I do feel, and that only makes it more difficult."

She was saying almost what he wanted to hear. Almost. "Shouldn't that make it easier?"

"No. I wish it did. I can't marry you, Brady, until I look into the mirror and recognize myself."

"I don't know what the hell you're talking about."

"No, you can't." She dragged her hands through her hair. "I barely do myself. All I know is that I can't give you what you want. I may never be able to."

"We're good together, Van." He had to fight to keep from holding too tight. "Damn it, you know that."

"Yes." She was hurting him. She could hardly bear it. "Brady, there are too many things I don't understand about myself. Too many questions I don't have the answers to. Please, I can't talk about marriage, about lifetimes, until I do."

"My feelings aren't going to change."

"I hope not."

He reeled himself back, slowly. "You're not going to get away from me this time, Van. If you cut and run, I'll come after you. If you try to sneak off, I'll be right there."

Pride rose instantly to wage war with regret. "You make that sound like a threat."

"It is."

"I don't like threats, Brady." She tossed her hair back in a gesture as much challenge as annoyance. "You should remember I don't tolerate them."

"And you should remember I make good on them." Very deliberately, he took her by the shoulders and pulled her against him. "You belong to me, Vanessa. Sooner or later you're going to get that through your head."

The thrill raced up her spine, as it always did when she saw that dangerous light in his eyes. But her chin came up. "I belong to myself first, Brady. Or I intend to. You'll have to get that through your head. Then, maybe, we'll have something."

"We have something now." When his mouth came to hers, she tasted the anger, the frustration, and the need. "You can't deny it."

"Then let it be enough." Her eyes were as dark and intent as his. "I'm here, with you. While I am, there's nothing and no one else." Her arms went around him, enfolding. "Let it be enough."

But it wasn't enough. Even as he rolled onto her, as his mouth fastened hungrily on hers, as his blood fired, he knew it wasn't enough.

In the morning, when she woke—alone, with his scent on sheets that were already growing cold—she was afraid it would never be.

Chapter 11

Nice, very nice, Vanessa thought as Annie worked her way through one of her beloved Madonna's compositions. She had to admit it was a catchy tune, bold and sly by turns. She'd had to simplify it a bit for Annie's inexperienced fingers, but the heart was still there. And that was what counted.

Perhaps the improvement in Annie's technique wasn't radical, but there was improvement. And, as far as enthusiasm went, Annie Crampton was her prize student.

Her own attitude had changed, as well Vanessa admitted. She hadn't known she would enjoy quite so much influencing young hearts and minds with music. She was making a difference here—perhaps only a small one so far, but a difference.

Then there was the added benefit of the lessons helping her keep her mind off Brady. At least for an hour or two every day.

"Well done, Annie."

"I played it all the way through." The wonder on Annie's face was worth the few sour notes she had hit. "I can do it again."

"Next week." Vanessa picked up Annie's book just as she heard the front screen slam. "I want you to work on this next lesson. Hi, Joanie."

"I heard the music." She shifted Lara to her other hip. "Annie Crampton, was that you playing?"

Braces flashed. "I played it all the way through. Miss Sexton said I did a good job."

"And you did. I'm impressed—especially because she could never teach me anything beyond 'Heart and Soul.'"

Vanessa placed a hand on Annie's head. "Mrs. Knight didn't practice."

"I do. And my mom says I've learned more in three weeks than I did in three months up at the music store." She flashed a final grin as she gathered up her books. "And it's more fun, too. See you next week, Miss Sexton."

"I really was impressed," Joanie said as Annie slammed out the front door.

"She has good hands." She held out her own for the baby. "Hello, Lara."

"Maybe you could give her lessons one day."

"Maybe." She cuddled the baby.

"So, other than Annie, how are the lessons going? You're up to, what—?"

"Twelve students. And that's my absolute limit." She pressed her nose against Lara's and had the baby giggling. "Absolutely. But, all in all, they're going fairly well. I've learned to check students' hands before they sit at the piano. I never did figure out what Scott Snooks smeared on the keys."

"What did it look like?"

"Green." She laughed and bounced Lara. "Now we have an inspection before each lesson."

"If you can teach Scott Snooks anything other than murder and mayhem, you're a miracle worker."

"That's the challenge." And she was beginning to enjoy it. "If you've got time, I can defrost a can of lemonade."

"Miss Domesticity." Joanie grinned. "No, really, I only have a couple of minutes. Don't you have another student coming?"

"Saved by the chicken pox." With Lara in tow, Vanessa moved to the living room. "What's your hurry?"

"I just stopped by to see if you needed anything in town. Dad and Loretta will be back in a few hours, and I want to see them. Meanwhile, I've got three dozen errands to run. Hardware store, grocery store, the lumber place. I still can't believe Jack sweet-talked me into that one." She plopped into a chair. "I've spent most of the morning picking up behind Lara the Wrecking Crew as she single-handedly totaled the house. And to think I was thrilled when she took her first step."

"I could use some sheet music." Vanessa gently removed Lara's grasping fingers from her necklace. "I tell you what, I'll write down the titles for you, and in exchange I'll babysit."

Joanie shook her head and rubbed a hand over her ear. "Excuse me, did you say babysit?"

"Yes. As in you-can-leave-Lara-with-me-for-a-couple-of-hours."

"A couple of hours," she repeated slowly. "Do you mean I can go to the mall, alone, by myself?"

"Well, if you'd rather not—"

Joanie let out a whoop as she jumped up to kiss Vanessa and Lara in turn. "Lara, baby, I love you. Goodbye."

"Joanie, wait." Laughing, Vanessa sprang up to grab her arm. "I haven't written down the titles for the sheet music."

"Oh, yeah. Right. I guess I got a little too excited." She blew her hair out of her eyes. "I haven't been shopping by myself in...I forget." Her smile faded to a look of dismay. "I'm a terrible mother. I was happy about leaving her behind. No, not happy. Thrilled. Ecstatic. Delirious. I'm a terrible mother."

"No, you're a crazy person, but you're a wonderful mother."

Joanie steadied herself. "You're right, it was just the thrill of going to the hardware store without a stroller and a diaper bag that went to my head. Are you sure you can handle it?"

"We'll have a great time."

"Of course you will." Keen-eyed, she surveyed the living room. "Maybe you should move anything important up a couple of feet. And nail it down."

"We'll be fine." She set Lara on the floor and handed her a fashion magazine to peruse—and tear up. "See?"

"Okay...I nursed her before I left home, and there's an emergency bottle of apple juice in her diaper bag. Can you change a diaper?"

"I've seen it done before. How hard can it be?"

"Well, if you're sure you don't have anything you have to do."

"My evening is free. When the newlyweds get home, I only have to walk a half a block to see them."

"I guess Brady will be coming by."

"I don't know."

Joanie kept her eye on Lara as the baby pushed herself up and toddled to the coffee table. "Then it hasn't been my imagination."

"What?"

"That there's been a lot of tension between you two the last week or so."

"You're stalling, Joanie."

"Maybe—but I am interested. The couple of times I've seen Brady recently, he's been either snarling or distracted. I don't want you to tell me it was wishful thinking when I hoped you two would get back together."

"He asked me to marry him."

"He— Wow! Oh, that's wonderful! That's terrific!" As Joanie launched herself into Vanessa's arms, Lara began to bang on the table and squeal. "See, even Lara's excited."

"I said no."

"What?" Slowly, Joanie stepped back. "You said no?"

She turned away from the stunned disappointment in Joanie's face. "It's too soon for all of this, Joanie. I've only been back a few weeks, and so much has happened. My mother, your father…" She walked over to move a vase out of Lara's reach. "When I got here, I wasn't even sure how long I would stay, a couple of weeks, maybe a month. I've been considering a tour next spring."

"But that doesn't mean you can't have a personal life. If you want one."

"I don't know what I want." Feeling helpless, she looked back at Joanie. "Marriage is… I don't even know what it means, so how can I consider marrying Brady?"

"But you love him."

"Yes, I think I do." She lifted her hands, fingers spread. "I don't want to make the same mistake my parents did. I need to be sure we both want the same things."

"What do you want?"

"I'm still figuring it out."

"You'd better figure fast. If I know my brother, he won't give you a lot of time."

"I'll take what I need this time." Before Joanie could argue, she shook her head. "You'd better go if you want to get back before my mother and Ham come home."

"Oh, you're right. I'll go get the diaper bag." She paused at the door. "I know we're already stepsisters, but I'm still holding out for sisters-in-law."

Brady knew he was asking for more grief when he started up the walk to Vanessa's house. During the past week, he had tried to keep his distance. When the woman you loved refused to marry you, it didn't do much for your ego.

He wanted to believe she was just being stubborn, and that backing off and playing it light would bring her around. But he was afraid it went much deeper than that. She'd taken a stand. He could walk away, or he could pound down her door. It wouldn't make any difference.

Either way, he needed to see her.

He knocked on the wooden frame of the screen but got no answer. Hardly surprising, he thought, as the banging and crashing from inside would have drowned out any other sound. Maybe she was in a temper, he thought hopefully. Enraged with herself for turning her back on her chance at happiness.

The image appealed to him. He was almost whistling when he opened the screen and walked down the hall.

Whatever he'd been expecting, it hadn't been his niece gleefully banging pots and pans together on the floor while Vanessa, dusted with flour, stood at the counter. Spotting him, Lara hoisted a stainless steel lid and brought it down with a satisfied bang.

"Hi."

With a hand full of celery, Vanessa turned. She expected her heart to do a quick flip-flop when she saw him. It always did. But she didn't smile. Neither did he.

"Oh. I didn't hear you come in."

"I'm not surprised." He reached down to pick up Lara and give her a quick swing. "What are you doing?"

"Babysitting." She rubbed more flour on her nose. "Joanie had to go into town, so I volunteered to watch Lara for a couple of hours."

"She's a handful, isn't she?"

Vanessa blew out a weary breath. She couldn't bear to think about the mess they had left in the living room. "She likes it in here."

He set the baby down, gave her padded bottom a light pat and sent her off to play with a small tower of canned goods. "Wait until she figures out how to rip the labels off. Got anything to drink?"

"Lara's got a bottle of apple juice."

"I wouldn't want to deprive her."

"There's a can of lemonade in the freezer." She went back to chopping celery. "If you want it, you'll have to make it yourself. My hands are full."

"So I see." He opened the freezer. "What are you making?"

"A mess." She brought the knife down with a thunk. "I thought since my mother and Ham were due back soon it would be nice to have a casserole or something. Joanie's already done so much, I wanted to try to—" She set the knife down in disgust. "I'm no good at this. I'm just no good at it. I've never cooked a meal in my life." She whirled as Brady came to the sink to run cold water into a pitcher. "I'm a grown woman, and if it wasn't for room service and prepackaged meals I'd starve to death."

"You make a great ham sandwich."

"I'm not joking, Brady."

With a wooden spoon, he began to stir the lemonade. "Maybe you should be."

"I came in here thinking I'd try to put myself into this little fantasy. What if I were a doctor's wife?"

He stopped stirring to look at her. "What if you were?"

"What if he were coming home after taking appointments and doing hospital rounds all day? Wouldn't I want to fix him a meal, something we could sit down to together, something we could talk over? Isn't that something he would want? Expect?"

"Why don't you ask him?"

"Damn it, Brady, don't you see? I couldn't make it work."

"All I see is that you're having trouble putting—" He leaned forward to look at the disarray on the counter. "What is this?"

Her mouth moved into a pout. "It's supposed to be a tuna casserole."

"You're having trouble putting a tuna casserole to-gether. And, personally, I hope you never learn how to do it."

"That's not the point."

Struck by tenderness, he brushed at a streak of flour on her cheek. "What is the point?"

"It's a little thing, maybe even a stupid thing. But if I can't even do this—" she shoved and sent an onion scampering down the counter "—how can I work out the bigger ones?"

"Do you think I want to marry you so that I can have a hot meal every night?"

"No. Do you think I want to marry you and feel inept and useless?"

Truly exasperated, he gestured toward the counter. "Because you don't know what to do with a can of tuna?"

"Because I don't know how to be a wife." When her voice rose, she struggled to calm it. Perhaps Lara was too young, and too interested in her pans and cans, to detect an argument, but Vanessa had lived through too many of her own. "And, as much as I care for you, I don't know if I want to be. There's one thing I do well, Brady, and that's my music."

"No one's asking you to give that up, Van."

"And when I go on tour? When I'm gone weeks at a time, when I have to devote endless hours to rehearsals and practicing? What kind of marriage would we have, Brady, in between performances?"

"I don't know." He looked down at his niece, who was contentedly placing cans inside of pots. "I didn't know you were seriously considering going on tour again."

"I have to consider it. It's been a part of my life for too long not to." Calmer now, she went back to dicing vegetables. "I'm a musician, Brady, the same way you're a doctor. What I do doesn't save lives, but it does enrich them."

He pushed an impatient hand through his dark hair. He was in the business of soothing doubts and fears, as much as he was in the business of healing bodies. Why couldn't he soothe Vanessa's?

"I know what you do is important, Van. I admire it. I admire you. What I don't see is why your talent would have to be an obstacle to our being together."

"It's just one of them," she murmured.

He took her arm, slowly turning her to face him. "I want to marry you. I want to have children with you and make a home for them. We can do that here, where we both belong, if you just trust me."

"I need to trust myself first." She took a bracing breath. "I leave for Cordina next week."

His hand slid away from her arm. "Cordina?"

"Princess Gabriella's annual benefit."

"I've heard of it."

"I've agreed to give a performance."

"I see." Because he needed to do something, he opened a cupboard and took out a glass. "And when did you agree?"

"I signed almost two weeks ago."

His fingers tensed on the glass. "And didn't mention it."

"No, I didn't mention it." She wiped her hands on her thighs. "With everything that was happening between us, I wasn't sure how you would react."

"Were you going to wait until you were leaving for

the airport, or were you just going to send me a post-card when you got there? Damn it, Van." He barely controlled the urge to smash the glass against the wall. "What the hell kind of games have you been playing with me? Was all this just killing time, lighting up an old flame?"

She went pale, but her voice was strong. "You know better."

"All I know is that you're leaving."

"It's only a single performance, a few days."

"And then?"

She turned to look out the window. "I don't know. Frank, my manager, is anxious to put a tour together. That's in addition to some special performances I've been asked to do."

"In addition," he repeated. "You came here with an ulcer because you could barely make yourself go out onstage, because you pushed yourself too far too often. And you're already talking about going back and doing it again."

"It's something I have to work out for myself."

"Your father—"

"Is dead," she cut in. "He can't influence me to per-form. I hope you won't try to influence me not to." She took a calming breath, but it didn't help. "I don't believe I pushed myself too far. I did what I needed to do. All I want is the chance to decide what that is."

As the war inside him continued, Brady wondered if there could be a victor. Or if there would only be vic-tims. "You've been thinking about going back, start-ing with Cordina, but you never talked to me about it."

"No. However selfish it sounds, Brady, this is some-thing I needed to decide for myself. I realize it's unfair for me to ask you to wait. So I won't." She closed her eyes tight, then opened them again. "Whatever happens, I want you to know that the last few weeks, with you, have meant everything to me."

"The hell with that." It was too much like a goodbye. He yanked her against him. "You can go to Cordina, you can go anywhere, but you won't forget me. You won't forget this."

There was fury in the kiss. And desperation. She fought neither. How could she when their mirror images raged within her? She thought that if her life was to end that instant, she would have known nothing but this wild wanting.

"Brady." She brought her hands to his face. When her brow rested against his, she drew a deep breath. "There has to be more than this. For both of us."

"There is more." With his thumbs under her jaw, he tilted her head back. "You know there is."

"I made a promise to myself today. That I would take the time to think over my life, every year of it, every moment that I remembered that seemed important. And when I had done that, I would make the right decision. No more hesitations or excuses or doubts. But for now you have to let me go."

"I let you go once before." Before she could shake her head, he tightened his grip. "You listen to me. If you leave, like this, I won't spend the rest of my life wishing for you. I'll be damned if you'll break my heart a second time."

As they stood close, their eyes locked on each other's, Joanie strolled into the room.

"Well, some babysitters." With a laugh, she plucked Lara up and hugged her. "I can't believe I actually missed this monster. Sorry it took so long." She smiled at Lara and kept babbling as she fought her way through the layers of tension. "There was a line a mile long at the grocery." She glanced down at the scattered pots and canned goods. "It looks like she kept you busy."

"She was fine," Vanessa managed. "She ate about half a box of crackers."

"I thought she'd gained a couple pounds. Hi, Brady. Good timing." His one-word comment had her rolling her eyes. "I meant I'm glad you're here. Look who I ran into outside." She turned just as Ham and Loretta walked in, arm in arm. "Don't they look great?" Joanie wanted to know. "So tanned. I know tans aren't supposed to be healthy, but they look so good."

"Welcome back." Vanessa smiled, but stayed where she was. "Did you have a good time?"

"It was wonderful." Loretta set a huge straw bag down on the table. There was warm color on her cheeks, on her bare arms. And, Vanessa noted, that same quiet happiness in her eyes. "It has to be the most beautiful place on earth, all that white sand and clear water. We even went snorkeling."

"Never seen so many fish," Ham said as he dropped yet another straw bag on the table.

"Ha!" Loretta gave him a telling look. "He was looking at all those pretty legs under water. Some of those women down there wear next to nothing." Then she grinned. "The men, too. I stopped looking the other way after the first day or two."

"Hour or two," Ham corrected.

She only laughed and dug into her bag. "Look here, Lara. We brought you a puppet." She dangled the colorful dancer from its strings.

"Among a few dozen other things," Ham put in. "Wait until you see the pictures. I even rented one of those underwater cameras and got shots of the, ah, fish."

"It's going to take us weeks to unpack it all. I can't even think about it." With a sigh, Loretta sat down at the table. "Oh, and the silver jewelry. I suppose I went a little wild with it."

"Very wild," Ham added with a wink.

"I want you both to pick out the pieces you like best," she said to Vanessa and Joanie. "Once we find them. Brady, is that lemonade?"

"Right the first time." He poured her a glass. "Welcome home."

"Wait until you see your sombrero."

"My sombrero?"

"It's red and silver—about ten feet across." She grinned over at Ham. "I couldn't talk him out of it. Oh, it's good to be home." She glanced at the counter. "What's all this?"

"I was…" Vanessa sent a helpless look at the mess she'd made. "I was going to try to fix some dinner. I…I thought you might not want to fuss with cooking your first night back."

"Good old American food." Ham took the puppet to dangle it for the giggling Lara. "Nothing would hit the spot better right now."

"I haven't exactly—"

Catching her drift, Joanie moved over to the counter. "Looks like you were just getting started. Why don't I give you a hand?"

Vanessa stepped back, bumped into Brady, then moved away again. "I'll be back in a minute."

She hurried out and took the stairs at a dash. In her

room, she sat on the bed and wondered if she was losing her mind. Surely it was a close thing when a tuna casserole nearly brought her to tears.

"Van." Loretta stood with her hand on the knob. "May I come in a minute?"

"I was coming back down. I just—" She started to rise, then sat again. "I'm sorry. I don't want to spoil your homecoming."

"You haven't. You couldn't." After a moment, she took a chance. Closing the door, she walked over to sit on the bed beside her daughter. "I could tell you were upset when we came in. I thought it was just because... well, because of me."

"No. No, not entirely."

"Would you like to talk about it?"

She hesitated so long that Loretta was afraid she wouldn't speak at all.

"It's Brady. No, it's me," Vanessa corrected, impatient with herself. "He wants me to marry him, and I can't. There are so many reasons, and he can't understand. *Won't* understand. I can't cook a meal or do laundry or any of the things that Joanie just breezes right through."

"Joanie's a wonderful woman," Loretta said carefully. "But she's different from you."

"I'm the one who's different, from Joanie, from you, from everyone."

Lightly, afraid to go too far, Loretta touched her hair. "It's not a crime or an abnormality not to know how to cook."

"I know." But that only made her feel more foolish. "It's simply that I wanted to feel self-sufficient and ended up feeling inadequate."

"I never taught you how to cook, or how to run a household. Part of that was because you were so involved with your music, and there wasn't really time. But another reason, maybe the true one, is that I didn't want to. I wanted to have that all to myself. The house, the running of it, was all I really had to fulfill me." She gave a little sigh as she touched Vanessa's rigid arm. "But we're not really talking about casseroles and laundry, are we?"

"No. I feel pressured, by what Brady wants. Maybe by who he wants. Marriage, it sounds so lovely. But—"

"But you grew up in a household where it wasn't." With a nod, Loretta took Vanessa's hand. "It's funny how blind we can be. All the time you were growing up, I never thought what was going on between your father and me affected you. And of course it did."

"It was your life."

"It was our lives," Loretta told her. "Van, while we were away, Ham and I talked about all of this. He wanted me to explain everything to you. I didn't agree with him until right now."

"Everyone's downstairs."

"There have been enough excuses." She couldn't sit, so she walked over to the window. The marigolds were blooming, a brilliant orange and yellow against the smug-faced pansies.

"I was very young when I married your father. Eighteen." She gave a little shake of her head. "Lord, it seems like a lifetime ago. And certainly like I was another person. How he swept me off my feet! He was almost thirty then, and had just come back after being in Paris, London, New York, all those exciting places."

"His career had floundered," Vanessa said quietly. "He'd never talk about it, but I've read—and, of course, there were others who loved to talk about his failures."

"He was a brilliant musician. No one could take that away from him." Loretta turned. There was a sadness in her eyes now, lingering. "But he took it away from himself. When his career didn't reach the potential he expected, he turned his back on it. When he came back home, he was troubled, moody, impatient."

She took a moment to gather her courage, hoping she was doing the right thing. "I was a very simple girl, Van. I had led a very simple life. Perhaps that was what appealed to him at first. His sophistication—his, well, worldliness—appealed to me. Dazzled me. We made a mistake—as much mine as his. I was overwhelmed by him, flattered, infatuated. And I got pregnant."

Shock robbed Vanessa of speech as she stared at her mother. With an effort, she rose. "Me? You married because of me?"

"We married because we looked at each other and saw only what we wanted to see. You were the result of that. I want you to know that when you were conceived, you were conceived in what we both desperately believed was love. Maybe, because we did believe it, it was love. It was certainly affection and caring and need."

"You were pregnant," Vanessa said quietly. "You didn't have a choice."

"There is always a choice." Loretta stepped forward, drawing Vanessa's gaze to hers. "You were not a mistake or an inconvenience or an excuse. You were the best parts of us, and we both knew it. There were no scenes or recriminations. I was thrilled to be carrying his child, and he was just as happy. The first year we were married, it was good. In many ways, it was even beautiful."

"I don't know what to say. I don't know what to feel."

"You were the best thing that ever happened to me, or to your father. The tragedy was that we were the worst thing that ever happened to each other. You weren't responsible for that. We were. Whatever happened afterward, having you made all the difference."

"What did happen?"

"My parents died, and we moved into this house. The house I had grown up in, the house that belonged to me. I didn't understand then how bitterly he resented that. I'm not sure he did, either. You were three then. Your father was restless. He resented being here, and couldn't bring himself to face the possibility of failure if he tried to pick up his career again. He began to teach you, and almost overnight it seemed that all of the passion, all of the energy he had had, went into making you into the musician, the performer, the star he felt he would never be again."

Blindly she turned to the window again. "I never stopped him. I never tried. You seemed so happy at the piano. The more promise you showed the more bitter he became. Not toward you, never toward you. But toward the situation, and, of course, toward me. And I toward him. You were the one good thing we had ever done together, the one thing we could both love completely. But it wasn't enough to make us love each other. Can you understand that?"

"Why did you stay together?"

"I'm not really sure. Habit. Fear. The small hope that somehow we would find out we really did love each other. There were too many fights. Oh, I know how they used to upset you. When you were older, a teenager, you used to run from the house just to get away from the arguing. We failed you, Van. Both of us. And, though I know he did things that were selfish, even unforgivable, I failed you more, because I closed my eyes to them. Instead of making things right, I looked for an escape. And I found it with another man."

She found the courage to face her daughter again. "There is no excuse. Your father and I were no longer intimate, were barely even civil, but there were other alternatives open to me. I had thought about divorce, but that takes courage, and I was a coward. Suddenly there was someone who was kind to me, someone who found me attractive and desirable. Because it was forbidden, because it was wrong, it was exciting."

Vanessa felt the tears burn the back of her eyes. She had to know, to understand. "You were lonely."

"Oh, God, yes." Loretta's voice was choked. She pressed her lips together. "It's no excuse—"

"I don't want excuses. I want to know how you felt."

"Lost," she whispered. "Empty. I felt as though my life were over. I wanted someone to need me again, to hold me. To say pretty things to me, even if they were lies." She shook her head, and when she spoke again her voice was stronger. "It was wrong, Vanessa, as wrong as it was for your father and I to rush together without looking closely." She came back to the bed, took Vanessa's hand. "I want it to be different for you. It will be different. Holding back from something that's right for you is just as foolish as rushing into something that's wrong."

"And how do I know the difference?"

"You will." She smiled a little. "It's taken me most of my life to understand that. With Ham, I knew."

"It wasn't." She was afraid to ask. "It wasn't Ham that you... He wasn't the one."

"All those years ago? Oh, no. He would never have betrayed Emily. He loved her. It was someone else. He wasn't in town long, only a few months. I suppose that made it easier for me somehow. He was a stranger, someone who didn't know me, didn't care. When I broke it off, he moved on."

"You broke it off? Why?"

Of all the things that had gone before, Loretta knew this would be the most difficult. "It was the night of your prom. I'd been upstairs with you. Remember, you were so upset?"

"He had Brady arrested."

"I know." She tightened her grip on Vanessa's hand. "I swear to you, I didn't know it then. I finally left you alone because, well, you needed to be alone. I was thinking about how I was going to give Brady Tucker a piece of my mind when I got ahold of him. I was still upset when your father came home. But he was livid, absolutely livid. That's when it all came out. He was furious because the sheriff had let Brady go, because Ham had come in and raised holy hell."

She let Vanessa's hands go to press her fingers to her eyes. "I was appalled. He'd never approved of Brady— I knew that. But he wouldn't have approved of anyone who interfered with his plans for you. Yet this—this was so far beyond anything I could imagine. The Tuckers were our friends, and anyone with eyes could see that you and Brady were in love. I admit I had worried about whether you would make love, but we'd talked about it, and you'd seemed very sensible. In any case, your father was raging, and I was so angry, so incensed by his insensitivity, that I lost control. I told him what I had been trying to hide for several weeks. I was pregnant."

"Pregnant," Vanessa repeated. "You— Oh, God."

Loretta sprang up to pace the room. "I thought he would go wild, but instead he was calm. Deadly calm." There was no use telling her daughter what names he had called her in that soft, controlled voice. "He said that there was no question about our remaining together. He would file for divorce. And would take you. The more I shouted, begged, threatened, the calmer he became. He would take you because he was the one who would give you the proper care. I was—well, it was obvious what I was. He already had tickets for Paris. Two tickets. I hadn't known about it, but he had been planning to take you away in any case. I was to say nothing, do nothing to stop him, or he would drag me through a custody suit that he would win when it came out that I was carrying another man's bastard." She began to weep then, silently. "If I didn't agree, he would wait until the child was born and file charges against me as an unfit mother. He swore he would make it his life's work to take that child, as well. And I would have nothing."

"But you...he couldn't..."

"I had barely been out of this county, much less the state. I didn't know what he could do. All I knew was that I was going to lose one child, and perhaps two. You were going to go to Paris, see all those wonderful things, play on all those fabulous stages. You would be someone, have something." Her cheeks drenched, she turned back. "As God is my witness, Vanessa, I don't know if I agreed because I thought it was what you would want, or because I was afraid to do anything else."

"It doesn't matter." She rose and went to her mother. "It doesn't matter anymore."

"I knew you would hate me—"

"No, I don't." She put her arms around Loretta and brought her close. "I couldn't. The baby," she murmured. "Will you tell me what you did?"

Grief, fresh and vital, swam through her. "I miscarried, just shy of three months. I lost both of you, you see. I never had all those babies I'd once dreamed of."

"Oh, Mom." Vanessa rocked as she let her own tears fall. "I'm sorry. I'm so sorry. It must have been terrible for you. Terribly hard."

With her cheek against Vanessa's, she held tight. "There wasn't a day that went by that I didn't think of you, that I didn't miss you. If I had it to do over—"

But Vanessa shook her head. "No, we can't take the past back. We'll start right now."

Chapter 12

She sat in her dressing room, surrounded by flowers, the scent and the color of them. She barely noticed them. She'd hoped, perhaps foolishly, that one of the luscious bouquets, one of the elegant arrangements, had been sent by Brady.

But she had known better.

He had not come to see her off at the airport. He had not called to wish her luck, or to tell her he would miss her while she was gone. Not his style, Vanessa thought as she studied her reflection in the mirror. It never had been. When Brady Tucker was angry, he was angry. He made no polite, civilized overtures. He just stayed mad.

He had the right, she admitted. The perfect right.

She had left him, after all. She had gone to him, given herself to him, made love to him with all the passion and promise a woman could bring to a man. But she had held back the words. And, by doing so, she had held back herself.

Because she was afraid, she thought now. Of making that dreadful, life-consuming mistake. He would never understand that her caution was as much for him as it was for herself.

She understood now, after listening to her mother. Mistakes could be made for the best of reasons, or the worst of them. It was too late to ask her father, to try to understand his feelings, his reasons.

She only hoped it wasn't too late for herself.

Where were they now, those children who had loved so fiercely and so unwisely? Brady had his life, his skill, and his answers. His family, his friends, his home. From the rash, angry boy he had been had grown a man of integrity and purpose.

And she? Vanessa stared down at her hands, the long, gifted fingers spread. She had her music. It was all she had ever really had that belonged only to her.

Yes, she understood now, perhaps more than she wanted to, her mother's failings, her father's mistakes. They had, in their separate ways, loved her. But that love hadn't made them a family. Nor had it made any of the three of them happy.

So while Brady was setting down his roots in the fertile soil of the town where they had both been young, she was alone in a dressing room filled with flowers, waiting to step onto another stage.

At the knock on her door, she watched the reflection in the dressing room mirror smile. The show started long before the key light clicked on.

"Entrez."

"Vanessa." The Princess Gabriella, stunning in blue silk, swept inside.

"Your Highness." Before she could rise and make her curtsy, Gabriella was waving her to her seat in a gesture that was somehow imperious and friendly all at once.

"Please, don't get up. I hope I'm not disturbing you."

"Of course not. May I get you some wine?"

"If you're having some." Though her feet ached after a backbreaking day on her feet, she only sighed a little as she took a chair. She had been born royal, and royalty was taught not to complain. "It's been so hectic today, I haven't had a chance to see you, make certain you've been comfortable."

"No one could be uncomfortable in the palace, Your Highness."

"Gabriella, please." She accepted the glass of wine. "We're alone." She gave brief consideration to slipping out of her shoes, but thought better of it. "I wanted to thank you again for agreeing to play tonight. It's so important."

"It's always a pleasure to play in Cordina." The lights around the mirror sent the dozens of bugle beads on Vanessa's white dress dancing. "I'm honored that you wanted to include me."

Gabriella gave a quick laugh before she sipped. "You're annoyed that I bothered you while you were on vacation." She tossed back her fall of red-gold hair. "And I don't blame you. But for this, I've learned to be rude—and ruthless."

Vanessa had to smile. Royalty or not, the Princess Gabriella was easy to be with. "Honored and annoyed, then. I hope tonight's benefit is a tremendous success."

"It will be." She refused to accept less. "Eve— You know my sister-in-law?"

"Yes, I've met Her Highness several times."

"She's American—and therefore pushy. She's been a tremendous help to me."

"Your husband, he is also American?"

Gabriella's topaz eyes lit. "Yes. Reeve is also pushy. This year we involved our children quite a bit, so it's been even more of a circus than usual. My brother, Alexander, was away for a few weeks, but he returned in time to be put to use."

"You are ruthless with your family, Gabriella."

"It's best to be ruthless with those you love." She saw something, some cloud, come and go in Vanessa's eyes. She would get to that. "Hannah apologizes for not coming backstage before your performance. Bennett is fussing over her."

"Your younger brother is entitled to fuss when his wife is on the verge of delivering their child."

"Hannah was interested in you, Vanessa." Gabriella couldn't resist a smile. "As your name was linked with Bennett's before his marriage."

Along with half the female population of the free world, Vanessa thought, but she kept her smile bland. "His Highness was the most charming of escorts."

"He was a scoundrel."

"Tamed by the lovely Lady Hannah."

"Not tamed, but perhaps restrained." The princess set her glass aside. "I was sorry when your manager informed us that you wouldn't spend more than another day in Cordina. It's been so long since you visited us."

"There is no place I've felt more welcome." She toyed with the petals of a pure white rose. "I remember the last time I was here, the lovely day I spent at your farm, with your family."

"We would love to have you to ourselves again, whenever your schedule permits." Compassionate by nature, she reached out a hand. "You are well?"

"Yes, thank you. I'm quite well."

"You look lovely, Vanessa, perhaps more so because there's such sadness in your eyes. I understand the look. It faced me in the mirror once, not so many years ago. Men put it there. It's one of their finest skills." Her fingers linked with Vanessa's. "Can I help you?"

"I don't know." She looked down at their joined hands, then up into Gabriella's soft, patient eyes. "Gabriella, may I ask you, what's the most important thing in your life?"

"My family."

"Yes." She smiled. "You had such a romantic story. How you met and fell in love with your husband."

"It becomes more romantic as time passes, and less traumatic."

"He's an American, a former policeman?"

"Of sorts."

"If you had had to give up your position, your, well, birthright, to have married him, would you have done so?"

"Yes. But with great pain. Does this man ask you to give up something that's so much a part of you?"

"No, he doesn't ask me to give up anything. And yet he asks for everything."

Gabriella smiled again. "It is another skill they have."

"I've learned things about myself, about my background, my family, that are very difficult to accept.

I'm not sure if I give this man what he wants, for now, that I won't be cheating him and myself in the bargain."

Gabriella was silent a moment. "You know my story, it has been well documented. After I had been kidnapped, and my memory was gone, I looked into my father's face and didn't know him. Into my brothers' eyes and saw the eyes of strangers. However much this hurt me, it hurt them only more. But I had to find myself, discover myself in the most basic of ways. It's very frightening, very frustrating. I'm not a patient or a temperate person."

Vanessa managed another smile. "I've heard rumors."

With a laugh, Gabriella picked up her wine and sipped again. "At last I recognized myself. At last I looked at my family and knew them. But differently," she said, gesturing. "It's not easy to explain. But when I knew them again, when I loved them again, it was with a different heart. Whatever flaws they had, whatever mistakes they had made, however they had wounded me in the past, or I them, didn't matter any longer."

"You're saying you forgot the past."

She gave a quick shake of her head, and her diamonds sizzled. "The past wasn't forgotten. It can't be. But I could see it through different eyes. Falling in love was not so difficult after being reborn."

"Your husband is a fortunate man."

"Yes. I remind him often." She rose. "I'd better leave you to prepare."

"Thank you."

Gabriella paused at the door. "Perhaps on my next trip to America you will invite me to spend a day in your home."

"With the greatest pleasure."

"And I'll meet this man."

"Yes." Vanessa's laugh was quick and easy. "I think you will."

When the door closed, she sat again. Very slowly she turned her head, until she faced herself in the mirror, ringed by bright lights. She saw dark green eyes, a mouth that had been carefully painted a deep rose. A mane of chestnut hair. Pale skin over delicate features. She saw a musician. And a woman.

"Vanessa Sexton," she murmured, and smiled a little.

Suddenly she knew why she was there, why she would walk out onstage. And why, when she was done, she would go home.

Home.

It was too damn hot for a thirty-year-old fool to be out in the afternoon sun playing basketball. That was what Brady told himself as he jumped up and jammed another basket.

Even though the kids were out of school for the summer, he had the court, and the park, to himself. Apparently children had more sense than a lovesick doctor.

The temperature might have taken an unseasonable hike into the nineties, and the humidity might have decided to join it degree for degree, but Brady figured sweating on the court was a hell of a lot better than brooding alone at home.

Why the hell had he taken the day off?

He needed his work. He needed his hours filled.

He needed Vanessa.

That was something he was going to have to get over.

He dribbled into a fast layup. The ball rolled around the rim, then dropped through.

He'd seen the pictures of Vanessa. They'd been all over the damn television, all over the newspaper. People in town hadn't been able to shut up about it—about her—for two days.

He wished he'd never seen her in that glittery white dress, her hair flaming down her back, those gorgeous hands racing over the keys, caressing them, drawing impossible music from them. Her music, he thought now. The same composition she'd been playing that day he'd walked into her house to find her waiting for him.

Her composition. She'd finished it.

Just as she'd finished with him.

He scraped his surgeon's fingers on the hoop.

How could he expect her to come back to a one-horse town, her high school sweetheart? She had royalty cheering her. She could move from palace to palace for the price of a song. All he had to offer her was a house in the woods, an ill-mannered dog and the occasional baked good in lieu of fee.

That was bull, he thought viciously as the ball rammed onto the backboard and careened off. No one would ever love her the way he did, the way he had all of his damn life. And if he ever got his hands on her again, she'd hear about it. She'd need an otolaryngologist by the time her ears stopped ringing.

"Stuff it," he snapped at Kong as the dog began to bark in short, happy yips. He was out of breath, Brady thought as he puffed toward the foul line. Out of shape. And—as the ball nipped the rim and bounced off—out of luck.

He pivoted, grabbed the rebound, and stopped dead in his tracks.

There she was, wearing those damn skimpy shorts, an excuse for a blouse that skimmed just under her breasts, carrying a bottle of grape soda and sporting a bratty smile on her face.

He wiped the sweat out of his eyes. The heat, his mood—and the fact that he hadn't slept in two days—might be enough to bring on a hallucination. But he didn't like it. Not a bit.

"Hi, Brady." Though her heart was jolting against her ribs, she schooled her voice. She wanted it cool and low and just a little snotty. "You look awful hot." With her eyes on his, Vanessa took a long sip from the bottle, ran her tongue over her upper lip and sauntered the rest of the way to him. "Want a sip?"

He had to be going crazy. He wasn't eighteen anymore. But he could smell her. That floaty, flirty scent. He could feel the hard rubber of the ball in his bare hands, and the sweat dripping down his bare chest and back. As he watched, she leaned over to pet the dog. Still bent, she tossed her hair over her shoulder and sent him one of those taunting sidelong smiles.

"Nice dog."

"What the hell are you doing?"

"I was taking a walk." She straightened, then tipped the bottle to her lips again, draining it before she tossed the empty container into the nearby trash bin. "Your hook shot needs work." Her mouth moved into a pout. "Aren't you going to grab me?"

"No." If he did, he wasn't sure if he would kiss her or strangle her.

"Oh." She felt the confidence that had built up all

during the flight, all during the interminable drive home, dry up. "Does that mean you don't want me?"

"Damn you, Vanessa."

Battling tears, she turned away. This wasn't the time for tears. Or for pride. Her little ploy to appeal to his sentiment had been an obvious mistake. "You have every right to be angry."

"Angry?" He heaved the ball away. Delighted, the dog raced after it. "That doesn't begin to describe what I'm feeling. What kind of game are you playing?"

"It's not a game." Eyes brilliant, she turned back to him. "It's never been a game. I love you, Brady."

He didn't know if her words slashed his heart or healed it. "You took your damn time telling me."

"I took what I had to take. I'm sorry I hurt you." Any moment now, her breath would begin to hitch, mortifying her. "If you decide you want to talk to me, I'll be at home."

He grabbed her arm. "Don't you walk away from me. Don't you walk away from me ever again."

"I don't want to fight with you."

"Tough. You come back here, stir me up. You expect me to let things go on as they have been. To put aside what I want, what I need. To watch you leave time and time again, with never a promise, never a future. I won't do it. It's all or nothing, Van, starting now."

"You listen to me."

"The hell with you." He grabbed her then, but there was no fumbling in this kiss. It was hot and hungry. There was as much pain as pleasure here. Just as he wanted there to be.

She struggled, outraged that he would use force. But his muscles were like iron, sleeked with the sweat that heat and exercise had brought to his skin. The violence that flamed inside him was more potent than any she had known before, the need that vibrated from him more furious.

She was breathless when she finally tore away. And would have struck him if she hadn't seen the dark misery in his eyes.

"Go away, Van," he said tightly. "Leave me alone."

"Brady."

"Go away." He rounded on her again, the violence still darkening his eyes. "I haven't changed that much."

"And neither have I." She planted her feet. "If you've finished playing the macho idiot, I want you to listen to me."

"Fine. I'm going to move to the shade." He turned away from her, snatching up a towel from the court and rubbing it over his head as he walked onto the grass.

She stormed off after him. "You're just as impossible as you ever were."

After a quick, insolent look, he dropped down under the shade of an oak. To distract the dog, he picked up a handy stick and heaved it. "So?"

"So I wonder how the hell I ever fell in love with you. Twice." She took a deep, cleansing breath. This was not going as she had hoped. So she would try again. "I'm sorry I wasn't able to explain myself adequately before I left."

"You explained well enough. You don't want to be a wife."

She gritted her teeth. "I believe I said I didn't know how to be one—and that I didn't know if I wanted to be one. My closest example of one was my mother, and she was miserably unhappy as a wife. And I felt inadequate and insecure."

"Because of the tuna casserole."

"No, damn it, not because of the tuna casserole, because I didn't know if I could handle being a wife and a woman, a mother and a musician. I hadn't worked out my own definition of any of those terms." She frowned down at him. "I hadn't really had the chance to be any of them."

"You were a woman and a musician."

"I was my father's daughter. Before I came back here, I'd never been anything else." Impassioned, she dropped down beside him. "I performed on demand, Brady. I played the music he chose, went where he directed. And I felt what he wanted me to feel."

She let out a long breath and looked away, to those distant Blue Mountains. "I can't blame him for that. I certainly don't want to—not now. You were right when you said I'd never argued with him. That was my fault. If I had, things might have changed. I'll never know."

"Van—"

"No, let me finish. Please. I've spent so much time working all this out." She could still feel his anger, but she took heart from the fact that he didn't pull his hand away when she touched it. "My coming back here was the first thing I'd done completely on my own in twelve years. And even that wasn't really a choice. I had to come back. Unfinished business." She looked back at him then, and smiled. "You weren't supposed to be a part of that. And when you were, I was even more confused."

She paused to pluck at the grass, to feel its softness between her fingers. "Oh, I wanted you. Even when I was angry, even when I still hurt, I wanted you. Maybe that was part of the problem. I couldn't think clearly around you. I guess I never have been able to. Things got out of control so quickly. I realized, when you talked about marriage, that it wasn't enough just to want. Just to take."

"You weren't just taking."

"I hope not. I didn't want to hurt you. I never did. Maybe, in some ways, I tried too hard not to. I knew you would be upset that I was going to Cordina to perform."

He was calm again. After the roller-coaster ride she'd taken his emotions on, his anger had burned itself out. "I wouldn't ask you to give up your music, Van. Or your career."

"No, you wouldn't." She rose to walk out of the shade into the sun and he followed her. "But I was afraid I would give up everything, anything, to please you. And if I did, I wouldn't be. I wouldn't be, Brady."

"I love what you are, Van." His hands closed lightly over her shoulders. "The rest is just details."

"No." She turned back. Her eyes were passionate, and her grip was tight. "It wasn't until I was away again that I began to see what I was pulling away from, what I was moving toward. All my life I did what I was told. Decisions were made for me. The choice was always out of my hands. This time *I* decided. I chose to go to Cordina. I chose to perform. And when I stood in the wings, I waited for the fear to come. I waited for my stomach to clutch and the sweat to break out, and the dizziness. But it didn't come." There were tears in her eyes again, glinting in the sunlight. "It felt wonderful. I felt wonderful. I wanted to step out on the stage, into those lights. I wanted to play and have thousands of people listen. *I* wanted. And it changed everything."

"I'm glad for you." He ran his hands up and down her arms before he stepped back. "I am. I was worried."

"It was glorious." Hugging her arms, she spun away. "And in my heart I know I never played better. There was such…freedom. I know I could go back to all the stages, all the halls, and play like that again." She turned back, magnificent in the streaming sunlight. "I know it."

"I am glad for you," he repeated. "I hated thinking about you performing under stress. I'd never be able to allow you to make yourself ill again, Van, but I meant it when I said I wouldn't ask you to give up your career."

"That's good to hear."

"Damn it, Van, I want to know you'll be coming back to me. I know a house in the woods doesn't compare with Paris or London, but I want you to tell me you'll come back at the end of your tours. That when you're here we'll have a life together, and a family. I want you to ask me to go with you whenever I can."

"I would," she said. "I would promise that, but—"

Rage flickered again. "No buts this time."

"But," she repeated, eyes challenging, "I'm not going to tour again."

"You just said—"

"I said I could perform, and I will. Now and then, if a particular engagement appeals, and if I can fit it comfortably into the rest of my life." With a laugh, she grabbed his hands. "Knowing I can perform, when I want, when I choose. That's important to me. Oh, it's not just important, Brady. It's like suddenly realizing I'm a real person. The person I haven't had a chance to be since I was sixteen. Before I went onstage this last time, I looked in the mirror. I knew who I was, I liked who I was. So instead of there being fear when I stepped into the light, there was only joy."

He could see it in her eyes. And more. "But you came back."

"I chose to come back." She squeezed his fingers. "I needed to come back. There may be other concerts, Brady, but I want to compose, to record. And as much as it continues to amaze me, I want to teach. I can do all of those things here. Especially if someone was willing to add a recording studio onto the house he's building."

Closing his eyes, he brought her hands to his lips. "I think we can manage that."

"I want to get to know my mother again—and learn how to cook. But not well enough so you'd depend on it." She waited until he looked at her again. "I chose to come back here, to come back to you. About the only thing I didn't choose to do was love you." Smiling, she framed his face in her hands. "That just happened, but I think I can live with it. And I do love you, Brady, more than yesterday."

She brought her lips to his. Yes, more than yesterday, she realized. For this was richer, deeper, but with all the energy and hope of youth.

"Ask me again," she whispered. "Please."

He was having trouble letting her go, even far enough that he could look down into her eyes. "Ask you what?"

"Damn you, Brady."

His lips were curved as they brushed through her hair. "A few minutes ago, I was mad at you."

"I know." Her sigh vibrated with satisfaction. "I could always wrap you around my little finger."

"Yeah." He hoped she'd keep doing it for the next fifty or sixty years. "I love you, Van."

"I love you, too. Now ask me."

With his hands on her shoulders, he drew her back. "I want to do it right this time. There's no dim light, no music."

"We'll stand in the shade, and I'll hum."

"Anxious, aren't you?" He laughed and gave her another bruising kiss. "I still don't have a ring."

"Yes, you do." She'd come, armed and ready. Reaching into her pocket, she pulled out a ring with a tiny emerald. She watched Brady's face change when he saw it, recognized it.

"You kept it," he murmured before he lifted his gaze to hers. Every emotion he was feeling had suddenly doubled.

"Always." She set it in the palm of his hand. "It worked before. Why don't you try it again?"

His hand wasn't steady. It hadn't been before. He looked at her. There was a promise in her eyes that spanned more than a decade. And that was absolutely new.

"Will you marry me, Van?"

"Yes." She laughed and blinked away tears. "Oh, yes."

He slipped the ring on her finger. It still fit.

* * * * *

NORA ROBERTS

28594	O'HURLEY'S RETURN	__	$7.99	U.S.	__ $9.99	CAN.
28590	SWEET RAINS	__	$7.99	U.S.	__ $9.99	CAN.
28588	NIGHT TALES:					
	NIGHT SHIELD & NIGHT MOVES	__	$7.99	U.S.	__ $9.99	CAN.
28587	NIGHT TALES:					
	NIGHTSHADE & NIGHT SMOKE	__	$7.99	U.S.	__ $9.99	CAN.
28586	NIGHT TALES:					
	NIGHT SHIFT & NIGHT SHADOW	__	$7.99	U.S.	__ $9.99	CAN.
28578	THE LAW OF LOVE	__	$7.99	U.S.	__ $8.99	CAN.
28182	SOMETHING NEW	__	$7.99	U.S.	__ $8.99	CAN.
28181	PLAY IT AGAIN	__	$7.99	U.S.	__ $8.99	CAN.
28180	A CHANGE OF PLANS	__	$7.99	U.S.	__ $8.99	CAN.
28172	WHISPERED PROMISES	__	$7.99	U.S.	__ $8.99	CAN.
28171	FOREVER	__	$7.99	U.S.	__ $9.99	CAN.
28170	REFLECTIONS & DREAMS	__	$7.99	U.S.	__ $8.99	CAN.
28168	CHANGE OF HEART	__	$7.99	U.S.	__ $9.99	CAN.
28167	CHARMED & ENCHANTED	__	$7.99	U.S.	__ $9.99	CAN.
28166	PLAYING FOR KEEPS	__	$7.99	U.S.	__ $8.99	CAN.
28165	CAPTIVATED & ENTRANCED	__	$7.99	U.S.	__ $9.99	CAN.
28162	A DAY AWAY	__	$7.99	U.S.	__ $9.99	CAN.
28161	MYSTERIOUS	__	$7.99	U.S.	__ $9.99	CAN.
28160	THE MacGREGOR GROOMS	__	$7.99	U.S.	__ $9.99	CAN.
28159	THE MacGREGOR BRIDES	__	$7.99	U.S.	__ $9.99	CAN.
28158	ROBERT & CYBIL	__	$7.99	U.S.	__ $9.99	CAN.
28156	DANIEL & IAN	__	$7.99	U.S.	__ $9.99	CAN.
28154	GABRIELLA & ALEXANDER	__	$7.99	U.S.	__ $9.99	CAN.
28150	IRISH HEARTS	__	$7.99	U.S.	__ $9.99	CAN.
28133	THE MacGREGORS: SERENA & CAINE	__	$7.99	U.S.	__ $9.99	CAN.

(limited quantities available)

TOTAL AMOUNT	$ _____
POSTAGE & HANDLING	$ _____
($1.00 FOR 1 BOOK, 50¢ for each additional)	
APPLICABLE TAXES*	$ _____
TOTAL PAYABLE	$ _____

(check or money order—please do not send cash)

To order, complete this form and send it, along with a check or money order for the total above, payable to Harlequin Books, to: **In the U.S.:** 3010 Walden Avenue, P.O. Box 9077, Buffalo, NY 14269-9077; **In Canada:** P.O. Box 636, Fort Erie, Ontario, L2A 5X3.

Name: _____

Address: _____ City: _____

State/Prov.: _____ Zip/Postal Code: _____

Account Number (if applicable): _____

075 CSAS

*New York residents remit applicable sales taxes.
*Canadian residents remit applicable GST and provincial taxes.

Silhouette®
Where love comes alive™